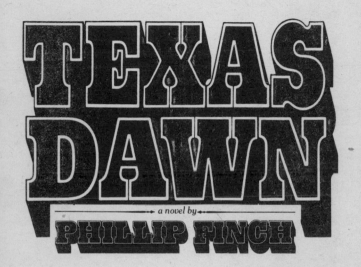

TEXAS DAWN

→ a novel by ←

PHILLIP FINCH

BERKLEY BOOKS, NEW YORK

This Berkley book contains the complete
text of the original hardcover edition.
It has been completely reset in a typeface
designed for easy reading, and was printed
from new film.

TEXAS DAWN

A Berkley Book / published by arrangement with
Seaview Books

PRINTING HISTORY
Seaview Books edition published 1981
Berkley edition / September 1982

All rights reserved.
Copyright © 1981 by Phillip Finch.
This book may not be reproduced in whole or in part,
by mimeograph or any other means, without permission.
For information address: Seaview Books,
747 Third Avenue, New York, New York 10017.

ISBN: 0-425-05492-6

A BERKLEY BOOK ® TM 757,375
Berkley Books are published by Berkley Publishing Corporation,
200 Madison Avenue, New York, New York 10016.
The name "BERKLEY" and the stylized "B" with design are trademarks
belonging to Berkley Publishing Corporation.
PRINTED IN THE UNITED STATES OF AMERICA

FOR ROBIN

Donnie Lee

We got off school early to go to the funeral. They chased us out after lunch, all of us, even the Mexicans from down-valley that didn't know Miz Rose Ellen Sample—which was how I heard her called for most of sixteen years—from Sam Houston. They raced out the doors happy as you please and run up on the buses and rode down the highway.

Though when I thought about it for a minute it made sense, since the classrooms would have been damn near empty anyways if they had let out just those that was going to see the old lady buried.

We stood out front, Tom Holloway and me, and waited for our mamas to pick us up and take us to the church. I peeked out the corner of one eye at Sue Everitt to catch her looking at me. Tom had joshed me pretty good at lunch about me wearing my Sunday suit, clean and pressed with the creases so sharp in the pants. I did feel a mite strange until I saw Sue E. look at me and give a sort of sideways up-and-down look at my suit, and then a smile full-on. I stuck my shoulders back and smiled back at her.

My mama and Tom's come along directly, together with our sisters, in the new Buick that was my daddy's to drive, him being straw boss of the southern division of the Circle Three Bar, biggest ranch in this part of the state of Texas. Tom's daddy had come by in the morning with the pickup that he drove as straw of the Box CF, Rose Sample's place, and he and my daddy had left together.

1

That was something you might not have seen two years ago. Some say there was bad blood between the two outfits. I don't know that I would go along with that, but I'd allow that there was something, all right. You might be pals with a fella for as far back as you could remember, then one day get into a spat and all of a sudden he'd be calling you a Circle Three bastard and you'd call him a Box C son of a bitch and the fists would start to fly. It happened more than once with me and Tom.

Tom and I squeezed into the back of the Buick. His mother shoved a tie and a suit coat at him and told him to get himself presentable.

Riding through town was right peculiar. It was shut down like Sunday midnight, and this was a Wednesday afternoon. Everybody was going to the old lady's funeral. There wasn't a soul on the sidewalk but those that was walking to the church, and not a car or a truck on the streets that wasn't heading to the same place. You can imagine what a tangle of cars and people there was when we got there.

Our daddies was already waiting in the church. We slid into the pew, about halfway between the altar and the last row. Ahead of us was family of all sorts and the mayor and commissioners from six counties and some people I did not know, plus the foremen of the two ranches and their families in the pew right in front of us. Behind us were hands and their kin and what few of the plain townsfolk as could squeeze in. The rest was outside and was to listen to the preaching, if you can believe it, over loudspeakers borrowed from the school stadium.

The organ was lowing already, even slower and sadder than usual. Soon the preacher begun to pray. While I did not listen to all the words he said, I felt sad all the time. She was a good old lady, from what little I knew of her—which wasn't much, her being Box C while my family and me was Circle Three folk. I met her once in a while on the street and called her Miz Rose the way she liked, and she always smiled at me. It did upset me some to think of her there in that wooden box.

Finally the words was finished, at least that part of it, and we took turns, row by row, getting up out of the pews and leaving church. Then it was off to the cemetery, where there was an even bigger crowd.

And the flowers! For everybody bunched around the grave, there must have been a dozen roses. Not to mention the other kinds. This time I could not get in close enough to hear the words that was said. I caught sight of Sue Everitt, and I must have been making eyes at her because my sisters giggled and my daddy reached his arm around me and squeezed my shoulder until I thought he would break it and he said, Damn your hide, show a little respect. This was a fine lady. That shut my sisters up right quick and I did not look at Sue E. again. I stared down at the tips of my boots sticking out from under my cuffs until one of my sisters give me a push and then I looked up and seen that there was a line headed up to the grave and we was supposed to be in it.

Everybody who passed by grabbed a flower out of the bunches that was setting there and tossed it into the grave. The casket was gone, and I knew it was down in the hole. The line moved slow, and this gave me a chance to look around when I got closer.

There was two headstones side by side, white marble the both of them. The words on the one beside hers said RAY-MOND NEWSOME and then in smaller letters CATTLEMAN and the dates, September 2, 1866–April 11, 1950. Green grass was just now sprouting out of the fresh earth over the grave, for this was the second time in just six weeks we had missed an afternoon of school for a burial. I looked over at the old lady's headstone to see whether they had put Sample or Newsome on it. But what it said was ROSE ELLEN FOWLER. I thought we was at the wrong funeral at first. It was the first time I ever heard the name in the valley. Under the big letters of the name was the same CATTLEMAN, which didn't strike me funny until later, and the dates: January 9, 1865–May 28, 1950.

I grabbed a rose and threw it in without looking.

On the way down the hill from the cemetery everybody drove a sight faster than they had driven up, and drove faster the farther down the hill they got, kicking up a hell of a cloud of dust. My daddy was with the rest of our family in the

Buick now, and Tom's mama and daddy and their family in the pickup.

Side by side forever, said my mama in the front seat. She said, I think that is so sweet, the two of them together like that until the end of time.

From the back seat, I seen her reach across and squeeze my daddy on his gear-shifting arm. Myself, I could not see what the fuss was about.

Though I suppose you could not argue with what my daddy said as we turned off the dirt road and on to the highway— which was that she was a woman like they don't make anymore, and had done a heap of living in her time.

Chapter 1

Side by side, they tramped down the road, three men weary from war, the trousers of their grey uniforms coated with dust from the road.

"How far, Charlie?" one of them asked.

"Four and a half miles. Two and a half to the crossroads and two more past there."

Charlie Fowler was coming home. He was going to see his wife and his baby daughter, born since his last furlough. He thought of his wife, tried to imagine her face when she heard his plans.

"These are our partners," he would tell her. "Earl Newsome, Orrin Sample. They are going to Texas, and so are we. You and me, dear, we're going into the cattle business.

"Go from eighty acres to eighteen thousand," he would tell her. That would swing it. Olive always wanted them to get ahead.

They had been married a year when the war came. He had been nineteen, and a farm boy with his own patch of ground when they married. She had been barely sixteen, a girl from the town four miles away. They were different, he knew. He could not make her feel the pleasure he got from his eighty acres, from the hard work with its harvest dividend. She had been unhappy, unsatisfied with the farm.

Now he had to sell her on Texas and a cattle ranch. He would do it. He wanted her to be happy; he did not live well with discord and tumult around him, and after five years of war he craved harmony more than ever.

"Eighteen thousand acres," he would tell her. "Think of it, Olive dear. Eighteen thousand!" Now they had a daughter, he would say, and this was their chance to make something for her sake and their own.

"Charlie," Newsome said, "you change your mind, it is no hard feelings with Orrin and me. A thousand in gold is a lot to go putting these days into something you never seen. You got a family and a farm. Me and Orrin got nothing to lose."

"What are you saying? I want to do this."

"So do we. You know how it is, though—you hatch up something the way we done, it makes the time go faster. But sometimes it don't seem so appealing out in the light of day."

"I wasn't passing the time," Fowler said, "nor talking to hear my own voice. We are going to buy that ranch."

They had met at a Confederate field hospital three months earlier, all wounded in the same nameless skirmish, five days before the end of the war. They were in three cots at one end of the hospital tent, with the smell of carbolic and dying all around them.

They had talked. Sample was nineteen, infantry, from Port Arthur, Texas. Newsome was twenty-two, cavalry, Front Royal, Virginia. Fowler was twenty-four, artillery, from Monroe County, Georgia. They had in common their wounds and pain and fatigue. By the end of the fourth day they were closer than some brothers ever are. And after the surrender they made plans.

Sample had the ranch. Not the title, not even the money, but the dream. He knew about the land, eighteen thousand acres belonging to his mother's cousin. She was a war widow, and wanted to sell. And Orrin Sample had never owned land.

Fowler had the down payment. Almost a thousand in gold, some inherited and the rest from selling off his stock and his single slave before the war. He had seen the bad times coming and had buried the gold before he went off to fight.

The two couldn't leave out Newsome. He was one of them. Besides, he could ride. It was the three of them together, or not at all. They were going into the cattle business on land that only one of them had ever seen, and that they did not yet own.

They walked along the road, closer now to Fowler's eighty and the farmhouse.

"A year before the war," Fowler said, "I rented that forty here on this side of the road, raised up a real nice crop of cotton. And that fellow, there in that house yonder, sold me my first plow horse for ten dollars. A hell of a good draft horse."

Fowler was walking between the other two. The three of them, together this way, made him feel confident and sure, as if there were no limit to what they could accomplish together. They believed in themselves, and in each other. They could do things. At Fowler's right was Sample, squat and strong, with the face of a fat bashful boy on the body of a blacksmith. To the other side was Newsome, the tallest of the three, and the most handsome. His face was burnished and tough, with a crescent scar on one cheek. The nose had been broken once, and set at an abrupt angle. Two fingers of his right hand were bent and crooked now. All these suggested to Fowler a man who had done things, and would do more. And there was Newsome's way of moving, the unhurried and athletic way he moved his body, stretched his legs, reached across a table.

Now Fowler was almost home, and he thought again of Olive watching the three of them approach, her husband and the two strangers who were his friends and partners. His left leg had been shot clean through by a rifle ball, and the wound still hurt, but he began to walk faster anyway.

Hedgerows lined the road. Through a break in the bushes he saw the house, on the far side of his eighty. Fowler ran. He burst through a break in the hedge, jumped over a fence, and ran through the tall grass that now grew in his fallow fields. Burrs and foxtails stuck to his pants. He heard Sample and Newsome thrashing behind him.

He was halfway across the field when a hint of dread made him stop. Something about the house, something not right, a dark whisper. Then he ran towards it faster. But no longer with joy; he was frightened of what he might find.

The house was empty, the front door half open in a sad,

wanton welcome. Weeds grew around the foundation. Fowler stood staring and then threw his head back to scream at the sky.

"Damn those bluebellies," he said. It came out in a loud moan.

Newsome and Sample followed him into the house. Dirt had blown in from the fields. There were cobwebs in the corners. Cornmeal spilled across the pantry from a hole that mice had gnawed in the burlap.

"Damn those bluebellies," Fowler said. "Damn them to hell."

But when he walked through the pantry to the back of the house he saw that the Yankees had had nothing to do with this. Behind the house, where he had buried his gold, the ground had been turned over and thrown aside in three different ragged circles. There were other, smaller holes in the red hardpan. A spade and a pick had been left beside one of them. When Fowler saw this, he knew that Olive had left, and had tried first to find the gold.

She had never been able to remember his directions for finding the cache. One line from the north corner of the henhouse to the door of the shed. Another line from the house's back door to the big elm. Where the lines crossed, the gold was buried two feet down. He found it, in the tobacco sack he had filled five years earlier. The gold pieces were heavy in the hand.

Fowler looked up at Newsome and Sample. He felt the urge to apologize, explain.

"She up and left me," he said. "Seems plain to me. She never was sweet on this place. And five years is a long time to be gone. So she up and went."

He had to leave now. This was no longer home. He could get by without her—five years of war had taught him to get by—but not if he stayed here. He had another reason now for wanting Texas and a cattle ranch.

A vague sense of duty made him set out to visit the neighbors to ask about Olive. He told himself that he ought to know where she had taken his daughter.

Fowler looked back once when the three of them reached the road.

"It was a fair farm," he said. "Not so sorry. She could have done worse."

The nearest neighbor was half a mile east down the road. The family there knew nothing. Nor did the family that lived another half-mile farther east. So they turned back and walked to the farm that bordered Fowler's on the west.

A baby was squalling in a crib that sat on the front porch. Fowler stood over the crib and watched.

"That is your daughter," a woman's voice said behind him.

Fowler did not turn. He peered down at the bawling baby for a few moments and then picked her up. He cradled her in his arms and held her tight against his chest. Her yelling grew louder at first but then subsided. When she was silent Fowler sat on the edge of the porch, bending over her so that his body blocked the afternoon sun from her face.

"This is my daughter, boys. I told you about her," he said. "Rose is her name."

She reached out with a pudgy hand and grabbed his chin.

"And damn me if it ain't fitting. Will you look at the color in her cheeks?"

The woman's name was Amelia Williams. She was in her forties, pudgy and greying, a matron already. Her husband was Noah, ten years older. They'd had two boys, lost one at Chickamauga, the other at Gettysburg.

"It's near five weeks that we've had her," Amelia said. "A lieutenant come through on his way home from the front, stopped here on his way. We said that we would feed him as well as we could. Your Olive come back that evening with the baby the way she did sometimes—we just loved to see that child—and he begun talking Charleston to her."

"If I'd known," Noah said, "I'd never have let him in here, I swear to the Almighty, Charles."

Fowler shook his head silently, as if to absolve him.

"She brought the baby here next morning," Amelia said. "She said she couldn't take it with her but that you would be home soon."

"You cared for her," Fowler said. "That is plain."

"We love the little thing. She is a pure joy," Amelia said. Her husband nodded.

"You've had no trouble keeping her fed?"

"Olive brought the milk cow with her. She said we could keep it. But you'll be needing the milk now that you have the child."

Fowler rocked the baby, dipping one shoulder. "I have to be leaving her," he said. "Me and the boys are off to Texas to be cattlemen. It will be some time before I can come back for her."

"Why, you can leave her, sure enough," Amelia said. "Leave her as long as you please. The place would be terrible quiet without her."

Noah Williams killed a rooster that afternoon, and Amelia fried it; Charlie Fowler deserved a welcome home from the war. And there remained a splash or two at the bottom of Noah's squeezins jug. After dinner the men went to sit on the front porch. They sipped corn mash from the crock and watched the moon slide up over the trees.

"Noah," Fowler said, "I want to thank you for what you've done, caring for my daughter the way you have. I'm obliged, and don't know how to repay you."

"It is the proper thing," Noah said, "and not such a trial as that. Little Rose gives Amelia something to wake up for, mornings. And I don't mind having that child around myself."

"Still, I'm obliged."

"The fact is that I want to talk to you about her. Don't misunderstand me. I ain't saying you wouldn't be a fine father. But I want you to know if . . . if you should come across trouble in Texas . . . or if you can't make it back as soon as you plan . . . you can rest easy about Little Rose."

"I know that," Fowler said. The couple would be happy, he thought, if he never returned.

"Amelia raised two boys up to be fine men, and we ain't so old that we are going to die and leave the girl alone before she is of age."

"I understand," Fowler said.

"I wanted you to know that," Noah Williams said. "We both want you to know that."

Fowler and Newsome and Sample slept that night in the Williams' barn. Before he left the next morning, Fowler walked to the baby's crib and held her up at arm's length to

study her. He wanted to remember her in his hands, her
laugh, the curl of the tuft on her head, her tiny clutching
fingers.

He kissed her on the forehead and laid her down in the
crib. He thanked Noah and Amelia and walked down the path
and into the road, with Sample and Newsome behind him.

Sample's parents lived a few miles from the Gulf of Mexico,
not far from the Louisiana line. They were renters, farming a
cotton patch. His mother's cousin, Eliza, had been with them
for nearly a year since her husband's death. She was ready to
sell her ranch. But not to family.

On an evening in late August, Fowler and the others bar-
gained with her.

"How much are you asking?" Fowler said.

"There are eighteen thousand acres. I would have to get
ten cents an acre."

"Stock?"

She laughed. "It's yours if you can find it. Beeves and
horses both."

"Buildings?"

"There was a house where I lived with my husband."

"What about barns, sheds, and the like?"

"You seem to have the idea that this is some sort of
plantation. I want you to understand what we are talking
about. Not some spread with fences and hands and water
wells. I and my husband hung on there for thirteen years and
never did we feel that we owned the place. We had legal title,
as far as that goes, but the place belonged to the Indians and
the floods and the drouth and the heat and the chill. We was
tenants just as sure as Orrin's folks are here."

Newsome spoke for the first time. "People say there is
money in beef."

"There is. Out there a million cows is running free, waiting for somebody to catch 'em, and every one will fetch at
least twenty in St. Louis."

"Running wild?" Fowler asked.

" 'Wild' is the word," she said. "Wild as any deer. You
would sight rather try to catch a buffalo than a Texas steer."

"Twenty dollars a head," Sample said.

"If it was as easy as picking apples," she said, "everybody would be out there doing it. But not everybody can. That's why I don't believe I want to sell to kin. I don't wish to pass on to my family the heartache and the trouble and the disappointment that go with the place."

They needed two days of talking to convince her to sell if Orrin was to be one of the partners. She saw that he wanted to be a part of it and finally that moved her—that and the fact that a stranger's money was to be down payment. Fowler paid her six hundred in gold. She took a note for twelve hundred more, payable in a year. At least, she told herself, Orrin would be wasting no more than time.

The place was easy to find, she told them before they left. Follow the Brazos River fifty miles past the end of the white man's territory. South then until they found the biggest valley they ever saw. The ranch was there, in Mansos Valley.

"It's a Mex word," she said. "*Mansos* means 'tame.' Somebody had a real wit."

She drew a map and wrote out a list of provisions and supplies. These, and two mules to carry them, and horses for the partners, brought them close to the end of Fowler's gold.

The days were hot as they rode, and the men were grateful that Eliza had insisted on wide-brimmed hats. As they left behind the lush coastal plain, the land grew hilly and arid. Sample had seen the ranch once, on a visit one year before the war. He pointed one morning to a ridge that he recognized. From there, he said, they would be able to see the spread.

The horses' flanks grew wet and slick as they climbed the incline. The men put up hands to shield their eyes from the midday sun.

They reached the crest. The land they had been seeking, the land that would provide their life's work and fortune, lay before them.

They saw a vastness of grass and trees and gullies and brush. The grass made a tall carpet pocked by thickets of oak and laced by deep gullies—arroyos, the native-born called them—where manzanita and prickly-pear cactus grew among the rocks.

The scope of it awed them. The ridge on which they stood

was part of the valley's eastern boundary. The unbroken hills to their right and left stretched, north and south, beyond the eye's reach. To the west, across the valley, was another line of hills that formed a boundary on that side. They were high hills but were so distant that the men saw them only as wrinkles on the horizon.

Below him Fowler could see mountain laurel on the hillside. A breeze came out of the west and showed itself in ripples that spread over the grass. Fowler's eye caught movement at the foot of the hill. A rabbit, he thought at first. But he blinked and leaned forward in his saddle and then he saw that it was not a rabbit but a she-deer leaping over the flat.

Fowler looked around him. Sample and Newsome were staring out from their horses, out at the valley. He saw on their faces what he had seen so often in the last five years. It was the look of men about to go into battle.

Chapter 2

The life that lay before them was fraught with every possibility of failure. But the three men sitting straight up in their saddles to see all they could of the country before them were, together, as fit for it as any could be.

The future would need men with deft hands, quick eyes, and the skills to use them well, men who could *do*. Earl Newsome was such a man. He could ride, shoe, and doctor a horse; could carve a wheel spoke, frame a house, and braid a lariat; could sharpen an axe, sole a boot, put a bullet where he aimed it.

In seventy years it would be a Texan's conceit to imagine himself the man that Earl Newsome was: capable and laconic and built with just the right angularity and slimness of hip, breadth of shoulder. He was a tall man, and there was a masculine grace in his stride. His face was lined already, and tanned. He was a man of actions, quick decisions, impulse.

The new life would demand physical strength, too. Orrin Sample had that, and the will and tenacity to use it fully. He was short. His frame would have suited a less spectacularly muscled man. As it was, the heavy shoulders, wide chest, and stocky legs gave him a chunky appearance that was not pleasing to the eye. He was not handsome, not even plain. His ears were too large and too prominent, the neck thick and stubby, the eyes shadowed by overhanging brows, the nose and jaw lumpy, asymmetrical.

He had been a clumsy child, and slow learning to speak.

This had convinced his mother that he was dull-minded. She told him so often as he grew, and he had no reason to doubt her. Grown, he sometimes moved slowly, and his speech was deliberate, hesitant, as though he feared to betray his deficiency. In fact, he was less intelligent than some, more intelligent than others. He was also a kind man, gentle in most situations, always unassuming. These traits usually are prized. But Sample with his slow ways gave the impression that they were innate, not cultivated, which somehow diminished their value to most people.

Sample had been a fierce fighter in the war. Of the three partners, he had been the bravest and the most loyal soldier. He had not questioned orders, nor fought with anything less than his utmost. Yet he was not a violent man. He had simply accepted fighting as another job, having never in his life shirked a task or left one unfinished. He had been a good worker even as a child. But he failed to get full credit even for this; the assumption that his was a simpleton's diligence was the cruelest slight of all.

That left him only his strength, which could not be denied, ignored, or misunderstood. He brought muscle to the partnership—and more than the other two would have guessed as they sat overlooking the valley that hot day in early September.

Finally, the new life would need thinkers. Skills and strength needed direction, and a vision beyond the next job. Charlie Fowler was a thinker. This would have surprised his two companions that day, for he showed none of the vagueness or indolence that they associated with thinking men. Fowler was direct. He had energy. He could ride passably, and shoot, and drink, and say what he meant when he spoke. He could read, but to Sample and Newsome this was a pardonable eccentricity, in light of his other qualities.

All the same, he was a thinker. His acts were rarely reflexive. He considered consequences, possibilities. He glimpsed the faint thread that ran from an act one day to its result later. He sensed the future's lunging and staggering course, read portents, augured with present fact as others once had done with entrails.

He had bothered to glance up and look at the future that sprawled ahead. This made him different. His partners sensed this, though they could not explain it. Already they were deferring to his judgment, waiting for his decisions. If they had thought about this, they would have said that his word was final because his gold had bought them this chance. But it went beyond that, though years would pass before his partners knew why.

That was the partnership. It was ideal for what the three men faced. They were suited to one another and to the dream they shared; and as long as it was intact, only good would come of it.

Chapter 3

There is no longer any job like the one that faced the three partners that first year in Mansos Valley. The land will never again be so gloriously, frustratingly open. The cattle will never be so wild. Now there are fences and pens, and the cattle roam only within these bounds.

Sample, Fowler, and Newsome made their first camp that year on a patch of grass between the Mansos River and what was left of the homestead: a four-room board-and-batten house with a sagging roof, a lean-to shed on one side, and two corrals that were the only man-made enclosures for twenty miles in any direction.

The partners' wealth was all around them for the taking: thousands of long-legged, lean-flanked cattle that roamed the arroyos, hills, open grasslands, and dense thickets that made up the property. Some of the cows bore the brand of the ranch that the partners had bought, and thus were theirs by law if not in reality. Others showed the brands and ear cuts of the two neighboring spreads, both abandoned during the war. Others, never marked, would belong to the first person who could mark their hides with a hot iron. All were cautious and quick to flee the approach of a man. The partners planned to brand as many cattle as they could that fall and winter, then start a roundup in the spring for the drive to a market. With the money they got there, they would have to pay Eliza's note and buy supplies for the next year.

Sample knew something of cattle ranching, and Newsome

something of horses. Both agreed that the mounts they had bought in Port Arthur would not be enough for the work they had to do. Each man would need a cutting horse for close work in a herd, another for rim-riding the canyons with their steep slopes, one for fording rivers, and another for night-riding the herd on the drive.

There were horses for the taking, too, out there with the cows. The partners chased horses for three days before finally trapping half a dozen in a narrow, closed arroyo. They got ropes on four of them and led them back to the corral, and Newsome spent the next three weeks breaking them to bit and saddle. During the last ten days he drew a chestful of pain with every breath; a truculent mare had planted a hoof in his ribs after throwing him to the dirt of the corral. When he was finished the animals still were not docile, but they were strong and steady, and they could be ridden.

The ranch's old branding irons were in the lean-to; these would have to do for a season. The partners wanted to put that brand on as many unmarked cattle as they could, to establish their claim in the spring. Once branded, the cattle were set loose, for there was no place to keep them. The men had hoped to add hundreds to their legal herd this way, but they found the cattle quicker, more skittish, and more long-winded than they had expected. The cows plunged through thickets and leaped gullies and matched the fastest horses' speed across flat land. None of the men could throw an open noose. Their best hope was to run a cow into mesquite so thick that it repulsed even those surging muscles, then slip a noose over the head of the cow as it struggled in the brush. Usually one rope was not enough, and the nooses had to be wide enough to clear the spread of the cow's horns and slide down around the neck. Sample and Newsome were the best riders. They roped the cows, while Fowler heated the iron and pressed it into the hide and then notched the ears.

They did not catch many cattle this way. Their bodies ached from lumps and cuts and bruises and saddle sores. The idea of putting together a herd of these creatures and driving them several hundred miles as a group seemed more improbable every day.

They were ready for Paco Alvarez and Camilo Ortiz to

come riding toward the campfire one evening. They were young men, not yet thirty, on their way home to Matamoros, they said. They needed a meal; Fowler motioned them down.

"We are *vaqueros*," Alvarez said. His English was good. "We been north to find work. But we didn't find nothing. No better than when the war was on."

"What kind of work does a *vaquero* do?" Fowler asked.

When Alvarez realized that this was not a joke he said, "A *vaquero*, my friend, works with cows."

"Sure," Sample said. "A cowboy."

"How long have you been doing that work?" Fowler asked.

Alvarez shrugged. "I start when I am a boy in Mexico. Six years there. Then nine years a *rancho* up the Nueces. I learned to speak *americano* there. Then the war came and I had no job, so I went to Mexico again."

"Can you rope cows?" Fowler said.

Alvarez searched for the obscure humor that Fowler so obviously intended. But he saw no hint of it in Fowler's eyes, steady on him across the campfire, so he straightened his back and said, "I told you I am a *vaquero*."

Fowler stood. "If you sat on your horse where it is now, and I stayed here, could you throw a rope around me?"

The horse was five, six paces away. Alvarez wanted to be a good guest. He made an effort not to appear offended. "With my eyes closed," he said.

"Suppose," Fowler said, "I hold out my arms like this. Could you throw the rope past my arms and catch me around my stomach?" Fowler raised his arms above his head, spread wide in a rough semicircle.

"Yes," Alvarez said.

"And if I was running away from you, fast as I can? Could you still do it?"

Alvarez smiled then. "I understand," he said.

He stood and walked to his horse, stepped up and into the saddle, and picked up a coiled rope from where it lay slung across the saddle horn. The rope was stiff and heavy. Alvarez held the rope in his left hand and took several coils in his right.

"I understand," he said again, and once more he smiled.

"You are the cow, yes? And you want me to throw the *reata* over your arms and around your belly, yes? Over your horns and catch your neck."

"Yes," Fowler said. "Just show me."

"But that is not how a *vaquero* would do it."

"Then do it your way," Fowler said.

He ran, arms spread above his head. Alvarez waited until Fowler was at the dim edge of the campfire's light, and then he threw. The rope floated out, kicking loose one coil after another. Fowler, feet slamming against the earth, glanced over one shoulder and looked toward the sky for the rope that he knew must be descending on him.

At that moment the ground fell away from his feet. His chin was the first part of his body to touch earth again.

He lay still so long that Sample and Newsome began to rise and Alvarez kicked his horse into a canter toward him. Then Fowler rolled over on his back and looked down at the rope looped around one of his ankles.

"Look at that," Fowler said as he sat in the dirt. "Will you look at what he did? That is a marvel, for certain."

He looked up at Newsome and Sample. "Partners," he said softly, "we need these boys."

They struck a deal; the Mexicans hired on through the spring drive, working for food and ten percent of the take at the end of the trail.

They had a good winter. By breaking camp once a week and moving to another part of the range, they could rope and brand thirty head on a good day. At first, Alvarez and Ortiz did all the roping. But the others took turns riding with them, and by January every one of them could cut a cow out of a bunch in open country, rope it, and tie it.

The cold nights brought them together around the campfire. While the fire blazed they tried to teach Ortiz to speak English. Alvarez, in turn, threw Spanish and cowboy slang at his riding partners during the day. Ortiz one night broke silence with a song. A few nights later Fowler did the same, and then Newsome and Alvarez, and later they found that Sample could sing, too, more clearly and sweetly than any of them.

Sometimes they talked as they lay in their bedrolls. It was

easier to talk of serious matters this way because they did not have to look at each other as they spoke. They could say the words to the sky and the stars. Sometimes the talk was of women, of loves won, lost, and imagined. In other places this would have been wrong; the thought of women would have magnified the longing that they all felt. But here women were an abstract. Women had nothing to do with this reality.

Fowler alone did not talk of women. He had loved his wife, and her leaving had brought him a sadness he was only now beginning to feel. There was a hole in him that he was filling with work and with dreams.

He knew, too, as the others did not, that they would not be living this way long. He knew that men need women. There would be women here soon, he thought, and the place would be better for it.

Chapter 4

By the end of January they had covered the range twice and they were ready to herd. They needed men, and food for the drive. Alvarez rode south to Matamoros, and Newsome rode with Fowler to buy supplies with what remained of the gold. They bought a wagon and two more mules, and they spent the rest on coffee, rice, sugar, flour, beans, and a three-legged dutch oven. It was a slow trip back, and two days after the wagon reached the spread Alvarez returned with five more *vaqueros* to work the drive for a percentage. Fowler took them on.

Sample and Ortiz had not been idle. Before he left, Alvarez had found a box canyon on one corner of the property, a half-mile long, the mouth perhaps one hundred feet across, the sides too steep for even a longhorn to climb. There was a spring on the canyon floor, and some grass. They would need a place to keep the herd, he said, and this would be small enough to keep the cows together but not so close that they would be likely to panic. Sample and Ortiz had been left to close off the mouth of the canyon, leaving only a gate. They used fencing they scavenged from the old homestead, trees they cut and split, brush they cut and piled and wove together— anything to keep the cows from getting a look at open spaces, as Alvarez put it.

They began to herd at the end of February, and within a week they had put almost nine hundred cows inside the canyon. They could have tripled the number, but the grass

25

was gone after a week and the cows were hungry and restless. It was time to move them, time to drive, so on the evening of the seventh day of herding, Alvarez gathered the *vaqueros*. He told them to eat their fill and to sleep well and to choose their strongest horses from the *remuda*. They were going to stampede the cattle in the morning and run the meanness out of them.

Sample and Fowler were the weakest riders. They stayed with the wagon, and watched at dawn the next day when Newsome and the *vaqueros* opened the gate and stampeded the herd. At first the cows poured through the gate. Then the fence came down and the cows broke through the barrier of brush, and the canyon was empty in less than a minute. The herd was a dark, squirming blot of noisy life that shook the earth as it passed. But it was together, with mounted men strung out beside it to keep it contained.

Soon it was out of the sight of Sample and Fowler. Sample chucked the reins on the mules and pointed the wagon toward the spot on the horizon where the animals had disappeared.

Newsome and the *vaqueros* kept the charging animals together for an hour. Then they hit an oak thicket and the herd spread, and it was another hour before the riders could nudge the fringes back to the rest of the pack.

The wagon caught them that afternoon. The path of the herd had been easy to follow, and at about midday Fowler and Sample crested a rise and saw in the distance a cloud of dust that rose high in the air. They needed two hours to reach it; it did not move as they approached, but continued to waft up into the air. Finally they saw its source: the herd was milling in a circle, the cattle moving at a mindless trot. The *vaqueros* had turned the stampede into itself, and now only rode the edges of the circle to keep the outside cows from straying. By evening the cattle were walking, and Alvarez sent men into the knot of animals to break the circle and begin to drive the cows again. Now they were too weary to run. The *vaqueros* drove them all that night, and the next morning. He allowed them all a few hours' rest that afternoon, men and cows, before they drove again through the night. The men slept in their saddles—the pace by now a slow canter—and snatched food from the wagon when they could.

They did this for four days and three nights. On the fourth night they made camp. The cattle were a true herd now, not tame but at least pliant. They would go where the *vaqueros* pushed them, and go as one.

On this, their first drive, Newsome and Sample and Fowler were lucky men. None of the rivers were flooding when they forded. Though they passed through Indian Territory, they did not face Cherokee warriors. The herd found water, if only from potholes and seeps. Men, horses, and cows stayed healthy. For the last two months of the drive the grass was good, and the cattle put on weight as they grazed up through the Kansas grasslands. And when the herd arrived in St. Joe the price of beef was up. The stock brokers, pens empty, were crying for cattle.

The herd checked in at 811 head. Fowler got an offer of $31 a head from the first broker he visited and talked him up to $35. He left the office with a draft in his pocket for $28,385.

Newsome, Sample, and Alvarez were waiting outside the door. They looked at his face, searching for a sign, as he stood before them.

"Well?"

"We are rich men," Fowler said, and he held the piece of paper up for them all to see. Then he walked across the street to a bank.

They took hotel rooms. A double eagle slipped across the registration desk quieted the mutterings about greasers. They bathed and got haircuts and bought clean clothes, and that night they ate French food, all ten of them at one table.

They whooped and shouted and sang and they were all drunk when they left the restaurant, stumbling, leaning against one another for balance.

Sample bumped into Fowler and grabbed at the lapels of his coat. "Charlie?" he said. "Is this real? Is this for certain happening to us?" He did not wait for an answer, but wheeled and followed the others.

Fowler hung back and found Alvarez at his side. "Paco, can we do this every year?"

"The cows are there. They keep making more cows. Next year you will bring twice as many, maybe."

Fowler leaned back against the wall. "This is lunacy. How can this happen to me?"

"You're a *ranchero* now," Alvarez said. "Don't you know? You own land as far as you can see. You own more cows than you can count. Maybe you didn't understand that when you were riding in your wagon and sleeping in your blankets like the rest of us. But now you see."

"Paco, you have to stay with us. You'll stay, won't you?"

"This is much money, my share. I could buy a farm. Or a store, maybe. I could find a wife, maybe. Get out of this wandering life."

They were sober the next morning, and silent with awe at the reality of it now. It faced them when they went to the bank to pay the Mexicans. Every one of the *vaqueros* put more money in his pocket that morning than he had ever had before, and what remained after that stunned the three partners— Sample and Newsome because they had never had so much and were sure that they never would again, and Fowler because he saw what the capital could do for the ranch.

They took their money in cash, sold their horses and wagon, and with their earnings hidden in three new carpetbags, took passage on a riverboat south.

One evening as they traveled, Fowler prodded the others into making plans. They had to spend their money well. Another year's supplies, of course. Lumber and mortar to repair the old house, if they could find a way to ship the material such a long distance. New saddles and ropes and guns and bedrolls and wagons and mules to replace everything that they had sold or discarded in St. Joe.

"That will still leave a heap," Newsome said.

"Yes," Fowler said. "And I think that we ought to buy land."

Sample was no orator. He left the protest for Newsome.

"Land! How much land do we need, Charlie? None, if you ask me, long as there are cattle and range. It ain't only our cows that tallow up on our grass, and ours don't know where the property line is either, for that matter. I don't see it, Charlie."

"It can't hurt," Fowler said. His reason was more specific than that. One evening the past winter he had looked at the valley and pondered what it would mean if someone one day put a fence around his own property and chased out all but his own animals. Then you would need land and grass and water of your own, and the more you had of those things the more cows you could run. Anyone could see that; if cattle cannot graze where they wish, he thought, they will eat up what they have, right to the edge of the fence, and then bawl for more.

But Fowler said none of that. Newsome and Sample would never see that far. But he knew how to reach them anyway.

"Earl," he said, "how much land have you ever owned before?"

He knew the answer already; Newsome's lips formed a silent "None."

"And you, Orrin, your folks are tenants. You never owned a place that had your name on the deed, up to now, did you? Not that I'm bragging. The best I could do until I met you boys was eighty acres of red clay. Not much of a kingdom.

"But now we have a chance," he said. "Eighteen thousand acres doesn't take such a big bite out of Texas when you think about it. If we are going to be men of property, we might as well do it right, go all the way with it. I wouldn't care if it took my nearest neighbor a day's ride to get to me. Damn me if I would.

"And what else would we spend it on? Once we got a roof to keep out the rain, and food in the larder, and tools, what are we going to buy?"

He paused to give them a chance to come back with an answer. There would be none, he knew. None of them had ever had enough money to seriously desire luxuries, and Fowler knew that such tastes usually are acquired by proximity. Having been assured of a home and food and a job for a year to come, Newsome and Sample were utterly satisfied. They could not imagine wanting more.

It was time for Fowler to finish it.

"Besides," he said, "if we can buy the spreads beside ours this year, our job will be that much easier. We won't spend half our time running down cows that turn out to have somebody else's brand on 'em. We'll know that every cow on our range will belong to us."

That was a luxury with some appeal. Maybe some more land would be a good idea, after all.

There was one thing, Sample said. He spoke slowly, watching the faces of the other two.

"We ought to have our own brand," he said, "that never belonged to nobody before. Something that is ours. We can start to use it this winter and in a few years there won't be a cow on the range that doesn't have our mark on it."

"Sure," Fowler said. "Don't you think so, Earl? We will all think on it some and try to come up with a proper one."

"I been thinking already," Sample said. He brought from a pocket a piece of paper. The symbol drawn on it showed three horizontal parallel bars within a circle.

"These lines," Sample said, pointing with a stubby finger, "is us. One is you, Charlie, and the other is Earl, and the third one, that's me. And the circle is because we are all three together in one, see? So it would be the Circle Three Bar."

They had never heard such talk from Sample. Fowler wondered what else was in him that Sample had never showed.

Fowler left the steamer at Vicksburg, where he bought a horse. He knew that now, if ever, he had to claim his daughter. She was his in name only, and if he waited another year he would never be able to take her from the only home she had ever known.

It would be a cruel thing to do, and already difficult as it was.

Noah Williams was in the fields when he saw Fowler coming up the road. He walked to where Fowler had reined in the horse.

No greeting.

"You've come for your daughter," Noah said.

Fowler nodded.

"Let me tell Amelia you are here. Will you give me that?"

Noah rode ahead on the horse. That left Fowler to walk the rest of the way. When he reached the house he saw Noah and Amelia standing at the door. The little girl was between them, eyes wide and unblinking, holding the woman's cotton skirt.

"Charlie Fowler," Amelia said. "I mean you no harm, but I hoped I'd never see you again."

"Amelia," Noah said.

"No, I understand," Fowler said. "But she's my daughter and I want her with me."

Amelia reached down, took Rose's hand from her skirt, and turned away into the house.

"Understand," Noah said, "that she loves the child so. She don't mean to be cruel."

"I know that."

"Child," he said, "this is your father."

The little girl looked at Fowler.

"We have told her about you," Noah said. "I don't know how much she understands, but we have told her anyway."

He spoke to Rose again. "This is your father," he said. She looked at Fowler and edged closer to Noah.

Fowler watched her all day, trying to comprehend the truth that this being, this miracle, was his daughter and part of him. Rose Ellen was nearly two years old now, and could walk, and could speak some words clearly enough that even Fowler with his unpracticed ear could understand them. She played with a calico kitten and a cloth doll stuffed with straw, and when Amelia took up a broom to sweep the floor, Rose held one cut down to her own size and brushed behind her.

She did all this while Charlie Fowler watched. He was shocked. He had imagined her still an infant in her crib. That evening, when they ate, she ate with them at the table and used a knife and fork.

"You'll be taking her tomorrow morning?" Amelia Williams asked during dinner.

"Waiting will only make it harder."

"I want to ask you something about this place you're taking her to."

Were there children nearby? she wanted to know. Women to care for her when the men were working? Schools? Doctors? Would she have a bed? And then, "Do you even have a house, I hope, for her to live in?"

"Not yet," Fowler said.

Amelia Williams stabbed with her fork at a scrap of food. "We won't let her go with you alone," she said. Her face was calm, her voice level.

"Even if she is your daughter, what you are going to do is

wrong. This so-called ranch is no place for a child who does not have a mother to care for her. No place for a child at all, likely. You can take her if you want, but you take us, as well, if you do. We will make the best of whatever we find there.''

So they went with Fowler and Rose Ellen to the ranch in Mansos Valley. In two days they sold their farm to the first taker; Fowler already had decided to keep his eighty. They loaded their belongings into a wagon, and the four of them traveled by road, ferry, and trail to the ranch.

When Rose Ellen first saw what would be her home for the rest of her life, she was playing with a thimble that she slipped from one finger to another. Noah hoisted her up on the front seat. "Look, Little Rose," he said. "This is your daddy's land."

But the land looked like all the rest to her, and in a few minutes she was asleep.

Chapter 5

The child found her new existence even richer than the other had been. She had attention, love, care, and food. The isolation of the place, its loneliness, and the obstacles it threw up to the men did not concern her. She had Noah and Amelia, and now her father and his partners. The ranch house and the grass outside the front door were fully as fascinating as the cabin and the clay she had known in Georgia.

She drew the soft side of the men to her. She bore them no threat, and repaid love with love. Sample sang to her, bounced her on one big knee, raised her over his head and flew her around the room mornings and evenings when he was not on the range. Newsome made gifts for her. He carved stick figures, built a crude house for her doll, even fashioned a bed from oak and dried rawhide when she outgrew her crib.

In her father she inspired wonder, for she was so unlike anything he had known and yet was part of him all the same. But soon she ceased being a curiosity. He learned to care for her, to speak to her so that she would listen, to answer her questions in words that she understood. That was the beginning of an uncomplicated love that lasted as long as he lived.

She was happy, in part, because the men were, too. She was sensitive, as children are, to undercurrents of emotion. During her childhood the partners were pleased with themselves and with their work, potent, capable, full of optimism and belief as the ranch grew. She sensed this and it brought her security.

She first sat on a horse when she was three years old. Her father had taken her riding before that, holding her in his lap. This time, though, he stood to the side and held her up to the saddle. She was startled, but tried not to give away her fright. She knew that this was important to him, and she wanted to please him. By now she wanted nothing more than his approval. After a few moments he lifted her away. The next time he put her up in the saddle, the sensation was not so bad and the perch did not seem so high. After that, when he took her riding he let her hold the reins. She learned the subtle and gentle pressures that a good horse expects on the traces. One day not long after her fourth birthday Fowler returned from a two-week trip to Austin with a small saddle in the wagon and a tired little runt of an Indian pony trailing behind. That was her first horse; she rode alone before she was five.

Amelia began teaching her to cook about that time. By then, her father was already spending evenings with her when he could, teaching her words and numbers. She learned spelling and arithmetic as quickly as she learned to ride.

It would not have mattered then if she had been homely. No one would have loved her less, the partners and the hands would have been no less captivated. But she was not homely. By age three she had outgrown her infant chubbiness. The features of her face were delicate and symmetrical, except for a chin that soon asserted itself, strong and prominent but not overpowering. It was the only jarring note, and by the time she was four Fowler and the others realized that she was blessed not merely with an absence of faults but with a natural beauty. There was no telling yet just what her bony body would become, but her mother had been lean and lithe. She was, Amelia assured Fowler, taller than most boys at that age.

Except for Amelia, she knew only men. She admired her father and the others and tried to imitate them. She acquired many of the skills that are supposed to be masculine: roping, shooting, hitting a nail on its head until it is buried. Less apparent, but just as real, were the confidence, pride, and self-reliance that she took from her father and the others. These traits were a natural legacy and would mark her forever.

She had lived more than four years on the ranch when the

life that had been so benign and so full of love was interrupted. Neither it, nor she, ever was quite the same again.

Rose awoke before first light that day, a morning in early
spring. Newsome was already out on the range with most of
the hands, roping horses for a *remuda*. Sample and Fowler
had stayed behind to hire more hands for the spring drive.
Now the hiring was finished, and they were going to ride out
to join Newsome and the others. Fowler would return in the
evening or the next morning. He was spending more time
now with contracts, lawyers, and ledgers than with cows and
horses.

Amelia was up before anyone, cracking eggs into a skillet
and boiling water for coffee. Rose Ellen had her own room,
in a loft over the kitchen that caught all the noise from
downstairs, so she was next to rise and come shuffling into
the kitchen.

"What are you doing awake?" Amelia said. "You need
your sleep, child."

"Papa is going away today."

"Not for long."

"I want to talk to Papa."

The men followed the aroma of the coffee and the hissing
of the eggs into the kitchen. Sample was wearing heavy chaps
with the hair turned out, spurs that rattled when he walked, a
slicker tied around his neck, and a sombrero.

"Orrin," said Amelia, "I won't have any hats at my
table."

He took it off his head and put it down on the child's. It
was a high-crowned hat, and so wide that it rested on her
shoulders.

She squealed.

"I'll swap you a kiss for that hat," Sample said.

She climbed into his lap. She felt the coarse hair from the
untreated cowskin of the chaps. Sample smelled of gun oil
and leather. His cheek was prickly from two days' beard
when she kissed him.

Then she slid down from Sample's lap and clambered into
her father's.

"How far are you riding today, Papa?"

"Up where the Mansos forks. Do you know where that is?"

She had not traveled more than three miles from the house since the day she arrived. But there was a hand-drawn map of the property tacked on one wall of her father's office. She studied the map often, and listened to the men's talk, and asked questions.

"Yes, Papa. That is where you catched the big roan last year that was such a good swimmer."

"Where we *caught* it. Yes, that is the place."

"Is it far?"

"About ten miles."

"From here to the sweetwater spring is about one mile," she said. She had been there with her father and she used that as a measure.

Fowler turned her face toward his. "Rose Ellen," he said, "what are you talking around?"

She looked back at him. "Papa, I want to ride with you today. I can go that far. I can ride as far as the spring ten times."

"No," he said. He bent to sip the coffee that Amelia poured for him.

"But Papa, I want to go."

"No. And if you want to know why, it is because you don't ride well enough yet. You just aren't strong enough to ride that far back. There is work to do when we get there and maybe I will have to stay overnight."

She put her lips into a pout.

"And last of all, you don't belong out there," he said.

That brought a slight, satisfied smile to Amelia's face. She did not approve of Rose Ellen riding, or learning to shoot a rifle (which she had, six months earlier), or wearing britches (which she did, at least half the time). At least Charlie Fowler was not ready to drag the child across the wilderness. Not yet, anyway.

"Is that settled?" Fowler said.

The child nodded.

"Maybe you can go over your lessons, the ones we learned last night," Fowler said. "We have time for that, Orrin."

The night before, as they had often done for the last two years, they had spent an hour beside a coal oil lantern, her father teaching her some of the things she would have learned at school, if there had been one within twenty miles. Fowler had bought a globe, book, pencils, and paper during one trip to Austin. Sometimes they learned together. Fowler had not finished eighth grade and sometimes he had to teach himself before he could teach Rose Ellen.

Lately it had been multiplication tables.

"Two times one," he said. She was in his lap, facing the table, with a paper in front of her and a pencil in hand.

"Two," she said.

"Write it down."

She did, in large and rambling figures.

"Times tables," Amelia said. "Charlie, you push that girl too hard."

"She can do it. Can't you, Rose? Two times two."

"Four!" Rose Ellen shouted.

"See? She can do it. Okay, write it out."

The sun had risen when they finished breakfast. Rose Ellen stood in the door after her father had lifted her up to kiss her. She clutched one leg, then released him, and stood watching as Fowler and Sample mounted and rode off. She watched until they were out of sight.

Amelia heated water for dishes. She did the washing; Rose Ellen dried. Then Rose Ellen went upstairs to make her bed as she had been taught (Amelia, the teacher this time, was determined that the child would learn two of women's ways for every masculine one she got from her father and the others). The day was the warmest in several weeks, so when she had finished the bed she went outside to play in the sunshine, with the hills and the plains and the openness all around her.

After lunch, Amelia made her practice her manners, by which the woman meant her own faulty version of a curtsey, which she had last seen twenty years earlier. When she was alone again Rose Ellen sat at the dining table to practice her figures and her letters. She would write her name ten times on a page; that would make her father happy when he returned.

She was fashioning the letters when she heard an unfamiliar noise from the back of the house, where Noah and Amelia were putting in a garden. It was a few steps to her father's office, where she could stand on a chair and look out to the back.

She saw four men she did not know beating Noah and Amelia. One of them was raising Amelia's shovel and swinging it down on her head, first bringing her to her knees as she slumped in the grasp of another stranger, the second blow knocking her face-down on the ground, the third coming as she sprawled and tried to crawl away. Two others were on Noah, one grappling with him, the other bringing the butt of a pistol down and down on Noah's face.

She had been at the window long enough to glimpse the violence, to see the blows falling, when she heard a noise at the front door, then the scrape of boots on the floor.

She hid. She hid in the first place she saw, a cabinet with solid doors. She climbed in and pulled the doors closed until only a thin slice of light fell through to her.

It was the cabinet where her father kept guns. Guns and bullets and caps and powder and some of the new waxed cartridges.

Guns were a tool then. Men carried pistols where they might find rattlesnakes, which was almost everywhere. They carried rifles to chase off coyotes and to hunt deer, and shotguns to kill squirrels and rabbits. Fowler had taught his daughter to use guns because they were useful.

Now she heard the footsteps crossing the front room, scraping toward the kitchen, pausing there, and thumping up the stairs toward her bedroom. But only partway up the stairs before descending. She heard a moan, and knew it was from Amelia.

She became aware of the butt of a pistol against her shoulder. It was the approach of those scraping footfalls that made her reach for the gun, cock the trigger, and hold it with both hands out in front of her. The footsteps grew louder, and she told herself that she would have to disobey her father.

He had told her, the first time he took her shooting, "Don't ever point a gun at a person. And don't ever, ever use it against anyone. Shoot animals if you must, but not people. Never people." The urgency in his voice, and the way he phrased it, had told her that this was no ordinary command. It was something special.

So she was going to have to go against her father. She thought: He might never love me again.

Her finger was on the trigger. She followed the sound of the footsteps around the room—to her father's desk, the drawers flung open and thrown to the floor, papers rustling. More footsteps, and talking, in the front room. Then the scraping soles were closer, and a shadow fell across the slit of light between the two cabinet doors.

The doors swung open. She looked at the face of a man she had never seen before. She pulled the trigger.

This was before smokeless powder. The cabinet, the room, the whole world (it seemed to her) filled instantly with blue-grey smoke. Her eyes burned and the noise left a numb ringing in her ears. The pistol jumped back in recoil and slammed against her face. The sear of the trigger gashed her above the nose. She had not expected that; her father had taught her to shoot a heavy muzzle-loader with quarter-charges, which made nothing like the kick of this lighter gun with a full load in the barrels.

She noticed none of this at first, not the sound nor the recoil nor the cut on her forehead. She saw the cap's flash in the somber light inside the cabinet, saw the man thrown backwards before the smoke obliterated her vision, heard his body hit the plank floor. Shoulders first, then boots.

The smoke cleared. Rose Ellen looked through it, out to the front room, where another man stood with his pistol drawn. Three others came running through the front door. These four she had seen beating Noah and Amelia, and she knew they meant her harm. They all looked at the body on the floor and then at her.

She heard them speak.

"It ain't but a child. A girl, I b'lieve."

"Hid in the cabinet."

"Just a tiny thing."

"Big enough to snuff out Jim's lamp."

"He dead?"

"Look at that hole in his head."

"What's she got? Look, a hawg-leg. That thing is 'bout bigger than she is."

"Go get it, Willie. Take it away from her."

"Yeah, Willie. Go get that thing from her."

The one closest to her stuck his pistol into his waistband and began to walk toward her. He walked slowly and spoke in soft tones. "Now, little girl, we won't hurt you. Just give us the gun, you don't want to make the big noise again. It's all right, sugar, just give me the gun."

She had disobeyed her father once. A second time would be easier.

She lifted the pistol up and rested it on her knees—her legs tucked in front of her—and she pulled the trigger back again. The two metallic clicks and the third, louder click when the trigger notched into place were louder than the man's voice, and carried across the room.

The man stopped.

"Go get it, Willie," one of the others said.

"She won't use it again, Willie."

The man in the middle of the room drew three breaths. In those moments Rose Ellen knew that she would do anything to keep on living. So far she had acted out of fright. Now she knew that she wanted to live. If that meant killing she would kill.

But the men withdrew. They would tell each other later that there was nothing worth stealing anyway, no sense in staying.

Rose Ellen crouched in the cabinet until her legs ached. By then the four men had fled. She climbed out of the cabinet and walked outside to where Noah and Amelia lay. She sat beside them and sobbed. Red ants were crawling over Amelia's arm, and over Noah's face. She brushed the ants away. Her hands became bloody. The ants crawled on her arms and stung, but she kept brushing them away from Noah and Amelia.

Her father found her that evening beside the two bodies. Her arms were swollen and red. She pressed her face into his chest and begged to be forgiven. She wanted him to hold her there forever.

Donnie Lee

We had dinner after the funeral, and when I was done I asked to be excused.

For what? my mama said.

Maybe go run down by the river, I said.

She said, It won't hurt you to spend some time at home. I never see you anymore, you're always running off to some place or another, you might as well be a boarder here the way you come and go as you please.

Why she was being that way I did not know, but I took it wrong and opened my trap too wide. I said, There's nothing to do around here.

Well, go visit your Gandy Meacham, she said. You ought to spend more time with him. We all should. You can just go set with your Gandy Meacham instead of running off tonight.

I could have got out of it if it was just me and her, but then my daddy looked up like he was hearing it for the first time and he said, Yes, that's a good idea. You can just go set a spell with Gandy Meacham.

And there was no getting out of that.

I stuck my hands in my pockets and fussed until my daddy looked up again from his plate and then I went to set with Gandy Meacham. The shades was down, as usual, and the room was dark and quiet. Gandy Meacham was there in the bed asleep, or so I thought. He had been there in that bedroom for a month and sometimes did not move out of bed once a day, even for the bathroom. He didn't eat or drink more than a baby.

He was my mama's grandfather. She gave him his name when she was small, so the story goes, because that was as close as she could come to saying granddaddy. He lived most of his life in Wyoming, so I hardly knew him. But when Gandy Meacham took sick it fell to my mama to take him in after he couldn't care for himself.

They tuck him off the train in Austin and brought him to the house and fixed him up in the back bedroom that we never used but for company. They stuck him back there and that was all we seen of him, except to go set with him and bring him his meals and help him to the bathroom once a day if he was feeling spry.

I don't mean no disrespect. He was dying, and I knew it even if nobody come right out and said so. I knew it was a cancer, too, though the way we acted you would have thought it was some kind of sin to say the word. Okay, he had a cancer and he was dying. But I have to say that Gandy Meacham wasn't nothing to me. He never once did come to visit us in Texas, until he was ready to die. He stayed up there in Wyoming, as I could see, and did what he pleased.

That was how I seen it.

There was a chair beside the bed. I set myself in it and looked at the old man.

He didn't sleep, exactly. Not once did I see him snooze and snore in the normal way. Every time I would look in on him, he was laying there in that dark room with his eyes cracked open, not moving, his chest barely heaving the covers up and down. He breathed faint, like a sick little bird with a busted wing, just barely there.

It was the pills, I think. My mama gave him pills from a prescription. Not for what ailed him, but to keep him quiet so that he wouldn't hurt so much.

For some time, there was just him and me not saying a word in that room, whilst the light grew dim outside, me not moving any more than him, for I was thinking about Sue Everitt. How much time passed I do not know, but you could have knocked me down with a feather, I was so surprised, when the old man said, in an old man's voice but still clear as you please, What day is it, boy?

I looked down at his face. There wasn't much light, but I could have swore that even though his face hadn't moved, and his eyelids was still down over most of his eyes, the part of the eyes that you could see had shifted around and was now fixed on me.

I didn't say nothing. I couldn't, I was so surprised.

So he said again, I asked you what day is it.

I found my voice. Thursday, I said.

Morning or night? he wanted to know.

Night, sir, I said.

There was not a word from him. But for the first time since he had come to stay with us I heard the sound of the old man breathing. Damn if I didn't hear him draw a couple of breaths before he spoke again.

I wanted to go, he said. I heard him draw another breath. He said, I wanted to go real bad.

I got up from my chair and went to him. I was going to help him, though I didn't want to have to tote him out of bed and into the hall.

It's okay, Gandy Meacham, I said. You can go now. I'll help you go right now if you want to go.

You have to remember that the few times I had heard the old man talk in the past month, he had not said one thing that really made sense. He talked like he was out of his head and I didn't figure this was any different. I could see why he would make a big thing out of going to the bathroom if that was all he ever did in a day. I thought I would help the old guy along, so I bent over to grab him.

He seen how I took his meaning, and how I was mistaken. He put up his hands to stop me. Not that, you damn little fool, he said, real sharp.

I sat back in my chair. I'm sorry, Gandy Meacham, I said.

Now I could tell for sure that he was looking at me. He had his eyelids peeled halfway back and his head was turned to me. He said, Why do you call me that?

That is how my mama told me to call you, sir, I said.

My name is Quiller, he said. Quiller Meacham.

Yes, sir.

I ain't your gandy anyways, am I? he said.

No, sir.

He said, That's right. You could call me Mr. Meacham, but I ain't been called Mister in twenty years. So Quiller it will have to be. Man to man. Does that suit you? he asked.

I didn't know what to say. I was just getting the idea that he could think and talk like everybody else. So I answered slow. Yes, sir. Okay, Quiller, I said.

He said, You thought I was asleep.

Yes, I said.

He said, I want to show you something.

Ever so slow, he reached around his body with his right hand and stuck it under his pillow. He pulled his hand out again and opened his fist and showed me two pills like my mama would give him.

I don't always swaller, he said. If I took every pill they give me I would never be wide awake again. When your mama leaves the room I spit them out and throw them down the toilet first chance I get.

He stopped talking for a minute. I didn't know whether I was supposed to say anything to that.

So I said, That's right clever of you.

He didn't say anything back at first. I looked in the dark to see if he was looking at me still.

Then he said, Even so I get in a haze and forget what day it is. I wanted to go to that funeral real bad.

Not till then did I realize what he had been talking about, that it wasn't the shitter after all.

I asked myself why Gandy Meacham, who had lived probably fifty years without setting foot in Texas, far as I knew, would care about the old lady's funeral.

When he spoke again his voice was even weaker than before. He wanted to know if there was a lot of people at the services. I told him there was, and how they closed down the schools and how the whole town of Luray had been shut down so people could crowd into the church.

Humff, he said, or at least made a sound like that. Then he said, Everybody knowed her, it seems.

Just about, I said.

He said, Well, I would expect as much. And everybody loved her too, I 'magine.

No, sir, I said, I don't think you could say that. Not rightly so. She had her enemies.

Humff, he said again. Well, that don't s'prise me neither, now that I think about it.

I was ready to ask him how he knew her, him being in Wyoming whilst Miz Rose lived all her life here in the valley, when I remembered that in the olden times there was not so many people around and that likely almost everybody knew everybody else then.

I also recalled that Quiller's brother Lynn, who was my mother's great-uncle, had lived in the valley. It was his family that my mama had come to visit when she met my daddy in Luray. I figured that maybe old Quiller had come to see his brother at some time and had met Rose Ellen Sample then.

I snuck it in on him. I said, That must have been back when you was visiting your brother down here.

No, he said after a time.

I heard his breathing again. Then he said, I lived here for a spell.

I said, I didn't know that.

It took him a while to answer, in a voice so quiet I could barely make it out. He said, That was some time ago.

We run out of conversation, I guess, because we just sat there for a while in the dark like before, though now I knew he was not asleep after all.

He spoke next and said, She was a mighty fine woman.

This time I knew what he was talking about. He meant Miz Rose Sample. I set there in the chair and tried to think of those two being young without lines on their faces and crooks in their backs. But I couldn't do it. Even in my mind they didn't come out right. I could see them with hair that wasn't grey, maybe, but their shoulders would still be stooped. And if I got the shoulders square, their hands would be wrinkled and they would still be walking with old people's creaky steps.

He said, I reckon you have things to do.

Oh, no, I said, I'm just fine.

He said, Well, so am I, right here as I am. Maybe I will take those pills after all. You go run along. Maybe go watch that new tellyvision.

The truth was that I was getting itchy to leave. I heard folks talking in the front room. We had the first TV on the ranch, and we could get a station in Austin, so folks would drop by evenings to watch with us. It was about time for Hopalong Cassidy, if I guessed right.

Maybe I will be getting along, I said.

He did not answer. He was just the way he'd been when I walked in the room, stock still with his eyes about closed.

So I left the room. I found a spot right in front of the screen and I stretched out to watch Hoppy. It was a good show, as I recall, but I could not keep my mind on it. I kept thinking about Gandy Meacham and Rose Ellen Sample, and wondering what she had meant to him.

Chapter 6

With Amelia gone, Rose Ellen was the only female on the Circle Three Bar. The closest woman was the wife of a neighboring cattleman, twenty-four miles away. The ranch was the only home that Rose Ellen remembered, for she was seven years old and had been living there for the last five. Men and ranch had changed during those years.

Their eighteen thousand acres had become two hundred thousand. Having convinced his partners to buy land with the profits of their first drive, Fowler bought. An old land grant of thirty-four thousand acres that first year, another of twenty-seven thousand the next, smaller parcels of a few hundred to a few thousand in succeeding autumns. One bad drive was all the burden most spreads needed then to sink, and Fowler was there to claim the remains. Then the big one, a grant of seventy-seven thousand acres owned by a family in Mexicali that had not been on the place since the start of the war. He got it by searching out the owners, knocking politely on their front door, and opening a satchel full of bank notes when he made his offer.

The partners had worked hard, and had had some luck, and Fowler had filled in when the luck fell through. They had two good drives in a row their first two years. The third year they waited three weeks trying to cross the Red River in spate. Here fortune and Fowler both were with them; as they waited, word came trickling down the trail of poor markets this year,

47

prices so low that some ranchers were selling to tallow factories instead.

Fowler and Sample galloped back to the ranch, brought
back cash, and spent the next six weeks buying stock at
bargain prices from drovers unwilling to face a three-month
drive with no reward at the other end.

That cost them their capital. For the next year they slid by
on credit and a smile. But a year later their herd was three
times larger than it had ever been before, and prices were up
again. It all meant money for improvements, and for more
land.

Their holdings were mostly contiguous, though occasion-
ally Fowler would buy a spread that did not touch the edges
of the main property. Then, inevitably, he would buy up the
intervening land as well (though he always tried to avoid the
semblance of urgency in these dealings) until the Circle Three
Bar had reached out to claim its satellite.

It seemed logical to Fowler that their ranch should spread
over every acre of the valley in which their first eighteen
thousand acres had reposed. Mansos Valley is more than
thirty miles wide. The bordering hills on the east and west
sides stretch more than seventy miles from north to south. At
the western edge of the valley, hugging the base of the hills,
is the Mansos River. Along its banks was the old ranch
house. As cranky and sporadic as its flow might be—swift
and muddy during the rainy weeks, little more than ankle-
deep during dry spells—the Mansos was the most important
and enduring source of water in that territory. Except for
isolated seeps and springs, there was no other place where
men or cattle could expect to find water during the dry
seasons, which could last eight, nine months, sometimes
longer.

To Fowler, the hills, with the vital ribbon of water between
them, seemed logical brackets for the ranch that he envi-
sioned. This ideal took its form from the sprawl of the land.
If the valley had been narrow, then so his vision would have
been, for he was not acquiring out of greed or compulsion,
but to satisfy an instinct for tidiness, order, wholeness. He
was far past the point of being awed by the distances involved.
He, who once had stood on the middle of his eighty acres and

admired the breadth of his property, now could add five thousand to the Circle Three Bar as casually as most men might buy a wagon or a rifle.

Six years after the partners first had ridden into this country, their property reached from one ridge of hills to the other, a thirty-mile stretch across the middle of the valley. This strip, roughly ten miles from north to south, slopped over the ridge on one side where property lines had not respected topography. To Fowler, this was surplus, and a clutter. Having bridged the valley, the ranch now could expand within the bounds of the ridges, north and south. Fowler was beginning to believe that this creation of his might cover the entire valley. It could be done, he told himself. Somebody had to own the land.

As the ranch grew, so did the ranch house. After six years its additions had engulfed the original four-room structure. The three partners and Rose Ellen all had rooms. Fowler had an office, and there was a front room, a dining room, and a proper kitchen. In Fowler's office, inked by hand on brown wrapping paper, was a map of the ranch drawn and charted by Newsome, showing landmarks like springs and canyons and arroyos. In another year, as the place grew, Fowler would hire a surveyor and commission a map of the entire valley, and Newsome would draw in the boundaries and the features of each new acquisition.

There were no fences or other means of marking land borders, and they were not needed. The growth of the ranch was reflected only in legal records, not by the look of the land, which had changed little since the partners arrived. But the house was different. They were proud of this tangible symbol of all that they had achieved. It grew with the ranch. It was built of carpenter-finished wood, with glass windows and solid floors—not like the mud-and-stone huts that still survived on some of the smaller spreads.

Surrounding the back lot behind the house were corrals, sheds, and a barn, a bunkhouse for the four cowboys who were kept on full-time, and a cabin for the foreman. This was Alvarez, the *vaquero,* who had returned one year after that first drive, broke and looking for work, having discovered that he was neither storekeeper nor husband.

The competition was spare, but the Circle Three was the finest ranch in the valley. And it marked the three partners as the wealthiest men in the valley, though their fortune was not in cash, but in the land and the stock.

The men themselves were different now, too. But they had changed so subtly and slowly that none of them was aware of it. They still worked hard and sweated and slept with bones and muscles sore, but they no longer were grubby adventurers. They bossed men, actually had hired a man to boss for them, and owned so much land that if they set out from one end and rode toward the rising sun in the morning, that sun would be at their backs and low in the sky before they reached the other end. This lent them a certain stature and dignity. They walked now with the air of men who had accomplished something admirable. If they did nothing else, they would still have the Circle Three Bar to point to.

Chapter 7

With Noah and Amelia gone there was nobody to care for Rose Ellen during the drive that summer. She was too young to travel with the herd, so Fowler was left to stand beside the child and watch his partners and their hands move the bellowing, milling mass of dirty hair and horns their first steps north up the trail. It seemed to him that Sample and Newsome were dragging his soul up the trail with them.

The herd left, as usual, from the box-canyon pen. When they were gone it was as if the place had been disemboweled. Take away the cows from a cattle ranch and there is not much left. Fowler and Rose Ellen rode without a word from the canyon corral to the ranch house. Fowler made coffee and the two of them sat silent at the kitchen table.

"Papa," Rose Ellen said, "don't be sad."

She reached across the table to touch him. He covered her hand with his own, the palm rough and scaly but warm. He squeezed her hand.

"Don't concern yourself," he said.

"Papa, I'm sorry you feel bad."

He reached for her, brought her face against the stubble of his own, held her tight. He should feel joy at this, he told himself. He would have weeks with his daughter. The drive would go on without him. The men would get the cows to market and return with money in the fall.

And he found as the days passed and the herd moved

farther north that he began to welcome this chance for rest
and for peace and solitude with his daughter.

But she was unhappy. Barely three weeks had passed since
the killings, and she was changed. Fowler had noticed that
she was more subdued than usual, nothing more. He was not
sure how a child was supposed to react to such a shock. But
the second day the two of them were alone together, when he
decided to finish spading the garden, Rose Ellen refused to go
with him. He watched her more closely after that, and saw
that she seemed to avoid his office. If she walked past, her
eyes would find another place to rest. He caught her standing
outside the room where Noah and Amelia had lived; she was
standing in the doorway, looking inside. One night he woke.
He thought he heard her calling to him. When he went to her
room he found her crying.

He held her as she wept, and he felt helpless.

Before a week had passed, Alvarez returned, riding slowly
up to the house. His left foot was bootless and swollen, and
hung free of the stirrup. Fowler helped him down from the
saddle, and supported him as he limped into the house and
slumped into a chair. The *vaquero* told his story. The first
camp they had made, the evening of the very first day on the
trail after they had barely reached the northern end of the
valley, he had shaken the dirt out of his boots and walked
barefooted to the edge of the Mansos for a drink of water. He
had stepped on a rattlesnake.

It had been a big snake, he said, but not big enough to kill
him. Two days of pain and delirium and he had beaten the
worst of it. The others, of course, had moved on with the
herd, leaving a man behind to look after him. But Alvarez
had sent him up the trail soon enough. As soon as Alvarez
was able to ride, he had pulled himself up on the saddle and
returned.

They gave Alvarez the room that belonged to Sample.
There he recuperated. Fowler cooked the meals and Rose
Ellen brought them to him in bed, carefully and gravely
balancing the platters. In a week Alvarez left the bed and in
two he could walk. He would be able to care for himself and
to look after the ranch, Fowler knew.

One night soon after Alvarez had taken his first steps,

Fowler visited his daughter in her room to hear her prayers. When he pulled the covers over her, they spoke.

"I notice you ride right straight in the saddle these days," he said. "You are growing into old Scratch, it seems."

"My feet come down to the stirrups," she said.

"You ride real good, Rose."

"Scratch is a good pony. I can take him where I want to go."

"Do you get tired? Does the saddle make your bottom sore?"

"No, Papa."

"I want to ask you something, then, and I want you to tell me true. Suppose I asked you to ride with me as far as the sweetwater spring and back two times. Can you feature that? Do you think you would get too tired?"

She squealed, sat up straight in bed, put her hands on the collar of his shirt. "Oh, no, Papa! I can do that."

"And if I asked you to do the same the next day, maybe a little farther?"

"Yes, yes, Papa!"

He wanted to take her away from the garden and the office. And he wanted to begin showing her the property that was as much her own as his. It was time she saw some of it.

"Then maybe you would care to go riding with me tomorrow. Just to have a look at things. We may be gone a few days. We will sleep out in the open. Maybe it will rain and maybe the sun will be hot. You understand?"

"I can do that, Papa."

"Then you must sleep hard tonight so you won't be tired in the morning."

She did not sleep, except in brief snatches when her mind hummed with dreams and her body thrashed the blankets. She was awake when her father lighted the fire in the kitchen. She dressed quickly and ran downstairs. On the kitchen table was a pile of food in sacks and cartons, four canteens, and fresh bedding in a roll with the white canvas duck still spotless.

"I stayed up last night and made up your soogans. The blankets will keep you warm and the canvas will keep you dry. We will take a mule so Scratch does not have to carry so much. We will ride easy anyways, just mosey around some."

When they had eaten breakfast they packed the mule. Fowler showed Rose Ellen a packer's knot, told her to remember it and to practice it because he would have her loading the mule herself before the end of the trip. They filled their canteens and said their good-byes to Alvarez, then mounted and rode.

They rode side by side for a while with the mule trailing behind on a lead. Rose Ellen did not look back at the house. The place was stained and her vision of it was murky and grey; that was because of the killings. She did not know why, but the house was different for her and she was not sorry to leave it behind.

Instead she studied the ground that they covered. Soon they were in territory she had seen only from a distance before. The horses' legs swished in the grass, stirring up insects that fluttered in the air and came to rest again. Fowler took them past a field of bluebonnets, more flowers in one place than she could have imagined. She made her father stop so she could pick some. She grabbed them in clumps and bunches that she stuck in his pockets, and her own, and under the flaps of their saddlebags, and in the mule's harness. When she had picked as many as she could she stood back and looked, and thought that there were more bluebonnets standing now than there had been before. She lay down in the middle of them and looked up at the clouds.

They rode five miles that day. The distance exhilarated her, the house so far away. She took comfort in that. Yes, they still owned the land out here, her father told her. She was glimpsing for the first time the size of the ranch and feeling for the first time how good that size could be.

Fowler knew a camp spot where water trickled most of the year out of the side of a knoll. Beside the spring was an outcropping of rock and a big boulder that gave shelter on three sides. It shielded them from a strong afternoon wind. Fowler built a fire and cooked a dinner of beans and molasses. The wind blew over their heads and bent the grass on the range. Their niche in the rock opened out on the west, so they watched the sun go down. There were storm clouds, purple stained with sunset orange and red.

Home was that way, her father told her, but they had come

so far she could not see the house. It was no threat now. The impossible stretch of land gave her sanctuary. She felt lost and untouchable here.

They washed their dishes in a puddle that the spring made in the grass. Fowler crouched over the puddle to swish his plate in the water and she did the same, imitating him exactly, balanced as he was on the balls of the feet and bending at the knees, leaning forward. She was studying him, as she had studied him already to duplicate the angle of the John B. on his head, to mimic exactly the lay of the scarf across his chest.

Her hair, grown long, was stuffed up into her hat. The cuffs of her pants were shoved into her boots, just as his were. She stood up at the moment he did, and her version of his walk away from the puddle was as close as it could be without the bow of the legs, which put a natural rolling hitch in his stride.

He put more wood on the fire. She nestled up against him, with her head on his shoulder, and he pulled blankets over them. The side of the boulder was orange from the flames. He held her and told her stories about his first year on the range. She heard thunder and sat up while he talked. To the west she could see lightning, so far away that she could not match the thunderclaps with the flashes.

"Don't be scared, Rose," her father said. "It is going past us. I don't believe we will even get wet."

"I don't mind if we do," she said.

She went to sleep happy. She knew something now that would never leave her: the land could make you feel good. It was big enough to let you escape from what bothered you and it could give you back what you had lost, fill you up again where you had gone empty. The land could do all that.

One day they stood on a promontory along the western range of hills.

"This part is ours," he said, "and down there in that arroyo is about where the spread stops. Royle Evans and his wife own past that. Maybe I can talk them out of it this winter. I think maybe she is weary with this hard work and would like to be done with it."

"Do they have as much land as we do, Papa?"

"No. Not a third as much. I don't suppose you understand that most people don't own as much land as we do, you and me and Earl and Orrin. There are some that don't even own a scrap of it, do you understand?"

She shook her head, no. She had never considered that.

"I can't explain it any better. They don't own any land, is all. Like, you own Scratch there. Some little girls don't have a pony. And some papas don't have any land. Some of them own some, but so little that if you put a hundred of them together—you remember that number, one hundred?—well, that's a whole lot of folks, and if you put them all together maybe they still wouldn't have as much land as we do."

He turned and looked down at her. "It's good to own a lot of land," he said. "Land is different from anything else. You wouldn't want to own more jewels than anybody else, or more clothes or more food. There wouldn't be a point to that—it would be just greed and pride that made you do it.

"Do you understand any of this? No, I don't imagine so. Well, that part about the jewels and the clothes is not as important as the rest. But I want you to remember this about the land. We want to have the best ranch there is, Rose. And with a ranch it's the land that counts. The more land we have the better this ranch is—just remember that, Rose. Remember that much."

He suddenly felt silly, talking this way to a child. He looked back over the valley. She did not grasp the sense of his words. But she felt the emotion behind them, and she knew it had to do with the land, and that part she did not lose.

They returned home and stayed for six weeks. To Rose Ellen, the place was once again the sanctuary she had known. The killings, when she thought of them, seemed to have happened someplace else, someplace to which she would never return.

Fowler was restless, for the ranch was dormant during a drive. He decided to travel to San Antonio, and he took Rose Ellen with him. And on this trip, too, she learned more about herself and about the way she was living. This time she learned by contrast.

They traveled seven days and rode into the city in the middle of an afternoon rainstorm. Fowler boarded the horses at a livery. He asked there for the name of the best hotel in town; across the street, a stable hand said. So Fowler and Rose Ellen threw their saddlebags over their shoulders and marched in tandem across the muddy street. The door of the hotel was polished hardwood, with etched glass and brass handles. Fowler swung one of them open for his daughter, and stepped through behind her. They clopped across the floor, over the plush carpet, up to the front desk with its ornate carved facing. Rain dripped from their slickers and from the brims of their hats, and spattered on the floor.

Rose Ellen had never seen anything so fine. She took it all in while she stood beside her father at the desk.

Across the desk, the clerk's eyes narrowed. "Sir?"

"I'd like a room. Your best. And two beds."

"And how long will you and your boy be with us?"

Rose Ellen sensed some contempt there. She looked at the clerk and waited for her father to correct the mistake.

"About a week," Fowler said.

"Papa!"

"Yes," Fowler said quickly. "She's a girl. My daughter. Take off your hat and show the man, Rose."

She snatched off her Stetson; dirty, matted clumps fell down to her shoulders. A man and a woman watched from a red velvet banquette not far from the desk. The woman drew in a breath and put a hand to her mouth.

Rose Ellen glared up at the clerk.

"Of course," he said. Now there was no mistaking the contempt. This man, Rose Ellen told herself, thinks he is better than me and my papa.

The clerk reached back for a key but withheld it. "We must ask for a deposit of twenty American in advance," he said.

Fowler slipped the saddlebags from his shoulder; made a show of unbuckling one of the bags, reaching inside, finding a leather drawstring purse, and dipping two fingers inside to come up with a gold twenty. He slapped it down on the desk and held out his hand for the key.

Then the two of them walked across the lobby and up the wide staircase, leaving gradually diminishing traces of mud in the shape of their bootprints.

"Papa, I don't like this place," Rose Ellen said when they reached the corridor at the top of the stairs.

"Hush, we'll have a grand time. Keep walking, Rose, don't look back at them folks. Here, this way."

Their room was at one end of the corridor, on a corner of the building.

"Will you look at this?" Fowler said. "You could run a fair-sized herd of cows in a place this big."

The suite had three rooms, two beds. In one room was a brass-rail bed, in another a canopied four-poster. Fowler swept his daughter up and tossed her onto the mattress of the four-poster.

"Ain't this fine? A featherbed, soft as can be. You've got a roof over you, too, in case the rain comes through the ceiling. This beats soogans on hard ground by quite a ways, I'd say."

But she would not be distracted from the new and startling fact that somewhere people lived differently from the way she and her father did, and that people in this place for some reason thought badly of her.

And something else bothered her.

"He called me a boy, Papa, that man down there."

"He didn't look close enough, is all."

"I'm a girl, though."

"So you are. But folks sometimes expect girls to dress a bit more fancy than you are right now. Maybe we can get you some girl clothes while we are here."

They stayed three days in the city, bought clothes and gifts, and ate every evening in the hotel's dining room. Fowler wore a suit of houndstooth check and he made her wear a flounced dress of pink silk.

She noticed that people treated them with more respect then, and nobody mistook her for a boy. But the city was loud, busy, seemed to be running a dozen different ways at once. The evening of the third day she asked her father when they could go home.

"Any time we choose," he said. "This is our holiday. But don't you think this is a fine place to be?"

She shrugged.

"Then we can go," he said, "if that makes you happy."

The next morning they slipped into jeans and cotton shirts and boots and hats once again. They strode out through the lobby, retrieved their horses, stuffed their purchases into another set of saddlebags and rode out of town.

Two days beyond San Antonio they stumbled across a sight that thrilled her more than any of the city's novelties. They had awakened before daylight. The sun was ten minutes risen when they came over a hill above a watering hole and surprised a herd of wild horses. There were hundreds, and they moved, startled, in a fluid formless unit. They flowed up the side of a ridge, then along the crest, silhouetted against the bright new sun. They raised dust, and their manes and tails flew, and the special light of dawn burst through the dust and waving hair in star-burst patterns. Then the horses were gone. Rose Ellen and her father had not moved, and they remained still as the dust settled and the silence restored itself, and there was only the copper sunlight glinting off the water.

She never had a summer like that one again. It remained in her memory like a series of vignette photographs, bathed in that same warm tone that had crashed through the manes and the tails of the wild horses, and they were images of nothing but happiness and love.

Fowler, Rose Ellen, and Alvarez stayed alone in the ranch house until the end of September. Rose Ellen, playing in front of the house, was first to see the riders making their way up the trail. She shouted to her father, and ran up the road with him. The men on horseback were Sample and the four full-time cowboys.

"We had a good drive, Charlie," Sample said as a greeting. He was flushed, excited. This was a triumph. "Good drive," he said. "Two thousand one hundred and seventeen head to market, and we got thirty-eight and a quarter."

"Where is Earl?" Fowler said.

"Natchez, last I seen of him," Sample said. He jumped down from his horse. "Damnedest thing," he said. "Earl has hisself a lady."

Chapter 8

Every year it was the same, the libidinal stirring that began as a faint flutter in the spring and grew to a frantic urge by the time August and Abilene arrived. You could mark with it the progress of the Circle Three Bar's herd up the trail.

Fording the Colorado, the first landmark barrier in their path, told them that they were truly on their way and awakened the desire that they all worked so hard to keep buried during the winter. It might be ignored at first. At the Brazos and the Red it was more insistent. The state line, and Indian Territory, marked the point at which desire usually grew beyond control, dominating their thoughts as they rode during the day and tormenting them at night. Once they reached the Kansas line their soogans were stiff and foul. No amount of hard riding or sweating on the shadowless prairie could blunt the itch that bedeviled them now. They were hounds on a scent, their noses pointed north and twitching. They swore at the unhurried meandering of the cattle.

When they finally collected their pay and burst out into the fleshpots they were sure that no amount of rutting would satisfy them. That illusion persisted no more than a night. Within two days, or three, they guarded what remained of their money with a baleful vigilance and strained to remember what had driven them to such expensive foolishness, assuring themselves and each other that they would never need a woman again.

Sample and Newsome were different because they had

been a part of that cycle for so long now. They knew the
relentless growth of desire and the cathartic abandon at trail's
end and the emptiness that was its residue. They had been
through it all so often that they could anticipate the ritual.
They knew the aching and yearning, the compulsion that
would send them out into the bawdy houses of Abilene, and
what would follow. But knowledge conferred no dispensa-
tion. They were as bound to the rite as any of the others.

They tried to deny it. This time, a few days out of Abilene,
Sample told Newsome that this year maybe he would try to
keep his money in his purse, no reason to go spreading it
around the way he had in the past. He was older now, not one
of these young bucks that had to get his wick dipped or
choke.

Newsome nodded in agreement as the two of them rode
point at the head of the herd.

"It ain't like them calico queens make you feel good,"
Sample said. "I mean, you feel good for the time being. But
it don't last."

"I know what you mean," Newsome said. "Exactly."

"So I believe I will lay low in Abilene. The boys can go
out and chase the painted pretties if they want. I got better
things to do with my spondulix than to leave it on some
chippy's night table. You?"

"Me?" Newsome asked. "Well, I don't know." Newsome
cleared his throat, adjusted his hat, frowned, and answered
without looking at Sample. "I imagine I will indulge," he
said. "Not the way I done when I was a young blood, five or
six years ago. I don't aim to wear myself out. But hell, Orrin,
a man's a man. I'm going to step out some."

"Not me," Sample said. "Not this time."

When they reached Abilene they went first to the brokers'
offices, then to a bank. They booked rooms for the group at a
hotel, and in the large room that Sample and Newsome shared
they doled out the hands' pay. The cowboys took the money,
broke off into groups of three or four apiece, and left shouting
and hooting. Sample and Newsome, on the third floor, could
hear the noise from downstairs when the cowboys exploded
out onto the street.

"Damn fools," Sample said. "They won't have half of it by morning."

"No," Newsome said.

"Me, I will settle for a few simple pleasures. Like a warm bath and a cold beer. How 'bout it, Earl?"

They each paid a dollar for a wooden tub full of steaming water, six bits more for a shave and a haircut. They bought clean jeans, shirts, underwear. It was early evening now, and they ate dinner and drank six schooners of beer between them.

In their room again, Sample let himself fall back on one of the two beds. "There ain't nothing I can add to that," he said. "I might just sleep until next Tuesday."

Newsome was standing by the open door, rocking on the heels of his boots. "I feel restless yet," he said. "Maybe I will wander about some, see how the town has changed in a year."

"*Adios.*"

"Have a drink or two of *aguardiente*," Newsome said. "Maybe try my luck with the cards."

"It is all the same to me if you want to go get roostered."

Newsome shouted his reply. "Damn it, Orrin, I am tired of pulling my pizzle. It won't do anymore, not when the real thing is out there waiting. When you turned into Saint Humping Gabriel I don't know, but I am going to take my pleasures when I can."

"Do what you want."

"That is exactly what I intend. I will do my best not to wake you if by some chance I make it back before next Tuesday."

"Thank you."

Newsome paused in the act of closing the door. He turned and spoke in softer tones. "Orrin," he said, "maybe I am weak. But I need a woman. I do. Them chippies are a poor substitute but they are the best I see on the skyline. Winters are so damn long, and right now all I can think about is the nights I laid in my bed last December, January, thinking I would give my right arm to have a soft, warm body beside me. Maybe I ain't man enough to pass up the chance now that I got it. Maybe I ain't. That's how it is."

He returned two hours later to the dark room, eased himself down onto his bed, and stretched out full length. He heard a horse's hooves on the sidewalk across the street. Somebody's cowhand, maybe one of his own, was riding for a night in the hoosegow. There were slurred shouts; the hooves clapped against the wood in a series of short, nervous, mincing steps. Newsome sat up and looked from the window in time to see the cowboy fire off five rounds from a pistol pointed at the moon. Each shot blazed brilliant orange, and the flashes lit up the cowboy's face.

Sample spoke without preface. He had been lying still and silent. "Gunfight?"

"No. Some boy hellin' 'round, is all."

No novelty in that. Newsome slid back upon the mattress.

"And how is the town?" Sample said.

"Oh, 'bout the same as usual. Maybe shrunk some. The whiskey still bites and so do the women, if that's what you want to know."

"The Red Dog still nasty as ever?"

"I didn't stay long enough to find out. I don't dive that low no more. Anyways, hurdy-gurdy houses always was too loud for me. I just went up to Big Nose Annie's for a spell."

"There is a woman ugly enough to curdle a rattlesnake's blood."

"Annie weren't there. She sold out to a bunch of French chippies."

"French. They's some good-lookin' gals, the French."

"There was a couple I wouldn't mash if I shook 'em out of my boot."

Sample took this in. "French. . . ." he said. Then: "Hell." He turned on his side. "Earl, you done for the night?"

"Anybody that's been throwed as much as me is always ready for another ride."

"Maybe you'd ankle it up with me to that place. Just to look around."

"Whatever happened to Saint Humpin Gabriel?"

"Pard," Sample said, "I feel 'bout as hard as flint and long as a wagon track. If I go another five minutes without a woman I just may boil."

Before the cowhand on the sidewalk could reload his Colt, they were dressed and out the door.

They were men who knew women mostly from memories and dreams. Women were a mystery to them, and a vexation. Not just women, but women's allure and the need they evoked in men. The chippies could help you ignore the need for a while but they could not diminish it. The gap remained after the grappling was done. Contact tantalized more than satisfied, and the men were left wanting they knew not what. This was the vexation. In every other way these men—Newsome, Sample, Fowler, and almost every other range-riding cowboy and cattleman—were used to doing for themselves. They could create or at least simulate everything else that they required. But what they needed from women they were powerless to provide on their own. They could not even put the need into words.

Women were troubling. The less to do with these foreign creatures, the better. They complicated an otherwise simple and satisfying life. Yet troubling as women might be, they still drew men like Sample and Newsome to a respectful, timid proximity.

Each year, as they returned from the drive, the men rode by train to St. Joe and from St. Joe to New Orleans on a riverboat. Newsome, feeling flush and fancying himself a dandy, visited a tailor this time through St. Joe. He had money and he wanted to show it. No popinjay planter in the social hall or the dining salon would outshine him this time. In the tailor's shop, he shrugged off suggestions of tweeds, somber twills, sturdy woolens. Silk blouses were closer to what he wanted. He bought three, collarless, with pleated breasts and loose sleeves. He wanted pantaloons striped black and white, two pairs. Then a pair of kid leather gloves, the color of a fawn's underbelly. He paid and was leaving the shop when he saw the sash: satin, red, six inches wide. He tied it around his waist.

So he was in full splendor two days later when he first saw the woman standing on the loading platform in St. Louis. He and Sample had ridden a packet down the Missouri and were waiting for the southbound *Robert E. Lee*. The woman stood ahead of them in the line at the ramp. She was tall for the day, and slender. She wore a bonnet that would have suggested dowdiness but for the clean lines of her face and the sheen of her blonde hair. She held a fringed parasol over her head, balancing it on one shoulder with the tips of three fingers touching the knob in delicate, negligent fashion.

She was alone, Newsome noticed. Unescorted. The sun had found a way around the edge of the parasol. It lit the hair on the back of her neck.

Newsome, held by the sight, nudged Sample.

"Orrin, looky there."

"Some woman."

One of the four hands making the trip with them leaned close. "Where's her man, I wonder."

"She don't appear to have one," Newsome said.

"A woman like that always has a man," Sample said.

They spoke too softly for the woman to hear, but she sensed their boyish excitement anyway. She got plenty of this attention and she knew how to deal with it. She turned her head back, as though to peer over one shoulder, but her eyes remained downcast. Then she brought them up to briefly confront her admirers. This was an art, letting the eyes flick up long enough to disarm, but not so that she seemed bold.

Her glance burned the men. They were silenced and they looked away. She should have turned away then, her work done, but her eyes lingered. They lingered on the pants, the blouse, the hat, that sash. Most of all, that sash.

She smiled.

Newsome writhed within, a splendid agony. He wanted to be anywhere but under her gaze; he wanted to be no place, unless closer to her. Nothing was ever simple with women.

They met that afternoon. Newsome was walking the upper deck when he saw her at the rail, looking down into the water. He walked to within a few feet of her, though two men were between them. That was the limit of his daring. He looked out across the river and tried to see what he could of her without turning his head. She seemed unaware of him, as the two men chatted between them. In a few seconds the men moved away and that left only a few feet of empty rail between Newsome and the woman with the parasol.

Newsome gripped the rail, swallowed against a sudden

constriction in his throat, and adjusted the angle of his vision enough to include the woman at the edge of his eye. She was beautiful. He wished he could see more without being forward.

She turned and smiled at him, casual and open, as though they were old friends. "Lovely day," she said. The voice was too soft for the chuffing of the engines, the splash of the water, and the six feet her words had to travel.

"Pardon?" Newsome said.

"Lovely day," she said, loud enough now.

"Surely," he said.

She nodded and smiled again. She looked at him, as though expecting something more, then turned her face to the opposite bank. Newsome wanted to do whatever it was he should be doing, wanted to step confidently to her side, lean in close so that she would not have to shout; wanted to speak the right words to make her laugh, open her smile to its full brilliance.

He stood, rigid and miserable, managing only to breathe, and that with some effort. He told himself, Say something. Say something before she leaves. You'll hate yourself if you don't.

"Whar-bouts you from?" he yelled.

"Natchez."

"That is on the river. I been past it."

"Yes?"

"Every year, me and my partners and our boys ride the *Robert E. Lee* from St. Looie to N'Orleans."

"Cowboys?"

"They is cowboys, the hired hands. Me and my partners—there's one that ain't with us this trip—are cattlemen."

"Texas?" she said.

"That's right."

"Do you have a large ranch?"

As she asked the question, she made the first symbolic step across the chasm between them. This was going better for Newsome than he had dared to hope. He, too, stepped closer.

"Fair size," he said. "Bigger'n three hundred sections. A section is a mile square."

"You own all that?"

"Free and clear. We had a good drive and I 'magine we'll be adding a few thousand more acres come the winter."

"And cattle to go with all that land?"

"Oh, yes, ma'am. More'n we could bother to count."

"That sounds positively fascinating," she said. "You must tell me more about it sometime."

Newsome by now was oiled with courage and ready to talk.

"The ranch is south of the Colorado, north of the Nueces, but inland a ways. We call it the Circle Three Bar—"

She cut him off. "I should return to my cabin now," she said. "The sunlight goes to my head, it is so strong."

"Yes, ma'am," Newsome said. "It's been my priv'lege."

She was gone before he could say more. No matter. In their few moments of conversation, he felt, he had leaped miles into alien territory. His head was awash with possibilities; he must go to the saloon, have a whiskey, contemplate all the ramifications of the amazing situation.

By that evening Sample and the hands had heard of the encounter. They were still full of questions as they ate in the dining salon.

"What did she say, Earl, when you said you was from Texas?"

"She said . . . I don't remember what she said. No, wait, she was the one that figured out the Texas part."

"What color are her eyes?"

"Blue. Green, maybe. Oh, I don't know."

"You don't know? What was you looking at, her shoes?"

"Did you touch her?"

"No. It wouldn't have been proper."

"She's a long one. Come up about your chin?"

"A little higher, maybe."

"Her skin looked white as bone when we seen her this morning."

"Pale," Newsome said. "But not sallow. She had some blood in her face."

"I wonder what she is doing alone. Only one kind of woman I know, looks like her, rides a riverboat alone."

"She ain't that," Newsome said. "I know that kind when I see one."

"What did she smell like, Earl? You can tell that way."

"She didn't smell like nothing. Yes, she did, now that I think of it. She smelled right sweet. But flower sweet, not like the polecats we know, that splash on a scent so as to cover up their stink.''

"She has money. Quality. You can see that right off,'' one of the hands said. "That is plain.''

The group fell silent. Eyes rose and focused somewhere behind Newsome, who sat with his back to the door. He turned. Across the room, the woman was following a steward to a table. She sat in a chair that the steward held for her.

"There she is,'' Sample said. "She is a sight.''

"Lookit that woman,'' said a hand.

"Now shut your traps,'' Newsome said fiercely. "Don't you make a fuss, you damn bunch of yahoos. Y'all act like you never seen a lady in your life.''

She seemed not to notice that he was in the room. Maybe, Newsome thought, she did not recognize him from his back. If she saw his face, he knew, she would smile. That would please him so, to have her lavish a smile on him while he sat among Sample and the hands.

"Boss, she looked over. She looked right over here.''

"Will you shut your damn mouth or do I do it for you?''

"She did it again, Earl,'' Sample said.

Newsome swallowed. He tried to affect nonchalance in turning around in his chair, looking back at her. But he caught her with eyes down, studying a menu. He turned back. The second time he turned, a few moments later, she was sipping from a glass, apparently absorbed in thought. With each attempt the cowboys held their breath, waiting, anxious for the connection of eyes across the dining room. They were one with Newsome. His thrill would be their own, though the risk was all his.

The third time, their eyes met. Again that smile, as though she were just now noting his presence.

She raised her hand in a tiny wave, then returned to her menu.

"Boss, that lady has eyes for you.''

"She's sweet on you for sure. Look out for that filly.''

Newsome set his mouth in a hard, even line, and spoke through clenched lips. "Please don't raise a commotion.''

Sample alone was exempt from the command. "What're you going to do, Earl?''

"I don't plan to do nothin'."

"She's about invited you to go over there with her. There she is, lonely as a stranger in town."

"I don't know, Orrin."

They finished their dinner without another word. Newsome did not look back at the woman. He stayed locked in his seat, staring down at his plate. When the table had been cleared he ordered two whiskeys in five minutes, and drained each with a swallow.

Finally he asked Sample, "She still over there?"

"Yep."

"Still eating?"

"Just this minute put down her fork."

"Look ready to leave?"

"Any time. Best make your move if you're gonter." When Newsome did not move, he added, "Make like she's a wild mare and you have to break her."

"Hell, if it was as easy as that, pard. . . ."

But he rose, and walked toward where the woman sat. He felt the eyes of the men follow him. The woman noticed him when he was a few steps away and beginning to falter.

"How nice to see you," she said.

"I wanted to say how d'you do."

"I'm glad you did. Won't you sit down, please?"

"You don't mind?"

"I wouldn't offer if I did."

He felt giddy as he slipped into a chair.

"We should have an introduction, you know, to make this proper by the book," she said.

"Earl Newsome," he said. His right hand went up to the brim of his old Stetson, hesitated, then pulled the hat away. He jammed it between one thigh and the chair, out of sight.

"And you, miss?"

"Mrs. Irene Weaver," she said. She saw his shoulders slump. "Please. I don't believe the late Mr. Weaver will object."

She suggested champagne. He ordered a bottle of the most expensive. She asked him about Texas, about the ranch, about the drive he had just finished. She allowed no slack in the conversation. Newsome had never suspected that a woman could care so about land, cattle, cowboying, partnerships, prices.

It would have been perfect except for the buzzards who leered across the room at them. She noticed him glance back at them. Maybe, she said, he would walk with her about the upper deck. The sun was down now, and the night was mild.

"Perhaps," she said, "you think I am presumptuous. Most women would have been more reticent. That is not my way, sir. I simply don't hold with some of the popular conventions. You understand? Not that I overstep the bounds of propriety. Has anything occurred between us that is improper? I think not. But this trip is too brief, as life itself is, for some of the silly rules that others thrust upon us. Don't you agree?"

He did. Indeed he did, if he understood half of what she was saying.

They disappeared through swinging doors, out onto the deck. Two of the hands were for following them, trying to stay out of sight. Sample stopped them. Earl will have enough problems as it is, he thought.

Sample went to his cabin. The engine's vibration lulled him to sleep. He was dozing when Newsome burst into the room and shook him. "Orrin, wake up, pard. I need some money."

"Money? How much? Five? Ten?"

"Couple hundred, maybe."

"What in blazes for?"

"Don't fight me on this."

"No fight. But we don't have that much here. We have to go to the captain and have him open the strongbox."

"I know, that's why I'm here. He said the two of us together had to be there. Come on, Orrin, hitch up your trousers and come along with me."

Sample followed him up to the texas, where the first mate waited beside a safe. "Both you gents put the bag in there, both has to be here when I open the box. That's the rule."

"Well, open it, then—open the damn thing," Newsome said.

When the safe was open the mate pulled out a small locked satchel that they had left there that morning. The two partners took the bag into a corner.

"You got the key?" Newsome said.

"Here. Earl, what is this all about?"

"Tell you when I got the time, pard."

Newsome jerked the lock away and shoved a hand into the bag.

"Earl, how much you need?"

"I ain't certain. I'll put back what I don't use. I ain't took a cent outta this ranch in seven years, and I ain't going to bust us tonight, neither."

He turned to the first mate. "Does greenbacks spend good hereabouts?"

"Good as gold."

Newsome nodded, and counted off fifteen twenties. He slapped the lock through the hasp of the bag and snapped it. Sample stayed long enough to see the bag replaced in the safe. Then he hurried after Newsome and caught him in the social hall, given over at this hour to five games of poker.

Newsome was walking from one table to another, scrutinizing the players. At the third table he stopped and snatched a gold pin from the lapel of a thin, sharp-faced man in gambler's blacks.

"Hey, mister. . . ." the gambler said.

Newsome seemed oblivious. He was holding the pin up to a lamp that flickered from the ceiling. There was a diamond at the head of the pin, and Newsome watched the way light broke through it. "This thing real?" he said.

"You appear to be the expert. You tell me."

Newsome held the pin under the gambler's nose. "Is it the real thing?" he said.

"Yes."

Newsome held it up to the light again. "How much?"

"I don't wish to sell."

"I'll give you three hundred in greenbacks," Newsome said. The money was in his left hand. He flung the bundle down on the table.

"Sold, it appears," the gambler said. Newsome was gone.

Sample followed him until they reached the upper deck. Then he saw the woman waiting there. Newsome walked to her. The pin was clenched in one hand. He brought the fist up and opened his fingers. She took the pin, then handed it back to him.

"You do it," Sample heard the woman say. "You're giving it to me, you find a place for it."

Newsome held the sliver of gold between thumb and forefinger, hesitated, then sunk it into a fold of fabric high on her bodice. The woman raised herself on her toes to kiss Newsome's cheek. Sample watched. The act, so simple and unaffected, brought a rush of emotion to him that he tried to understand as he left, as quietly as he could, and returned to his cabin. There was embarrassment; he had been an intruder there. Some jealousy, maybe. She was a beautiful woman and Sample told himself that the miracle that had befallen Newsome could as easily have been his own. And, when he considered it, there was just a touch of fear. But that was loco, he told himself. He had nothing to fear from a kiss on Newsome's cheek.

Newsome joined him soon in the cabin. There was awe in his voice when he spoke. "Pard, that is some woman. Some woman. I can't believe all that has happened to me. Irene is her name, Irene Weaver. A widder lady. Every now and then I seen ladies like her. I always figured that they was too good for me, that them and me would have nothing to talk about.

"But it ain't so, Orrin, not with Irene. We talk about every damn thing you can imagine. And she listens to me. Like she cares, what I got to say.

"God, I wanted to show off for her. I wished that the meanest, wildest horse you ever seen was on that deck, so's I could ride it, show her what I can do. I wanted her to see me riding a fast horse flat out, roping a cow that is burning the breeze to get away from me. I wanted to tell her, 'Irene, there's a thousand things I can do that you got no idea of.'

"That was why I got the pin. I shouldn't've took the money, maybe, but I had to do something to show off."

Sample understood: you would want to show a woman like that what a man you are. "The money is part yours," he said. "Charlie won't care."

Newsome, silent for a moment, groped for his next words. "I wanted her to come with us, Orrin. I wanted her to see the ranch. She said that wouldn't be right." He coughed softly.

"But she said I was welcome to get off the boat at Natchez, get myself a room, and keep seeing her there. That is what I will do."

"Why, you old fox," Sample said. "Looks like you found yourself a lady. Go to her, Earl, if that's how it is."

Sample tried to sound hearty and full of cheer. But that was difficult. Because even as he spoke all the envy and fear that he had felt earlier surged inside him again.

Chapter 9

In her cabin, Irene Weaver unfastened, one by one, the buttons at the back of her dress. While her fingers worked, her mind turned over the day. She had to think it all out. She could not afford a mistake, not her, not now. She had to be cautious, had to be sure. She would only have so many chances in the time she had left.

Poverty at least gave you that advantage. It taught you how seldom opportunity came within reach, and what value that opportunity had. The poor learned to make the most of their chances.

And she had been poor, born into a family with four children when she arrived, with five more to come. Her father was a blacksmith in Shreveport, Louisiana. A smitty's earnings made thin slices when divided among a family that size, and even after two of her brothers died of scarlet fever and a sister was taken by pneumonia there never was enough. The house went without paint, the children without shoes. Irene's mother had a gift for sewing and patching and making clothes out of scraps that others would have discarded—and sometimes had. She was proud of these creations, something from nothing. But Irene despised them. Doing without was bad, but tolerable. Doing without while others had plenty, that hurt the most.

She was born beautiful and somehow stayed that way. The beauty had survived bad food, home remedies, drafty walls, and coarse lye soap. It managed to make itself obvious even through the patched dresses and the severe bun of hair—both her mother's doing. When she was sixteen years old she married the pharmacist who recently had bought a shop on the street where Irene lived with her family. Everhall Weaver was thirty-three years old, dour beyond his years, mired in bachelorhood. He owned his shop, and a carriage with a matched set of greys, and a gingerbread cottage across town. That clinched Irene. She settled into the cottage and tried to avoid the old neighborhood. She visited her parents as often as she needed to forestall their visiting her.

Once she recovered from the heady excitement of her own home, a well-stocked pantry, and store-bought clothes, Irene examined more critically the life to which she had committed herself. It had its drawbacks, though Ev was not one of them. She could say truthfully that he was all she wanted in a husband, dull as he was, for her requirements were different from most. He seemed to be a good pharmacist. But Irene sensed that there was a practical limit to how high any pharmacist would climb in life.

The tidy cottage closed in around her; Irene saw dozens of houses nearby that were larger and more opulent. The carriage seats needed new upholstery and the greys were looking sway-backed.

With a suddenness that startled Ev, they were living in a larger home in Natchez, he was owner of a drayage company, and they were the parents of a baby boy. Irene had found the drayage company for him; it belonged to a distant relative of one of her friends. Ev had not been able to resist her, not with a baby on the way and Irene insisting on only the best for their child. Never had his life changed so quickly, and never had the changes been so momentous. The shell-game slipperiness of it all bothered him. He felt as if it had all happened just beyond his reach, slightly faster than he could follow. Now you see it, now you don't. He had never really had hold.

Irene reassured him. She pointed out that their new house in Natchez was better than the one they had left. The drayage company would be a money-maker, properly run. He could see that. Their debts were greater, but so were their earnings.

Best of all, he was a businessman, no longer a shopkeeper. They were moving up.

The movement, however, was mostly hers. She had social aspirations, and within a year had bought the dresses and attended the dances and sponsored the parties that were her admission to Natchez society. She needed fine clothes, new furnishings for the house, a nursemaid for the baby. A nursemaid! Ev was appalled. They were living in a world that he barely knew. Other people did these things, not Ev Weaver.

The scope of their expenditures was awesome when he compared it to the budgets he had drawn up for himself as a bachelor. He had paid cash, had spent judiciously, most of all had abhorred debt. Irene scolded him now when he hesitated to take on new obligations. They had the money, she told him. The debts always were paid.

They were, for he was putting all of his effort and most of his hours into spurring on the business. It was growing, though no faster than their debts and Irene's capacity for spending. Ev wished he had more time for his son. He was a poor father, he told Irene once. But she consoled him. He couldn't do everything, she said. Little Ray loved him all the same, and one day would appreciate all that his father had done for him, the selfless and magnificent way he had provided.

Seventeen minutes after midnight, three days short of his fortieth birthday, Ev Weaver died in his chair at the drayage warehouse. He slumped forward and his head hit the desk where he had been working. His body lay there until the next morning.

Irene failed to realize the implications at first. Seven years of security had lulled her. She had taken for granted the supply of funds that her husband had squeezed out of the business. When he died the money faltered but the debts did not. She knew nothing of the company, had left those details to Ev. Now she was unsuited to replacing him. It was a lesson learned. Never again would she fail to know, to understand, and most of all to control the sources of her financial security.

She promoted Ev's assistant to general manager. Still the profits flagged. Six months after Ev had died, she sold the company. Once she had satisfied her own creditors, and the company's there was little enough left.

Already she had begun to look for another husband. Her inheritance would buy her some time. She told herself not to panic, that the suitors would come calling once the arbitrary, inflexible period of mourning had passed. But as she looked out at Natchez through a black lace veil, she despaired of her prospects in a city that now seemed hopelessly small and backward. She could not marry just anybody now. It would take a special kind of man, a generous and substantial man, to fill her material needs. Such men were rare. She had risen to the top of Natchez gentility, and from that perch her view was commanding. She could see few matches at her own level, and she would not marry down. That would be starting over, unthinkable. There were no pharmacists in her future now.

Her mother died about that time, and Irene returned to Shreveport for the first time since she had moved to Natchez. What she saw frightened her. She had forgotten how bad it was, the hopelessness, the dreariness of poverty. She left terrified that she might once again be forced to live that way.

In a letter of condolence a friend in St. Louis had invited her to visit. Irene found a family to keep her son. She put away her widow's weeds and traveled upriver to St. Louis. This was no Natchez. St. Louis had money, men, prospects. She stayed there a month, long enough to convince herself that if she was to find the right man she must leave Natchez and establish herself in St. Louis; most important, she must continue to live as though her resources were without limit. The certain man that she wanted would want only a certain kind of woman.

So she was racing time—racing the inevitable depletion of her funds and racing age as well. She had not withstood the years as easily as she would have liked. She saw the beginnings of lines at her eyes, at the corners of her mouth. Her face was showing the first signs of an unhappy, strained pinch. The effects were slight enough so far. They could be ignored or at least disguised. But she knew that time was against her here as well.

She had been returning to Natchez when she met the cowboy. She had to trust her instincts, she knew, and her instincts told her that this man owned all that he claimed and was what he seemed to be. That had been the most difficult part, believing that a man could be so boyish, so abashed, so vulnerable to feminine ways. But it could not be an act, she decided. It was too perfect, too complete.

Still, she would have to be cautious. The man she chose would have to be a particular sort. Wealth was only part of it. He had to be the kind of man who would not fight her inclinations, a pliant man. She was different from most women, and the man she chose for her next husband would have to be accommodating.

Texas was far from Natchez and genteel society, all that she knew and valued. But she had never before met a man who was partner in three hundred square miles of land. If need be, if she chose that way, she would change Texas to suit her tastes. For this she believed above all else: that there was nothing that could not be altered if one made enough effort.

October passed, and November. One evening Fowler told Sample that they might have to make plans to buy Newsome's share if he did not return. That would mean a loan, maybe even selling some property to raise the capital. There would be hard times for a while if Newsome wanted his share in cash.

But Newsome rode up the trail to the house in mid-December. He was at the reins of a covered buckboard, with a woman beside him. A young boy rode in the back seat with trunks, cartons, hat-boxes. While Sample, Fowler, Alvarez, and Rose Ellen stood outside the door of the house, Newsome climbed down from the seat, walked to the other side of the carriage, and put out an arm for the woman to hold—just to touch, really, as she stepped to the ground.

Newsome made the introductions. He wanted everybody to meet his wife, Irene, and their son, Raymond.

Donnie Lee

It was history class, and what the teacher called a Living History project, that got me together with Sue Everitt.

History was third period, and the best part of the day for me, since my seat was beside Sue E.'s. I could never get close enough to her. I felt good being next to her that way, but I had trouble keeping my mind on what was said. This was double bad because Sue E. was the straight-A type and I wanted to look sharp for her. Most times it didn't work that way.

The day after the funeral she was dressed right pretty, with a skirt and a sweater that she wore pushed up around her arms, and her hair pulled back in a ponytail. We walked together to the cafeteria and she said would I eat lunch with her because there was something she wanted to talk to me about. That turned out to be this Living History project.

The teacher had throwed that right past me in class while my mind was on the skirt and the sweater and the ponytail. I caught enough to know that we was supposed to team up with somebody else in the class, and do a composition on something that had to do with the history of the town or the valley. It had to be something that wasn't in the books, something we got from talking to people who actually knew the way it was way back when.

Sue E. said, What do you think is a good topic, Donnie Lee?

I wished right then that I could have been back in class to

pay more attention this time, listen real close and then think hard so that when Sue E. asked me that question I would have a string of good ideas and she would think I was something. But all I did was hem and haw and chew on my sandwich until she saw that I didn't have a clue.

Lord, I felt dumb.

Well, she said, I've been thinking I would do Rose Ellen Sample.

I piped right up. I said, I thought this was supposed to be a Living History project. I recollect we buried that old bag yesterday.

Soon as I said it I was sorry. I was trying to be smart, is all. But Sue E. took it wrong. She looked at me like I was a big *cucaracha* that just climbed out of the crack in the wall.

I might have expected something like that, she said.

I'm sorry, I said. Please believe me. I didn't mean it. And I didn't. I had nothing against the woman.

You shouldn't make fun of the dead, Sue E. said. Especially not a woman like her. Did you ever stop and think of all Miz Rose must have gone through? Did you ever consider how hard even men had it back in those days, and how much harder it must have been for women?

I don't suppose you ever thought about all she must have gone through in her life, Sue E. said, like she was scolding me.

I reckon not, I said.

I have, she said. That is why I want to do a project on her. She must have been a great lady.

I reckon you're right, I said.

Do you think so? Sue E. asked me. Do you really think she was a great lady?

I said, She must have been. Everybody says so.

Then maybe you'd care to work with me on the project, she said. I think we can help each other out on this. You know the people in the valley, you know who we can talk to.

Nothing ever made me feel better, or feel more proud, than hearing that. Like I was special. Like she thought I had the goods to help her with her A. Right then I knew I was in love.

Naturally lunch went by so fast I hardly noticed it, and Sue

E. had to go. When the bell rang she told me, Donnie Lee, you think about a list of people we can talk to. You think about that and maybe Saturday we can start on this project.

I floated through the rest of the classes, went home, ate supper, all in a fog. All of a sudden I was at the end of the day without knowing how I got there, my mind was so stuck on that girl. I still had not done a lick of thinking about my project or anything else, but damn if I was going to look like a dummy in front of her again.

I made myself concentrate on who to talk to. Tom Holloway's daddy, who was Rose Ellen Sample's straw. That would be one. Stallworth the banker did business with everybody in the valley. But he was not nearly as old as she'd been. I kept trying to come up with somebody who'd have known her from a long time ago.

Then it hit me.

Gandy Meacham, right under this same roof, in a room that was right under mine. Gandy Meacham went back that far, and he knew her then. He said so.

I had to talk to him. Right then it had to be. I knew Sue E. would be real proud of me and would think I was really something if I come up with Gandy Meacham, who nobody else even knew was in town.

I jumped out of bed and went downstairs. The house was quiet and I tried not to make any noise. I tiptoed past my parents' room and went into Gandy Meacham's.

He looked the same as ever. But I knew from the night before that that didn't mean anything.

I bent over him and said his name, his real name like he told me.

I said it again. Quiller, I said. Then, Gandy Meacham, you awake?

He just barely budged, opened his eyes like they was sewed shut.

What is it? he said.

I said, I thought maybe we could talk. Like last time. Maybe we could talk about Miz Rose Sample.

What you want to know about her? he said.

All about her, I said. What she was like, the way she acted—all such stuff.

It took him a while to answer, a few words at a time. Not now, he said. Too tired. My head's woozy. Come back tomorrow, you hear?

Yes, sir, I said.

He reached out and took me by the arm. He give me a squeeze, about as hard as he could. He closed his eyes. I could tell when he went back to sleep, for his hand on me relaxed and he let go. I pulled my arm loose as gentle as I could, and I laid his hand back on the bed where it had been.

Chapter 10

The grown-ups set aside the fight long enough to eat supper. They were silent when the cook brought the steaming porcelain tureen of soup, and they ate with their eyes down at their food, silver clicking against the glazed plates.

That suited Ray and Rose Ellen. It meant they could slip unquestioned away from the table while the adults stewed over the latest sharp words. The boy and the girl glanced at each other. No words. They understood. Rose Ellen left first, crossed the parlor, and went outside through the front door. She walked to the stable, threw a blanket across the back of her new mare, and was drawing in the straps of the saddle when Ray appeared. She knew, without asking, that he had waited a moment to rise from his seat and had left by the back door. When he led his pony out of the stable she was mounted and waiting for him.

"Where to?" she said.

"We got a couple more hours' light."

"Indian Oak," she said. It was their name for a lone tree on a hill nearby. Rose Ellen kicked the horse into a half-circle to point it toward the hill, but Ray already was in motion before she moved, before she had spoken or even had thought the name.

They rode at a canter until they were out of sight of the house. They both knew the spot, a bend in the trail that hooked around a knoll. The other side of the rise was blind from the house. When they made the turn each one put spurs to horse.

The animals gathered up beneath them and then exploded forward, surging down the twin ruts of the wagon trail. They rode side by side and followed the trail until it veered away from the hills. There the riders cut off into the open country, and at a gallop picked for themselves paths through the brush, the rocks, and the gullies. Each was intent now, alternately crouching low for speed and sitting up in the saddle to guide the horses through the shadows of the evening sun. Their paths separated for a time, then drew closer together, and crossed when Rose Ellen found in her mare a reserve of speed that let her pass the boy in the flat, let her flick across his field of vision, across and back again, so close she could hear his pony snort from the dust kicked into its nose.

He drew even at the base of the hill. Then it was straight up, the horses straining. Ray had his hat in his right hand and was pounding it against the pony's side. Rose was bent over the pommel, the reins loose in her left hand while the right found a grip in the mane.

It was the mare by a head as they charged over the top. Then Rose Ellen was up in the saddle, tightening the reins as she vaulted out of the stirrups. She hit the ground with legs moving and dived across the brown grass to slap the tree's trunk.

He was half a step behind her, and he sprawled across her legs as he reached for the tree.

"Mine," she said, breathless.

"God damn."

"Don't you curse around me, Raymond Newsome."

"I reckon I will if I want."

She pulled herself from the ground, sat against the trunk so that she could look out over the valley. He sat beside her.

They were children no longer. They had grown into skinny and bony parodies of the adults they would become. Rose Ellen had her full growth, but the sharp edges of her elbows, knees, and cheeks were more obvious than they would be soon. Ray was already showing the long legs, wide shoulders, and strong arms of a man.

Below them the river was luminous, the low sun at an angle that let its light reflect off the water.

"Don't get sore," she said, "just because I beat you to the top again."

"I ain't sore. Who says I am?"

"It happens often enough. It seems to me a body would be used to it by now, and might learn to take second best without cursing to wake the dead."

"That mare there has got speed to waste. Look at the long legs on 'er. Give me that mare, I could beat you to the top and whistle Dixie while I was doing it. I wouldn't have to go throwing myself 'crost the dirt to do it, neither."

"It ain't speed. It's heart. That mare has got more sand in her than the whole Mansos River. And there ain't nothing wrong with your pony that a fair rider wouldn't straighten out."

He said nothing to that. She looked at him. His jaw was set and his eyes had narrowed into slits. She knew that she had gone too far. She thought, That's just the way he does when he is stung, puts on like he is so tough and can't nothing hurt him.

She said, "You about flew over that *hondo* back there."

He said nothing, but his jaw relaxed.

"That's a deep one," she said. "I was just behind you when we come up on it. I says to myself, There ain't no way he's going to jump it. It's too wide for that. He'll go down it and come up, for sure. But there you went, like it wasn't but a crack. I said to myself, Well, if he can do it on that pony I reckon I can do it on this long-legged mare. But I wouldn't have tried it if I hadn't seen you do it first. You rightly flew over that arroyo."

He rubbed his eyes with the backs of his dirty hands. "It weren't so much," he said. "It's a good pony. Jumps a long ways when it has to."

Then it was better, and they could put the race behind them and look out over the valley together, back to the way they were most of the time, which was more as one person than two.

She was thirteen years old now, he more than a year younger. They were rarely apart from the beginning of day to bedtime, and it had been that way almost from the start. That first day, when the adults had sat stiffly in the front room making polite conversation, Rose Ellen had taken Ray outside, showed him the horses and the barns, and led him down to the river. She had coaxed off his brogans and teased him across the river with his pants rolled up around his knees. He had been something of a frail little boy then, frightened and unsure. It was a new life and a new country, all so different from what he had known. She had decided to cure him of his fright. After eight years of living with adults, she was ready for the company of a child, and she was going to teach him her ways.

She had pursued his friendship. He would be her pard, she decided. She taught him to ride—on the sly, using her little pony—so that when Earl decided his new son ought to learn something about horses Ray shocked him by climbing into the saddle, sitting just as a horseman should, and urging the horse into a trot around the corral. Rose Ellen had been there on the fence that morning, watching it all, proud of the surprise on Earl's face. She had watched Ray bounce in the saddle with his head held erect and had thought, Yes, this boy will do right well.

Their being together was natural. When Rose took her lessons from her father, Ray was there too, learning the same things. If Rose weeded in the garden, the job went twice as fast with two. It became his job to curry the horses, but there was no reason why a girl should not help. And if one was going to ride in the hills for the sheer pleasure of it, the other would follow, of course. That was safer; it made sense, plain enough.

Soon they had their own existence that only incidentally touched that of the adults. Irene had tried to keep them apart at first. She had wanted to keep Ray indoors. This was all new to him, she argued, and he ought to step into it gradually. But he had confounded her by leaping into the new existence, abandoning himself to the new ways. He had prospered. He grew nine inches in two years, showed muscles in his arms and shoulders for the first time, turned acorn brown in the sun. His mother could not hold him back.

Ray and Rose Ellen were growing up together in a universe

of their own design, with compacts and understandings that
the others never suspected. They knew about each other all
that was worth knowing. When they were alone together they
could go hours without speaking. They had intuition and
empathy that sometimes were better than words.

Yet even with this melding they were different, one from
the other, in ways beyond gender. Rose Ellen was the talker
if there was talking to be done. Ray kept his feelings close;
there was no telling what she might blurt out, or when. They
could both be hurt. And the closer you were, she was learning, the easier it was to hurt and be hurt. But Ray would take
the hurt like he could take it forever, and never cringe. She
cried out against it.

Rose Ellen realized the differences. She grasped all this
because she had observed, considered the matter, and judged
it. Ray took it in without question, and there was the biggest
difference. She was her father's daughter this way above all.
And he was his stepfather's son, by inclination and by imita-
tion. In this way and in half a dozen others, he was taking on
Earl's manners.

Alone on the hilltop, they picked up stones and flung them
down toward the valley. A hawk slid by, dipping one wing to
wheel in a circle above them. Ray ran to his pony and slid his
repeater from the sheath on his saddle, but she stopped him.

"I can hit that bird easy," he said.

"I know that," she said. "You think you have to waste
good powder to prove that to me?"

He stuck the rifle into the sheath. Such a beautiful bird, she
thought. She didn't want to see it gone.

They climbed the oak, she boosting him up to the lowest
branch, then taking his hand and scrambling up the trunk.
Together they went hand over hand to the top, until each
could stand on a thin upper branch and feel daring.

In the house, down in the valley, the four adults were
sitting in the room that they now called the parlor, once the
original front room of the old house. The ranch had changed
in the last four years. As usual, the most obvious changes had
been in the house: partitions, additions, refinements. Irene
had wanted them all, had pushed for them and had overseen
them.

First a new room for the two of them, Earl and Irene. That was fitting, they all had agreed, husband and wife apart from the others. The new room became a new wing soon. They had wanted Ray nearby, and there had to be closets for Irene's clothes, and Earl deserved an office of his own like Fowler's, and the Mexican woman she found to cook and clean house needed quarters, too.

After a few months Irene had sent for her furnishings. They filled the house and she wanted rooms for the excess. She wanted the house as elegant as the furniture; they kept a carpenter on salary for eight months making the changes. They ate with silver, from china plates, and walked on plush rugs, and sat on chairs covered with velvet. This was her world, within the walls of the house. She cared about the workings of the ranch, too much for Fowler's tastes, but she got what she needed to know from the men and from ledgers. No need to walk out into the sun and the dirt. That was for the others. She sat in the house, happy to be alone. She read and did knitting or needlework. And all the time her mind was working, working.

"I know we can work this out someways," Sample said. He was at one corner of a triangle, with Fowler to one side of him, diagonally across the room from Newsome and Irene. Sample balanced a cup and saucer and tried to look at both corners as he spoke.

"Let's just talk this thing out some more," he said. "If we hack away at it we can come up with something we all like."

This bickering had plagued them for the last several years. It had forced Sample into the role of conciliator and mediator, making him open up and trust his own words.

"Orrin, you'll spill your coffee and ruin the rug," Irene said.

"We can talk around it all you want," Fowler said. "I still can't see buying stock now. I might not put up such a fight if we didn't have better things to do with our money. But I think we can get the Taylor spread now, and if that means buying no stock this year then so be it. It ain't as if we don't have cattle. We could bring three thousand head to market next year and still leave some behind. The Taylors have some anyways, which would go in the deal."

"You aren't trying to tell us that it is the Taylor stock you are after," Irene said.

"I'm saying they have stock that will go in with the deal."

Irene said nothing, but looked at her husband and put a hand on his shoulder so solidly that it was almost a nudge.

Newsome cleared his throat. "Now, Charlie, what we was thinking—Irene and me that is, and maybe Orrin won't give us much of a fight on it either—is that it don't make sense to spend money on land the way we done.

"It's . . . it's cattle that brings money from the brokers, not land," he said. He glanced at his wife, saw her head tip forward slightly. Doing fine. He rolled on. The words he was supposed to say were coming easier now.

"Now, land, the way it works in these parts, don't mean much at all. There is folks in this valley running five hundred head that don't have much more land than what their house sits on. Their cows roam over the land, and the land is open. Like Tom Adams, that sold his six sections to us a while back. He took his money and bought himself a herd down Matamoros way and here he is back this winter running them Mexican cows right on the same land again. Ain't nothing changed except our money is in his pockets now and his cattle is running on our land 'stead of his. Now, dogged if he didn't make us look like a bunch of halfwits with that. Dogged if he didn't. Irene . . . that is, we . . . we don't see the sense in it."

She put a hand on her husband's arm. "Why buy the Taylor place when our cattle graze on the land already?" she said.

"You wouldn't understand," Fowler said. This dream of his, this vision of a single ranch up and down and across the valley's sprawl, he had never shared. And he would not. He believed that it would mean nothing to them. He also believed that they would be grateful for the land one day.

"Can you answer that?" Irene said. "See if we don't understand whatever reason you have."

"What if it changed?" Fowler said. "What if it wasn't like this all the time, and we had to keep our cows only on land that we owned?"

Newsome again: "How, Charlie? How we going to make

our cows stay where they belong? You can throw up a splitrail fence around eighty acres to keep your herd in, but how in hell can you fence all the land we own and keep the fences standing? It can't be done. You're talking crazy. You don't need fences when you got brands."

Fowler was motionless in his chair. He stared at them.

"If we had the money we needed for everything else," Irene said, "I could indulge you in this. But it was just last week you protested when I wanted to send to New Orleans for that pianoforte I saw there in the fall. Save our profits for the ranch, you said. But for land? When we already have so much more than anyone else in the valley, so much that we are laughingstocks? We're land-poor is what we are, Charlie Fowler, and I for one don't see a reason for that."

Fowler neither moved nor spoke. But within himself he damned small minds, small visions.

On the hill, high in the oak tree, Ray and Rose Ellen looked out at the flat light that the evening sun threw across the valley. The light had lost the stark midday glare and its shadows were longer and softer than they had been two hours earlier.

"Where does the river go, do you reckon?" the boy said.

"My papa says that after a piece it leaves this valley and goes into the Nueces. And then the Nueces goes into the Gulf, he says."

"I wouldn't mind follerin' her to the end, someday."

"Me, I want to go to Wichita with the drive. I could do that."

Ray moved out on the branch. "I can go way out here," he said.

"Don't you fall."

"I won't fall. And I can go out way farther. See, way out here. And even farther."

"Don't, Ray." The sight of him halfway out on the limb made her chest tighten.

"I ain't scared."

"I know. You're real brave. But don't."

He edged out, beyond his last handhold, arms extended for balance.

"Ray," she said.

He moved for the trunk when he heard the first crack. But the wood splintered in front of him and he fell.

He hit two more limbs on the way down and he broke them both. His body thumped heavily on the ground, and he lay there fighting for the air that the blow knocked out of his lungs. She jumped down from the last branch, ran to him, and turned him face up. She was crying.

Breath came; he gulped it and spoke. "Don't cry. Rose, don't do that."

"You hurt bad?" she said.

He gave a tentative flex to neck, legs, arms, fingers. "Shoot, no," he said.

She sniffled and blotted her eyes on a shirt sleeve. "You're a sight," she said.

His shirt was ripped, front and back. His pants were torn down one leg. His face was unmarked, but both arms, and his chest, and the one exposed leg, showed deep scratches where blood was welling. He sat up and raised his right arm; it was scraped raw where he had hit the earth.

"My maw is going to tan me," he said.

"I ought to do it first."

"I can't let her see me."

"You can't go in looking like that. You have to clean out the scratches, too."

They rode slowly down the hill, across the road to the edge of the Mansos. He obeyed when she told him to take off his shirt, sit on the bank, hold his arms out. She shook dust from her bandanna and dipped it into the river. She held it in a ball to wipe the cool cotton down his wounds, first his arms, then his chest, his back, his legs. Then she put the bandanna into the water again.

"Pull down your britches," she said.

"Rose."

"You got scratches there on your seat and I can't get to them under your pants."

"Let me do it, then."

"You think I care whether I see your old backside? Just pull down your britches and let me do it. You'll never get it clean. It's a nasty one."

He did as she had told him, and felt a flush on his face and across his chest.

"Pull 'em up," she said. "We got 'em cleaned out but you still need more. Luz has a salve that she keeps for when she gets a burn. That would be dandy, don't you think?"

"Hold it, Rose. We can't let my mother see me like this. She'll keep me beside her for a month."

"Then we won't let her see you."

They rode home. From inside the house there was shouting. No one noticed as they crossed the corral and rode into the stable.

"You stay," she said. "Wait. I'll take care of you, Ray."

The shouting stopped when she was a few feet from the back door. She came in, trying to be quiet. She looked around a corner to peer into the parlor. Four in there, she saw, and Luz in her room, where she always went when the talking turned to shouting.

"There's no need for that," Sample was saying. "We all want the same thing. We want the best ranch in the territory. We don't all agree on how to do it, sometimes—that's our problem. Charlie, maybe it don't matter if we don't get the Taylor place. We could spend less and get some smaller spread. And Earl, Irene, we don't have to sink all our money into stock. We can buy some cattle and some land, work it that way."

Rose reached Ray's room without crossing the parlor, so it was easy to get the clean jeans and the shirt that he needed. She left the clothes at the back door and walked through the dining room. The voices were lower. Irene saw her as she walked toward the kitchen.

"Where's Ray?" she said.

"In the stable, ma'am."

"It's late now. I don't want him running off this time of day."

"He'll be in directly, ma'am."

Irene looked back at Sample. Rose Ellen walked into the kitchen, found the tin of salve in a cupboard, and stuck it into a back pocket. She crossed the dining room again, gathered up the clothes, and ran to the stable.

"Good as done, Ray. Here, slap some of this on before

you change. You can do your backside yourself if that makes you feel better.''

The sky was smudged black over red when they walked together into the house, front door this time. He must be hurting, she knew, but he walked as if he did not carry a mark. And there were none that the fresh clothes did not cover.

The adults were rising out of their chairs in the parlor.

"Raymond, I never see you around here," Irene said. "Where do you spend your time? I don't like the way you make yourself so scarce, mornings through to night.''

And Fowler spoke, more sharply than usual. "Rose Ellen, you've got lessons to do. Am I raising some sort of ignorant savage? I regret the day I stuck you on a horse the first time.''

The two children caught each other's eyes. Then Ray turned for the kitchen and Rose Ellen walked to her room.

She closed the door behind her. She pulled off her boots and stretched her skinny body on the bed. With her arms folded beneath her dark hair she watched the last minutes of sunset stream through her window and play out on the opposite wall. She was occupied with Ray, not so much thinking about him as feeling him. And though she had no word yet for the feeling, the truth was that every bit of her was suffused with a young girl's love for Raymond Newsome.

Orrin Sample left the house and walked to the tack room beside the stable. He was alone. He stuck two fingers into a jar of saddle soap, soft and fragrant with a rich smell that he liked. He brought out a dollop and smeared it on the saddle that lay before him on a bench. He spread the saddle soap over the smooth leather until he had covered the seat with a thin, opaque film. Then he worked it into the leather, moving his hand in circles, pressing hard with the fleshy part of his palm.

This argument had drained him, as they all did. Irene and Earl tugged at him one way, and his loyalty to Fowler drew him in a different direction, though Charlie never tried to sway him as the Newsomes did.

He could not fault Charlie Fowler for the way he had run the ranch. Sample could look around and see what Charlie had done in eleven years, see the changes that Charlie had brought about. A house that was as good as a storybook mansion. Land almost without end. Money—plenty of money. And something better than money. Power might be the word for it. When he rode the range and when he walked the streets of Abilene, Austin, San Antonio, Sample stepped aside for nobody. For the first time he was part of something important, something that mattered.

He yearned sometimes for the simpler life they had known before the ranch had grown so large. They had been three together in their work and in their hunger. They had agreed. Agreeing had been easy then because their needs and their aims had been so simple. Earl wouldn't have argued then about buying land or cattle.

Sample rubbed the cream into the leather and thought, I am the same, at least. I haven't changed. And a moment later: The hell you haven't. You are older and you want more money just the way Earl and Irene do—just the way Fowler does, too, if you look close enough at him—and in some ways you want more than you ever dreamed of, and there are some things that you dreamed of once that you know you will never have. Like a woman. You dreamed once about a woman, but you know that it is not for you now. You will never find one to care for you the way you want. That is one dream that has shrunk down to nothing.

But everything changes, he knew. Even Texas was changing, with towns where once there had been grass; schools and churches; county commissioners; roads, including a regular corridor from south Texas to Kansas with not a single unfriendly Indian in the way. People were raising crops and children in parts of Texas that the Cherokee had held as their own five years earlier.

Everything changes, Sample told himself. You can't cry over what is lost because everything changes.

He dug out another hunk of saddle soap and slapped it so hard on the leather that his palm stung. Everything changes, he thought. Maybe so. But it was a damn shame that they hadn't held on to a few things just a while longer.

The sun was dropping behind the hills, throwing shadows across the valley, when Charlie Fowler left the house. He walked down to the Mansos and sat against a high bank that the floodwaters helped cut every year. He felt the evening stillness of the land that surrounded him.

Maybe he was wrong, he thought. Maybe it was all fool-ishness, the idea that he had carried with him all these years. Even if it came to fences, they still owned more land than they would need for a fine cattle ranch. Life would be smoother in the house if he were not so stubborn. Maybe it is pride alone that keeps me battling, he thought. And pride is a poor reason.

He listened to the stream running over the rocks, and considered the dream that had moved him along, given him something to chase. Having a fine ranch wasn't enough. They'd had that for years. Having the biggest, and the best, was something to look at in the distance when he raised his eyes from his boots and the Texas soil.

He might have done it, he thought. Once the times had been right and luck had been with him. Most important, Sample and Newsome had been with him, and for a while he had almost believed that they could do anything, the three of them.

But now he had doubts. The dream seemed more distant than ever. There had been changes on the Circle Three and in the valley. People were taking hold. He was not alone in making bonds with the land. Others wanted a part of this valley, too.

He stood up slowly and looked around. He saw that the far hills to the east still reached into daylight. He realized that he had never seen the valley, one end to the other, at one time. No mountain on either side of the valley was high enough to grant such a view. Fowler did not know how high a man would have to climb to see every square mile of the valley at one time.

Higher, he thought, than he could reach.

Earl Newsome watched Fowler walk slowly up from the stream, head down. Looking like a beat man, Newsome thought. He did not want to hurt Charlie. But he wanted more to please Irene, and she had ideas, things that he would never have realized without her help. Damn Charlie for being so mulish, he thought. No reason to behave that way. There was plenty for all on this ranch.

Earl paced the kitchen while his wife knitted in the parlor. He was full of desire tonight and he knew that she would not disappoint him. Not tonight. Not after he had done so well this evening, speaking up to Fowler as she had urged him.

The clock rang seven-thirty. Irene did not look up from her knitting. Newsome took a rifle from the rack on Charlie Fowler's office wall and brought it to the kitchen with a can of oil. He checked the action and oiled the moving parts and wiped the barrel clean. He did this with five guns and was working on his sixth when Irene rose, put her knitting into a basket, and left the parlor. She walked down a hall and around a corner into their room.

Newsome replaced the rifle in the rack and met her in the room. She was bending over a dressing table with a lamp burning before her, examining her image in a mirror.

"Hello, darling," she said, and she showed him a smile that Newsome wished he saw more often. It warmed him this time, as always, and it gave him courage now. He walked to her side and kissed her on the nape of her neck. This time she did not seem to object. He had learned to be careful; often his attentions annoyed her. She never said so, but made it plain enough. He had accepted that there were times when he should not touch her, or even try. He had not married a cow-town chippy. Irene was a lady.

Tonight she was open to him. She turned from the mirror, put her arms around his neck, and kissed him on the cheek. "I want to thank you," she said. "You told him all the things that needed saying tonight, and with more force than I could have put behind them. I'm so proud of the way you stand up for me, Earl."

"I will do anything for you," he said, and he meant it.

She pressed her lips against his, and in a moment opened her mouth to his tongue. This was a rare treat. It inflamed him and he felt for the stays of her dress.

She pushed herself away. "Wait, Earl," she said. "Just a minute."

He stood beside the bed, pulling off his clothes, while she extinguished the three lamps around the room. He heard her dress hit the floor in the darkness, then slips and petticoats that he still did not completely understand.

Then he heard the bed creak.

"Earl, are you ready?"

It was one step to the bed. He was on her, his hands working over her body. He touched her breasts, stroked down to her hips, feeling the curves of the flesh. He leaned against her. He felt her legs part under his weight. She reached down, found him rigid, touched him in a way that made him arch his back. She was deft and sure in finding the place for him.

He writhed, bucked, grunted. No resistance, not tonight. Tonight she was all his, and that was worth all the turmoil. Her arms were around him. Her fingers clutched his buttocks; that brought him closer, closer to the edge. He finished with an ecstatic spasm that left him dizzy, jubilant, and feeling like a man again.

Chapter 11

That spring Sample alone took the herd and the hands to Abilene. Fowler stayed behind again. He could not run the ranch from horseback on the trail. And this time Newsome, too, stayed back. That was Irene's idea. If Fowler could skip six months' riding, so could her husband. More than one man bossed the Circle Three now.

Sample found a good market. When he returned, Earl and Irene were gone from the big house. They were building four miles up-valley, Fowler told him, living in a cabin now with their new home half finished.

Better for all concerned, Fowler told him.

That was one change. He discovered another a few minutes later. He answered a knock on his bedroom door to find Rose Ellen, come to welcome him home. She greeted him as she always had, with arms around him, holding him tight.

"Orrin," she said. She stepped back to arm's length and looked at him. "I'm happy to see you back. I missed you. I always do."

She squeezed him again. The body that he felt against him was different now, changed in just a few months. Sample felt womanly contours under his hands. Breasts pressed against his chest, and he felt a tightening in his groin that embarrassed him.

She sat with him in his room and talked, and all the time the excitement stayed with him. He saw that she was no longer a girl. She had some growing yet to do, but she was going to be a beautiful woman. He could see that.

There had been terrible fights while he was gone, she told him. They would start over any small thing, turn to shouting for a few minutes, and then a silence that might last for days. You had to be careful what you said, she told him, because everybody had a short fuse.

That night, when he should have been sleeping, he thought of Rose. He remembered her body under his hands. The girl that she had been had never affected him this way. She had been Rose, sweet Rose who was his friend's daughter and a joy to them all.

This was different. The changes in her stirred him and awakened longings that he had been so careful to keep in check. He wanted to touch her again.

Then he told himself that this was wrong, thinking this way. She was no woman yet. And she was still Charlie Fowler's daughter.

He tried not to notice her the next day, and the days that followed that one. He did not want Charlie ever to suspect what she was doing to him. But when he knew he could watch her, with nobody aware of it, he gave in. He watched how her hips were filling in the boy's pants, how her breasts showed through the loose fit of her cotton blouse.

After a few days of this he told Charlie that he would be spending some time with Earl and Irene, maybe camping there nights. They needed help with their new place, and work was slack around the ranch now.

He did it to get away from Rose Ellen. He thought his fascination might pass if he didn't see her for a few days. But during his second day there—they had found a nice rise of ground, not far from the river—she rode up the trail with her hair flying behind her. Sample was on the roof, straddling a rafter. Rose Ellen pulled up and called for Ray. The boy came out from the frame of the new house.

"Ray, can you go riding?" she said.

"Pa?"

"I want you to finish up on the floor before sundown."

"I will."

"No more'n an hour," Earl said from inside the house.

The boy went for his pony, tied to a picket stake nearby. Rose Ellen looked up at the skeleton frame. She saw Sample for the first time, waved, and called his name. At that moment Ray swung up into the saddle and the two of them rode off together.

And Orrin found himself envying the boy, wondering what the two of them did when they were alone like that. Mostly he envied the time Ray had with her and the way Rose's eyes followed Ray every moment that the two of them were together.

He knew then that soon he would have to leave the house where she lived. He knew that this would go hard with Charlie. But he also knew that he had to be away from her.

In two weeks the Newsomes' house was framed and roofed and walled. Earl hired a carpenter from San Antonio for the rest, so Sample returned to the old ranch house. Soon Newsome removed the furnishings that Irene had brought from Natchez: the china and the silver, the rugs and the velvet chairs and the standing clock. Irene hired away the housekeeper, too, so the first evening without her Fowler cooked for three, steak and potatoes and pickled beans. They ate together at a kitchen table, Fowler and Sample and Rose Ellen, using tin plates from the chuck wagon. Irene had taken all the rest.

They ate without speaking. Rose Ellen excused herself to finish a book. That left the two men alone with the remains of the meal. Neither had eaten half of what Fowler had put on the plates.

Sample poked with a fork at the food before him. "Charlie," he said, "you up for some talk?"

"Talk? If you want."

"This is hard," Sample said.

"Don't matter. We're pards. You can tell me what you want."

"I don't know which foot to lead off with."

"Orrin, don't go coyoting 'round it. You come straight out and say it. It can't be all that bad."

Sample sucked in a breath and spoke. "Charlie, I think I'll be going off on my own to live."

"You don't like your room? Take your pick. There's plenty now."

"It ain't the room. I need a change of scenery."

Fowler sat back in his chair. "Damn," he said.

"Don't take it personal, Charlie," Sample said. "It's got nothing to do with you."

"No. Course not. All my friends are up and leaving me alone in this house we built for ourselves. But it's got nothing to do with me."

Sample didn't want to wound Charlie this way. But he knew he could not tell him why he was leaving. Charlie would have to take it without a reason.

"I tell you, it's got nothing to do with you."

"Well, hell, get on with you. I ain't keeping you, I hope. You don't have to feel obliged to wait for the end of dinner—just pack up and go."

"Damn it, Charlie, things is changed."

"You ain't just blowing through a whistle they have."

"I mean here in the house. With Earl gone it ain't like three partners sharing everything. This house is yours now, yours and Rose Ellen's. I'm just a maverick here with no place to call my own."

"We'll split the place down the middle if that makes you feel better. You take one side, leave the rest to me and Rose. We can work it that way."

"No. Only one way to make it right in my mind."

Fowler put his hands to his face, ran his fingers over his chin. "I am done with this crap. It appears I have lost the touch I once had with beef and pataters. What do you say to a swallow or two?"

They took two cups and a bottle and they walked outside, beside the stable where they had a view of the valley. In the bunkhouse they heard Alvarez and one of the hands crooning to chords strummed on a guitar. Fowler filled one of the cups, handed it to Sample, filled the other, and corked the bottle.

He drank from the cup.

"Somewhere we lost it," he said in a moment. "Not all of a sudden, but gradual, so nobody noticed it for a long time. But it is gone now, plain enough."

"Maybe it ain't really lost."

"Oh, it's lost, pard. It is lost all right. Things won't ever be the same as they were when we started out, just the three of us trying to make something out of nothing here. But maybe it ain't so much to lose.''

Another gulp. Sample waited.

''I mean,'' Fowler said, ''there was the three of us, young bucks, we thought we was something special. We thought we could lick the rest of the world if we but stood back to back and fought with all the grit we had in us. But maybe we weren't so special after all, more lucky than special, and maybe we haven't lost so much.

''Could be we got too big,'' he said. ''Maybe that was our mistake. We did right fine when we had to scrap to make our way. But things got easy and it all went to hell.''

He drank once more, and this time Sample spoke. ''We couldn't help getting big, Charlie. We wanted it. Not one of us would have raised a hand to stop it even if we knew how it would turn out. We wanted it too much, all of it.''

The next morning Sample packed his belongings to leave. He discovered that for the first time in his life he owned more than he could carry on a single horse. He had to load a second with a pack saddle.

He was cinching the rope when Rose Ellen came out of the house. She walked up to him. ''Papa told me,'' she said.

He thought he would have to console her—tell her, ''I'm not going far, and I'll be 'round all the time.'' But she seemed to be taking it. Not as if she were happy about it, but as if she understood.

She guessed that she had caused this. Orrin was her friend and she did not want to see him go. But he was a man, too, and she sensed a change between them. There was something different in his eyes now when he looked at her, and she knew that his leaving had to do with that.

Orrin kissed her on the forehead, pulled tight the last hitch on the pack, and rode up the trail toward the house where Earl Newsome and his family were living now. The cabin beside it was his until he built a place of his own. Irene had offered it already. She seemed always there to help when he needed it.

Chapter 12

Earl Newsome, if he had known the depths and the power and the subtlety of what churned within his wife, would have said that she was a right quick study. Sharp as mesquite. Clever as a coyote. Could lay lower'n a lizard at high noon.

After five years of marriage he suspected no such thing. He would have been surprised to find these qualities even in a man. For a woman, his wife, to possess them was unthinkable. He would have been astonished to learn that within her first week at the ranch she had decided that she had married the wrong partner in this enterprise. Before she had washed all the dust from her clothes, she had realized that the place swung around Charlie Fowler.

It was easy enough, she had thought, to say that he had the brains. Look closer and you could see that none of them was stupid. But Charlie knew how to use his mind, and he trusted it. That put him one big step up on the others. The most elusive answer in her deductions came when she asked herself why Charlie had not gotten rid of the other two already. She watched more and retraced her thinking and could not escape the unlikely conclusion that he was a decent man who cared as much for his partners as he did for himself.

As she saw more of Fowler and learned more about the ranch, she marveled at what he had accomplished in so few years. It would have been beyond most men. Left alone, he might do great things in the valley.

But so would she. And Irene would not be happy with her

own destiny in the hands of another, no matter how capable.

Sample had been in the cabin five days when she asked him to dinner. By now, she thought, he'll have had enough of his own cooking.

She found Luz in the kitchen. "Mr. Sample is coming to dinner tonight," she said. "He likes that tamale pie of yours, the one you do with the cornbread. I want you to make it for him. And I believe we will have wine, a good bottle from that case that was shipped from New Orleans."

Sample and Newsome were gone roping and branding for the day. They had men to do such work, but somehow the stiff muscles and bruises were important to them. Hard work kept them busy, and they had nothing else to do. Ray had gone riding with Rose Ellen. Once the children had worried her, living in the same house, beyond her control. That changed with the new place; now Irene thought that she could end the friendship when she wished.

She had Luz heat some water. She washed her hair and sat doing needlework beside a window in the front room. By afternoon the sun had dried her hair, and she could brush it down her shoulders. She wet the tip of one finger with perfume and tapped it against her neck, below the ear. From a closet she pulled a dress that she had not worn since she came to Texas. The dress had a high, tight bodice, and it was nipped in at the waist. Earl would like that dress, she thought. And so would Orrin. Tonight she wanted Orrin to like her.

Sample came to dinner still dirty from his day, but with fresh clothes and clean boots. No need to have dressed for dinner, she told him. They were friends. She wanted him to feel at home here. This was a place, she said, where he could come for food or for talk or for no other reason than to be friendly. She hoped he wouldn't need an invitation next time.

He drank wine before dinner. Irene kept the glass full. The tamale pie was as good as he had ever tasted. It was his first meal in a week that hadn't been burned. After dinner there was more wine and talk. Sample was tired and he did not fight when she offered him a soft chair in the parlor.

Somehow the talk drifted to Fowler and the ranch. Sample wasn't sure how that had happened, but he felt he ought to defend Charlie. Charlie was his friend. "I won't speak against him," Sample said.

"That's very loyal," Irene said. "I admire that in a man."

"You don't know how far we come since the end of the war."

"But you all had a part in that, didn't you? It took the three of you to do it. I know Earl did his part and I'm sure you did, as well."

He nodded. "I did, some," he said.

"Don't think that I'm attacking Charlie Fowler," she said. "I give the man his due. That much, but no more. Not as much, perhaps, as he gives himself."

"Charlie is a good man."

"He is your friend. I know. And I'm not one to say anything if you happen to be content with the way you've been treated."

There was more talk, but Sample went home turning that phrase over. "If you happen to be content," she'd said, "with the way you've been treated." Sure, he was content. Damn right he was content. He had no reason not to be. Or none, anyway, that he knew.

Dinner with Earl and Irene became a habit. Luz could cook; Sample was hopeless with a stove. The cabin was lonely after twelve years in the big house with the others. Being alone would not have been so bad, not if he could have been truly alone. But the Newsomes' house was there at the top of the hill from his cabin, and he could not ignore the light that glowed from the windows when the darkness came.

Sometimes they did not bring up Fowler. They could go all evening without mentioning his name. But just as often Irene would have something to say, and it would always be in words that disturbed him later. Sometimes she referred to Fowler without ever using his name, and always her words confused Sample and troubled him.

They did not need such a large house, she said one night, or furnishings that were so expensive. They could get by with much less. But this was their way of getting money out of the ranch, money that was theirs by right. Otherwise, she said, the profits disappeared after every drive.

Was it difficult, she wondered another time, to run a ranch? Didn't he think he could do it if he had to?

One night she asked Orrin how often he went over the ledgers. He answered, "Oh, now and again." He was ashamed to admit that he had never thought of questioning Charlie's figures.

Fowler and Newsome were still speaking, rigidly civil but at least talking. They still worked together. When the drive was a month away they spent a day roping and branding. For Fowler this had overtones of days past, sharing jobs and sweating together. Earl seemed friendlier than usual. At mid-afternoon Newsome stopped, reined in at a spring near the branding fire, and crouched over the water. Fowler saw him drink and splash his face. He pulled his horse in beside Newsome's and joined him at the pool, squatting beside him.

"It is ungodly warm for this time of year. It appears we will have a hot one this summer," Fowler said.

Newsome looked at him and nodded.

"The cows get stronger and spryer every year. Or maybe it is just me slowing down," Fowler said.

"Maybe some of both."

"There's something to that."

Newsome said nothing in return, and moved as if he were ready to stand up and leave. So Fowler spoke.

"Earl," he said, "you and me go back some."

"Yes," Newsome said.

"We been through a lot together."

"We have." Newsome's answer was cautious, neutral.

"I want to talk to you now," Fowler said. "About something important. But I don't quite know the words to use."

"That ain't like you, Charlie. You always had the right words."

Fowler caught the sarcasm but did not check himself. "Things have changed," he said. "They are not the way they used to be with us, the three of us."

"There's four of us now, Charlie."

"That's so. And that gets straight to what I want to palaver about. Things have changed, as I say. Not for the good, I don't think. You think so? You think we're better off now than when we started out?"

"Some things is better."

"But the way we lock horns now over every damn thing. That ain't right."

"That seems to be the way things come out."

"But why? Does it come from inside of us? When it was just us three, did we ever once gouge each other the way we been doing the last few years?"

The two men stood, and Newsome said, "What are you telling me, Charlie?"

"I'm saying maybe we should look and see where all this bad will comes from. I know Irene is a fine woman, and you love her, but look at what has happened since she settled here."

"Maybe you said enough, Charlie."

"And maybe you ought to be your own man again instead of letting a woman speak for you."

Newsome's right hand drove into Fowler's stomach, bent him over with his arms grabbing his midsection. Newsome took him by the shoulders, tossed him to the ground, and went toward him again. Before Sample and one of the hands could pull Newsome away, Charlie Fowler was dazed, bloody, and beaten.

That night Irene told Newsome that she was pregnant. She said she had been saving the news until she was sure. "I think it is time we set out on our own," she said. "Don't you?"

She needed six days to sway Sample. On the seventh they called on Fowler. He looked at them through eyes puffed nearly shut, spoke with lips stiff from half-healed cuts.

"You look as if you've come to do business," he said. They stood in the archway of his office.

"We want to split the place up," Newsome said.

Fowler stared at them, Newsome and Irene stolid and unmoving, Sample a step or two behind, more diffident, hesitation in his face.

"You too, Orrin?" Fowler said.

Sample looked at Newsome and Irene, and he nodded.

There were some pens in a jar on Fowler's desk. He pulled them out one by one until he found one with a broad nib. "Equal thirds," he said. He took an inkwell in hand and walked to the surveyor's map of the valley. He dipped the pen in the ink, placed the point down carefully, and drew a heavy black line across the northern section of the ranch. "That one," he said, "may be a mite smaller than the other two. But it has good springs and some nice bottomland beside the river."

He dipped the point again, placed it down on the map, and once more pulled a black line of ink across the paper. This line bisected the lower section of the ranch. "Those two match up with the other, near as I can tell," he said. He put down the inkwell and the pen.

"Sliced in three," he said, "like carving a roast. Lines run east to west across the valley, so we each get a piece of the river and some good grassland. You can have your choice. I'll be happy with whatever you leave me."

Newsome and Irene walked to the map.

"This line," she said, "it runs between the two houses?"

"I did it that way."

"Orrin, we would like to have the piece that the new house is on. Does that suit you?"

"Sure," he said. "You'll want to keep the house."

"Then we'll take this one," she said. "The northerly one. As long as the house is inside the line."

Fowler said, "Up to you, Orrin."

"It don't matter. If they's all the same, you keep the piece with your place on it."

"Then yours is the third one in the stack," Fowler said. "I am in the middle, with a fine lot of neighbors to the north and south of me. We will have to do this legal. This time of year there ain't much money, but we can divvy that up when you please. We got a job branding cattle but we will get it done."

He was trying to keep his voice under control. He was angry but he did not want to lose his dignity.

"Is that all?" he said. "You got what you come for? Irene, you don't think I've pulled one too fast? You sure you're getting your due, Orrin?"

He waited; they were silent.

"Then get the hell out," Fowler said. He pointed a trembling finger at them. "Get the hell out of my house, all of you."

They left. Fowler saw Rose Ellen standing outside the

office. She looked frightened. That was unlike her, and the sight of her troubled face drew Fowler to her. He put an arm around her.

"You heard?" he asked.

"Yes."

"Do you understand?"

"I think so."

"Earl and Irene and Orrin are not happy being partners with me anymore. They want their own spreads. So it won't be the Circle Three Bar anymore. It will be three ranches, and you and I will own one. I like that idea, Rose. It will give us a spread all our own, and we won't have to share it any longer."

"Can we still live here?"

"This house is on our part. We can live here if we please, and I don't see why not. Now there's nobody to tell us what to do or when or how. Nobody to answer to."

"Can I still be friends with Ray?"

Fowler was angry. His voice rose. "Now, why in hell you want to hoot around with that bunch? His ma and pa just told me they want nothing to do with us. Earl and Irene are no good, and the apple doesn't fall far from the tree. He'll show the same stripe as them one day and I don't want you near when he does. No, I expect you can find better than a Newsome for a running mate."

Her eyes filled with tears. She turned from him and ran to her room. He heard a sob burst out as she shut the door. He had to swallow the urge to go to her room, tell her that he was wrong, that she could be friends with the boy if she wished. He knew that would make her happy. But he wanted to spare her the rough handling that she would get from any child of Earl and Irene.

Later that day Ray heard the same. The order came from Earl Newsome. Earl surprised Irene by telling the boy, without prompting, to have nothing more to do with Rose Ellen. With a ranch of their own now, Earl said to Ray, he would have to learn the business. It was time he worked instead of riding the day away with Rose Ellen.

The next day, and every day for a week, Ray and Earl rode together. The man and the boy chased cows and practiced roping. Earl gave him a horse from his own string, a nimble cow horse with good speed and quick feet, able to match a heifer's dodge and feint. The boy knew horses. He rode as if born to the saddle. Newsome decided that with more time roping and watching cows, studying their ways, young Ray would be a hand worth having.

So he doubled the boy's work, pushed him from first light to sundown. Ray would bolt down his supper and then collapse in bed, each night more exhausted than before. Sleep was never long in coming, and he slept numb, drugged.

But there were moments before he slept, and moments in the saddle during the day, when he thought of Rose Ellen. He wished she could see him now, roping and chasing cows. She would be proud. He imagined her watching him, and in his imagining all his throws were perfect: every rope caught a cow, every noose snagged a neck or an ankle, he tied every calf's legs while the dust from its fall was still in the air, and the calves never kicked free. He wished Rose Ellen could see all this.

After a week's work Earl took a day off. He had lawyer business with Fowler. He told Ray to go out alone and work. But Ray did not push himself as hard as Earl had pushed him. That night he did not lose himself to sleep as he had before. He had more time to think about Rose Ellen. He wondered whether he would see her again. Maybe it would be years before Earl let him go to visit her. Maybe never.

No, not years. He sat up in bed. Right now, as soon as Earl and Irene were asleep. He waited to hear the door of their room close, forcing himself to be patient until he thought he could stand it no longer. When he was sure that they slept, he dressed, picked up his boots, and crept into the hall. Luz's room was across from his own. He could hear her snoring. His parents were at the other end of the house. He walked down the dark hall and stood at their door. Once again he waited, and heard nothing, and saw no light under the door.

He left the house. When he was outside he pulled on his boots and walked to the horses. No stable yet; they stayed tied to a picket line. The horses knew him. They stirred when he walked to them but they made no sound. He found his new horse, raised a hand slowly to stroke the animal's jaw. The horse flapped its tail and nickered.

His saddle and blanket were inside. He knew he could do without them. He untied the horse's reins from the picket rope. With both arms around the horse's neck, he swung one foot up and jumped with the other. That gave him the push to roll up on the horse's back. He rode away at a trot.

The night was murky black, with a quarter-moon rising over the far hills. The boy pinched his knees around the horse's middle while he peered ahead into the darkness. He reined in at a tree about a quarter of a mile from the old house and walked the rest of the way.

There were no lights. From the back door, he thought, he could get to Rose without coming near Fowler's room. There was no lock. With feet bare again, he was silent in the house until he pushed the door of Rose's room. The hinges squeaked and the noise woke her.

"Papa?"

"Hush, Rose," he hissed.

"Ray!"

"Keep your voice down, girl."

He walked to her bed. She rose up and grabbed one of his forearms, held it tight. She was wearing a nightshirt. It had ruffles around the high collar and around the cuffs. Something—something about the darkness, the nightshirt, her touch, the danger—thrilled him. He pulled his arm away, though that was not what he wanted at all.

"You came," she said. "Came to see me. I thought you would never come to see me again."

"My pa told me no."

"Mine, too."

"But I got a notion to come," he said. "So I did."

"Good to see you," she said.

"Get your clothes on," he answered.

"Clothes?"

"We can't talk here. And I didn't come all this way just for a howdy-do. I got something to show you."

"You wait outside," she said.

He sat on the back-door step. The quarter-moon was higher in the sky now. When she met him he pointed her toward the tree where he had tied his horse. They walked together, their shoulders touching. She reached down and took his hand. He felt a swelling in his pants. This was new to him. He held tight to her hand, feeling a warmth and a pleasure he had never known before. It had everything to do with Rose, with the feel of her hand in his, and with her wanting him to be here, her caring for him and being glad that he had dared to come to her. Somehow all that was part of what was happening to him.

When he saw the horse she let go of his hand and ran. "Ray! Yours?"

"Yep. I call him Rojo. His hair is brown, but it does look red when the sun hits it right."

"I don't see the sense of going back directly," she said. "If Papa was going to miss me he'd have done it by now. A horse this big can carry both of us, wouldn't you say?"

He helped her up and took her hand to pull himself onto the horse's back. She put her arms around his chest, and though her touch was light the breath left his lungs.

They had touched before, touched often. What was happening now was a mystery to him. But it was an even greater mystery that until now he had felt nothing when they touched. Now he could not imagine her failing to arouse him. He wondered how he had ignored it.

They rode across the hills. There was more light from the moon now, and when open space stretched before them he gave the horse more rein. They rode until she tugged at his shirt and told him that she ought to go back. She was afraid that her father might wake early.

He brought her to the tree where he had tied the horse. She slipped down to the ground.

"You got yourself a fine horse there, Ray," she said. "I want to tell you that. And I want to tell you that you made me real happy, coming to see me like this."

"It made me happy, too."

"You come to see me again?"

"If I can."

"We got to. We got to keep friends even if our folks can't abide each other. We got to find a way."

"We will," he said.

"This is Thursday. We'll meet someplace, try for Sunday. Sunday, after everybody is asleep. If one of us can't get out Sunday we'll try for Tuesday, and if we don't do it Tuesday it'll be Thursday a week. That suit you?"

"Uh-huh."

"Don't let me down, Ray."

"I come here tonight, didn't I?"

"We got to keep friends," she said.

"We will."

She reached up and touched his elbow. He knew that he was supposed to bend down toward her. His heart sank but he moved, as if a hand were pushing him down. Someone else, not him, was bending down to her.

He stopped with his face an inch from hers. She raised up on her toes to meet him the rest of the way, and she placed her lips against his, both hands on the back of his neck.

Then she was leaving. He had to speak to stop her.

"Rose," he said. "We have to decide. Where we supposed to meet?"

She thought for a moment. "Indian Oak," she said.

"Indian Oak."

She ran toward her house.

His own home was dark when he got there. Luz still snored behind her door. He knew that he should be sleepy, but he had never felt more charged. Something was happening, something between him and Rose. He had to find out more about it, feel it again and explore it. He would understand it better then.

But one thing needed no studying. Already he knew that he would not be kept from Rose Ellen Fowler.

Chapter 13

When they should have been driving cattle to Kansas, they were splitting up the ranch. All that they had held in common they divided equally.

The money was easiest. The land took longer; they needed a surveyor and a lawyer to do it right. They picked over guns, horses, tack.

Some things, though, defied division. Fowler, Sample, and Newsome gathered the hands one day and told them that they could have a job with any of them. Alvarez looked at them and allowed that he was not the sort to be changing his scenery too often. He would keep his bedroll where it lay, in the bunkhouse that now belonged to Charlie Fowler. One of the others asked Fowler if he could make their pay for the rest of the season. He could, and that decided it. They would all stay with Fowler and Alvarez.

When they left the hands in the bunkhouse Fowler walked to a shack and came back with the branding irons. The long rods were black, but the shaped metal of the brand was burned white by years of fire.

Fowler thrust the irons at them. "Maybe one of you knows how we can slice this up like the rest. It was your idea, Orrin. You can have it, if that doesn't offend Earl. But you be careful. Earl is always jealous of getting his fair share."

Sample dug the toe of one boot in the dirt and said, "Charlie, you keep it. You might as well."

"I don't want them around here," Fowler said. "These

119

brands belong to a ranch that doesn't exist anymore. I've got new ones being made up, and I don't need these.''

He spat. "For any reason at all,'' he said.

Newsome held out a hand. "I'll take them,'' he said, "if neither of you will. It's a good brand. You can read it in the moonlight.''

That left the cattle—wealth that they had never counted. They might have fought over this, but Sample was ready with a way of dividing them. Starting at one end of the range and working their way to the other, they would rebrand every cow that bore the Circle Three Bar mark. There would be three different irons in the fire. The brander would use each one in turn. One cow for Fowler, the next for Sample, the third for Newsome. They would brand every cow they found, and after they had finished, any cow that bore only the old mark was fair taking for any one of them.

There were thousands of cattle. Sample tried counting but gave up the effort after the second day. He was missing too many, and anyway the number was growing so great as to be meaningless. Even divided by three, the herds would be huge.

Fowler stayed away. He sent Alvarez and two hands. Newsome took Ray with him; it was the boy's first trip to work on the range. They made Ray the branding boy. They trusted him. For twelve hours every day he kept the fire hot and the tips of the irons glowing red. He laid the irons in order across the fire. For Fowler it was a Diamond Five—he had cut a deck of cards; for Sample, an O–Bar–S. Newsome chose an inverted V that was to be placed above the old brand, forming rafters over the old Circle Three Bar mark. In a few years the rafter markings would be useless, and would disappear from the brands on Earl Newsome's cows.

Hundreds of times a day, Ray would snatch up the next iron in line and knock it against the side of his boot to clean it of clinging ashes and coals. He would run with it to where a cowboy had dumped and tied the cow, and would press the brand in until he could smell burned hair. His body was occupied by the mechanics of stoking the fire and choosing the iron and branding, but his mind was with Rose. It was fixed on the memories of her touch, of her arms around his chest, of her lips on his. She could not know what he was doing. The first Sunday night, and the next Tuesday, and the Thursday after that, he thought of her going at night to the oak tree, waiting for him in the dark.

She'll think bad of me, he told himself. She'll start to doubt. She'll go the second time, and maybe again after that, but no more. He thought it unfair, that he should care for her and think so often of her without her being able to know it. He imagined himself holding her, whispering in her ear, telling her words that would make it all right.

His first night back was a Sunday. He was exhausted, but he fought sleep while he waited for Earl and Irene to go to their room.

The night was brighter this time when he rode to the top of the hill. He sat beneath the tree. He could see bats fluttering overhead, scattering from an owl that dove with its wings spread and steady. He dozed for a while but soon he woke, sure that she was on her way.

He stood. In the valley was a figure on a horse, traveling fast and trailing a plume of dust. Soon he could hear the horse's hooves beating against the ground. The horse leaped over the brow of the hill.

She reined in, climbed down, her eyes on him. "H'lo, Ray. Your pa put you to work, it seems." She was trying to be calm, but the quaver in her voice gave her away.

"You knew."

"I puzzled it out. I thought you might have weaseled out on me. I did, at first. But I figure you for better than that. I knew if you didn't come you'd have a reason. Maybe off with the crew. Paco came home today, so I knew if you were ever going to come it would be tonight."

"I did," he said.

She moved to him, put a hand on his face. It trembled against his cheek.

"I was afraid you wouldn't be here," she said.

He thought they might kiss again, right then. He wanted to hold her and kiss her and tell her all the words that had swum in his mind when he lay alone on the range. But he hesitated, and she pulled her hand away and made him sit beside her under the tree.

They talked, safe trivialities. He barely heard the words. Even when he spoke to her his head spun with excitement, with strategies, with self-reproach for having been so timid.

He realized that they had stopped talking. She was looking at him and smiling. "Your head is still on the cows," she said.

"Oh, no, it ain't. I seen enough of cows to last me some time."

She held his hand, and shifted her weight so that their arms touched as they sat side by side. The pressure of her body against his spun his head even faster. Only one way to stop his mind from whirling.

He turned and kissed her. She returned the kiss. Her arms were around him.

She tilted back her head and spoke. "Ray, don't push so hard. You hurt my lips."

"I reckon I kiss passable well."

"You don't if you hurt my lips," she said.

"Then maybe I just ought'n to kiss you again."

"Maybe not."

She stood, and brushed her hands against the seat of her jeans. "I am sorry," she said, "that I troubled both of us to come up here tonight. We would have done a heap better with sleep instead."

He regretted his temper. Its flaring had come from nowhere. Now it was gone already and he was contrite, abashed. "I'm sorry," he said. "I got hot when you said you don't like my kissing—too quick to rile. I'm sorry if I hurt your lips."

"I like your kissing just fine," she said. "It would be even better if you didn't push so hard against my lips."

"Maybe we can try again," he said.

"No. But maybe if you can get away Tuesday."

She rode away and left him alone on the hill.

Lamps were burning in the house when he returned. He considered at first riding away. If they had missed him, there would be hell to catch.

He walked in by the back door, and heard voices in his parents' room. Maybe, he thought, he could bluff his way through this one. He went to his room, pulled off his shirt, and walked back into the hall in jeans and an undershirt. Earl was in the hall, walking toward him without seeing him. His face was pale.

"What's wrong?" the boy asked.

Newsome looked down at him, recognized him for the first time. "Your mother," he said. "Didn't you hear us? Your mother is ill, boy."

Ray looked into his parents' room. Irene lay on blood-blotched sheets, her face a drained and pallid grey. He sat beside her bed and soon Earl joined him. They stayed with her that night. First Ray felt guilty for having been gone when his mother took sick. But he knew that his being gone had nothing to do with that. He made himself consider the fact that his mother might be dying, that he might be without her forever. He asked himself whether he could do without her. And he decided that he could. He would mourn her, and her dying would hurt him, but he knew that he could survive it.

At first light Ray rode for a doctor, thirty miles distant in a cow town called McPherson, below the valley's south end. It was late evening when he returned with the doctor.

The doctor looked at Irene's face and sent Ray and Earl out of the bedroom. He closed the door. The pendulum of the big standing clock in the parlor rocked behind a gilt-glass plate. It hit a quarter-hour chime and then struck eight before the doctor came out. She had lost the baby, he said. Now she needed rest, six weeks at least.

Newsome kept watch over Irene. When she was awake he was there to talk to her, or to be silent, as she wished. He held her bowls of food, and when she was too weak to feed herself he spooned the gruel and creamed corn and mashed potatoes into her mouth.

Ray had spent a night and a day trying to make himself strong against the possibility of his mother's death. When he saw that she would survive, her illness became an inconvenience. His father's restless vigil stopped Ray's trips to the oak tree. There was no predicting when he might be awake.

But the boy's days were his own. He made forays into the Diamond Five property, and one day he saw Rose Ellen riding alone. She seemed happy to see him. She understood, she said, and she hoped that his mother would get well soon. If he wanted to come calling anytime during the summer, she would be living with the family called Peeples, up-valley. Her father was leaving soon on a drive. And Mrs. Peeples would not object to her having a polite caller.

Fowler had decided late that spring to lead a drive. It was an impulse. He still had a foreman and a crew. They gathered the herd and pushed up the trail in mid-May, the latest he had ever started a drive. But he was happy to be in the saddle again, once more in the business of selling cattle.

He was the only one of the three to leave with a herd that year.

While Newsome nursed his wife and Fowler drove his herd, Sample was building a cabin. He alone had not had a house when the ranch was parceled out. He could stay in the cabin on the Newsomes' property, Earl had told him. But that was an empty offer. Sample could not run his ranch from a house ten miles distant. So he dismantled the cabin where he had been living, stacked the lumber in wagonloads, and carried it to his own property. He knew a spot in the middle of the valley's width, a place with trees and a good spring that was wet all year. There he rebuilt the cabin.

When he had finished he had no time for a drive. The grass on the trail would be gone, and the rivers would be flooding. He had no help, anyway. He had not taken on hands, and most of the good cowboys were hired and were on their way to Kansas.

He told himself that he could get by until the next spring. He had some money from his share of the Circle Three Bar's cash reserves, and he could live with few expenses. He would survive.

Newsome, too, lacked help. But even if he had had a crew, he would not have left Irene. He would stay beside her until she was well again.

The doctor's six weeks became twelve. Irene spent mornings out of bed, and took solid food again. The pallor left her cheeks. Newsome began spending his days away from the house, and sleeping beside his wife in their bed.

One day he looked at her, and she seemed as healthy and as lovely as she had ever been. He saw her as a woman once more, no longer an invalid. His desire welled up once again.

When she blew out the lamp in bed that night he reached to touch her.

"No," she said. "Please, Earl, not that."

He turned away, tried to sleep and to swallow his hurt.

The next day when he came home he saw Luz with an armful of his clothes, moving down the hall. He followed her into a third bedroom that was beside Ray's. She was putting the clothes into a chest of drawers.

She looked at him in the doorway. "Senora Newsome. . . ." she said.

He found Irene in a chair beside their bed. "Luz is moving my things," he said.

"Close the door," she told him. When he had shut it she motioned him to the side of the bed. "I wanted to discuss this with you," she said, "but you were gone so early this morning. I think it would be better, darling, this way."

"Me? In there?"

"Please understand."

"We are husband and wife," he said. He had to keep himself from shouting. "I don't believe I care for this."

"Do you want to lose me?" she said. Her voice was loud, too loud for him. He didn't want Luz, anybody, to hear what she was telling him. "I can't be pregnant again, Earl. I can't take that chance again, can't let it happen. I don't want ever to have to go through what I've just survived.

"Next time," she said, "I might not be so fortunate. Surely your rights aren't so important to you that you would put me in jeopardy so that you can be satisfied."

"No," he said. He wrung his hands together. His forearms rested on his knees and he looked past them to the floor. Then he looked at her face. "You don't have to put me out of here," he said. "You don't. I swear you don't, Irene. I wouldn't let anything happen."

He meant it. He knew he could stop touching her if she wanted. But he did not want to be put out of their room for Luz and Ray and the world to know.

"We can't take the chance," she said. She was quiet now, placating him. "You're a man, Earl. That's why I married you. And that's why we can't be together, my darling. . . . Do you understand?"

He nodded down to the rug on the floor.

"Nothing else has changed," she said. "I want you to know that. I still feel about you as I always have. We are still partners in every other way, aren't we? And don't you know that this is as difficult for me as it is for you?"

She watched his head bob again.

"Then kiss me, Earl, and show me that you still care for me."

He bussed her on the cheek and left the room. He went outside and did not come to dinner. He watched the sunset and he thought of Charlie Fowler, lucky to be out on the trail, bedding down in the grass and looking up at the stars.

When he came into the house, the door to her bedroom was closed. He went to the room where Luz had carried his clothes. He lay across the bed. The mattress was stiff and unfamiliar. He wished he had been able to get a herd together. He wished he were on the trail now, lost to the world somewhere north of the hills.

Chapter 14

As Sample had been a year earlier, Charlie Fowler was astonished at six months of change in Rose Ellen. He had known, before he left on the drive, that she was no longer a little girl. When he saw her again she was a woman. It was that simple. His daughter was sixteen years old, and a woman now.

He looked at her and imagined how she would strike a man. Strike him silly, he guessed. She was a beauty, even in men's clothes. Long legs, a fresh and pretty face when she kept her hair out of it, and a shapely form. Still, she was not ordinary, even for a pretty girl. There was her jaw, which was strong and sharp. And there were her eyes, which were dark and alive and in their own way strong and sharp as well.

A few days after he had returned he watched her hard all morning, so intent that she caught him once and asked him what was troubling him. He noticed the delicate movements of lips and hands when she ate, and he watched her walk, just the way a woman walks—How did she ever learn that? he wondered—through the corral to the stable. He suddenly felt that this place was wrong for her. She was too good for the rough textures, for the gritty dirt and the hills strewn with rocks, for the coarse shirt and jeans that she wore.

He thought of her in a brocade gown and evening slippers, perfumed and with her hair done in fashion, not stuffed as it was now beneath the crown of a wide-brimmed hat. She would be beautiful.

She climbed into the saddle of her horse as he watched. She did it as ably as any man could. When she rode away, he realized that some men would be grateful to ride so well.

This brought regret to Fowler. She had become what she was because he had brought her here, for his own sake, for his own happiness and satisfaction. She diminished the loneliness of the place, cut it down to a size he could manage. But, he thought now, he had considered too much his own welfare, and hers too little. What did she know now of being a woman? She would be a freak anyplace else. Women would laugh at her in New Orleans. And she couldn't very well expect to impress a man with riding and shooting.

Fowler resolved to think of Rose's interests now, put her above himself for once. Maybe she knew nothing of what a woman was supposed to know. But she had a good head. She could learn.

The next morning they rode to McPherson to buy supplies. When they had finished they ate lunch. Fowler excused himself in the middle of the meal and told her that he had business at the bank.

Fowler knew that the banker had a daughter a few years older than Rose. She had gone to a finishing school, and had come back a lady.

The banker gave him the name and address of the school. In Denver it was, the Hardy Academy for Young Women. Fowler used the bank's stationery to write a letter of application. Then he posted the letter and joined Rose Ellen at the restaurant.

Two months later the notice of acceptance from the headmistress was waiting for him at the post office. Fowler scribbled a second letter and enclosed a fifty-dollar deposit.

For a few days he said nothing to Rose Ellen. He felt that he had done wrong by acting without telling her. The argument that it was all in her best interests sounded feeble when he repeated it to himself. He searched for a way to tell her what he planned.

He found it the night he saw her leave the house and ride for the hills.

He woke without knowing why, listened for a sound, heard nothing. He was ready to give himself up to sleep again when he heard a scuffling outside. His room was at a corner of the house and from one window he could see the lot out front, and the corral and the stable. He rose from his bed and looked through the window.

Rose Ellen was leading a horse from the stable. She walked the animal toward the back of the house until she was out of view. He moved to another window and saw her leading the horse away from the house, toward the hills. When she was so far away that he could not hear the horse's hooves scraping in the dirt, she mounted and rode slowly away.

He swallowed an urge to call out her name. Instead he dressed quickly and saddled his own horse. He prodded the horse into a gallop. Soon he saw her again. She was riding for a high hill, then up the side of the hill.

He had reached the hill's base when she was at the top. He reined up and waited. It wasn't right to follow her, he thought. He ought to have faith in her, ought to trust that she would do nothing wrong. Then he saw a second rider coming from the north, with his horse pointed toward the hill that Rose Ellen had just climbed. The man—Fowler could see that much— seemed not to notice him, and rode to the top while Fowler watched.

Fowler dismounted and climbed on foot. He would be quieter than the animal on the steep and rocky hillside.

He climbed carefully when he got close to the top. One last step up. He saw his daughter. She was lying with her back toward him, a pair of arms wrapped around her. She was kissing a man whose face Fowler could not see.

Fowler kicked at the earth. Rose Ellen turned, startled. She moved her mouth but could not speak. Fowler saw the arms release, saw the face pull away from hers.

It was the Newsome boy. But not such a boy anymore. Fowler heard words coming from his own mouth. They were hollow, lacking body, penetrating just the edge of his consciousness. The rest was taken up with rage.

"Like animals," he was saying. "Like animals."

Rose Ellen stumbled trying to reach her feet. Fowler took two steps forward, caught her by the wrist, pulled her down again so that she was on her knees. Ray reached for Rose Ellen to pull her free.

Fowler was ready. He flung a forearm at the boy's face, and the force and the anger behind it sent Ray sprawling.

Fowler walked with Rose to where her horse was fastened. There was no resistance from Rose when he pulled her down the hill, her wrist in one hand and the horse's traces in the other. Rose lost her footing twice; he dragged her until she found her balance again.

His anger had ebbed by the time they reached the house. He was thinking instead, and now he knew what he must do.

He told her that he was sorry for having lost his temper that way. She was wrong to sneak off, he told her, wrong to be doing with a boy what he had found her doing, and wrong especially to be doing it with that no-good. He hoped he hadn't hurt her in any way. Then he told her to sleep well and be ready to ride early.

He did not have to warn her against leaving again.

The next morning he told her to pack her bags, all the clothes she owned worth wearing, and not to bother with too many pants or cotton shirts or hats or pairs of boots.

She cried when he told her what he planned. She cried and turned alternately petulant, contrite, and sullen as they rode to Galveston, ferried to New Orleans, rode by steamer up the Mississippi to St. Louis, and west from there by train.

When the train passed through Topeka she told him calmly that they were both going to feel terrible if he went through with this. He told her then that she was right, most likely.

But until he left her at the school in Denver, carried in her trunks, and walked down the stone steps without her, he did not know how right she had been.

Donnie Lee

All morning I run over in my mind how I would let on to Sue Everitt about Gandy Meacham. She wanted an A, and I had the fella that would help us get it, who knew Rose Ellen Sample from way back. The question was, how should I tell her?

Should I come right out and say so?

Or should I string it out, and bring Gandy Meacham out of the north forty while she wasn't looking? I wanted to make her happy, and make her proud of me.

I tried out both ways in my head, but come the end of history class I still hadn't made up my mind. The bell cut loose and I told her I wanted to talk to her about our project.

She said, I'm sorry, Donnie Lee. Prom committee meets this lunch hour. You should have talked to me before class.

But then she said, Why don't we get together after school? T.J.'s, if that suits you. You can catch the late bus.

T.J.'s was a hamburger shack across the road from school. I faked a bad ankle in the last five minutes of gym class, last of the day. That way I got out early and beat the crowd. I got a booth and held on to it so long I thought the girl would never get there. Then I seen her in the door, and yelled at her, and it was just the two of us in a booth ordering pop and fries.

I decided straight out was the best. When the waitress left I said, Sue, I got our A living right in my own house. My

131

Gandy Meacham, my great-granddaddy, he knew Miz Rose when they was young.

She said, How far back?

I said it was fifty years or so since he had been in the valley.

She wanted to know how well they was acquainted, and I told her it sounded like they was real good friends back then.

The pop and fries come, and she chewed on the end of a fry and got a look in her eye like her mind was someplace else, and then she looked at me and said, Bet they weren't.

Weren't what? I said.

Weren't friends, she said. Not just friends, anyways.

I told her I didn't get the idea that they was enemies.

She said, I don't mean that, silly. I bet they were—you know—boyfriend. And girlfriend. Like that.

In my mind I thought, Ain't that just like a girl to get such a notion? But I was learning to keep my head a good long step ahead of my mouth when I was around Sue E.

Could be, I said. You never can tell.

She said, I bet he could tell all manner of stories if he had a mind. Maybe we could see him tonight.

I told her that might not be such a good idea. I wanted to talk to him some alone and prime the pump. I didn't know how Gandy Meacham would take to Sue E., who was, much as I liked her, the flighty sort. I had a notion she might get under his hide.

I said, Let me talk to him tonight. He takes medicine and sleeps an awful lot and he don't always make sense.

Then you have to tell me about it, she said.

First thing Monday, I told her.

She said, Not on your life. I don't want to wait that long. Make it Saturday. You call me right up on Saturday and tell me what he had to say.

I had a better idea, but it come out in a mumble.

She said, What was that, Donnie Lee?

I said, Oh, I was just thinking maybe you and me could get together tomorrow night and I could give you the lowdown on what Gandy Meacham had to say and we could see a picture and drive around a bit while we was at it but it prob'ly ain't a very good idea and it was just something that popped into my head don't pay it no mind.

She said, Why, that sounds like fun.

Well, great, I said. My hands must have jumped when I said it because I hit my glass and spilled pop all over the table.

I could hardly get my tongue out of its own way for telling her how sorry I was.

But she didn't seem to mind. She said that was okay, like she meant it. About then my late bus pulled up in front of school and I had to go catch it. But before I did she asked me what time I wanted to meet her and I said I would get my daddy's car to pick her up at seven.

Now I had to talk to Gandy Meacham. When I got home I threw my books and my jacket on the bed and went down to his room. I was hoping he would be awake. But his eyes was closed shut and I couldn't get a rise out of him when I called his name. I left him, thinking he would be in better shape later.

I thought I would give him a hand, so that night at dinner, in the middle of talking and eating so that nobody took much notice, I said, I think I will go set with Gandy Meacham this evening. I can give him his pills if you want.

That's thoughtful of you, son, my mama said. But it won't be necessary. The poor old fellow was restless this afternoon, so I gave him a double dose to help him get some relief.

The pain is terrible, she said. I don't know how much longer he can go on this way. Even so, I had to poke the pills down his throat to make him swallow.

A double dose.

I expect that will knock him out for a spell, I said.

All night, I hope, my mama said. Poor fellow, I believe he is half out of his mind. Today he was talking about you, Donnie Lee. He told me to tell you that he didn't forget about you.

And him, she said, who hardly even knows you, Donnie Lee.

Chapter 15

By their will, Sample and Newsome and Fowler had changed the valley, not so much the look of it as the way it was used and what it would become. With work and luck and persistence they had begun to shape the place as a blacksmith shapes an ingot.

But there were events beyond their reach that would determine the future of the valley as much as the three men ever had. That year there occurred two oblique events, independent of each other and hundreds of miles apart, that would alter the valley forever.

The first came a few days before Christmas, 1880. A man named Hart drove his one-horse carriage up the road that ran the western length of the valley. The carriage was overloaded in the back. Its springs creaked, and Hart felt the jolts from every bump and hole. Hart was from Illinois. He was a salesman, six days on this job. He did not care for Texas and he had developed a definite aversion to cattle folk, with their closed minds and set ways. He did not see how they could do business without the special product he was selling. They threw up a wall of indifference at him when they should have been hurrying up the road to greet him. They shunned him and snickered at this marvel.

He was young, with a young man's impatience and zeal. All morning he followed the road north up the valley. He passed the smaller ranches, for he was after the leaders in this territory. He knew that every region has its leaders; get them going your way and the others will follow. He would call on the three big spreads that were, he had heard, stacked one atop the other in the middle of the valley.

He did not stop at the first. That place looked like a squatter's cabin. The second one, up the road a few miles, seemed more likely.

Charlie Fowler met Hart on the front porch.

"I'm a wire salesman, sir," Hart said. "And a fencing salesman as well. I mean, the product I'm representing is both at the same time."

"I never heard of a wire fence that would stand up to cattle," Fowler said.

"This one will," Hart said, "because it is different."

Hart opened (as he always did at this moment) the leather case that he carried with him. He held it open for his prospect to inspect the specimens mounted inside. There were also loose lengths of wire. Fowler reached for one and held it between thumb and forefinger of each hand.

"What are these things?" he said.

"They are prickers," Hart said. "Barbs, if you will. Mr. Glidden, who holds the patent, calls this a barb fence. Feel one. Touch it."

A second later he added: "But not too roughly."

But he was too late with the warning. He always, intentionally, was. Fowler drew back his hand and stared at his thumb. He put it to his lips and tasted blood.

"Sharp," he said.

"Yes, sir, sharp it is."

"But cowhide is a sight tougher than mine."

"No matter. A cow wouldn't want to tangle in this any more than you would. You can five-strand it if you want, but four will do just fine. Draw it tight with a team, tack it good to a stout post, and no cow will try it twice."

Fowler looked closer at the wire, saw how the thin barbed pieces were wrapped around the heavy-gauge wire. He imagined a cow running into it. This was some idea.

"Maybe you heard," Hart said, "about the demonstration our Mr. Gates put on not long ago in San Antone. He put up a corral in the city plaza, using this very same product. Posts and barbed fence, nothing else. Then he drove one hundred of the fiercest steers he could find into that pen and sent men in with blazing torches to scare the steers and set them running against the fence.

"The steers charged until the men couldn't get them to charge once more. Not one of those steers got through."

Fowler held the strand of wire out. "This is a wonder," he said.

Not once since Hart had been in Texas, selling his fence, had he gotten this far with a cattleman without encountering laughs and a skepticism so deeply rooted that it would not be budged. But this man was different.

"Maybe you would care for a demonstration on a small scale," Hart said. "In my wagon I have a spool of the wire. You surely have fence posts. We can build a small pen and see how a few of your animals take to it."

"No," Fowler said. "You don't have to do that. I believe you. Yes. I believe what you're telling me."

"Then you'll be wanting to place an order."

"I don't think so," Fowler said. He replaced the strand of wire in the leather case.

"You are here too soon," he said. "You are ahead of your day, at least as far as cattlemen are concerned. We have no reason yet to confine our cattle this way."

"So I've been learning," Hart said.

"I mean," Fowler said, "that you won't sell to cattlemen until they have a reason to keep others' cows out. Don't you see? It won't be keeping in his own stock that will sell a cattleman. We have no reason to keep our cattle from chewing our neighbor's grass, and right now our neighbors don't object. So far there is enough grass to go around.

"But that will change one day," he said.

Fowler watched the salesman turn away, climb into his carriage, slap the reins, lurch down the road. "This is a great thing you've got," he shouted to Hart. "Don't give up on it, hear? Your wire will have its day in this country."

He watched the carriage bounce away and he thought, So now it begins. It had to happen sometime.

Irene Newsome was in an upstairs room when she saw Hart pulling up at the house. She was downstairs a minute later, in time to hear Earl sending the stranger away. "What is the matter, dear?" she said.

"No matter," Newsome said. "This fella is trying to sell me some wire fence, is all. And I have been trying to tell him that any cow that tries is going to walk through any wire fence a man can put up."

"Not this one," Hart said. He held out a piece of the wire for Irene.

"You'll notice the sharp barbs, which intimidate the animal," Hart said.

"You know about cows, do you?" Newsome said. "I have been a rancher for fifteen years and I think I know something about cows. And I say that this puny wire will not stop one, barbs or no."

Something in the salesman's face made Irene look closer at the wire, reach out for it, and touch only the smooth wire, not the barbs, when she did. "You seem to believe in this," she said.

"I've seen it work."

"Mister," said Newsome, "I will let you water your horse, even stay for dinner, since it is about that time. But don't try to sell me any more wire fence, because I'm not fool enough to buy."

"I would like to keep this," Irene said.

A week later she made a rare excursion out of the house. Her face shaded by a wide-brimmed bonnet, she had one of the hands drive her to Sample's cabin. There she told him that she had business with him. She wanted to talk about buying land.

That same day, in an apartment in Washington, D.C., a man and a woman sat together on a couch and spoke. The woman was nearly forty years old, plumper than she had been as a young woman but with a straight back and skin still smooth. The man was fifteen years older, balding and big-bellied. He wore a swallowtail coat and spats and grey trousers. There was a stiff celluloid collar across the neck of his starched shirt. A gold watch chain spanned his girth, circling the roundness of his stomach.

They sat at opposite ends of the couch, their demeanor and

the distance somehow suggesting estrangement, not unfamiliarity.

"There must be something you can do," the woman said.

The man's voice was a raspy bass. "How many times in the last month have we been over this?" he said. "The answer is the same. I can do nothing. I am finished here. I must return home, and I cannot possibly take you there with me. A small town like that, it would be unthinkable."

"After twelve years," she said. "Finished, like that."

"You knew this could happen," he said. "The voters grow weary. They clamor for change. Even a U.S. senator is not immune to the effects of the fever."

She stood with her back to the man. "Surely you can make some arrangements," she said.

"It is beyond me," he said.

"Don't you care?' she said. "Doesn't it matter to you, what happens to me now that you're gone? I can't stay here after you leave. People know me. They know who I am. Even after you leave they will still fix me with you. Doesn't that move you at all?"

He stood, walked to her, put a hand on her back. "Of course it does," he said. "I care very much. We don't have to discuss that now." He put an arm around her waist and kissed her on the side of her face.

She pulled free, her face hard. "No more," she said. "No more until you take care of me the way you should."

The man backed away, tugged at his lapels, walked to a mirror, and ran a hand over what remained of his hair. "I don't have time anyway," he said. "My wife will be expecting me home early now that I am out of a job."

"What are you going to do for me?" the woman said.

The man walked to the door and let his hand pause on the knob. "The lease is up at the end of the month," he said. "But it is paid until then."

She stayed for a while in Washington. She had made friends who would help her through this, she thought—would introduce her to other people. With the new term there were new faces at the dinners and at the parties. She held on to the hope that she would be discovered again as she had been discovered twelve years earlier. She could serve a man well now, with all that she knew of the city and its workings. She would give herself until spring. Spring, she told herself, was a good season in Washington. Then spring was summer, hot and miserable Washington summer when you sat quietly in the shade and breathed carefully to keep the sweat from bursting forth on your body. The invitations became fewer, and that fall the dinners and the parties went on without her, and she knew that she was finished in Washington.

In the last week of October, while Charlie Fowler drove his herd to Kansas, the woman was on a train bound south through the Virginia countryside. She had searched for choices, and had found two. Being on this train bound south was the alternative to suicide.

From Atlanta she took a branch line to the county seat. There she walked from the depot to the county building, and she found the tax collector's office. A man looked up from his work and saw her at the counter which ran across the front of his office.

"I need some information," she said. "I am trying to contact a man, an old friend with whom I've lost touch. He lived in this county until after the war. I don't know if he is still hereabouts. This was in south county. He owned eighty acres. Fowler was his name."

The man knew of him. He still owned the land; taxes paid in full. A queer business. Not a seed planted on the property for twenty years, but every spring the tax bills went to some place in Texas and every summer the money came back.

McPherson was the name of the town in Texas. And, no, nobody knew where that might be.

She took a room that night, and asked herself again whether she needed to go on with this chase. She did, was her answer. Very much indeed.

She was at the ticket office of the rail depot the next morning, first in line when the agent opened the curtain across the front of his booth.

"I need to get to Texas," she said.

Chapter 16

In the daytime Rose Ellen could see the mountains from her dormitory window. The far peaks were sharp-edged and steep, with blue-grey facets of rock poking through the snow. Sometimes she could see the wind toss the snow and swirl it into graceful mares' tails.

But she still preferred the rolling foothills that lay between Denver and the high peaks. They reminded her of Texas hills, especially now that the snow was receding, leaving the hillsides brown and bare.

As she watched another twilight, Rose Ellen leaned her head on the windowpane. The sun was dropping beneath the ridge of high peaks in the west, and the round hills were growing dark. Her breath condensed against the cold glass.

She wanted to be home.

She put a woolen shawl around her shoulders. She was cold beside the window. Without turning, she spoke to a girl behind her, reading by gaslight. "The cold makes my fingers hurt," she said. "Second week of April and the pond is still frozen outside."

The other girl laughed into her book. "Don't blame the weather for your fingers hurting," she said. "Miss Charlotte's hickory switch has more to do with it. If you don't mind your ways, you won't leave here with any fingers worth mentioning."

Rose Ellen pulled the shawl tighter. "I don't feel it anymore," she said. "She might as well be hitting a rock for all it hurts me."

Charlotte Ames was a small and fragile woman who, in words so soft they were barely audible, taught girls to be ladies. She carried a hickory stick as thick as a man's thumb. What her words lacked in emphasis, the hickory stick provided. A first offense against one of her rules of decorum brought the stick down on a table, or against the wooden arm of a chair. When the stick moved a second time it came to rest against the knuckles of the transgressor. Within a week after she had come to the school, Rose Ellen's hands were swollen and bruised. When she held a pen she could feel every knife improperly gripped, every verb misconjugated, every vowel broadened when it should have been clipped, every shoulder allowed to slump.

Rose Ellen had taken every blow. They were less frequent now than they had been. And she knew that she could endure anything once she had survived Miss Charlotte teaching her to walk.

She had been walking down a hall, her first day at the school, when Miss Charlotte beckoned to her and wanted to know what exactly she called that act that she was performing with her legs and feet.

" 'Walking,' ma'am," Rose Ellen said.

"You may call it 'walking,' " Miss Charlotte Ames said, "but I do not. Tonight you will come to the parlor and I will teach you how to walk."

In the parlor that night the woman told Rose Ellen to remove her shoes and to walk a straight line. Miss Charlotte knelt and bent close to the floor and held the hickory stick in her right hand.

First they would work on cutting down her stride, she said. She told Rose Ellen to take smaller steps.

Rose Ellen walked.

"Shorter," the woman said, and she banged the hickory stick on the floor.

Rose Ellen turned and walked again while Miss Charlotte leaned forward on her hands and knees to follow her footfalls.

"Shorter," she said again, fiercely, and this time she brought the stick down against Rose Ellen's bare toes.

A minute earlier they had been alone. Now ten girls watched Rose Ellen learn to walk. Her cheeks flushed red and she felt a moisture at her hairline.

She bit her bottom lip to keep from crying.

"Walk!" said the woman. And: "Shorter!" The stick bit Rose Ellen's toes. Rose Ellen learned to take smaller steps that night as the stick clapped down in front of her every time she moved her feet forward. If the step was small enough, her foot stopped short of where Miss Charlotte slapped down the hickory stick. Another night of this and the hip-rolling swagger was gone from her walk. She was putting the heel of one foot directly before the toes of the other, as if she had been doing it for years.

Lately Miss Charlotte had been improving her speech.

"I don't understand," Rose Ellen said now, "why we all must sound the same when we talk. I know I sound different from her but I don't see the harm in that."

"Miss Charlotte's way is the right way, she says."

"I know what she says. But until I came here I never heard such a way of talking. And I did fine."

"Miss Charlotte says it is coarse. And I must agree."

There were eighteen teenaged girls in the school, every one the daughter of a suddenly rich prospector, or rancher, or merchant, or thief. The times brought quick money to some. All of it was new money, and the girls under Miss Charlotte's care were reclamation projects, the first generation of their families to have manners equal to the money.

Those who had been at the school longest showed the fewest traces of their origins. Those most recently arrived spoke and acted as Rose Ellen had always known people to speak and act. The new words and the new ways of pronouncing old words felt clumsy in Rose Ellen's mouth, but gradually she became aware of a change. She was sorry to find the old ways disappearing in her. The newest student was a girl from Dallas, and Rose Ellen strained sometimes to catch snatches of her speech. The words had a comforting sound. Like the foothills, they summoned up memories.

She had nothing from Texas except those memories, a few clothes, and a slim packet of letters that she kept tied in a red ribbon.

All but one of the letters were from her father. There had been three in four months, two of them posted as he had returned to Texas from Denver.

He wanted her to understand, he wrote. This would be best for her. She would be taught things she should have learned already. She needed this to turn out right.

Those first two letters were plaintive. The third, sent from McPherson, was sturdy and full of forced good cheer

Not a word of Ray Newsome. But less than a week after her father's third letter she received a fourth, this one in an impatient scrawl that was different from her father's careful hand.

She took it to the room that she shared with two other girls. When she saw that she was alone, she broke the seal and read:

Dear Rose Ellen,

I hope this gets to you. I knew you was gone but I did not know where, then I heard the banker in town tell pa that you was at a school in Danver with this name, i hope it is right.

Then I had to go home and wate until the next time we went to town, which is suppose to be tomorrow and steal some paper and write this letter and hope I get a chance to post it. I hope I can.

Things are right fine in the new house. It is a cold winter, we had a norther blow down and freeze us a couple days, my rojo he stuck a leg in a hole and busted it but pa says thats all right, come spring I will get to ride the trail with him and his boys and I can have my pick of the string just like all the others, and maybe I can ride flank I ride so good.

Last week Thursday I think it was I rode up to indian oak and it made me feel sad. I miss you terrible and hope that maybee you and me will see us again.

My pa he hired a passel of hands name Skinner, Aldritch, Philips, Adams, Burgin and a mex named Pascual. He made Skinner foreman and Adams he is an old guy they say he can cook.

Who knows maybee I will have to ride up to Danver some day.

Yours very truly,
Raymond J Newsome

She had thought of him often, sure that he had forgotten her, that he was living in the valley and riding his horse and never thinking of her. Now she knew differently. Most nights she took her feather pillow in her arms, closed her eyes, and imagined that it was Ray Newsome. That way she slept easily, and happily.

"This book is about Boston," said the girl behind Rose Ellen. Her name was Amanda, and she was from Wichita. "I would like to go there, I believe."

Rose Ellen looked over her shoulder at her. "Boston? I don't know why."

"Boston is a great city. Women there wear beautiful dresses, the like of which we never see in Denver. All the men are gentlemen. Their behavior is perfect. It is the real thing, my dear, not the counterfeit article that Miss Charlotte passes off here. She thinks we are too backward to notice the difference. But I know. Miss Charlotte may be the best there is west of the Mississippi, but she is still a fraud."

Rose Ellen turned back to the window. "I don't care whether I learn the real way or not," she said. "It is all nonsense to me."

"How can you say that? I want to learn to be like the best people, to walk with them and live like one of them."

Rose Ellen looked out into the darkness beyond the window. "I don't understand how you can call them the best without even knowing them. They would have to be very good to be the best because I know some good folks back home that I would put up against anybody in Boston. I never met those folks you are talking about, and I don't expect I ever will unless they come to Mansos Valley someday, so what use do I have for their silly ways?"

"You mean you'd go back to Texas?"

"Sometimes I'm of a mind to start walking south and not stop until I get there."

"Whatever for?" the girl asked.

Rose Ellen imagined the shape of the bare hills, and thought that in the darkness the hills on the other side of the pane could be the hills enclosing her valley.

There was an oil lamp beside the window. Flecks of snow were falling now, and streaking white in the glow of the flame.

"Because it is my home forever," Rose Ellen said.

That night her father was sleeping under the sky, the herd bedded down on the trail just south of the Red River. They would ford the next afternoon. The storm that was bringing a spring snow shower to Denver was north of his camp, and when he lay face up in his soogans he could see the stars' pinpricks of light seeping through the blackness. He was bringing a herd of eight hundred and fifty that season. It would be a good year for the ranch.

He had worked his hands hard that winter. With Rose Ellen in Denver, the place had been empty for him. He had taken for granted the life she brought to the house. In its place was a terrible bleak loneliness that would not be banished. So he spent days at a time on the range, riding and roping with the hands harder than he had done in ten years, working them as hard as he worked himself.

When herd-gathering time came they were working together in a way that pleased Fowler. He could not remember the last time he had felt so good about his ranch. He thought he would make something of it yet.

Earl Newsome and his herd were twenty-seven days up-trail, far enough north to be on the periphery of the storm. The clouds were thin overhead. The moon shone through them and made them grey blots.

They had never left so early on a drive. They needed the days because they were trailing up to Wyoming to sell beef to the army. That winter a major had come riding through the valley, calling on ranchers, offering contracts of thirty dollars a head, on the hoof, at Fort Laramie. Irene thought they should take the contract. It was good business, she said, to sell to a buyer who spends someone else's money. They could get thirty dollars in Wichita, but there was no telling what arrangement Earl might be able to make with a generous quartermaster. Wyoming it was.

On this night Orrin Sample was alone in his cabin. For the second year in a row, he would be passing up the drive. That left time for reflection, for thoughts that he tried without success to push away.

Lately he had been looking back at his life, to see what he had done, what kind of man he had become. A fine occupation, he told himself, for someone more than halfway to the end of three-score-and-ten.

Before he had known Fowler and Newsome and the partnership, he'd not been a man to ask such questions of himself. Ten years into the partnership he would have answered them proudly: he was a man who could think and work; he knew ranching; he had opinions worthy of consideration; he was part of a great enterprise.

Now the doubts were strong. He had been making mistakes since they'd split the ranch. And maybe, he thought, before that. The success of the Circle Three Bar—not without effort, but predictable and almost inevitable—had deceived him. It was not so easy, he was finding.

He considered his mistakes. For the second year in a row he had been late hiring help for a drive, and help was hard to find. He had hired two saddle tramps to rope and brand strays. But then he had slipped patching his roof, and was hobbling when he should have been riding. The saddle tramps worked alone, and when they left him after two weeks it was to start a herd of one hundred and fifty cows—bearing a new brand—up the trail to Kansas. So for the second year in a row he would not be mounting a drive.

He had been weighing an offer of twelve dollars a head from a rancher on the Nueces when Irene came to call. She had stepped down from her carriage and stood until Sample, flustered and confused, offered her a seat inside the house and a glass of spring water.

"Orrin," she said, "I know you have found the going somewhat tough since we made the break. I feel badly, since Earl and I had a part in that. We would like to help if we could."

He said no, he did not need charity. Not yet.

"I don't mean charity, but a trade that would help us both."

He told her that he was about to sell five hundred head.

"Don't," she said. "What is he offering you? Sixteen dollars? Fifteen? You're giving the cattle away at that price. Instead of selling what is really valuable, you can get rid of what you don't really need."

"Besides cattle, I've only got land."

"That's what I mean," she said. "Land."

He refused at first. They both knew that land was worthless. He had heard her say so fifty times to Charlie Fowler. He thought this was just a clever way of getting him to take help.

In the end she talked him into it. He gave in when she agreed to take her choice of the land, whatever she wanted. Even so he felt like a cheat when he took the money: sixty-four hundred dollars at one dollar an acre to cover the ten sections of his land through which the Mansos River flowed, with its cool water and its grassy banks. He was grateful for her generosity.

He was not a happy man as he examined himself in the solitude of his cabin. He felt weak and vulnerable for the first time in many years. Never before had he doubted his decision in the Confederate hospital bed. Reality had always been equal to the best he could have imagined for himself.

Now he was not so sure. Chances and opportunities once spurned now seemed suddenly imposing. A wife, maybe, if he had not come to this remote place. Children. Maybe not so much land but a thriving life. A life in which he did not need the charity of his neighbors to survive. A life, above all, in which he would not be haunted, as he was now, by the looming, mocking specter of what might have been.

Chapter 17

That summer of 1881 Ray Newsome joined the company of men. He kept something of a boy's spirit but his body was a man's and he did a man's job on the trail. He rode beside men, and ate with men; he listened to their obscene stories at night and told bawdy lies of his own in a man's voice.

The change went beyond that, to depths that Earl Newsome did not recognize at first. Even Irene saw only the outlines of it. But what she knew of it she liked. As they rounded up the cattle for the drive she understood that for the first time her son was counting the cows and the ranch as his own. He was no longer a bystander. He had a share in it. She thought she glimpsed in him the first quickening of pride in what he had, and of wanting. Most of all, wanting.

Never had anything satisfied him as much as this drive, moving the herd, his herd, up the trail. He liked to push his body all day, then placate it with a full stomach and dreamless sleep at night. More important to him, he was doing something of his own, working for his own future. He thought this good job would be twice as good if they were driving twice the cows, for the ranch was nothing without cattle and the drive.

He was ready for the notion when it came to him, had prepared for it so that it arrived one night like a welcome and overdue guest. He realized: this ranch will be mine. And nothing will come close to my ranch. It will be the best.

He grew into the idea as they drove north. The stance

suited him, and Earl accepted it. Ray no longer rode flank, but took his place beside Earl, on point at the head of the herd. When it was payoff time at the fort, Earl and Ray walked together to the quartermaster's office, and together they gave the man a hundred dollars for counting a herd of nine hundred and thirty-two as one thousand and forty-five.

Fort Laramie was no cow town, and the men were ready to play. They were camped outside the fort; Earl called them together and told them to choose. They could have Cheyenne for a couple of days or they could have Denver—all the same to him.

Ray was sure that he did not draw a breath during the talk that followed. Cheyenne was closer, somebody said. They would be there sooner.

But Denver is a for-real city, said another.

All the more reason, said a third, to stay clear of it.

Then Burgin threw in a story about a dive in Denver where the barmaids walked about in shirts, nothing more. Shirts and a smile, he said. And Adams spat into the fire and recollected a show he had seen there—'77 it was, or '78—with girls dancing about in their scanties and going out into the crowd, and once every hour a lottery where the winner took his pick from the girls in the dancing line.

That carried the night for Denver. Ray, standing at the edge of the circle of men, expelled the air he seemed to have been holding for five minutes.

He knew what he would do. There would be no keeping him from it. Denver was a big city, they said. Maybe so. He would find her anyway.

And it was a big city, the biggest he had ever seen. Bigger than Austin, which he had visited once. Bigger than the image he had formed in his mind of San Antonio, from stories he had heard. Denver was so large it did not have one single main street, but a dozen at least that might qualify.

They reached town in the afternoon and found a hotel. The cowboys made plans in the lobby. One of them called to Earl, "Hey, boss, you going to let that younker bust loose tonight?"

Newsome looked at Ray standing beside him at the desk and said, "Reckon he can speak his mind if he has one."

Ray shifted his weight from one boot to the other, hands

jammed into the hip pockets of his pants. "I might like to look around some," he said.

"I thought you might," Earl said. "Go on, then. But don't do anything to make me ashamed of you, understand?"

They took Ray to the first saloon they found, around a corner from the hotel. They stood at one end of the bar. One of the cowboys ordered a round of whiskey for the bunch, but another said, "The boy don't need to start off with whiskey, a beer will do him fine."

"You ever drink whiskey?" Aldrich said.

"No," said Ray.

"Beer, even?"

"No."

"Make it a beer."

He drank it down. The taste was strong in his mouth, and swallowing was difficult. He wondered what part of the foulness was alcohol. Probably alcohol straight would not be so bad, he thought, so next time around he ordered whiskey and got no argument. That burned the throat at first, but at least it did not have the dense taste of beer, and after it burned the first time it slid down easily enough.

He ordered a second whiskey, and drank it.

The cowboys had begun to leave, first a pair, then a third, then two more until his second whiskey was down and he was alone at the bar with Adams.

"We got to go with the boys," Ray said. He had to say it slowly. His mouth was thick.

"You don't want to go where they are headed," Adams said. His hair was long and grey, curling up the back of his neck. "Next year, maybe, but not this trip. You stay. Get good and lathered, which ain't going to take you 'til the sun goes down, and then I'll show you home to your pappy. You got to take these things slow."

He nodded at the bartender. "Another whiskey for the young buck here."

Ray gulped this one. It went down easily. Whiskey, he told himself, did not take much getting used to. He could stand here and drink all night. He could, that is, if he had nothing else to do.

He put the glass to his lips and tilted his head back until he was sure the last drop had gone down his throat. He put the glass on the bar, tugged at the waistline of his pants, and told Adams thank you, he had something to do.

Denver was a big place and he did not want to walk from one end to the other. They had left their horses at a stable across the street from the saloon. Ray went there and got his horse.

"Lookin' for a school," he said to the stable boy. The words came out hard; Ray considered the possibility that he was drunk. "School for girls."

"Even if I knew of one," the boy said, "I wouldn't tell anybody else about it."

Ray stared down at him from the horse.

"But I don't, pard," he said. "I surely don't."

Ray rode his horse into the street, into the evening shadows. He swayed and held tight to the pommel and pinched the horse's spine between his knees for balance. The animal hesitated, unsure of these new commands. Ray chucked it forward and turned down the street, toward what seemed the busiest part of town.

For a while he rode from one edge of town to the other, hoping to find the school that way. But he could not remember which streets he had ridden. Twice he asked for directions, but the answers he got were useless to him. He could not remember the street names and the turns he was supposed to make. Then the sun went down and he could no longer read the street signs.

He felt sick. The motion of the horse made his stomach churn. He was away from the center of the city, on a street lined by houses, when he got off his horse and sat on the corner. He hoped that sitting would soothe his stomach. He tucked his head between his knees. When he looked up again he saw a man, strangely dressed, standing before him. The man wore a dark blue suit with brass buttons, and he carried a smooth club. There was a badge on the front of his jacket.

The man tapped the club into his cupped palm, tapped and tapped and looked down at Ray. "And," he said, "what manner of distress have we here?"

That evening Rose Ellen sat quietly through supper. She

listened to the crickets, and the songbirds, and the rustling leaves. Only eight students stayed at the school that summer, so they all ate with Charlotte Ames on the screened veranda. They took their main meal in the cool of twilight. Better for the digestion, Miss Charlotte said.

Rose Ellen went upstairs this evening, as usual, when she finished her meal. The other girls in the room had gone home for summer. She could be alone, open the window, smell these last days of summer.

Charlotte Ames gave herself credit for changing the rowdy bumpkin who had been dropped at her door nine months earlier into a credible version of a lady. Rose Ellen was sedate now, had achieved that languid and almost soporific state which was the Ames ideal. But what Charlotte Ames took for serene composure was actually no more than boredom.

Rose Ellen sat by the open window, lit a lantern at her elbow, and read. She was tired, for no reason. She had done no work in many weeks, had not run or ridden or even raised her voice. Still, she was tired. So she turned down the flame of the lamp, put the book aside, and closed her eyes. A man's voice woke her, a man's voice that she did not know, calling her name in the street. She looked outside. She saw only darkness at first, then the figure on horseback.

"Rose Ellen Fowler," the man's voice said.

She heard Miss Charlotte shout. Miss Charlotte leaned from a window and screamed for the man to go away. "I told you," she said. "Miss Fowler cannot see you. You are drunk and filthy and disgusting. Go away, please."

"Rose Ellen!" the man called again.

And then she knew. Something in the voice gave it away, changed though it was since the last time she had heard it.

"Ray?" she said from the window.

"Yep. You coming down, girl?"

"Well, I don't know that I can, Ray. What are you doing here?"

"Come to take you riding. They let you keep a horse here? No matter. We can double up on this one."

Miss Charlotte screeched up at her, "Stay where you are, young lady. Don't let that man near you. He will do you harm. Stay in your room until he is gone."

"Let's go, Rose."

"He won't hurt anything, Miss Charlotte. He is a friend of mine from Texas, having some fun. Maybe we can let him in the parlor for a few minutes. That will quiet him down—you'll see."

From below, a harridan's tortured howl: "No-o-o."

"Jump, Rose. It ain't far. You can do it."

"Miss Charlotte, please. Just to talk for a short spell."

"Clara, lock that front door. Ramona, see to the back. Young man, I'm warning you. Go away this instant."

"That's it. That ties it," he said.

There were three stone steps up to the front door, and a landing. Ray leaned down in his saddle and tried the door. When it did not budge he kicked the stirrup away from his right foot.

Rose Ellen stepped back from the window. She could not watch. She heard a succession of sounds: Ray's boot slamming against a door, a splintering of wood, shrieks and screams of shrill female voices, a shattering of the front door's etched glass, and a tinkling of its shards. She heard Ray's feet hit the landing, and heard his heavy boots clopping in the entryway, down the hall. Then louder, up the stairs.

She thought, My God, he is coming for me.

"Rose!" he shouted. His voice reverberated up the stairwell, breaking nine months of quiet. "Rose Ellen. Where the hell are you?"

She opened the door. He looked at her and grinned, the expression so ludicrous and the sight of him there so welcome that she smiled back at him.

"Let's go," he said.

He was different. The boy she had known would never have done this.

He walked to her and took her arm. They walked into the hall. Three girls stood there wide-eyed, watching her. Four more and Miss Charlotte herself were at the bottom of the stairs, watching. There was no movement.

They started downstairs. At the bottom of the stairs Miss Charlotte and the girls stepped back when they approached. Rose Ellen realized that they were afraid of Ray.

"I am going out," she said, "with my friend here. Please

don't worry about me. He won't let anything happen to me.''

On the landing he mounted and pulled her into the saddle behind him, and they rode. They galloped past the edge of town, leaving behind its houses. She clasped her arms around his chest and thought of stories her father had read to her from a book. They were stories of women trapped in castles and knights who came riding to rescue them. The stories had never meant much to her. But she had never before needed rescuing.

When they had put the city behind them he let the horse canter. "You ain't angry?" he said.

"No. I am happier than I have been since I don't know when. Since the last time we were together.''

"I had to come see you. Had to find you. First I thought I couldn't, but then I got some help from this fella said he was po-lice. I wasn't but a few houses away. I told him I was looking for my sister and he helped me out.''

They found a grove of aspens beside a brook. Ray pulled up there, jumped down, and helped her off the horse. He found a flat, clear spot among the trees, and they walked there hand in hand. Ray breathed in the night air. His head was clearing.

He looked at her, his hands on her shoulders, to make himself realize that they were together again. He pulled her to him and kissed her.

When they separated he said, "I thought of you every day. All the time.''

"I was sure you wouldn't.''

"You're talking crazy, Rose. I love you.''

The words made her heart skip. "I love you too,'' she said.

He put his lips against hers. They sank down to the grass. His hands moved over her body as she pressed against him. He felt her back, her shoulders, ran his hands down her spine, his fingers pressing against the fabric of her dress.

"Is it the same?'' he said. "Is everything the way it was?''

"Better,'' she said. "There is more of it. Understand?''

They looked at each other, not turning away or even blinking, each examining the other in the light from the stars and the moon. For some time they lay in the grass and kissed. His hands still searched, moving across her face, her arms, her spine, while he held himself against her.

"I want something," he said, "and I don't know how to ask, and I ain't even sure I am supposed to have it."

She stared into his eyes. Ray, no more a boy, she thought. Now a man, she could see.

"We've done everything else together," she said. She reached back for the top button of her dress and pulled it free. She unfastened them all while Ray watched.

He kissed her on the lips, then her neck, then down the bare curve of her shoulder where he had never kissed her before. He remembered: gentle, gentle, the way she likes. He put his hand under the strap of a camisole and slipped it over a shoulder, and when he pulled it farther he bared a breast. They each pulled free of their clothes, and when they held each other next it was skin on skin.

He rolled her on her back and found a place for himself between her thighs. They rested long enough to find the rhythms of their bodies. Only then they moved.

Later he cradled her against him, her head tucked under his chin. "I never knew," he said. "Never had no idea."

"That is the way it is supposed to be," she said. "I could see where it might go wrong. But the way we just did it is the way it is supposed to be."

For some time they lay that way. It was a warm night and the air felt good on their bodies. He became aware of a dampness on his chest. She was crying.

"Rose, I'm sorry. I'm so sorry. What did I do?"

"Not you," she said. "I was thinking. I don't want to do that with anybody else. It would be different. It would be wrong."

"I wouldn't let you," he said. "And same for me. I wouldn't do it with anybody else. You're the one I want, girl."

"Good," she said.

"We can't let anything come between us. Not after this."

"No."

He said, "We'll get married, I 'spect."

"It seems the reasonable thing."

"Not right off. I want to, but it will take some doing, from your end and mine."

"Then we will work on it, won't we?" she said. "If it is something we both want we will have to work on it until it comes out right."

"We can do what we please," he said. "We ain't children no more."

"Between ourselves we can be," she said. "Between ourselves it doesn't have to be any different than it was when we were little. But we have to show the others we are grown-up now, and can do what we want."

"Even if that is marrying," he said.

He helped her to dress, fastened all the buttons down her back.

"You know," she said, "you don't have to marry me to make this right. What we did tonight is right all by itself. You don't have to marry me for that."

"I won't. Oh, I ain't saying it is something I had on my mind for a long time, because it wasn't. I thought about you, but marrying looked a long way off. Like something that other people did. But if other people can do it, we can too. And when it popped in my head and right out my mouth it seemed like the best idea I could have. It still does. We can do it come morning if you like."

"No. Wouldn't be fitting. I want it done proper."

"Then ride back to Texas with me. At least do that. I will talk my pa into it. You don't want to go back to that place."

"I don't, but I will. That is the thing for me to do, face what I have to face there and then square things with Papa."

He knew there would be no arguing her out of it, not if anything of the little girl survived in the woman. He brought her back to the school, kissed her once more, and watched her walk up the stairs and through the broken door.

Finding his hotel took some work, and the room was dull with early light when he got there. He did not sleep. His mind was alive and it gave him no rest. That day, and the next, and most of the ride south to Texas he saw with the clarity of a traveler in a strange land. He found himself changed in every way, the transformation complete. Now he saw the world through new eyes, a man's eyes.

Charlotte Ames kept Rose Ellen confined to her room for three days, as though she carried a contagious fever. A girl brought meals to her door three times a day, knocked, then scurried down the stairs. Rose Ellen was grateful for the solitude. She wondered, with a detached curiosity, what sort of atonement the woman would extract. Rose knew she would live with it, whatever it was. The night had changed her, too. Suddenly she could not fathom the unhappiness and the torment that she had felt in this place. It was a triviality now, a nuisance. She was above it; it had nothing more to do with her and she could not take it seriously.

The quarantine ended with Miss Charlotte rapping on her door, telling her that her father had been informed in a most detailed letter. Her qualifications as a student at the school would have to be reexamined. Restitution would have to be made for damages. Apologies would be necessary. And her supper was on the table.

That was the end of it; her crime had exceeded Miss Charlotte's capacity for punishment. There was one final penance: the wondering stares of the other girls, who followed her with wide eyes wherever she went and jumped aside when she passed them in the halls.

After six days of this her father arrived, trail-weary from the drive to Kansas. Rose Ellen reached the front door first to answer his knock; she had seen him coming up the stairs. They held each other and she cried. Fowler, too, was seeing through moist eyes when Miss Charlotte, standing in the door of her office, arms crossed, requested him to do her the kindness of speaking privately with her. Now.

Rose Ellen waited in her room. For the first time she felt regret for what she had done. Her father would be hurt, and she did not want that. He was a good man and deserved better.

He walked into her room, closed the door, sat on the edge of her bed while she sat across from him in a chair. "She says you had some fling the other night."

Rose Ellen nodded.

"Who the hell was this young whelp, somebody you been carrying on with up here?"

"It was Ray Newsome," she said. "And he is no whelp."

"Son of a bitch," he said softly.

"Please."

"She said he was drunk."

"Maybe he was. He wouldn't have done what he did without some liquor in his belly. He is not that kind."

Fowler waved his hands in the air for a few moments before words came. "What is it?" he said. "What is it with you two?"

She knew she had to choose her words. Finally: "We don't like for people to try to keep us apart."

Another silence as he considered that. "Do you mean to marry this boy?"

"I do."

"Well, damn, I don't know what to do."

"If you would listen, Papa, I would tell you that he is good and kind. Different from you in some ways, Papa. Too quick to move sometimes. I wish he sat on things for a spell the way you do, to see what they will turn out to be. He doesn't. Doesn't have the patience, maybe. I wish he did, but he doesn't, and that is him.

"Some ways, though, he reminds me of you," she said. "Real proud. Like he cares about himself and knows that he is something special. I don't mean vain. That isn't becoming. Full of respect for himself is what I mean. That is a good thing for a man to have. Or a woman."

"I don't know what to say, Rose. I did not feel kindly toward him before I walked in this room and your words can't change that. I still think of you and him up on that hill and it makes me sick every time I do."

"I'm sorry."

"Sometimes I wish I had shot him right there. I think that would have made me feel better."

"Papa, no."

"No," he said. "Not me. That is not my way. I think too damn much."

"That is a good way to be," she said.

"When you went riding with him," he said, "the other night, I mean. You didn't do anything . . . anything that wasn't right."

"No, Papa," she said. "I didn't."

He cleared his throat. "That Miss Ames. She tells me you have been a trial for her."

"She has her ways. And I have mine."

"This school was a mistake. You don't belong in a place like this."

"It's a good school, Papa."

"For some, maybe. But it was wrong to stick you here among people who would try to change you, so far away from your home. I don't blame you for being happy to see a face that you knew."

"They changed me for the good, Papa. They did. I have learned all sorts of things that I didn't know before. I was terribly crude before. One could hardly have called me a female. And I got some book learning, too, Papa. That doesn't hurt."

She walked to where he sat, took his cheeks in her hands, knelt, and kissed him. "I'm grateful to you, Papa. You can't feel bad about what you did. You did the best thing for me, always have."

"Thank you."

"I know this place is expensive," she said, "so I wouldn't want to be more of a burden on you than I've been already. To be honest, I think I've gotten most of the benefit from this school that there is to be had. I would not want you to throw away your money on something that I did not need."

"Well, you do seem to be a finished woman," he said. "At least to my eye. You always did learn fast. If you went home now you would be the jewel of the valley."

"Let's go home, then," she said.

He stood. "I'm not saying yet on your Ray Newsome. But you do belong in that valley. You want to take the train and the steamboat?"

"I want to wear some pants and ride," she said.

They rode together as they had ridden that summer ten years earlier, mindless of care and time, covering the miles. Sometimes they rode side by side and talked. She told him stories of Miss Charlotte and the hickory stick in a way that made him laugh. They were out of Kansas and four days into Indian Territory before Ray Newsome's name came up. He mentioned it, in offhanded fashion. She knew then what her father had decided. Within a week they were discussing whether Ray might be able to court her without his parents' permission.

Charlie Fowler had taken his daughter's side, a move both emotional and pragmatic. He knew, having heard her speak about Ray Newsome, that she would not be shaken loose from her heart's hold. To stand against a stampeding herd of longhorns would be as fruitful. He knew, as well, that his daughter was strong and smart, and cared for her own self. If she felt so strongly about Ray Newsome, she might know something. But even if she were wrong, and Ray Newsome were no man at all, Charlie Fowler could not deny her what she wanted so much.

They had the house in sight one afternoon, their trek at an end, when Fowler looked at his daughter and said without preface or explanation, "If he is the man you think he is, and if he cares enough about you, he will find a way through this."

The next day she was in the front room of the house when she saw Ray in the distance, on horseback, half a mile or more away across the Mansos. She stepped out on the porch, waved, and called his name. He galloped up to her.

She squinted at him. His head blocked the high sun.

"Come down and greet me proper," she said.

"Your pa is gone?"

"He knows. He understands. Get off that horse and kiss me."

He did.

"You look right fine," he said. "Wearing a dress, I see."

"Around the house I do, unless I want to ride. It doesn't have those skirts piled together, so it is not too bad."

"Every day I could," he said, "I rode by the house. I was trying to see if your pa was back yet, to get up the grit to tell him what I had to say."

"And what is that?

"You know. That we are going to be married."

"I wanted to hear you say it again."

Fowler walked around the side of the house and saw them standing there. Ray stepped away from Rose Ellen, then toward Fowler, slow, calm. He stopped just close enough to Fowler that his speaking voice would carry.

"You don't like me," he said, "I know that. But before you throw me off your land I am telling you that I mean to marry your daughter."

"My likes don't seem to carry much weight anyway," Fowler said. "You don't have to stand there ready to scrap. It has been some time since I threw that punch at you and I wouldn't presume to start in again."

Fowler saw the young man's shoulders drop slightly, his arms relax at his sides.

"Maybe," Fowler said, "you would excuse yourself from my daughter and come have a few words with me."

They sat in the front room. Fowler studied him before he spoke. Still afraid, Fowler thought, but sitting on his fear so that it doesn't show. Ready to stand up for himself. Good for him.

"You won't have to come around here like a fox to a henhouse any longer," Fowler said. "My daughter says she wants to marry you. As long as that is so, and you behave, if you follow my meaning, then you will be welcome here."

"Thank you."

"Rose Ellen tells me that Earl and Irene have tried to keep you away from here."

"They tried."

"They won't be happy to hear of your plans, I'd think."

"I'll tell them. When I think of a way and I figure they're ready for it, I'll tell them. And it won't take me long. I'll get it down soon enough, so's we can get on with this marriage."

Fowler put up a hand. "The marrying will wait," he said, "if it is meant to be. Six months from now, or a year, if you two belong together you will still be ready for marriage. If you aren't, then you can be glad that you waited. I'm not rushing the marriage here. I want to know if you can court my daughter the proper way."

"I will," Ray said, the voice almost defiant. "I wouldn't do it any other way."

"Listen to what I say. Rose Ellen loves you. That means she wants to be with you, have some time with you, not just sit alone in her room and pine away and wonder when you are going to sneak off to see her, next week or the week after. I won't have you doing that to her.

"What you tell your parents is your own affair. I don't want to hear of it. I'm only telling you now to make your arrangements, whatever they may be, so that you can keep my daughter as happy as she deserves to be. That means being with her."

"I will. You can hold me to that."

"Damn it, I do have to say that they are short of sight and small of mind if they don't think Rose Ellen is fit to be with you. Because I think that she is, and you are the lucky one."

It was Ray who asked Orrin Sample's help. He called on Sample, told him he needed a favor. He wanted Sample to ask Earl for help, ask to have Ray work three days a week with him that winter.

"I need hands," Sample said, "but I can hire them. Earl doesn't have to send his boy down here to help me."

"This isn't for you, Orrin. It's for me. I want to get out of that house for a time so I don't have to account for every hour."

"What can you do here that you can't do at home?"

"Court Rose Ellen Fowler."

The answer shocked Sample, and touched off a welter of emotions that threatened to break out on the surface. Anger. Jealousy. A woeful sadness. He said nothing, let the feelings wash over him and subside, and wondered how much of them showed. Not much, he guessed. The boy still looked at him, puppydog-earnest, waiting for an answer.

Sample found his voice. "Planning to marry her, are you?"

The boy grinned, and Sample found himself hating him, wanting to pound the smugness out of him.

"Uh-huh," he said. "Soon as I can get my ma and my pa turned around in the right direction. 'Til I do, I have to find a way to see her without raising dust in the house. I thought, If I worked for you down here I could see her two–three times a week. You wouldn't have to run to tell tales if I passed my evenings at the Fowler place. And you'd get a good day's work out of me in the bargain."

Sample scrambled in his mind to find a way to refuse without betraying why.

"It seems underhanded to me," he said finally. "Telling lies, running from this place to there. I am your father's friend. Am I supposed to help you deceive him? Is that what you want me to do?"

Ray said, "Don't you care about Rose Ellen?"

"I have known her since she was two years old." Longer, he thought, than you have. "Natur'ly I care about her. Like she was my own daughter."

Ray said, "And don't you think she is a fine girl?"

This time Sample did not have to keep the truth out of his voice. He said, "I think she is as good a girl as the Lord put on this earth."

"So do I. Don't you see that puts you apart from my ma and pa? They don't care for her because she is Charlie Fowler's girl, and that is all they need to know. That ain't right."

Sample had no answer to that.

"I figured you would be on our side, Orrin, since you been friend to both of us for so long."

Sample sent him away with a promise to think about what he asked.

Sample knew that he still had not broken free of Rose Ellen, not if the thought of her marrying another man affected him this way. She did not dominate his thoughts as she had once before. But in the past year he had thought of her often all the same, and the thoughts sometimes were fantasies of her living in his cabin, sleeping beside him in his bed, having his children. He told himself that the thoughts helped him bear more easily the days strung onto more days when he saw no person, heard no other voice but his own, talking to himself.

He decided to speak to Charlie about this—Charlie, whom he had not seen in more than a year. It would not be an easy visit. A half-dozen times as his horse walked up the road Sample had to wrestle with the urge to tug one rein, turn back to the cabin, and leave Charlie Fowler undisturbed. And each time he fought it down with the thought that if he was lucky he would see Rose Ellen as well.

Fowler's greeting was friendly in a vague way. They spoke for a few minutes in the front room. Sample did not see Rose Ellen. He told Fowler that he needed his advice. Fowler nodded him to a chair.

The two men were straight-backed and stiff in their seats.

"I don't mind telling you, Charlie, I felt a mite odd coming up the road," Sample began. "You and me, not having said a word in some time."

"We have both been busy," Fowler said.

"Yes," said Sample. "I thought you might have some ill will to me, not that I would blame you if you did. I ain't sure that breaking up the ranch was the wise thing to do."

Fowler could not hold him at a distance. Not Orrin, not his friend. He smiled and saw Sample do the same.

"That isn't so, Orrin," he said. Then: "Ah, that is a lie. For a while there I hated you. I hated you for giving in. But that is ended now. You could not have kept the ranch together yourself, and lately I think that what happened was for the best."

For a while they talked in generalities, traded gossip, spoke of the weather. Rose Ellen came into the room, ran to him and wrapped her arms around him, then sat on the arm of her father's chair. That was good for Sample. He could watch her while he talked to Fowler.

"I came," Sample said, "to talk to you about something that has to do with you, Rose. And Ray Newsome. He said to me yesterday he was going to come courting you."

"He is, Orrin," she said. "I'm going to marry him."

Then it is true, Sample thought. Hearing it from her was even worse.

"I told him," Fowler said, "that he could call if he did it proper. He has trouble with Earl and Irene. That pigheaded pair don't want him around here. I said he was welcome if he found a way to keep company regular."

Sample told them what Ray Newsome had asked. Their reactions hit him hard. Rose Ellen seemed happy to hear it. And a slight smile showed on Fowler's face.

Sample had come to hear Charlie say that it was wrong, a crazy idea, have nothing to do with it.

But Fowler said only, "How about that? The young fella

acts like he is serious about getting what he wants."

Sample dreaded the answer he would get, but he asked the question anyway. He had to know. He said, "And how does it strike you, Rose?"

She looked hard at him. He thought he saw a wisdom there, an understanding. He could believe that she knew everything that was going on inside him.

"I don't know that I would want to make up your mind for you, Orrin," she said. "You do what you think is right. Lying is wrong and there are some who would call it a lie. I don't know. I don't want you to do anything that strikes you wrong. But if you can see your way through this, you'll make me very happy."

Her words made the difference. He wanted to see her happy, even if that meant helping Ray Newsome court the woman they both loved.

Earl was quick to grant the favor. Work was slow on his spread and would be for some time, he said. Better to have Ray helping a friend than to be idle. They settled on Tuesday, Wednesday, Thursday of each week. Ray could save traveling time by staying over with Sample those nights.

Ray arrived early the next Tuesday morning and worked with Sample building a corral until midafternoon. Then he wanted to clean up for the evening. Sample waved him off. Sample peeled carrots and potatoes for a stew, threw some beef into the pot, and made some gravy while Ray bathed in a washtub outside. The boy whistled while he splashed in the soapy water. He changed into clean clothes and came into the kitchen brushing his hair while Sample took the stew off the stove.

"I'll be leaving," Ray said.

"I made dinner. Look, fresh meat, and the carrots are good."

Ray turned away. "Thanks," he said. "But if I hurry I can eat with Rose Ellen."

Sample watched him run for his horse and gallop off.

Later that week, after Ray had returned home, Sample visited the big house again. Just to talk, he told Fowler.

The two men had a good evening together and the visits became regular, whenever Ray was not there. The hours

Sample spent with Fowler, quietly steeping himself in their shared understandings, were some of the best hours he had known in a long time. Earl treated him well and Irene always welcomed him in her distant way. But that was not the same. Earl was not the man he had been. With Charlie the illusion survived, however tenuously, that time's effects were not so great.

After one of these visits Fowler and Rose Ellen watched Sample walk, slightly drunk, to his horse, and ride slowly to the cabin.

She turned to Fowler and said, "I feel sorry for Orrin."

"He would not want to hear you say that."

"He makes me sad," she said. "Everything is changing around him and he is the same. Older, but the same."

"I feel sorry for him, too," Fowler said. He put an arm around her. "Because he has nobody like you in his life."

One night in late October Sample came to dinner. They were eating the last of the soup, and Rose Ellen was bringing a roast to the table, when they all heard the sound of a wagon on the path outside.

Rose Ellen put the platter down and went to the door. Fowler leaned back in his chair and strained to make out the faces of two figures in a buckboard. The light was gone from the sky and his eyes could catch no details.

The horses and the wheels stopped at the front porch, and he heard a man's voice asking whether this was the home of Charlie Fowler. A woman was climbing down, and the man stood in the buckboard holding a trunk.

"You want me to drop this-here on the porch?" the man said.

"Best wait a moment," answered the woman.

She looked at the figure silhouetted in the doorway. "You wouldn't be Rose Ellen?" she said.

"I would."

The woman stepped forward onto the porch and walked to within a few feet of Rose Ellen. She wore a black silk dress covered with a film of yellow trail dust. There was something disquieting to Rose Ellen about the familiar, almost nonchalant way the woman approached her and studied her face.

"You turned out beautiful," the woman said.

Rose Ellen heard her father behind her. She looked at him, and his startled, frozen face gave her a shiver of fear.

The woman looked past Rose Ellen. "Hello, Charlie," she said.

Fowler did not answer, did not move.

"Who are you?" Rose Ellen said.

The woman said, "Just your mother, Rose."

Chapter 18

The man standing in the buckboard asked once again whether he should put the trunk on the porch.

Sample remembered some leatherwork that needed finishing and said a quick good-bye.

Olive Fowler said, "Charlie, the question is whether the bags stay in the wagon and I go straight back to that town or you invite me in and the wagon goes back empty."

The man standing in the buckboard looked impatient. He put the trunk down and stood with one foot on it while he waited.

"Well. . . ." Fowler said. "Well. . . ." He looked at the man in the wagon and then again at Olive. "Well, you can't go back tonight," he said.

The man lowered the trunk and a portmanteau down to the porch. Rose Ellen stepped back; Olive walked a few steps into the house, stood, and waited.

The driver climbed into the buckboard and shook the reins.

Fowler found a box of matches. One by one, he lifted the glass chimneys of the oil lamps in the front room and touched match to wick. When he was finished the room was bright and an odor of phosphorus hung in the air.

"The chairs are for sitting," Fowler said. Olive took a seat near the middle of the room. Fowler hesitated. Rose Ellen guided him to the couch, where they sat together, looking across at Olive.

Fowler tried to sort out the emotions that fought to be

recognized. He was judging the effect of eighteen years on his wife, wondering which question should come first, and asking himself how he should react now, what would be the right word, the right response.

"Ummm, Rose Ellen, this is your mother," he said. "Damn if it isn't."

Rose Ellen was curious and startled. She studied Olive to find echoes of her own looks. She was angry at the intrusion, and unable to stifle a fear which she did not yet understand.

Olive Fowler was relieved. She had actually gotten into her husband's home, was seated in his chair, had not been laughed at or forced back to McPherson. She knew that surprise had served her well so far, but would soon lose its effect. She tried to stay alert to what was happening, to sense and ride the currents lapping around her.

Sure that silence worked against her, Olive spoke. "I paid the fellow ten dollars," she said. "It took him half the day to get here and he will have to drive back half the night. That seemed fair. Did I pay too much?"

"The job is worth what he can get for it," Fowler said.

When nobody spoke again she said, "I thought my journey was finally at an end when I got to that place, that McPherson. The people at the courthouse, there in Georgia, they said they sent your tax bill to that town and I thought you were living there.

"You can feature how surprised I was to find I still had more than twenty miles to go yet. I could have stayed there overnight but I didn't want to. I couldn't get this far and then wait longer.

"In town, they all knew of you. Everybody did. They say you have a real big ranch, Charlie."

Fowler nodded. She took his silence for animosity. Actually, he was trying to slow down the whirring of his mind, to seize just a part of what was happening, but she took his silence for animosity and reacted by talking, prattling.

"I had a devil of a time getting here. No trains, just two coaches a week to that McPherson. I was lucky, I spent three weeks asking about the place and nobody knew of it and then in Denison a man on the train heard me ask the question and told me how to get there.

"Rose," she said, "you are so lovely. I think she has your mother's eyes, don't you think, Charlie? And my mother's figure. My mother had such a fine form."

Fowler finally knew what he needed to ask. "Olive," he said, "why have you come here?"

"I got to thinking about you," she said. "And about Rose, too, wondering what she looked like and what had become of you. I went to Georgia to see you, and when they said you were in Texas, why, my curiosity got the best of me and I just had to come see what you were doing out here."

She looked at Fowler and at Rose Ellen. Their faces were immobile.

"That isn't the truth of it," she said. "Not all the truth, anyway. I got myself in a spot, Charlie, and had no place to go and nobody to turn to. I was at the end of the road, with money to last me maybe a year and no way of getting more.

"That is it, plain as I can make it. In a way, money was the least of it. Nobody to tell my troubles to and nobody who cared what happened to me made it even harder. I had my mistakes for company.

"I used to think of you and Rose all the time. Just think, I'll confess, never believing I would ever see you again. Then things got bad and I thought of you some more and I told myself, Charlie Fowler is the last man who ever treated you right, maybe he won't be too hardhearted if you go see him."

Tears dropped from the corners of her eyes and ran over her cheeks. Her face was dusty, and the tears made clear pink channels. She dabbed at them with a handkerchief.

"I was ready to come live with you on that eighty acres, if you'd have me," she said. "That place I left as if it were nothing, it began to look like paradise to me. It was all I wanted anymore."

She sniffled, and dabbed again with the handkerchief. The cloth left wet smears of dust.

"I don't know what to expect from you, Charlie. You are a good man, but there is a limit to anybody's goodness. After what I did to you—and to you, Rose—I wouldn't have been surprised if you'd sent me back to McPherson straightaway. I couldn't have blamed you."

The tears gushed now. She sobbed into her handkerchief.

Fowler started from his seat to go to her. He felt a pressure from Rose Ellen's hand, holding him back. But Olive sobbed again, even louder, and Fowler moved forward and Rose Ellen's hand fell away from him.

Fowler stood beside his wife's chair. He felt awkward in putting out a hand to lay on her shoulder. "Please don't do that, Olive," he said. "There's no call for that."

"I've been a horrible woman, Charlie," she said. "I don't deserve any kindness. But I need help. I don't know what you have in you to do for me, but any finger you lift would help me. Just letting me into your house like this—you've given me another night to go on living."

He said, "Sure, you'll stay here tonight. We've got plenty of beds. We'll fix you up with one, and we've still got a hot meal on the table. You must be hungry."

She shook her head. "My stomach is too tied up to be hungry. But I am tired and dirty. I wouldn't fight you if you offered me a hot bath and a place to sleep."

"We'll do it," he said. He was glad that she had stopped her bawling. "Rose will heat some water for the bath, it won't be long. Please, Rose? Be an angel and start that fire."

Rose Ellen left without a word.

"I don't believe she likes me, Charlie. I don't believe she is a bit happy about my being here."

"You've got to understand—"

"I do. Of course I do. I can't blame her. Suddenly the mother she never had appears at her doorstep. I understand."

She touched the hand on her shoulder. "Charlie," she said, "you never went to court against me?"

"Divorce, you mean? No, I didn't."

"Why? I don't mean that I'm sorry you didn't. But why not?"

"Never had a reason good enough. It is a long way to a courtroom from here, and it never seemed necessary, not the time nor the trouble nor the expense. So I never did."

She asked, "There was never anybody else you wanted?"

He forced a laugh. "Take a good look about you when the light is better in the morning. I mean, look around this valley, if you didn't this evening when you were driving up. This is not exactly New Orleans. It is not what you might call teeming with marriage prospects. There is only one woman in this valley that I know of now who isn't married and would make somebody a good mate. And she is my daughter.''

Later Fowler and Rose Ellen ate a cold dinner. Olive was asleep upstairs. They ate and did not speak until Fowler laid down his knife and fork and said, ''You think I did wrong, letting her stay tonight.''

''This is your house.''

''But you don't approve.''

''I don't, if you want my opinion. You're a kind man, and I love you for that, but I don't understand your kindness to her, not after what she did to us.''

''You'd have had me shut the door against her, send her away without a word.''

''Yes,'' she said.

''I couldn't do that,'' he said.

''I don't want her here,'' she said. ''She has no place in this house. She is from somewhere else. We built all this without her. We can enjoy it without her. I don't care for her.''

''I do,'' he said.

The words surprised her.

''You look at her and you see only what she is,'' he said. ''I can't help but see what she used to be, as well, and that makes me sad. You have nothing about her to remember, but that isn't so for me. She married me and bore me a child, and that isn't so easy to bury, the memory of that.''

Rose Ellen said, ''I would hate her if she had done to me what she did to you.''

''I did,'' he said. ''For a long time I did hate her. But hating can't live on itself. Not in me it can't. After a while I stopped hating her because I had no reason to do otherwise. Some of the love survived, though.''

''You don't love that woman,'' she said.

''No. But once I did, and there is something there anyway, something left. It stopped me from sending her away, Rose. If she'd given me a choice, while she was still at a distance, I'd have said no, she shouldn't come here. But I had no say in that, and she came, and I could not turn away from her.''

''What do you intend to do?''

"Help her, somehow."

"Give her money. We have enough. But don't let her stay here, Papa. She makes me afraid. I don't know why, but she makes me feel that something is wrong in this home of ours."

"Nothing is wrong," he said. "Nothing is changed. We are too strong together for that."

She listened to his words, but they did not ease her fears.

Chapter 19

Rose Ellen crouched at the edge of the Mansos. She dipped a soapy shirt into the stream and shook it until the flowing water had rinsed it clean. Then she twisted it dry and threw it with a pile of wet clothes that lay on a flat rock. Washing clothes was not a tedious job when she put the tub beside the river. She liked the sound of the water, and the high banks here made it a private place.

So she was doubly irked when she heard Olive Fowler's voice behind her from the top of the bank.

"You're making a terrible lot of work for yourself," she said to Rose Ellen. "I mean, carrying those clothes back and forth up the hill when you have a spring to draw water from right behind the house."

Rose Ellen twisted another shirt into a knot, twisted it until it stopped shedding water. She flapped it and laid it on the pile on the rock.

"Besides," Olive said, "the clothes don't get near as clean with the cold river water. They need heated water to come clean."

Rose Ellen stopped in the act of scrubbing a pair of pants and looked at her for the first time. "I have my reasons," she said. "They rinse out better when I can dunk them in the running water. That makes up for not having hot water. I like to sit beside the stream when I work. That helps the washing go faster. And if I make more work for myself I don't see it is anybody's affair but my own."

Olive looked past her nose at the pile of clothes on the rock, shifted her gaze to Rose Ellen, and said, "Tonight I am doing the dinner. You don't have to worry about it. I believe I will do beef in a pastry shell. It will be very tasty. I'm sure Charlie has never tasted the like of it."

Rose Ellen slapped the pants into the stream. "I wish you would try not to do that," she said. "It's very impolite."

"Make dinner?"

"I mean, ignoring what I say if you don't care to hear it. You have this way—I don't know whether it is habit or design—of pretending that what was said does not exist. You go off making your own trail in conversation whenever it pleases you."

Olive looked again at the pile of clothes and again at Rose Ellen. "I got the recipe from a French chef in Foggy Bottom. He cooked for Andrew Johnson's secretary of state. His sauces were delicious."

She walked up the slope to the house. Rose Ellen wrung the last drips from the pants and threw them on the pile.

Olive Fowler had been in the house ten days, and seemed to have rooted herself. Elementary physics applied, an object at rest tending to remain at rest unless acted upon by an outside force. Charlie Fowler showed no inclination to make her move.

Rose Ellen might have added a corollary in the case of household intruders: the longer an object remains at rest, the greater the effort required to make it move. Olive was becoming a fixture, part of the scenery, blending into the background of the house like a tawny mule deer against an October hillside.

Soon enough, Rose Ellen thought as she hung the damp clothes on a line, the woman would be claiming squatter's rights.

At first, Fowler had explained to Rose Ellen that he could not send her away. She was overwrought, he had said, apology in his voice. She did not seem stable. To put her out would be cruel. During that time, Olive said little, materializing and vanishing silently. She walked with her head slightly bowed, almost cringing, as if expecting the worst.

When the blow did not fall she became less cautious. She

spoke at the dinner table, asked questions, advanced opinions. Her first ventures were timid and hesitant. Lately they had become more definite.

More and more, Rose Ellen thought, she was acting as if she belonged here.

Rose Ellen hung the rest of the clothes in the sun and the breeze, and she went into the house.

Olive was in the kitchen, slapping and kneading dough. When she heard Rose Ellen she complained loudly about the quality of the flour—how could anyone be expected to make decently thin pastry with such stuff?—and when she got no response she clattered plates and pans.

Two days earlier, she had cooked her first meal. She had asked permission at the table, had ventured that she felt uncomfortable being waited on like this when she was perfectly capable of cooking. She would be much obliged, she had said, if they would let her do the next dinner; Charlie should let her earn her keep while she was resting.

That was the word she had used. "Resting."

The dinner had been delicious. Charlie had complimented her twice. Twice too often for Rose Ellen. That evening Olive had told a slightly ribald story she had overheard on the train from Atlanta.

Charlie had laughed at the story. Too loudly, for Rose Ellen. The story had been about three drummers and a farmer's daughter, not a story most women would tell men. The suggestion of intimacy, the forwardness, had irritated Rose Ellen.

Now Olive was taking a second dinner upon herself, no questions asked, just assuming that Charlie would want her to cook and that she had every right to be in the kitchen.

Rose Ellen heard the sound of tin and crockery being moved in a cupboard. She walked up the stairs to her room, and began to think about Ray. This was a Tuesday, and Ray would be coming.

Charlie Fowler, alone and on foot, heard the sound of his boots crunching in the gravel of a dry streambed in the hills. Five jackrabbit carcasses, tied by their hind legs with scraps of rawhide, dangled from his belt. Blood spotted and caked his pants above the knee. He thought that a sixth would give them a meal, with enough left over for stew.

He had not hunted in ten years, so six rabbits in a day would be a feat. This morning he had gotten the urge to hunt (as he sometimes did) and had dismissed it (as he always did). Then he told himself that there was no work that others could not do, that would not at least wait.

And Olive had mentioned rabbit the night before. *Lapin,* she called it. She said it was a delicacy in Washington City, served in all the best homes. The thought of surprising her, of flopping some rabbits down on the kitchen table, had given him the last nudge he needed to reach for his double-barrel, switch it in his saddle scabbard for the Winchester, and go hunting today.

Her third night in the house, Olive had mentioned Washington for the first time. She said it casually, and with her words implied that she had lived there a long time. The next night she had said so, specifically. Twelve years, she said, almost thirteen. But she said no more, and Fowler did not press for details. No reason to do that, he told himself. Nothing she told him could possibly please either one of them. She would share that with him when she was ready.

As he reached the edge of the dry streambed he brushed against a knee-high clump of sage, and the sound he made startled a rabbit at his right. Maybe twenty yards distant, to judge from the noise. The rabbit scurried through a patch of brush, across Fowler's line of sight, toward the open streambed.

He raised the gun to his shoulder. The wood of the stock was smooth against his cheek. He knew that the rabbit could clear the streambed in three bounds. But there would be a moment, in the middle of each leap, when the animal would hang in the air at the full reach of its spring before it hit the earth again and pumped its legs once more.

The animal broke out of the brush, and took a first jump into the streambed. Fowler brought the black lump of a sight in front of the rabbit's nose, swinging left all the while. The rabbit bounded again, and Fowler's finger tightened on the trigger. It leaped a third time, the brush on the far side close now, and Fowler squeezed.

The shotgun jumped in Fowler's hands and the rabbit spun

awkwardly, unnaturally, and fell to the ground. Fowler ran to it. It was a fat buck.

When he reached his horse, he tied all the carcasses together with a single length of rope, fastening each one with a hitch above the joint of a hind leg. He threw the string of rabbits over his saddle horn, put the shotgun into the scabbard, and rode home.

He smelled beef cooking when he came through the front door. There were loud voices in the hall. Olive and Rose Ellen were arguing about clean clothes and how they should be folded.

Fowler put the rabbits on the kitchen table. As he walked through the hall Rose Ellen brushed past him with clothes bundled in her arms and anger showing in her face. He was walking after her when he heard Olive's voice from the kitchen.

"Charlie! You brought rabbit!"

Rose Ellen turned into his bedroom. He stopped and said, "Yes. A couple of nice big ones in there."

She walked out of the kitchen, wiping her hands on an apron. Rose Ellen's apron, he saw.

"They are all nice and big," she said. "You didn't get them all on your own, I don't imagine."

He could not resist smiling, a silly, proud smile. "Every one," he said. "But I notice you have something else cooking."

"Nothing," she said. "The hands will eat it. It is no loss. We can't let this rabbit go wasting. You have wine? I once learned a tasty wine sauce for rabbit."

The rabbit was fresh and good. Rose Ellen ate a few bites before she got up from the table and said that she was anxious to see Ray. She would get on her horse and ride down the road to meet him if nobody objected.

"She has been cross the last week," Fowler said. "Not her nature, normally."

"Two women sharing a household is hard sometimes," Olive said, letting the phrase slip out as if it were a matter of fact that two women now shared this house.

She noticed that Fowler did not challenge her.

"May be," he said. He put a chunk of rabbit into his mouth. "She should not let it disturb her so."

Rose Ellen rode most of the way to Sample's cabin before she met Ray. They brought the two horses flank against flank and kissed, still in the saddles.

"Your pa at the house?" He wanted to be alone with her.

"Yes," she said. "But we don't have to go back there. I don't care if I don't see it for the next few hours."

They rode instead to Indian Oak.

They sat under the tree. Rose Ellen rested her head on his shoulder. They had not made love since the night in Denver. She liked to feel his arms around her and the touch of his lips, wanted to embrace him as she had that night. But she told him that she could do without babies now, and her will prevailed, usually finding as much struggle in herself as in him.

"Ray, you have to get me out of that place," she said.

"Things that bad with your ma?" he said.

"Don't call her that. She may be my mother but she doesn't deserve the name."

"I thought your pa would have throwed her out with the suet and the gristle."

"He has a soft spot as wide as this valley. And she found it without even looking too hard."

"She treats him real good, going on what I seen last time."

She kicked at a clump of dirt. "Men! Is that all that matters, somebody treating you good? Just anybody will do, I suppose, 'long as they treat you good. It appears to me that a man will bed down in a den of shake-tail snakes if they don't bite him first off."

"She can't be all that bad," he said.

"She is. You haven't been around her. All you saw of her, she was making up to you, flapping her eyes at you and telling you how handsome you are. You don't know what it is like in that place. Makes me sick from the bottom of my stomach clear to the top of my gizzard. If she doesn't leave, there won't be room for me. And I don't see Papa making her go. You are going to have to take me away from there, get our own house started so we don't have to let in anybody we don't want."

"I was thinking, maybe the drive would be a good time to

tell my folks about us. If I get Pa alone, I can get him seeing my side. Then Ma will have to foller along."

She kicked again at the clod of dirt. "I don't know that I want to wait that long," she said. "Don't know that I can. Do you want to marry me or not?"

"You know it."

She shifted, faced him. "Raymond," she said. "I don't want to push you. Don't want to rope you into something that you don't think is right—something that doesn't seem right in every bone under your skin. Like the way I feel about it.

"But if you love me, and you think it is right, I want you to marry me as soon as you can. Your ma and pa will have to hear it sooner or later. It won't be any easier eight or nine months down the pike. I know I was the one that said 'Wait' before. But that was different. I didn't have that woman crowding me then."

"I'll tell them," he said. "Friday, if you want, when I get back home."

"I have this terrible feeling," she said. "I do not know where it came from, and I never felt it before. But it is like something is closing in on us and we are running out of time to get away from it."

"I don't see anything like that," he said.

"Like when you run a cow into a box canyon," she said. "The cow just runs, like it always does. The cowboy knows what is happening but the cow doesn't realize. The cow always thinks there is a way out the other end of the canyon. Then, when the cow has run far enough, the cowboy stops and goes over to the gate and pulls the gate shut.

"Even then the cow doesn't see what is happening. Not 'til it runs to the end of the canyon and then runs back, and pokes all around. Finally it gets to the cow that it is in this spot and there is no getting out."

"I don't understand," he said.

"I feel like we—the both of us—are that cow," she said. "Something is running us toward a box canyon. We can't see daylight ahead of us but that doesn't bother us. We think there is always daylight at the other end. And now we are running out of time to turn away. Pretty soon that gate is going to clap shut behind us and we won't have any place to go."

She began to cry.

"Something is happening," she said. "Something is changing. I want to marry you, Ray. I want to be your wife forever and have a happy life with you. We think we have all the time to do that but maybe we don't. I want us to get together, because I know nothing can touch us then. I want us to grab it and hold to it while we have the chance."

She held her face against his shirt, and he put his arms around her.

In his dining room, Charlie Fowler swallowed the last scrap of rabbit and looked for more.

"No—we ate every bit? That was satisfying, Olive, best meal I've had in some time."

"I can cook the rest."

"Leave it. It will make good jerky. But if I had any more room I would take you up on it. You are a fine cook, Olive."

"Thank you, Charlie," she said. "I have to say that I have improved some over the years."

She was confident enough now to allude without fear to the past, and she got the reaction she wanted.

"Why, Olive, you were a good cook before. Not as fancy as you are now, but a real fine cook. I don't remember you serving me a single bad meal, not a one."

She took the compliment with her eyes turned down. Then she said, "Would it be forward of me to suggest a brandy to top off dinner? I noticed two decanters in the cupboard."

"That is port wine, and sherry. Been there a couple of years. I will have some port if you will."

She was on her feet before he could move. "Sit, Charlie. Relax yourself. You have been doing for yourself so long, you are jumping up every five minutes. Find a soft chair in the sitting room, and I'll bring the wine in there."

They sat together on the couch, clinked glasses in a toast to health. They drank.

"You have been here almost two weeks," he said. "What do you think of this spread?"

"It is big," she said. "So much land with nothing on it but cattle. And quiet. If the wind isn't blowing and there are no cows nearby, it is as still at noon as it is at midnight."

He considered that.

"Quiet? I never thought about that. I have been here so long I never notice the quiet. It's good that way, don't you think? Settles the nerves."

"It is a restful place," she said. "No disputing that."

They sipped again.

"The first few years, you must have missed having people around," she said. "There is that drawback."

He thought before he answered.

"We were busy," he said, "me and my partners. Work is a blessing that way. After some time we got accustomed to being alone here. We couldn't have everything."

He ran the edge of his tongue across the bottom of his mustache. There was a lie if he'd ever told one. They had learned to accept loneliness but it never got easier to take.

"I don't mean to say that we wouldn't have liked having more people around us. I did get lonely. What I would have done without Rose Ellen, I can't say."

"But a daughter can't be everything to you."

"No. She tries."

Olive moved closer to him. "Charlie, I want you to know . . . if I can do anything to please you . . . anything you need from me . . . well, we are still husband and wife, you know. That is not changed. I know it has been a long time, and I wouldn't blame you if you had put away those feelings for me some time ago. But if you haven't, why, you can make those demands on me anytime. I wouldn't mind, not in the least."

She drank the last of her port. "Enough for me. Will you want more? Then I'll put this away and go to bed."

He sat alone and thought of his daughter. She did not understand him—would not or could not. When Olive had first arrived, Rose Ellen and a part of him had wanted to send her away. He had silenced his own misgivings, but Rose Ellen was still strident.

He wanted to tell her everything he had told the protesting part of himself. He wanted her to know what a simple joy a man gets from a woman's smile, a woman's compliments. Sometimes that was beyond a daughter's doing. A daughter would not understand the power women had over men to raise them up and dash them down, turn them about-face with only a wink, a nod, a word.

Maybe, he thought, now that Rose Ellen was a woman she understood these things but did not believe her own father was subject to them.

Mostly he wanted her to see his vision of the life that lay ahead of him after she married. She had sustained him so long. Now he saw her married, and tending to another man in her own home. Little enough left for him then, and he would be needing her all the more.

He rose, and thought, I have to be looking after myself now.

He walked to Olive's room. The floorboards creaked. He was going to knock on her door but he saw that it was open a crack, with a line of light at the door's edge. He pushed it open.

A single low flame of an oil lamp lit the room. Olive was sitting up in bed with her back against a pillow, her hands clasped in front of her on the blankets.

Like she is waiting for me, Fowler thought.

She smiled at him.

The blankets covered her to her hips. She was wearing a lace peignoir. Her big breasts rose up and out of the lace when she breathed.

"I thought I would come visit," he said.

"Good."

"Your invite was more than I could turn down," he said. He reached out and put his fingertips on the skin that showed above the peignoir's neckline.

"Charlie," she said, "can things be the way they were before?"

"Yes," he said. His breath came hard now.

"I want it that way," she said. "Charlie, you wouldn't send me away now, not after this?"

"No," he said. His fingers worked down between the lace and her flesh.

"I deserve the worst. I know that. But you wouldn't use me this way and then send me off? I couldn't bear it if you did."

"I wouldn't," he said. "Believe me, I wouldn't do that."

She let him pull the lace away.

Donnie Lee

All along I thought that my mama would not want me bother-
ing Gandy Meacham about Miss Rose Sample. Like she
would think there was something wrong in reminding the old
man about past times.

But I had to do something, for in nine or ten hours I would
be at Sue Everitt's house and I still did not have a lick of
news to tell her about the project. When I saw my mama head
for Gandy Meacham's room with those pills in a bottle and a
glass of water, I knew I had to do something.

I said, Ma I wish you wouldn't give Gandy Meacham his
pills right off.

She wanted to know why.

I want him to talk to me, I said, and the words don't come
out right when he takes the pills.

She said, The poor man is sick. He hurts inside.

I told her I knew that. But I said, Gandy Meacham told me
he likes to be awake and he tries not to take the pills sometimes.

She set the glass of water and the brown bottle of pills
down on the table. Why, I had no idea you were such pals,
she said. What is so important that you two have to talk
about?

About the old days, I said. And I want to take what he says
and use it in a paper for history class. Actually, me and a girl
is doing this paper together.

I waited for the top to blow. But it didn't. Instead she said,
Donnie Lee, I think that is fine. That old man has a treasure

187

locked inside his head and it makes me feel good that somebody is taking the trouble to get at it.

She said, You go on and talk to Gandy Meacham. Get him to tell you all kinds of stories about his cowboying days. Just take these pills with you and make sure he takes two or three of them when he starts to hurt too bad.

Then she asked me who was this young lady I was doing the paper with. She wouldn't stop me from getting a good grade, would she?

I told her about Sue E., and how if anybody had reason to be afraid of coming out on the short end of the deal it was her.

My ma said, A nice girl, is she?

Real nice I said.

She said, You like her, Donnie Lee?

Yes, ma'am, I said. Fact is, I'm taking her out tonight to talk about the project and I wanted to know if I could use the Ford.

She said, That isn't for me to say. Your daddy will be home for lunch and you can ask him then.

But, she said, you behave yourself and I don't see that you will have any problem.

I took a pencil and a notebook with me into Gandy Meacham's room. He was awake, staring up at the ceiling.

Howdy, Quiller, I said.

Howdy, Donnie Lee, he said. He made a move like I was supposed to set in the chair beside his bed. When he did, his face puckered up like he had bit into a lemon.

I said, You okay, Quiller?

He said, I hurt in the mornings 'fore I take my pills. Once when I was in the rodeo—this was up in Calgary in Canada—I got throwed by a Bray-ma bull. That wasn't nothing new. But when I got up on my knees that bull hooked me with a horn. Stuck his horn in and pulled it out bloody. The way I felt for a month after that is the way I feel now when I don't take my pills.

I asked him if he wanted to take them. I didn't want him hurting so on my account.

Just one, he said. That will take some of the bite out of it without knocking me out.

After he took the pill he said, I recall you saying you wanted to talk to me. What was it exactly?

About the olden days, I said. Especially about Miz Rose Sample. For school. We are supposed to learn about historical people, not from books but by talking to people who knew them.

That is the best way, he said.

He laughed. Though it come out more a wheeze than anything, you could tell that something struck him funny.

Tell you one thing, he said. Back then didn't none of us think that school kids would be talking about us, or people writing books about us the way I've heard, or putting us in moving pictures, which we didn't even know of.

His face puckered up again, and this time his hands grabbed the blankets to hold on to until the pain let up.

Soon as it did, he started in talking.

He said, I had a brother a year older'n me. That was Lynn. Him and me cowboyed in the Panhandle country together on the XIT. I know you heard of that spread, the XIT.

Anyways, we cowboyed up Pandhandle way until one day in '90, I think it was, or '91, we decided to hoof it out of there. We traveled some and rode the grub line until we come to this here Mansos Valley. We stopped at the first spread we come to, which was the Circle Three Bar, and that was how me and Lynn come to work for Raymond Newsome.

He looked over at me and at the paper and pencil that was laying on my lap. What the hell is that for? he said.

I want to write down what you say, I told him. When you get to Miz Rose.

Go on, then, and write, he said. We are getting to her directly.

But he didn't say nothing at first. He just stared up at the ceiling, like there was something the matter with it. But there wasn't—he was just looking and not really seeing it at all, I'd guess.

I said, Quiller?

Life, he said. Life. You think you got a handle on it sometimes but you don't. Nobody does. You do things, simple things that you figure don't make a bit of difference one way or other but later it turns out they change everything.

Lynn and me, we didn't have to stop in this valley. We could have passed on through. And everything would of been different.

He said to me, You can get your pencil ready now.

He said, The first time I seen her she was in mud up to her knees. She was wearing a man's shirt and man's pants, and when she slogged out of the mudhole she had on a pair of men's brogans, shoes you would call them, that must of been at least four sizes too big for her. Not even cowboy's boots. See, the Box CF—that wasn't the name then, but it's the same spread—was not much of a money-maker. It rode drag to the Circle Three in this valley. She didn't have the money to throw away on a pair of boots and then go roon them in the mud trying to save a heifer. This was a drouth year and cows was getting stuck in the wallows all the time. So she had this pair of brogans that she carried with her and put on 'stead of boots when she had to walk in the mud.

She was a sight. She was trying to get the heifer out all alone, her and her horse, with a rope that the horse was pulling while she heaved on the heifer's butt end. The heifer was kicking and throwing mud, but Rose kept pushing, and I knew I couldn't let her go it by herself.

So I climbed through the bob-wire fence, he said. Ray Newsome's bob-wire fence.

He stopped talking and his eyelids closed up. Not like he was asleep. At first I could not figure what he was doing. When I seen him clench his jaw, I knew. He was hurting again, and he thought maybe he could fight it better if he did not show the hurt.

When he loosened his mouth he sucked in a lot of air, and let it out. Then he talked some more.

He said, I thought she was a beauty, right as she was. Most men today, if they seen her that way, would not say so. The years was tougher on females then, I believe, than they are today. You get a woman working out in the sun like a man, doing a man's job the way she done, it is tough on the looks.

He said, Prob'ly when she was younger she was the kind of beautiful everybody knows. Not so much, though, when I first seen her. She had been through a lot, though she wasn't yet thirty. She had a good form, but not soft the way women usually are. Wiry and tough is more like it. Her hair was down in her face, and even from 'crost a fence I just knew that her hands wasn't soft, that they was tough like a workingman's. Why not? She had done the work of a good man. Of two middling men.

He said, I still thought she was beautiful. It was the way she leaned against that heifer and pushed for all she was worth. Her heifer wasn't going to die in the mud if she had anything to do with it. That was all I had to see. I knew what I had to know. Sometimes it works that way. I said to myself, Now, there is a woman. She didn't have an ounce of quit in her, and she wasn't afraid to get dirty to do what she had to do.

Gandy Meacham stopped talking all of a sudden. He turned around on his side and propped himself up on his elbow. Then he said, See, Donnie Lee, s'pose that was a man instead of a cow in the wallow, a man that she cared about. You think she wouldn't do the same for a man, if she would get in the mud and get kicked and dirty just for a ten-dollar cow? The woman who will do that will go halfway to Hades and back for a man she cares about.

Leaning on his elbow was too much for him. He lay back against the pillow. Then he said, I ain't saying that she didn't have looks. Later, when I seen her out of a mudhole, dressed up like a lady, she was right purty. But purty ain't beautiful. And when I seen her pushing that heifer I knew she was beautiful.

He said, What do you want to know? You want to ask me questions?

Well, I said, what was she like? Did she really run her spread all by herself back then?

He wheezed out another laugh. He said, Run it? I bet it broke her heart when she had to hire help. That woman could do everything there was to do on a ranch, and better'n most men. She had a terrible time keeping hands. See, she was always getting into whatever was being done. If you was branding then she'd be there, not just roping but leaning over the irons to make sure you burned 'em just right. If you was running fence she wanted to be there too, making sure the posts was sunk deep and the wire was tight enough. You

couldn't do an hour's work without she would be there check-
ing to make sure it was done right.

So I heard, anyways, he said, from the boys who quit on
her, and I can believe it.

I said, I reckon it wasn't easy to work for a woman.

He said, Oh, she had her hard times over that. Nobody
thought a woman ought to run a ranch, though none had the
grit to say so to her face.

But I think it was mainly the way she run the ranch that
didn't set well, he said. Other bosses hired a foreman and
stayed out of the way, and a cowboy did his job without
somebody at his shoulder to make sure. That kind of thing
sticks in your craw. Hell, most fellas get into cowboyin'
'cause they want to be left alone. Later, when I found out
more about her and what she had been through, I understood why
she acted that way. When you are as smart as that lady was,
you don't have to be burned twice to stay clear of fire. Once
is enough. She didn't want to trust nothing to nobody if she
could help it.

He tipped his head toward me and said, What did you think
of her, Donnie Lee? You seen her, I know.

Not much, I said. Just around town some, and she acted
friendly to me. But other folks might say different.

Like what? he said.

Well, sir, I said, I heard she was a holy terror to get along
with.

The old man laughed like he was fit to be put away. I
didn't think he had that much energy in him. It was the pain
that finally stopped him, cut his laugh short and turned it into
teeth-gritting again.

When that was over he said, She had fight in her is what
she had. She had more fight in her than a barroom full of
drunk cowboys.

One more time he grabbed the covers. And he said, Donnie
Lee, better get me them pills.

He took them and he said, Sorry, boy, but I don't believe
I've got any more talking in me for today.

That's okay, Quiller, I said.

He said, You talk to me for a change. You are a fair-
looking fella. You must have a gal to tell me about.

I said, I got my eye on one. Her name is Sue. And I am talking to you for her and me both, since we are doing this project together.

Well, then, you got to bring her around, he said. Next time. I mean it.

I said I would. Then I talked about her for a while, and I didn't feel funny about it. I thought, There ain't nothing I can tell this old man that he ain't already seen and done himself. I figured he would understand.

After a spell his eyes closed and I thought he was asleep. But when I stopped talking he said, in the drowsy way he had with the pills, She sounds like a fine girl, Donnie Lee. I want to meet her.

Yes, sir, I said. Then I remembered one thing in particular I had to tell Sue E.

Quiller, I said, just one more thing. I know this is silly as all-get-out, but I have to ask you anyways. For Sue.

Go ahead, he said.

I have to ask you, I said, if you and Miz Rose was in love.

He turned to me and smiled and said, Hell, boy, ain't you figured that out yet? 'Course we was.

How do girls know these things?

Pretty soon he was asleep and I left him. When I found my mama and gave her the bottle of pills she said, Your father is home early for lunch. Why don't you ask him about the Ford?

Most of the time I have to work up to something like that, but right then there didn't seem to be any putting it off.

He was setting in the kitchen, drinking coffee and looking at *Life*.

I stood in front of him and he said, Is there something you want, Donnie Lee? Spit it out if there is.

I said, I wonder if I could use the Ford tonight.

What for? he said. Not to go out looking for trouble with a bunch of other boys, I hope.

No, sir, I said. I have to see this girl, it's about the history paper we are working on together, and I thought it would be a sight easier for me to drive myself than for you to be hauling me back and forth.

He said, Who is the girl?

I told him, and he looked at my mama, who had come in

the kitchen and he said, Cloyd Everitt's girl. The new doc in town. Nice folks, I hear.

Well! A doctor's daughter, my mama said.

I guess it would be okay, he said. Especially since it is for schoolwork. 'Course you will be back by eleven.

I said I would.

Good, he said. I'll knock off early today, so I'll see you before you go.

Lord, what a fuss they made over me before I left. Ma making sure my pants looked just right and my hair was combed, my sisters giggling and making faces.

Even daddy got into the act. He walked out with me on the porch and said, What do you plan to do with this young lady tonight? When you are not working on your school project, I mean.

I said, I thought we would go get a bite and maybe see a picture.

He said, You got money?

Two-fifty that I saved, I said.

He dug into his pockets for the keys to the Ford, a '40 model that we owned and not a ranch car. He come up with the keys and with two dollar bills, and he handed the lot to me.

He said, Better take this. I would not want you running out of gas.

My ma come out on the front porch. Crying, if you can believe it. And my sisters looked out the window. You would of thought I was going off to war, not just my first real date with a girl.

I was careful backing the Ford out of the driveway, and I drove slow down the road. I knew they was looking at me.

When I got out on the highway it was easier. I headed for town, thinking about the strange ways of kinfolk.

Chapter 20

If he was a man, he told himself, he should act like a man. So the day he returned from Sample's ranch, Ray Newsome told Earl and Irene that he was going to marry Rose Ellen Fowler.

Earl Newsome, as was his nature, exploded.

And Irene, as was her own, said nothing, but watched carefully.

She saw Earl's anger burn itself out quickly. Even its moment of incandescence was not especially furious. He seemed to react as a matter of course. His wishes had been subverted, therefore he was angry.

But she saw that his anger had little else to sustain it. Earl did not object to Rose Ellen herself. And his malice toward Charlie Fowler had spent itself as well. Now, once the rage passed, he was left only to fume and glower at Ray. Irene noticed that.

She also saw that Ray stood up to the anger. So he knows what he wants, she thought. No budging him. She took all that in and weighed it for a few seconds. Only then did she speak.

"Let us be calm about this," she said. "We don't need to raise our voices."

"I ain't shouting," Ray said. "I only want to tell you that I am going to marry Rose Ellen and nobody will tell me different."

That brought from Earl a momentary flash of anger. "We can send you away from here," he said. "You think she would care for you then, you a drifter with no place to go? What would you do then, go live with her and her father?"

"If that's what I have to do, I will."

"We don't want that," Irene said. "We don't have to speak of such things because it won't go that far."

"I will if it comes to that," Ray said.

She said, "Yes, I believe you, Ray. Earl, it appears that we have raised a strong-minded boy. And he knows what he wants."

Ray nodded.

"I assume that the two of you have talked this over."

"Over and over."

"Does her father know?"

"Yes. He is with us. Not at first, but he is now."

She threw questions at him, poked and probed, but found no seams in his resolution. He was determined. To all her questions he gave the same answer.

"Raymond," she said, "you must know that you've startled your father and me. We don't know quite what to say. We're not antagonistic, not at all. But we would like some time to discuss it between ourselves. Will you give us that? By tomorrow evening we will have had a chance to go over what you have said and to talk it over without shouting."

He saw it as a retreat, and was happy to cease fire. He walked away and left them alone in the room.

"If that don't blow me over," Earl said. "Him. Just a boy of sixteen. Telling us he is getting married, no two ways about it."

Time, she thought. Must have time. Ray is too strong now. Fight him now and you lose. But maybe time will change that.

"Darling," she said, "I don't believe we should go too hard on him. He seems to have given it some thought."

"You ain't saying you go along with him?"

"No," she said. "If I had a choice I would tell him to forget the girl. But I know him and I can see that he won't be talked out of it by anybody but himself.

"And if it does come to pass," she said, "would it be such a disaster? I don't know that I want Charlie Fowler for an in-law, but the girl has her qualities."

"Oh, I ain't saying that she don't."

"At least Charlie has some means. She is not some little flirt out to marry into cattle money."

"That is so," he said.

"Now, you know," she said, "young people do have a way of changing their minds. For this reason, or that, or no reason at all. I think that there is a good chance that if we give them time, one of those young lovers will have a change of heart. So much the better if that happens. If not, then maybe their marriage is not such a bad thing anyway."

She knew that she could never let it happen, not if she had a choice. Rose was strong-headed, and she had ideas. Irene did not need another such woman in the family.

Earl shook his head. "Woman, I can't keep up with you," he said. "I would have figured you dead against it, even more than me. Instead, here you are halfway to talking it up. Suits me. We will just get them to wait as long as we can before they go off and do it."

The next evening Ray rode down the trail to see Rose Ellen. He found her beside the Mansos, looking into the water.

"What are you doing here?" she said. "How did you get away? You came with news. You did, didn't you, Ray Newsome? You told them. Just the way you said you would."

She laughed and grabbed him by an arm. "Down here," she said. "Off that horse and tell me how it went."

He saw that her eyes were red, the lids puffed. "Who made you cry?" he said.

"Nobody but me. I got into a terrible fight with that woman. She came to me and said she wanted to be my friend even if I would not let her be my mother, and I got wild. I said I hated her for what she did to Papa and me, and if it was up to me I would kick her fat bottom back to where she came from. Then Papa stuck up for her and I didn't want her to see me cry, so I came down here."

She sniffled. "So how 'bout it, cowboy? You going to take me away from here?"

"Pretty soon."

"What is that supposed to mean?"

"I told them, just like I said I would. At first they tried to talk me out of it but I wouldn't listen. Rose, I stuck to it. Then today, before supper, we talked some more. They went along with it. They said if I was sure and you was sure we ought to do it.''

She leaped forward, hugged him, kissed his neck. "You did it, Ray!" she said. "We are going to get married. It is really going to happen.''

"Sure it is," he said. "Just as soon as we have a chance to get ready, so as to do it right.''

She stepped back. "What does that mean?''

"There is a whole heap of things we didn't think of, we was so busy loving each other up. Like, where are we going to live? Not in that house, with her?''

"No. Not since she got here.''

"You don't want to live with my folks.''

"No.''

"Well, they was real good about it. My pa, he said he would build us a house, a half-mile or so up from our place. Not too big or fancy, but enough for the two of us.''

"That is good of him," she said.

"But he can't do it until after this next drive.''

"No! Eight months? Nine, ten? I don't want to wait that long.''

"That's what I told them. But they said, We didn't want to get married, did we, and have me up and leave you right away and go off on a drive? I had to say, No, we didn't. I can't miss the drive. Pa needs me for that. So that is five or six months we won't be together anyways.''

He reached to hold her. She pushed him away.

"Oh, Ray, I don't like it, not a bit.''

"Anyways, maybe it wouldn't hurt us to hold off some and make sure we want each other. You don't know. You might get tired of me all of a sudden.''

"Where did that come from? You don't think that way. Do you? Answer me, Ray, Do you think we have to wait to be sure?''

"No.''

"Do you think waiting until next fall, sometime, is going to change my wanting to be with you, or your wanting to be with me?''

"No."

"Some things a person is sure of."

"Please, Rose. I done the best I could. It was hard enough as it was. I thought I done pretty good. I don't want them to hate me. I didn't want to have to yell and fight with them. I thought I done pretty good for the two of us."

She put her hands on his upper arms, felt the hard, thick muscles beneath his shirt. "You did," she said. "A month ago if you'd told me what you said right now, I would have been so happy I believe I would have floated right off the ground. And eight or nine months would've been nothing to wait. What is a few months when something you want so much is waiting at the other end?

"But that woman has made me impatient. That is all I can say. Impatient and unhappy and ready to change. They might be right. It won't hurt us to wait. I can if you can."

He held her in his arms under a purple Texas sunset. A bank of clouds splayed out dark and sullen across the sky. His shoulders were broad; he was a head taller than she, and the clasp of his arms was strong and insistent. He stroked her hair while he whispered in her ear, soft words like the gentle and mindless night songs of trail drivers, who hope to pacify the herd with a lullaby.

Chapter 21

One night Rose Ellen awoke in her bed, crisply conscious of
an escape from her quandary: She had to wait until the end of
the Newsomes' drive before she could be married; she did not
want to stay alone with Olive for half a year; but she loved
her father and would like to be with him once more before her
life changed.

She would go with him on his own drive.

The simplicity and logic of it thrilled her. She wondered
why the thought had not come to her earlier. Maybe because
it was so obvious. And maybe, she conceded, because women
did not go on cattle drives.

But she would, this once. She would talk her papa into it.

She did, though the talking was not enough. When he
balked she spent a day riding with him, showing him again
that she could chase down cows and rope charging steers and
ride steep ridges as well as any man he could hire.

Even that was not enough. He still refused. When she
pressed him he told her that he feared for her safety and her
chastity, trail-riding with a dozen cowboys.

"Who will be your pardner?" he asked. It was custom for
cowboys to work together and sleep shifts as a pair.

"You will," she said.

"The trail scout works long hours, rides twice as many
miles as anybody else," he said.

"I can keep up."

"The boys, they like to strip down and get themselves wet

when they get near water. It keeps 'em from getting too gamey. But you won't be able to do that.''

"I'll find a way.''

"Their language is the worst. Cowboys can cuss the spots off a pinto, and they won't alter their ways because a lady is around.''

"I don't expect they will," she said. "They have been cussing the same around me since I can remember. Maybe I will hear a word I don't know, but I doubt it. I believe I heard them all by the time I was six years old.''

"Rose," he said, "you don't know how it is with cowboys on the trail. They get wild. Their nostrils flare when they think of women, and they think of women all the time. There is no telling what one of them might try with you.''

"Papa, do you hire crazy men?" she said. "I mean, out-and-out howling-at-the-moon crazy men?''

"I try not to," he said.

"Then I don't believe I have a worry. Any cowboy who tries anything with me will have to think about what I'll do to him when he sneaks into my bedroll. Not to mention you. And then Ray Newsome, when he finds out about it. What I mean to tell you is that a cowboy would have to be pure loco to buck the three of us. And you say you don't hire crazy men.''

"If I say yes, will you wear your blouse and your pants loose? Will you keep your hair tucked under your hat the way you did when you were a little girl?''

"That is what I plan.''

He laughed. "Wait until they hear about this in Wichita.''

She had noticed before how straight the cowboys rode in their saddles when they began a drive. Manliness, she had always thought it. Something about going on a drive made men feel more like men.

On the morning the herd started up the trail she saw that she herself rode more erect, shoulders even more square than usual. She knew then that it was pride, not manliness, that swelled up inside the drovers at this moment. The start of a big job brought pride, if it did not intimidate. And there was also a touch of awe, because the herd was so large, so mighty. The cattle calls bellowed. The long raked horns jabbed up at the morning light like so many hundred dancing knives. But these few riders, with their horses and their wits, would move the roiling black mass up the trail, hundreds of miles to their goal.

She knew then why men rode so tall, first morning of a drive.

Alvarez was foreman of the ranch, and the job of trail boss fell to him by right of experience as well as position. In other outfits the trail boss usually rode well ahead of the herd, finding spots for a meal break and an overnight camp, seeking out the water and grass in dry country, and after storms searching the banks of high rivers for a likely ford.

With Fowler on the drive, Alvarez stayed close to the cattle and the cowboys. Fowler chose their camps and their fords. He called himself a trail scout. The work was hard. He enjoyed seeing the country that the herd would cross in a few hours, liked most of all being alone with his horse in the open spaces. This time Rose Ellen rode with him, and he liked that even more.

Six days out of the valley a rainstorm hit them. The rain came down in heavy drops that popped loudly against the brim of her hat, against her slicker, against the earth. The dry ground soon turned muddy. So heavy was the rain that it obscured vision beyond a few feet. At times the drops were so thick they formed an opaque grey veil that periodically dropped and lifted before them.

They pushed north for an hour. That brought them into flat and open land. The cattle trail in this region was a band several miles wide. In late summer it was easy to follow, from the millions of hooves that had pounded into the ground, from the grass eaten close to its roots. But they were early on the trail this year and the downpour was washing out signs of passage.

They rode for another half-hour until Fowler stopped and moved in his saddle. He looked out through the rain that cascaded in front of him.

Rose Ellen bent close to say, "I've never seen the likes, Papa." She had to shout to be heard through the hammering of the rain.

Fowler nodded.

She shouted again. "Which way is north?"

He looked at the sky, tilting his head back until the drops splashed into his eyes. He wanted to find a glare of brightness in the clouds that would show him the sun. But the sky was dark, the only light diffused and seemingly without source.

"They way we are headed, I think," he said. "You?"

"I was thinking we got off track back there."

He was using a Mother Hubbard saddle with a canvas apron that fastened around the leather to keep his legs dry. He shook the canvas to chase a puddle of water out of his lap, and he looked around.

"Might as well find the herd," he said. "I don't see us stopping to eat anyway. We aren't getting a hot lunch today, I don't believe."

They turned the horses around and rode slowly. A few minutes later they reached the edge of a ravine. There had been no ravine in their path when they left the herd. They knew then that they were off the trail. They rode for a few hundred yards along the ravine's edge, then back in the other direction. They hoped to find where it grew shallower and ended. But the ravine still went down as far as they could see in the rain.

"We'll wait," Fowler said. "This thing blows by, we will climb a hill and find the herd. It can't be far off."

So they sat in their saddles at the edge of the ravine, and they waited for the rain to stop. But they were not accustomed to standing long in one place. After about twenty minutes of this Fowler shouted to Rose Ellen.

"I reckon if we get to the bottom and follow it out to the end it will empty us out on the trail again and we will find the herd."

She nodded, and they started down the ravine. At first the ground was soft and the horses sank in to their fetlocks. But soon they reached rock, boulders smooth and rain-slick. They had to pick their way around the large ones. Sometimes there was no way around and the horses had to walk from one rounded rock to another.

Fowler had not ridden this horse on such terrain before. It was one of a string of horses that he had brought with him. Fowler liked this one for hard rides because it was long-winded and strong. But on the rocks now the horse was skittish. Rose Ellen's horse was more nimble. She took the lead. She gave it rein and the horse found its own way down, planting three feet before advancing a fourth.

She could not see the fall, but even through the drumming of the rain on her hat she heard the horse's hooves skidding behind her, heard its sound of fright from deep in its throat, heard Fowler's yell, angry and surprised.

She turned and saw the horse lose its balance, fight to regain it, tumble over sideways and send Fowler twisting, vaulting out of the saddle.

He landed hard behind a big rock, out of her sight.

Rose Ellen pulled hard on the reins. She jumped down and ran to her father. His head was against a rock. He was face-down and he was not moving. She tugged and pulled at him until his back was on the ground and his face was turned toward her. His Stetson was cocked to one side. His right forehead was exposed, and there was blood coming from a raw patch in his scalp. She pushed aside some of the hair matted in the wound, and she saw the white of his skull where the rain carried away the blood.

She felt sick and frightened. Behind her the fallen horse lay on its side, kicking and writhing and squealing. She put her father's hat over his face to keep the rain off, and then she went to the horse. She saw the broken bone that poked through the skin of one foreleg. She pulled her father's rifle from its saddle scabbard, levered a round into the chamber, and put the end of the gun barrel behind one of the horse's ears.

The horse stopped moving when the metal touched its head. It jerked once, and then the straining muscles under its brown skin lost their tension when she pulled the trigger.

She put the rifle into the scabbard and then ran to her father again. She knelt beside him and lifted his Stetson. His eyes were closed. She took off her own hat, crushed it and put it between his head and the rock. She cried. The tears were warm on her face when they met the cold rain.

He moved and spoke for the first time a few minutes after the rainfall became thinner. She was deciding whether to ride, try to find the herd, when he moved his right hand toward the hat on his face and mumbled some words into the felt.

She lifted the hat. "Papa, you're alive. How do you feel?"

"Like a steer danced a fandango on my head. Is anything broken?"

"Not that I can see. You got some scrape up there."

He stretched and moved limbs, muscles, joints, until he was standing. "All's well," he said. "The horse?"

"I had to put him down," she said. "Busted leg."

He rode her horse and she walked beside him, out of the ravine. When they were close to its mouth they heard cattle calls. It was their herd. During lunch Fowler cleaned his wound and bound it. But it still hurt. That afternoon the jogging of the horse sent surges of pain through his skull. He could not sleep that night. His tossing woke Rose Ellen and she stayed awake with him. In the morning light he looked haggard and drawn. The special life that had always danced behind his eyes was gone.

"You can't go on today," she said.

"Leave me here for a day. Stay with me and we can ride to catch up tomorrow."

"You need a doc. You should see the size of the lump on your head."

"I can feel it. Like an egg."

"You can't even talk without closing your eyes. Is it that bad?"

"I'm not complaining."

"No," she said. "You wouldn't."

"I have to be with the herd in Kansas," he said. "Work my bargain with the buyers. Paco can get the cows there, but it ain't his job to haggle. Those are my cows, not his."

She said, "They are mine, too. Don't argue. I can bargain. First I listen to talk about what the other outfits have been getting. Then, when I go to the buyer, whatever he offers, I hold out for three dollars more. No, make that four, four-fifty. Since I am a woman they will be starting low with me. Then I meet them somewhere in the middle, if it is on the high side of what everybody else is getting."

He smiled through the hurt. "Maybe you can bargain," he

said. "But you can't travel alone to Kansas with a bunch of trail hands."

"I can," she said. "And I will. I am sending you back with the rustler. I will do his job. He doesn't sleep anyway, except in the saddle. Nobody is going to try any foolishness there."

Fowler hurt too much to argue.

The rustler in every outfit was a boy on the edge of manhood, learning the cowboy's trade from the busy end: assistant to the cook; keeper of the *remuda;* square and errand-runner for the unkempt trail drivers; in general, the lowest-ranking member of the vagrant trail society.

This year, the Diamond Five rustler was a fifteen-year-old named Sam. This was his first drive.

Now Rose Ellen took him away from the *remuda* and explained what he must do. "Get him back to the ranch. Don't hurry him too much, but don't waste time, either. His head will hurt some no matter how slow you go. Give him the gentlest, calmest horse you got, I don't care whose string it comes out of. Take food with you, give him some if he wants but don't bother him with it if he doesn't. Let him rest if he feels like it. If he wants to sleep an extra hour in the morning that's okay. Otherwise, ride when you can see."

Sam nodded after a moment. "Okay," he said.

"What I'm trying to say is, get him home fast as you can without killing him."

"Yes, ma'am."

She held her father tight. Then she stood back as he slowly pushed himself into the saddle and swayed atop the horse.

"I'm fine," he said. "Just fine. It made my head throb to set down hard that way."

They rode off. Rose Ellen wanted to watch them leave, but the point riders charged in, yelling for new mounts, swimmers for a rising river ahead. By the time she had cut the animals out of the milling herd, the man and the boy were out of sight.

Fowler and Sam rode south that day. Fowler's head felt huge, distended. The pressure of the hatband was too much, more like a tight iron strap than thin leather. He cut a slit at both ends of the crown and tried to ignore the pain. It was with him constantly, so bad sometimes that it made his eyes blur.

He gripped the saddle horn as he rode. There was dimness at the edges of his vision. He felt weak, somehow lightheaded with all the hurt.

He pulled at the reins. "Got to stop," he said. His motion off the horse was almost involuntary, as much a controlled fall as a deliberate step. He sat heavily on the ground. His forehead was suddenly wet.

"I hear water running on the other side of that bush," Sam said. "I'll fill the canteens with fresh water and bring you some to drink."

The boy emptied the tepid water from the canteens, held them one after another in a deep hole of the stream, and let the air bubble out of them. He carried them back to Fowler and the horses. Fowler was on his side with his eyes closed.

Sleeping, the boy thought. He wondered what he should do now. Get him home, the daughter had told him. But let him rest if he wants. He decided to sit in the shade of a cedar tree and let him rest. Sam did not mind the wait. The grass was green, the bluebonnets were in bloom, and the air carried the fresh taste of spring.

Sam drank from a canteen and waited for Fowler to awaken. Soon his conscience nagged at him. He had given him rest. Now he should get him on his horse and on his way again.

He walked to Fowler and spoke his name. Fowler did not move. Sam bent down and said his name louder. This time when there was no response he put a hand on Fowler's shoulder and moved it gently.

It felt heavy.

"Mr. Fowler," the boy said, louder.

Sam shook Fowler for nearly a minute before he drew back his hand and looked hard at him. Having never before seen death in a human being, he was slow to recognize it in Fowler's face, his skin and his limbs.

He had no shovel. Somehow he got Fowler's body across the saddle of his horse and tied him down. He rode without stopping for a day and a half, returning Charlie Fowler for the last time to Mansos Valley.

Chapter 22

Olive sent the boy to tell Sample. After he had fed the boy and led him to bed Sample sat alone to prepare himself for the night and the day ahead of him. He felt grief for Charlie Fowler. He knew he had lost a friend, and he faced more closely than ever before the palpable fact of his own mortality. Then he put a saddle on a horse and he rode up the trail.

He stopped first at Fowler's home, and spoke to Olive. She seemed more frightened than bereaved, and begged him to take Fowler's body off the horse and lay it down in the stable. He carried the body into a bedroom instead. Then he left her and headed up the trail to the Newsomes' home.

In their parlor he told them what he knew.

"How?" Earl asked.

"He fell and hit his head. There is a mark there, doesn't look like much. He was coming back when he died."

"Poor Charlie. This is bad, Orrin."

"He'll have to be buried soon. This was yesterday morning it happened."

"First thing, then," Newsome said. "Poor Charlie."

"I better be leaving," Sample said.

Suddenly Newsome did not want to be apart from him. "Don't go, Orrin," he said. "Stay here for a time—you don't have to go home tonight."

"I can't stay. There is work to be done. You have a spade?"

"I want to help you, Orrin. We can do that together."

Sample looked at Irene and said, "That would be fitting."

"Spades and picks are in the shed, you know where," Newsome said. "Take what you need. I'll meet you in the stable directly."

Newsome came walking out of the house and toward the stable while Sample was throwing a saddle on the back of a horse. Newsome finished the cinching and looked up and said, "She wants to come for the burying, she told me."

"I have to say that is a surprise."

Newsome put his foot into the stirrup and climbed into the saddle. "Irene ain't one to do what you expect," he said. "You think she is going one way and then she goes another."

Like, Sample thought, she is playing a game by rules nobody else knows.

"I can't figure her," Newsome said. "I stopped trying a long time ago. She has her reasons, and they always make sense when you ask her."

Sample carried a spade across his lap, Newsome a pick. They paused at the gate in front of the stable.

"Where do we want to do this?" Newsome said.

"It doesn't matter, long as we don't have to go far in the morning. We have to get him in the ground."

"How about up on the hill where we used to chase the deer? Where the laurel grows so thick. There is a clearing that looks over his place."

"It wouldn't matter to Charlie. Any place in this valley would do for him."

"Then let's make it the hilltop there," Newsome said. "That is a good place."

For a while they worked together. The rainstorm of three days earlier had passed through the valley, too, so the ground was damp and yielded to the steel. As the hole became deeper, they took turns working. When his turn came Sample swung the pick hard, sinking the point deep into the earth, turning up clods of dirt where he pulled it free.

For Charlie, he thought. Dig it deep for Charlie. So deep the coyotes cannot get to him. Make it deep for Charlie.

"It pains me," Newsome said, "to think that Charlie went hating me."

"He didn't," Sample said, twisting the point of the pick in

the ground and pulling it free. He brought the pick over his right shoulder and swung it down again. The curve of the pick made a swift, vicious arc in the night air and struck with a force that Newsome felt through the ground.

"It wasn't in Charlie to hate for long," Sample said. "To keep hating is work. You have to have nothing else on your mind. That wasn't Charlie. He had plenty else to think about."

He twisted the point free again. "Anyways, it wasn't you that riled him. Don't take it wrong, but you know what I mean."

"I didn't think he was cheating us," Newsome said. "He didn't go about things the right way, but that was just his manner. Charlie wouldn't take anything from us."

Sample rested to catch his breath. He wiped a sleeve across his forehead. "I ain't the one to tell it to," he said.

"We done wrong, didn't we?"

"Prob'ly."

"We can put everything back together the way it was. I'll tell Irene. I'll make her see. Rose Ellen will go along with it, don't you think?"

"Ain't likely," Sample said. "Charlie wouldn't have done it, even if you'd asked, and I don't see Rose Ellen doing it. Anyways, you can't put back together something that was broken like that. You bust it up, it is gone."

"Charlie had ideas. He had big plans."

Sample turned to face Newsome. "Earl, this is just the wrong damn time to talk about Charlie's plans. Three or four days ago, or a couple of years back, Charlie would have been really happy to know you thought so high of them. But it's too late now. I don't imagine Charlie cares now about you or me or his plans. So don't go on about it now."

Sample felt the grief come over him. He swung the pick into the ground, again, again. He attacked his sorrow that way and when he had beaten it down he was ashamed for having spoken as he did to Newsome. He stepped out of the hole and sat beside him.

"Don't mind me," he said. "Who am I to tell you? If Charlie was here, he'd say, 'My plans weren't so much. Just work hard and turn this valley into cattle country.' That was all he wanted."

*   *   *

The two women, dressed in black, met for the first time that next morning. They rode together in a buckboard with Ray driving. Earl and Orrin drove a wagon with the body. It was wrapped in a shroud of canvas that Orrin had sewed during the night, and it rested in a coffin that Earl had finished just an hour earlier. There was a wooden headpiece with Fowler's name carved into it: Newsome's work also.

The three men lowered the coffin into the hole. There were no prayers. They all stood looking into the grave until Sample swore softly, reached for a shovel, and began flinging dirt on the top of the coffin.

Olive and Irene sat in the wagon, in a patch of shade beside the mountain laurel.

"This must be a shock to you, especially after being so long apart," Irene said.

"You can imagine," Olive said. "I thought my life was finally secure. I expected to spend the rest of my days here. I don't know what I will do. Rose Ellen won't have me stay. We didn't get along as we should have."

Irene watched Sample throw in the dirt while Earl banged the headpiece into the ground with the flat of a shovel.

"But she won't know for some time," Irene said. "Even if we could get a message to her in Kansas, it would be some time before she returns. Months."

"I'll have time to find myself a new place," Olive said. "But I know I'll have to move on when she returns."

Irene took her hand and patted it. "You must come with us," she said. "Stay with us a few days. You don't want to return alone to the house." She smiled.

"Besides," she said, concern in her voice, "it is possible that the future is not as dismal as it seems now."

Men had their tools: guns, horses, ropes. Irene saw that there was a limit to these things, and a limit to strength and hard work. They had their place, but Irene knew that the ranch existed first because of deeds and titles and phrases in lawbooks. The law was the ultimate tool, if you knew how to use it.

Irene did not act immediately. She waited until Newsome and Sample had combined their herds and had begun a drive up the trail a few days later. Then, with Olive a guest in her home, she sent to McPherson for the lawyer.

His name was Belford Tefler. He was sedentary in a community of active people, so his paunch, his big bottom and fat thighs, were unusual. But he carried his head and moved his eyes in the manner of a hungry hawk. Irene liked that.

And he seemed to know his law. He sat down with Olive and Irene, and before Olive had finished her story he was interrupting her with questions and talking about probate courts and rights of survivorship.

Irene listened to the strange words and thought, There are so many ways of getting what you want in this world.

Working north, by day and by night moving among the dozens of horses in the *remuda*, Rose Ellen made her way with the herd to Wichita.

For a few days she thought constantly of her father. Gradually, with the passing of days and weeks, the thought that he might have been seriously hurt seemed more and more improbable, and too great a burden to carry from Texas to Kansas.

She worked hard, catching and saddling horses, gathering firewood, filling water barrels, washing dishes. Usually there was no time for meals with the cowboys. She ate food that she snatched from the cook's wagon. She took her sleep in short naps, when she could get it, for even at night she had to supply horses for the changing shifts of riders who watched over the herd.

Within a week after her father had left the drive, she got her first indecent proposal. She discovered that a good laugh was the best rejection. It stopped the man without bruising him, gave him a chance to pretend that he had been joking, all in fun. Before they reached the end of Indian Territory she had laughed at least twice with every hand in the outfit.

The tactic failed only once. Even more exhausted than usual one night, she did not notice when one of the cowboys stopped where she was sleeping and opened her bedroll. She woke when she felt his hands on her. He was a saddle tramp that Alvarez had hired for the drive.

"You and me been apart too long," he said.

She reached behind her for the .44 that she carried on her

hip and used, with its holster and belt, for a pillow at night. Before he could react she brought up the butt of the gun and broke his nose.

Twice during the drive she went from rustler to decision-maker. Just inside the Kansas line, farmers met them on the trail. The farmers carried rifles and shotguns, and they wanted the herd to turn back. They were afraid of Texas tick fever, and they would not let the cattle pass.

Alvarez wanted her advice. He was trail boss, but the cows were hers.

She decided: turn the herd around, drop back a few miles, then turn around again and stampede. See if the farmers will stand up to six hundred sets of long, crooked horns.

They did not. She considered the seventeen head that they failed to retrieve afterward a small enough toll to pay for passage.

After that she returned to horse rustling and dishwashing until they reached Wichita. Then she had to sell the herd. She patiently endured the leers and the laughs from the cattle brokers. Then she talked them up to a good price.

Alvarez showed her the way to the hotel where they always stayed in Wichita. She paid for the rooms and signed the register. She was walking away from the desk when the clerk looked down at the signature and said, "Is that Fowler? Miss Fowler?"

"Yes," Rose Ellen said.

"Something for you," the clerk said. "It has been waiting a few weeks."

He disappeared behind the desk, ruffled through papers, and came up with an envelope. She took it from him and saw that it was in Ray Newsome's hand. She held it tight until she was alone in her room. Then she tore it open and read:

My darling Rose,

I needed to tell you this and so decided to write it to you and post it in Austin or Fort Worth or Red River station. Your pa is ded, he died on the way home after he hurt his hed, we buryed him on a hill behind the house.

You no how bad I feel for you. Rose I'm sorry really
I am.

Your darling
Raymond J Newsome

Chapter 23

That year the nesters in Kansas tried hard to stop the surge of beef up through their territory. Some of the drovers sold to brokers who had set up offices near the border. The prices were lower there, but the cattlemen saved time and aggravation.

Sample and Newsome were among them. So they cut two weeks each way off their drive and they returned to the valley before Rose Ellen and the hands from the Diamond Five.

Newsome was not ready for what he found there. Nothing could have prepared him for the news. After twelve years of marriage, he realized that he did not understand his wife. But he thought that at least he knew her limits, that she could no longer astonish him.

He knew he was wrong when she told him that they now owned the Diamond Five.

"We have a good name," she said. "I found the money without much problem. Twenty-five thousand is a bargain when you consider what we got. We can pay off some of it now if you want, with the money from the cattle. Olive was anxious to sell. She doesn't much care for Texas, and she was happy to get what she could."

Irene asked him whether he had heard of such a thing as a probate court. She hadn't, herself, until the lawyer told her about it. A probate court decided what happened to a man's property after he died. There wasn't one in this county;

they'd had to go to Austin. But it was worth the trip, when the judge decided that Charlie Fowler's ranch belonged to his widow.

Earl said, "Not a cent for Rose Ellen?"

"Olive had a good lawyer. The one from McPherson, named Belford Tefler."

"Not so long ago you were saying that land was the last thing we need."

"That was before. Now I think it is a good thing, to collect as much land as we can get."

"What the hell is going on? What are you trying to do? We bust up the ranch because Charlie Fowler is buying too much land to suit you. Then we go off on our own and buy more land than Charlie ever did. What the hell is happening?"

His voice was loud. She knew he was angry, and she knew his anger was always best met with calm.

"Think for a minute," she said. "Five years ago it was you and Charlie and Orrin, equal partners in the ranch. Except that Charlie was a little more equal than you and Orrin, and got things his way. Now it is just you and Orrin, and he doesn't even have his full share anymore, and you have all the rest, and you do things your way."

"Are you complaining, Earl? Because I saw a chance to make things better for us? The Diamond Five was a steal for the money. You think we could have gotten it for twice the price if Rose Ellen had returned and talked to her mother? Olive wanted to leave here, and she went off a sight wealthier than when she came in.

"Look," she said. "We own about all of the old Circle Three that is worth owning. Aren't you proud of that?"

He shook his head. "I should be, maybe, but I ain't. I can't be proud of something I had no part in."

Ray wanted Rose Ellen to get the news from him first. He told himself that he could control her anger, make her realize that this was not the disaster it seemed.

Every day, sometimes twice a day, he rode to the empty house and looked for her. After ten days he found her, sitting on the porch with tears in her eyes.

She held him tight.

"Oh, Ray," she said. "I cried for a long time after I got

your letter. My papa was dead and I was feeling what it was to be really alone. But I got over it and I thought I was done with crying.

"Then I saw this. The stable empty, cobwebs in his office. He loved this place so. He wanted so much for it. Now it is up to us, Ray. We have to make it all that he wanted."

She sniffled and rubbed her face against his shoulder. "At least Olive is gone," she said. "Cleared out, huh? That is something, anyway. I guess with Papa gone she had nothing to stay around for."

He felt helpless in the face of what he had to tell her.

"Rose, I want you to listen and stay together," he said. "You want to cry, I know that, but you got to keep hold of yourself. 'Cause there is something else you have to know right now."

Nothing to do but throw it out, plain and with all the edges exposed. He said, "A judge said the ranch belonged to Olive, since she was your pa's wife. My mother, she bought the ranch from Olive, and Olive is gone. The ranch don't belong to you, Rose Ellen."

He tried to avoid her eyes, swollen and red and now looking at him through a wet film.

"What?" she said. "I don't understand."

"The ranch belongs to my ma and pa now. But that's all right. It's all in the family, as they say, and since you'll be marrying me directly I don't see that it makes much difference."

Her eyes turned cold and furious. He spoke faster.

"See, in a way they was doing us a favor, my ma and pa. If Olive held on to the place, it would be out of your hands forever. But it ain't. Likely they will give it to us to run, just like our own—ain't that even better'n a house up the river like my pa said he would build for us?"

She stepped back from him. "I have to think this thing through," she said.

He tried to soothe her. "Not now," he said. "Not while you are still grieving your pa. Take some time. Rest up and get better and then think about it. You can stay in the house, long as you want. Nobody will care."

She shrieked, "No!"

Then, less shrilly, "No. I won't be a guest in my own house. I will find a place to think by myself."

"Don't run off. I want to see you. I been apart from you too long. I want to hold you and help you through this."

She held out a hand to stop him. "No. Let me be. Let me be alone. We will talk after a while, but right now you let me be. If you want to help me, get into the bunkhouse and tell Paco and the others what you just told me. I don't have it in me to repeat it."

Her horse was still saddled. She rode away from the house. She did not want to be near it. She rode with her mind fixed in sorrow, in anger, in hurt, unconscious of a destination. But when she reached it, she knew that she was where she wanted to be, and she got off the horse, drifted a few steps, and sat cross-legged in the grass.

She was looking over the valley from a hilltop. She could see the river bright in the high sun, could see the house where she had grown up, could see across the valley to the eastern hills. She saw these things but she did not examine them. She knew them. They comforted her.

She sat. For a time she wept, her chest heaving. She let the tears run down her face. The horse grew restless and wandered away. She did not notice. There was the evening sun and then the moon and the dark night. Still she sat and wept. She thought of her father, and of the house lifeless and empty below her, and of the land that she knew and loved stretched out in front of her. She forced herself to think of her father dead, and of the house and the land belonging to someone else now. She did not sleep. She thought of what she had seen of the world outside her valley, and she thought of herself being a part of that world outside. She, who had never been alone, thought of living a life apart from anyone else.

During the night a wind came up and rustled the grass, and blew brittle dead leaves against her, and dried the tears on her face.

Before the sun rose in her eyes the next morning, she had grasped that her father was truly dead and all that this meant. She understood that she had no place and no rights anymore in the only home she had ever known. She also knew that she could not leave the valley, that she must find a way to stay.

By midafternoon, when the figure on horseback rode toward her, she knew what she would do.

It was Ray, she saw. She stood, stirring for the first time. She brushed the dirt and some dry grass from her pants.

He stopped the horse a few feet from her. "I knew you'd be here," he said. "I knew it."

She did not understand.

"Indian Oak," he said, and he gestured with a hand.

"I didn't even notice."

"I'm worried about you. I came to bring you down."

"No need to worry. I was coming down anyways."

"You sound better."

"I am better now than I was when I rode up here. I had to think things out," she said.

He got off the horse and stood in front of her. "Me, too," he said. "Like about this buying the ranch. My mother, I think she wants to get back at you, Rose. I think she wants to stop us from getting married. She figures, if she gets you mad enough, you won't want any part of the Newsome family. She knows you get hot when you're riled. Ever'body knows that, if you pardon my saying so. Anyways, I know she don't want us married.

"So," he said, "she thinks if you get hot enough you will throw me over and that will be the end of us."

"Your mother doesn't like me," she said, "for the same reason she didn't like my papa. She isn't happy unless she is sure that she is smarter than everybody around her. She can hold on to you and run you easier if she doesn't have me in her way."

"Well," he said, "maybe that is so. Maybe that is. That part didn't come to me, but maybe it is so. Anyways, I know she don't want us married."

Rose Ellen said nothing.

"See?" he said. "That means we have to all the more. Right now. Without waiting. I mean, when you are done with your mourning. She won't like it, but she won't do anything about it. I'm her boy, she can't get rid of me. I'm the only one, see? They don't have another son."

"I can't marry you," she said.

"Rose, you don't know what you're saying."

"I know. I thought on it all night. That was the first thing that came clear to me, and it wouldn't go away. I can't marry you."

"This is silly. I don't want to hear it. You're down on me for what my ma did. I don't blame you. But you can't take it out on me. It wasn't me that did it. We have to get back at them, Rose. We will last the two of them out and then it will be all ours and it will be our laugh on them."

"That's why," she said. "You see? What was mine, she took away from me. I loved that place, Ray. I love this valley. I never want to leave. And now you come to me and say I can get back what is mine just by marrying you and waiting for your folks to die.

"Well, it is not so easy," she said. "One thing, that place isn't the same for me anymore. I never would have believed how fast you can hate something you loved. I feel like it's tainted somehow. It doesn't make me feel good the way it did. It just makes me remember what was done to me. It makes me sick to think about it, and that won't change. I have a long memory, and I am no good at ignoring what is shoved in front of me."

"Then we won't go near it," he said.

"Will that change her being your mother? I have been slapped in the face, Ray, and I can't pretend different. I don't have much room for fighting. But I have one thing. I can turn my back on her and you and all that belongs to the two of you."

"That is pure bullheadedness," he said.

"Maybe. I'll give you something that isn't. She's powerful smart, Ray. She is better than anybody I ever saw at getting what she wants, figuring out this and that to work her way around every little problem. I can't live with you knowing that she is out there, working the way she works, trying to get you free of me.

"Every day I would be wondering what she is doing, and wondering why, and asking myself what she is trying to get out of us, and being afraid that she is going to get me when I'm not looking. That is no way to live, like sleeping with one eye open all night. She has power over people, Ray. It is plain sense to stay clear of a rattlesnake if you have the choice.''

He held his hands up before her face, not a threat but a gesture of supplication. He clenched them into fists. His knuckles were white. "Do you love me?" he said.

"Yes."

"Do you want to marry me?"

"I wish things weren't the way they were, so I could marry you and feel right about it. But I can't shut my eyes to what is real."

"You want to live here in this valley?"

"More than anything."

He felt tears coming to his eyes. "But you won't make everything right and marry me."

"No."

"I don't understand," he said.

"I covered this ground back and forth a hundred times last night. I decided, the way a question is put to you can be more important than what you're asked.

"Like," she said, "if somebody stopped you out on the range, and pulled a pistol on you, and told you to take a drink of water from his canteen. It wouldn't matter how thirsty you might be—if it's put to you that way you wouldn't let a drop past your lips.

"I don't mean everybody," she added. "Some people would look right past the gun and drink away if they were thirsty. But not you, and not me. Not the way we are. Ray, I want to say yes, but the question has been put to me all wrong."

He stopped crying. He stared at her. "By God," he says, "it comes down to pride. It's pride that's behind all this."

"Call it what you want," she said. "I wish I was free of it, but I'm not."

"You'd make us both miserable for pride."

"It runs both ways," she answered. Her voice was soft and even. "You love me. You say you want to marry me. But I would bet my life you won't do the one thing that will keep us together. And it's a simple thing."

"The hell I won't," he said. "Just say it, and watch me do it."

"You won't," she said. "It came to me last night, but I knew it wasn't worth thinking about since you will never want to do it. I don't blame you. I wouldn't either if I were you. And I only say it to show that pride runs both ways here."

"I'll do anything," he said.

"Leave the valley with me," she said.

She let it hit him before she spoke again.

"That gets around all of it," she said finally. "You leave your ma and go so far away that she can't get to us and I can pretend she is no blood to you. You give up what is coming to you of the ranch so that it won't be like I am marrying you to get back what is mine. It won't be like I have a gun to my head making me drink that water I'm so thirsty for. We have to go away from the valley, but I can do that if I have to, if it means us being together. We start fresh, with nothing but our own selves."

"Now, Rose. . . . ." he said.

"I'm ready," she said. "Go down there and say your fare-thee-wells and come back and get me and I'm yours."

"I can't do that."

"You could, but you won't," she said. "I don't blame you, Ray. I already said, I wouldn't if I were you. It's a bad deal. You are in line to own the best part of this valley, and I wouldn't give that up if I was in your spot, not for anybody. People have their good and their bad, but this valley is precious."

"This isn't fair," he said. "You can't expect me to give all that up."

"I have to go now," she said. "I have something to do." She began to walk down the hill.

"As long as she lives," he shouted at her, "you will know that she beat you, that she got the best of you."

She did not turn around.

"If that fella," he said, "the one with the water, if he stuck that canteen in your hand and shoved it up to your mouth, I do believe you would cut off your own arm to keep from drinking."

She stopped and looked at him. "I would," she said. "And so would you, Ray Newsome. Besides me, you're the only one I know who would do that." And she walked away, and left Ray Newsome on the hill.

This time she knew where she was going. She found her horse at the bottom of the hill and rode south on the trail beside the Mansos.

Rose Ellen watched the valley as she rode. She wanted to embrace it and to make it part of her again. She told herself that she had been gone from it too long. Now she knew how much she cared for it, and all that it meant to her. So she watched it this day, trying to see and smell and feel all that it held out to her.

The day was bright and warm. Clumps of cattle drank at the river, which flowed low now against the cut banks and around high-lying islands of sand and rock. Rose Ellen stopped her horse once and looked down into a quiet backwater pool. She could see a big bass drifting along the bottom. Then she leaned over and the shadow of her hat crossed the pool. The bass flicked its tail once and was gone, leaving a swirl of sand where it had been.

After she had traveled a few miles south she cut off the trail and across the valley, south and east. An hour of riding brought her to a new, narrow trail that cut east to west across the valley. She rode east, and soon the trail brought her to Orrin Sample's cabin. It was a rectangle of unpainted shiplap siding with a shake roof and stone chimney. It sat beside a stand of trees, nestled in among them for shade and protection. The scene gave her comfort. It looked like somebody's home.

Sample was splitting wood behind the cabin. When he heard the horse he came around and saw Rose Ellen. She brought to him the racing of his heart that he could not control.

"Rose," he said. "Come rest yourself."

The porch was a wide front stoop. She sat down and Sample sat beside her. His face was red and wet.

"About your pa," he said. "You have my feelings, my sympathy. Oh, that ain't the word, anyways. I felt real bad, Rose, and still do. I miss him terrible. You know that."

"I know."

Her smile helped him put his awkwardness aside. He knew he could talk about something else now.

"I don't believe you seen the place before," he said. "Not since the cabin has been on it."

"You found a nice spot for it. I don't believe there is a prettier one in the valley. This is a real lovely little mott. Those are gum trees, I believe, and a couple of cottonwoods, too. You don't see many of them this far out in the valley."

"And a few loblolly pine," he said. "They like the water, you know. Right in this spot, I don't know why, the water is real close to the ground. It makes things green. And the trees keep the house cool in hot weather."

He stood. With a nervous gesture he slapped his palms against the sides of his thighs. "What can I do for you, Rose?" he said. "What brings you to these parts?"

"I need help, Orrin."

"I'll do what I can."

"You know what Olive and Irene did to me."

"Yes. You heard, then. I hoped it wouldn't be me to tell you. That is bad, Rose."

"Worse than bad. I am alone and I have no place of my own."

"Earl and me, we didn't know she was up to that. Earl would've stopped her if he'd known."

"Maybe," she said. "But it is done now. And I need help."

"Like I said. Whatever I can do."

She felt weary, beaten, old.

"Orrin, would you marry me?" she said.

"Now, Rose."

"Orrin, I need you to say yes."

"You are tired and all turned around. You don't know what you're saying."

"I am tired. But I never thought more about the words I spoke. I want you to take me for your wife. I don't know what I will do if you say no."

His next words gave her his answer. He paused and said, "What about Ray?"

"I can't marry Ray. Because he is Irene's son and because I am too proud to do it that way."

"You still love him?"

"Yes." She knew that her answer did not matter.

"You don't love me."

"Not in that way."

"I don't want you marrying me to get even with Ray."

"That is one thing I would not do. You are a good man, Orrin, and have been my friend as far back as I know. I wouldn't do that. You want to know why I ask you this? Because I want to stay in this valley. Because I need somebody to care for me. I wish I could go it alone, but I don't think I can.

"I can help you with this place, Orrin. I can make you a home here, do women's things for you. Have your children. Mend your clothes. Most of all, be good to you and kind.

"I wouldn't ask any more of you than what I know you've got, waiting to give to the right woman. I'd try to give more back than I ask. I even got a dowry, you might say. I brought good money back from the drive. We can use that. It's yours."

"You don't have to make it a business deal," he said.

"I want you to do it," she said. "And I wouldn't ask if I didn't know you wanted me. I cannot afford your saying no to me. Between Irene Newsome and my own contrariness, I have run out of chances."

"You say you still love Ray Newsome. There can't be three of us in this," Sample said.

"Have you ever seen me fail at anything I really wanted to do?" she said. "I won't say I'll stop loving him. I don't know about that. It will take time. But I promise to put him behind me and not look back. I promise to forget about him, and that's different from the other."

He nodded.

"One more thing I promise. If you marry me, I will be a better wife to you than you ever dreamed of having on the loneliest night of your life. I can do that, too."

The next morning they rode to McPherson, and when they returned in the evening they were husband and wife.

Every day for a week Ray Newsome rode to the old house

beside the Mansos, and to Indian Oak. He was looking for Rose Ellen. He did not find her. The hands in the Diamond Five bunkhouse said they had not seen her. He came home to dinner one night and found guests. John Sears and his wife owned ninety-five sections north of the Circle Three. They had been on the land since before the war, and Irene thought they might be ready to sell. So they had come to dinner.

In the middle of the meal John Sears said, "The talk is that an old bachelor bit the dust the other day. Another good man gone to ruin. Your old partner it was, Orrin Sample."

"Can't be," Earl said.

"Not Orrin," Irene said. "He would have told us."

"We was to McPherson the other day, and heard it there from Alvin Barber, who got it from the parson's wife."

"I can't believe it," Earl said. "Who would have the old bear?"

"That's the best part," Sears's wife said. "Just a girl it was. Charlie Fowler's daughter. Rosetta, was it?"

"Rose Ellen," Ray Newsome said softly. He put down his knife and fork, mumbled excuses, and left the room.

"And her," the woman said, "just a child, wasn't she? Though it has been several years since I seen her last. They do change fast at that age."

Later, when her guests had eaten, Irene went to see Ray in his room. "I know this is a shock to you," she said. "I don't know how she could have done this to you, Ray. Without even a word."

"I hate her," he said. "I hate you, too. You did this to me."

"I didn't. Did I push her into Orrin Sample's arms? Did I tell her to be so fickle? You know better. I tried to stop you from making a mistake, didn't I? I tried to tell you that she was wrong. I'm only glad you found the truth before it was too late. Poor Orrin, I pity him."

"I wish I was him. I would give anything to have her back."

"Be glad you are rid of her, Ray," she said. "What do you want with such a girl, so flighty and impulsive? She was too strongheaded for you, Ray. You don't want that in a wife. You'll find someone, soon enough, who is more suited to you.

"Someone," she said, "more . . . manageable."

Donnie Lee

There is nothing comes easy, my daddy says, that is worth having.

And when I picked up Sue Everitt on Saturday night, I had to believe him. I don't think I was ever more ready for anything than to be alone with that girl, have her to myself to talk to and smile at and show off for. But first I had to knock on her front door, and naturally I was early and she was late, so that meant sitting in the Everitts' front room and getting the treatment from her parents. Her mama was not so bad, only snuck looks at me from the dining room as she was clearing the plates from the table. But her daddy set right down in front of me and started asking me questions. Like how long did I have my driver's license? I wasn't planning on driving too far, was I? Wasn't my daddy the Bates who was straw boss at the Circle Three? Tell me a little bit about this history project you two are working on. And, at the end, I'd be sure to have her back before eleven, wouldn't I? A real pain.

Though when I seen Sue E. walk down the stairs I could see why he wouldn't want to take any chances.

She was wearing a dress. I believe it was blue, with a white belt, and what they call pleats below the waist. But I could not say for certain. Girls spend so much time picking the right clothes and getting their hair and makeup just so, when all the time it is not the hair nor the clothes that men look at, but the lady underneath it all.

231

And Sue E. was just fine that way, thank you.

I know the proper thing to do is to say something like that when it comes to mind. It makes a girl feel appreciated. But I couldn't, not with her parents there. I waited until after she kissed her mama and daddy good-bye, and after I remembered too late that I was supposed to open the car door for her, and after we talked about what we wanted to do and then drove to the Rialto, and after we sat through most of *The Sands of Iwo Jima*. I waited that long to get up the nerve.

Finally I said, Sue, you look real pretty. I whispered it in her ear, which was the closest I'd got to her all night.

Why, thank you, Donnie Lee, she said. These old things, I just threw them on.

Oh, how I wanted to touch her. I got my arm up on the armrest and put it against hers. She didn't seem to mind. I leaned toward her until my shoulder touched hers. That was okay, too. It took me a while longer to do what I really wanted, but eventually I just made up my mind and I done it. I put my hand on top of hers.

And she held on to it, sort of laced our fingers together and held on.

This happened right in the middle of the last big shoot-up in the picture, so it wasn't long before the curtain come down and the lights come up and we had to leave, and I had to take my hand away.

When we got to the car she said, We ought to talk some about the project. Did you see your great-grandfather today?

I told her I sure did, and maybe we ought to go to T.J.'s to talk about it. So we did.

She made me repeat, word for word, all that Gandy Meacham had told me. She listened to the story about the heifer and the mudhole and said, Uh-huh, yes, uh-huh. Nothing else.

Then she stopped me and said, Were they in love? Did you ask him?

Well, yes, he said they was, I told her.

She didn't give me any I-told-you-so's. She didn't have to.

I swung right into how Gandy Meacham thought Rose Ellen was beautiful, not just because of the way she looked but the way she acted, and that made Sue E. smile. Not like laughing, but like she was glad to hear what I was saying.

What a sweet thing, she said. That part about a woman doing all she can to help a man. I want to visit your great-grandfather and see him for myself.

Ordinarily I would have said no. But lately it seemed my mama liked my talking to Gandy Meacham about the old days. If we had time, maybe it would be a good idea.

And I have to admit I wasn't exactly ashamed for my mama and my daddy to see Sue E., beautiful as she was.

It was nine-twenty. I said sure, why not, and we got into the car and drove there.

My mama stared bayonets at me for bringing home somebody without her having time to clean and primp and such. But my daddy didn't mind, and seemed to take a shine to Sue E. He stood up and bowed real low to her, but not in such a way as to have it seem he was making fun of her, and he asked her about her daddy, and he told me git in the kitchen and bring some lemonade, where was my manners?

So we drank lemonade in the dining room, and my mama warmed up once she saw that Sue E. was just regular folks, even being a doc's daughter. Sue E. come straight out and said, I wonder if it would be possible to meet Donnie Lee's great-grandfather, I've heard so much about him.

My mother said, He isn't well, you know.

Yes, ma'am, Sue E. said. I know that and I don't want to inconvenience him. But if he hasn't turned in for the night it would be a privilege to meet him.

He would likely welcome the company, my daddy said.

My mama nodded her head. She said, He is due for his pills any time now. If I woke him up he ought to be able to talk for a spell.

That was what she done, and presently she come out of the room and said okay, and Sue E. and me walked in together.

His eyes looked bright, and if you don't mind my bragging I'll tell you that he acted right glad to see me.

I made the introductions. Quiller Meacham, I said, Sue Everitt.

He said, You must be the one Donnie Lee is doing the schoolwork with.

I knew then that if it wasn't for the pills he still had every card in the deck.

Sue E. said, That's me, sir.

Gandy Meacham crooked his neck and run his eyes up and down her. He said, Danged if you ain't a looker.

I don't believe Sue E. even blushed. She just said, Thank you kindly, sir.

Gandy Meacham give a smile I hadn't seen from him before, like to crack his face. He said, An old geezer like me can get away with such talk.

Why, Sue E. said, a gal doesn't mind what age fellow such talk comes from as long as he is a gentleman.

He said, So you want to know about times long gone.

About Rose Sample, she said, and about you, too.

He said, I would sight rather talk about her. But we will get around to me, too, if we talk about her long enough.

She was an unusual woman, Sue E. said.

For a fact, he said. Would nobody argue you on that one.

Must have had a lot of determination in her, Sue E. said.

He said, I never heard anybody put it that way before. That particular word, I mean. Not to say it ain't right, for I reckon it is. But the way I often heard it said was, she had a load of hell in her neck.

He said, You ever heard that one? That she had hell in her neck? It means if she went out after something she wouldn't be stopped. And if she had her head set one way, nobody and nothing would turn it.

He said, That was Rose Ellen. More hell in her neck than any woman or man I ever knew.

I seen him grit his teeth the way he did in the morning when the pain made him stop talking. But he didn't ask for his pills.

Sue E. must have known what was wrong. She didn't say nothing, just reached for the old man's hand and held it while his face twisted up. It was a strange sight, her smooth young hand on his, which was old and spotted, wrinkled and hard. It had one finger long ago broke and set crooked, and another, the little finger, missing down to the first joint.

Sue E. saw his face relax, and then, like nothing happened, she said, In what way do you mean?

The forehead over his eyes grew half a dozen new creases as he pondered that one. Sue E. waited for him to talk.

Finally he said, There's so many it's hard to pick just one. But like the town, he said. The one you go to school in and where you do your grocery-shopping and your clothes-buying.

That town, he said, was built by Ray Newsome. He done it at a time when Rose Ellen was down on him. Which was most of the time, from what I gather.

Gandy Meacham coughed and hacked a mite, and then he said, Now, Rose Ellen was sure that town was built out of spite for her. It all had to do with shipping beeves, you see, and him not letting the railroad down through his land all the way to the end of the valley. A hell of a mess.

He said, You read about any of this in your books?

We both said the truth, which was no, we hadn't.

He said, Then listen up. What I am telling you is true history about this valley and those people. For a long time, understand, Ray Newsome had a mad on for Rose Ellen. You best be ready to suffer the consequences if you ever said her name to his ears. He was that way, and she was the kind she was, which was why it took them so long to get together, I 'magine.

So, Ray Newsome had a mad on for her and would not let the railroad through to her land. He would not let her cattle cross his land either. And she said that was fine with her, she did not want to touch her foot down on his land. And by that time the rails was how everybody got their cattle to market.

Gandy Meacham said, The railroad people got on Ray Newsome about that and he backed down and said she could pass her cattle through, but she said to hell with him anyways, she would find another way of doing it. And what she did was to drive her cattle around the other side of the valley and skirt Ray Newsome's land, which took some skirting what with all the land he owned, and she took her cattle to some other station up north of the Circle Three.

Sue E. said, That is what I mean by determination.

He said, Maybe. Some would call it pure cussedness.

Sue E. looked at me and then at Gandy Meacham and said, Sometimes you need cussedness to get what's coming to you.

He said, I'll grant you that.

And she said, Not only that, but cussedness has one other thing going for it. Maybe it is not something you want in somebody who has it set against you. But it must be nice to have it in somebody who is on your side, and cares about you.

Gandy Meacham cracked that smile of his again, and I saw that he squeezed Sue E's hand. He said, Donnie Lee, where did you find this young lady?

You could have lit a football field with the look on Sue E's face when he said that. And I wondered to myself, Do you have to be eighty-some years old before you learn how to make a girl that happy?

Sue E. said, Donnie Lee, I'm going to get spoiled for attention if I don't get out of here. And I don't want to get home late my first time out with you. She said, Will you take me home?

I said I would, and we did our good-byes, and Gandy Meacham made Sue E. promise to come back and see him. He said he had plenty more to tell her.

I drove her to her house, and parked in her driveway. I was about to get out, for this time I remembered to open her door for her, but she looked at her wristwatch and said, Donnie Lee, it's only seven minutes 'til. No need to rush these things.

No, I reckon not, I said.

I knew she expected me to have something else to say, so I said, Sue E., I had a good time tonight. A real good time. I'm glad you said yes to going out with me.

She said, You haven't heard me complain either, have you?

I said, I believe my great-grandfather took a liking to you.

She said, Well, I like him, Donnie Lee.

And I like you too, Donnie Lee, she said.

Somewhere I found the nerve to lean over and kiss her on the lips. I must have done something right, because next thing she was moving over to me, and planting a kiss that like to curl my hair.

Chapter 24

They named the boy Charles, but Charlie it would always be. He was born pink and healthy one afternoon in October of 1885, in the cabin his father had built in a moist grove of gum trees and cottonwood and loblolly pine.

There was a newly hewed cradle in one corner of the bedroom, waiting with fresh bedding. After the child had been cleaned and dried and had fed for the first time from his mother's breast, Rose Ellen Sample stood and held him in her arms, walked slowly but steadily to the cradle, and laid him down there. Her legs were weak. With Orrin for support she stood beside the cradle and watched their newborn until after he had begun to sleep.

Rose Ellen was happy. She discovered that the marriage did not change her life so much from what it had been, though it was far from what she had imagined it might be with Ray Newsome. Orrin needed her, as her father had. She cooked for him and kept the house, as she had for her father when they were alone. Orrin needed her for her presence, her caring, and her femininity in a life that had been barren without it. And in that he was not so different from her father.

She still thought sometimes about Ray. But she had taken to heart her new life and her husband and now her child. She was happy with them, grateful for a home, glad to be surrounded by the hills and the valley.

Ray ran the Circle Three Bar now. Eight months after he

had helped to bury Charlie Fowler, Earl Newsome died in the saddle—of heart failure, the doctor said later. He was roping calves when he pulled his horse up short. The hands said he'd had a puzzled, uncertain look as he sat on his horse. Then he fell sideways and off the horse, dead before he hit the ground.

At Earl's burial Ray saw Rose Ellen for the first time since she had married Sample. She and Orrin rode in a buckboard to the top of the hill where Fowler's grave was. Ray's face burned when he saw them. He tried to keep his eyes down but could not stop looking at her. He saw her stay in her seat while Sample went around to the side to help her down. Then Ray saw why, saw her rounded belly and her full breasts. He wanted to turn and run.

He had not known that she was pregnant. News traveled slowly. The hands from one ranch might trade gossip with those from another, but at the Circle Three there was a chasm of class between the bunkhouse and the family home that the gossip did not leap.

So when he saw her beside Earl's grave, Ray knew for the first time that she was having Sample's child. She seemed even farther from him now, her departure even more outrageous. The sight of her on Sample's arm, her belly swollen, stirred what had been festering for months, a love turning incompletely to loathing and never far from his mind.

He was always aware of her, aware that she was living not many miles distant but in most ways far removed from him. He thought of her kissing Sample, and lying with him, and knowing with him the intimacies of childbearing. These thoughts, nurtured by his love for her, his jealousy, his imagination, assumed giant proportions in his mind. If he had seen her more often, seen the simple dimensions of her life, he might have been able to pare down his obsession one stroke at a time, whittle away at it until it was only a memory. But he had no chance to do that. His bitter love for her and his outrage at her leaving grew unchecked within him.

Irene noticed the change in him. She guessed its cause and she could see its effect. He sank himself deep into the ranch, becoming fixed on making it grow and prosper, dominate the valley. It did her work for her. He needed no goading, only infrequent direction; the compulsion did the rest. The Circle Three and Rose Ellen became tangled in his mind, one becoming an outlet for the frustrating other. After a while he could put it into words, and it came out simply enough: Make her sorry. Show her what she missed.

He bought land, and the ranch grew. The Newsomes' credit was good, and with Earl dead there was no more reason for restraint. They bought at the north end of the valley and at the south end as well. Soon their holdings surrounded Sample's land on every side. The Circle Three was Ray's now. Irene was happy enough to step aside. Her son was all that she could have wanted, as intent on buying, building, questing, as she had ever been.

She had one more bequest to make.

One evening they sat at the dinner table long after Luz had cleared away the dishes. They were talking about the rail line that ran to Denison from the north and the east. The railroad company was dropping its rates, and now they could consider shipping cattle by rail instead of driving on the trail half the year.

"I heard in McPherson that some of the ranchers on the Nueces are using the train this year," he said. "Some say the trail will be half empty above Dallas."

"You might think about it," she said.

"I have thought of it. I can save three months' pay at least for half a dozen men. And the cows lose weight on a long drive. Maybe they will fetch more at the other end if they have more meat on them."

"You could spend less time away," she said. "The more you are here, the better for this place."

"But I need to move a lot of cows," he said. "Two thousand, three thousand, maybe. We need more space."

She took it as a joke. "Could you ask for more than we have in this valley?" she said.

"More grass, then," he said. "More feed. There must be twice as many as there were ten years ago. And they do nothing but eat and make more cows. If they would fan out some it would be better, but they don't leave the water. There are places they have eaten down to the roots, bad as sheep."

Now she knew he was not joking. "So you want to clear out some of the cows," she said.

"Have to."

"But it won't do much good, will it, if the others don't do the same?"

At first he did not understand.

"I mean," she said, "you will only be making room for others' cattle to eat our grass." She meant Sample. Except for the O–Bar–S they owned every acre in that part of the valley.

She said, "What is the use of clearing the land of Circle Three cattle so that somebody else's stock can graze better?"

"The grass needs a chance," he said, "but I can't keep his cattle off."

She left the table and returned with a short length of barbed wire. It was the sample she had gotten two years earlier from the salesman. "Look at this," she said. She gave it to him. "It is time we talked about it."

He glanced at the wire and put it on the table. "Barb-wire fence," he said. "I've seen it."

"Where?"

"All over Kansas. I am sick of seeing it. The nesters use it to stop us on the trail. Last year we carried cutters to get through it."

"It works?"

"Like blazes. In Panhandle country they use it to keep the cows from drifting south in a storm. I heard stories in Wichita about the big freeze last year, whole herds bunched up against the fence. They wanted to go south for food. They will drift for miles if you let them."

"Maybe we need it," she said.

"We don't have freezes like that."

"Maybe," she said, "we need it for the same reason the nesters do."

Then he saw. In his mind he saw a fence across the land, dividing the valley.

"You could do so much," he said. "Keep your own cattle where you want them, let the grass grow in some places and then when it is high put the cows in again. Give the land a rest one place or another. But cattle folk won't like it. It ain't the cattle way.''

"The ways have to change sometime," she said. " We will show cattle folks.''

They were the biggest landholders in the valley. In the last ten years there had been an entrenching, a consolidation. The smaller ranchers had sold to the bigger ones, until by '85 there were only six spreads in the valley, the smallest seventy-four thousand acres. And this was cattle country, not an acre yet turned over by a plow except some patches of vegetable gardens.

The O–Bar–S was, by Ray Newsome's standards, a modest operation. Ray's house, whitewashed and roofed with tin, was the finest in the valley; Sample's cabin, weathered grey by sun and rain, was the most primitive. The Circle Three kept a dozen cowboys on permanent payroll; Sample kept two, including Alvarez, who had come over after Fowler's death. But they were degrees of the same prosperity. Even balanced against seasons of drought and down markets, these were good times for cattlemen. Sample and Rose Ellen still lived better than most people in Texas or out of it. They bought what they needed to be comfortable, saved some money, and lived their life together as they wished.

The difference was of vision. Ray Newsome's wealth and his holdings could not increase fast enough to suit him, while the land already was providing more for Sample than he had ever hoped to own. With Rose Ellen and his son in their cabin now, he had all that he had ever wanted.

And it seemed to have no end. People would always want beef, Sample told himself, and nobody could strip him of the land he owned. He was a happy man, and he found his greatest happiness in the cabin, with his wife and his son. Charlie seemed to change by the week. He was strong, perpetually hungry, full of an uncommon energy. He learned to crawl, and soon rubbed his knees and his hands red on the cabin's wooden floor. They started teaching him to walk, Sample coaxing him forward while Rose Ellen kept him upright.

They were playing with him one morning when a hand from the Circle Three rode to the cabin.

Mr. Newsome had sent him, he announced, to say that he would be building a fence around parts of his property. When the fence was finished, there would be room for Circle Three stock only.

He rode away. Sample and Rose Ellen and the child stood in the front door of the cabin and watched him leave.

"What does that mean, Orrin?" she said.

"It means he wants to be hard about it. He wants to keep his grass for his own cattle."

"Then we'll take ours off his grass. And he can keep his own inside his fences. We don't care, do we?"

She saw him lick his lips the way he did when he was troubled.

"Do we, Orrin?" she said. "This doesn't hurt us, does it?"

"No," he said. "He can keep his damn grass."

That afternoon Charlie Sample left his mother's arms, three times put one foot in front of the other, and collapsed into his father's big hands. They were his first unaided steps. And that evening Alvarez came to tell them that hands from the Circle Three were building a fence to keep them from the stream.

Rose Ellen brought her son with her. She carried him in her lap while she rode with Sample and Alvarez to the river. They found the Circle Three's hands working into the night, digging holes, planting posts. Rose Ellen saw spools of wire and piles of fence posts beside the canvas tents they had pitched on the land. They were east of the cabin, and at least a half-mile from the river.

Rose Ellen rode to the men and shouted at them. "You boys get going!" she said. "Get off this land with your infernal fence. You fence Circle Three Bar land if you want, but stay off ours."

Sample stopped beside her.

"Orrin," she said, "it appears that these boys are building a fence the length of the stream."

"We are," one of them said. "Ray Newsome's orders."

"You are putting it on our land," she said. "Work if you want, but we will tear down every post that is struck on our property."

Sample put out a hand to touch her. "Rose," he said, "just a minute."

"They can't put fence on our land," she said. "Tell them, Orrin—tell them they can't. Our cattle can't get to the water with this fence."

The hand who had spoken was the same one who had come to the cabin that morning. He looked up and waited for Sample to speak.

"Tell them," she said. "This is our land, Orrin."

Sample looked around, and across the grass to the arroyo that contained the stream. He said, "I don't believe so, Rose."

"Orrin," she said, "I'm sure you're mistaken. Our land goes across this valley from one range of hills to the other, clear across. My papa drew it that way on his map. I saw what he drew."

"I sold it," Sample said. "I sold it to Irene. She wanted to help me out, a couple of years back."

He looked down at the cowboy. "How far is this fence going?" he said.

"All the way, past your line to the south. And then across the valley just above your line, and across it again to the south. You are going to have fence on all four sides of you. Mr. Newsome says won't a one of your cattle set a hoof on his grass."

Rose Ellen found words again. "You sold it?" she said. "You sold your water? You sold the only thing that keeps your cattle going?"

Sample turned his horse and began to ride slowly to the cabin, head bowed. Rose Ellen held the child.

"How could he do it, Paco?" she said. "How could he sell off his water like that?"

She watched Orrin's horse clop off in the darkness and she saw the sag of his shoulders. The sight made her want to be beside him. She spurred her horse and caught him.

"I'm sorry," he said. "I never seen it coming."

"We will make do," she said.

"I didn't know what I was doing. What do you want with me? I ain't sharp enough to be doing this. Not like your pa was. I don't have it, Rose."

"We'll get by," she said.

"How? With the trickle from a few springs? You know how many cows I can water without the Mansos?"

Charlie held a tiny fistful of mane and made a loud, happy babble.

"We will get by," Rose said again.

The fencing took weeks. That gave Sample a chance to gather and sell most of his cattle. But it was a bad time to sell. In '85 the market was down and cattlemen were holding their beef out for the next season, hoping for higher prices. Sample shipped 500 head to Kansas City by rail, a mixed herd that netted him $8 a head after expenses. A ranch at the north end of the valley bought some of his best steers for $11; another outside McPherson gave him $7.50 for a mixed herd of about 1,500. Finally he found a packer near Corpus Christi who was offering $3 for any cow able to walk into his pens, and they drove a herd there.

Rose Ellen kept ledgers. Within three months they had sold 4,870 head for $18,990. And the fences were closing in. They kept out 300 head of the best, and five horses. Sample thought that the springs and the seeps on his land would support no more.

While the last section of fence closed around them, they rode early one morning up the valley to the Sears ranch. The man and his wife greeted them, cooed at Charlie, and asked them to stay for lunch.

In the middle of the meal Sample said, "You folks know this ain't purely a social call."

"I suppose not," John Sears said. "I have to say straight out, Orrin, that I can't buy your cattle. I am stocked to the limit now, my cash is low, and I can't handle a bigger herd until I sell off a slew of them next season."

"No," said Sample. "Rose and me are in the market to buy. We would like to buy your place."

Rose cut in. She said, "You might not be up for selling now. We understand that. But maybe the time is not so far off when you will be, and when that comes we want you to know that we'd like you to come to us."

Sample again: "We don't know that we could pay you

cash. But we could give you good money down and pay the rest in ten years, I 'spect.''

"The fact is," Rose said, "we are cattle people without the means to keep much cattle. We need a place with water."

John Sears tried twice to speak. The third time he found room for his words. "I would like to sell to you folks," he said. "Or talk to you about it, anyways. You are a fine sight, this little family of yours. It would be good to see you on the place when we give it up.

"But I can't sell to you," he said. "Ray Newsome come to us months ago with that lawyer of his, and they trotted out some damn deal. . . .''

Sears turned to his wife. "Eula," he said, "will you get that paper? It is in the file, in the bottom drawer of my cabinet."

Back to Rose and Orrin again. "Anyways, it was something I never heard of before. I thought it was nonsense, a waste of good money, though I imagine he has it to throw away if he wants. Talk is he trailed two thousand and a half head up to Denison last time, and that was when prices were up.''

His wife returned with a folded piece of foolscap. Sears squinted at it.

"The lawyer calls this thing an option," he said. "The way he explained it to me, what he bought with this thing when he paid us the money—"

"Two thousand it was," his wife said.

"Yes," said Sears, "what he bought was the right, he told us, of having first crack at buying our spread before we sold to somebody else. So I can't make a deal with you without talking to him first and giving him a chance to top you. So even if I was for selling, which I don't believe I am, I couldn't do it. I would have to go to Ray and give him his chance at it.

"I don't believe," he said, "that you two want to try outbidding the Circle Three Bar."

Sample swallowed. His throat was hard and dry. "You have a fine place," he said. "I can see why Ray would want to get hold of it when he has the chance."

"Oh, it ain't just us," the woman said. "The Pratts, too,

and the Hesselbarths that I know of for certain. I don't know about the Gilmers and the Martins except for talk. I do hear they signed, too. It looks as if Ray Newsome means to own this valley from bottom to top. And he might just be the young fella to do it.''

They were returning home, riding through the Circle Three when they met a cowboy on horseback. The fence was almost done, he said, and the boys had found a few head of Sample's stock. He told Orrin to claim them now or lose them forever.

"We have room for more?" Rose asked.

"Room. No water. We can't keep any more."

"Show us where these cows are," Rose Ellen said to the cowboy.

There were five, penned in a corral beside the Circle Three stables. When Rose Ellen saw the cows inside the pen she handed Charlie across to Sample and climbed down from the horse. Sample was carrying a Winchester in his saddle scabbard. Before he could stop her she pulled out the rifle and yanked the lever to push a round into the chamber.

Ray ran to the window when he heard the first shot. He looked out from the second story of his house and he saw Rose Ellen with one arm braced against a corral post, sighting down the barrel of a repeater. Her face was impassive, her lips thin. One dead cow was on its side in the pen. She fired again and another cow fell dead in the dust. The baby screamed. Rose Ellen fired again and again and then once more, and each time a cow fell dead in the corral.

Ray pushed open the window. He saw her shove the rifle into the scabbard, climb on her horse, take the child from Orrin. She said something to one of the Circle Three hands. Ray could not make it out. After she and Sample and the baby were gone, Ray sent for the hand and told him to repeat her words.

"She said, 'Tell Mr. Ray Newsome that he can keep our cows.' That's all," the cowboy reported.

Sample and Rose Ellen rode along the fence until they found a gate. The fence seemed to go on forever, following every contour of the terrain, a strange intrusion on the land. The fence surrounded them, and suddenly their thousands of acres seemed small, constricted.

"There are other ranches," Sample said. "Outside McPherson, up north. We can go someplace else."

"No," she said. "Not now. We are going to stick it out here."

One evening Irene asked Ray to take her riding in the wagon. She wanted to see the fence, she said. He drove her south in a carriage. When they reached the fence at the north end of Sample's land, she stepped down from the carriage and walked to the fence and she stood beside it. She looked up and down its length. She looked at Ray and she nodded her head once.

The fence would be her legacy. In two years she was dead of a stroke, lingering paralyzed for months before she finally expired. But she died knowing that her son and her ranch were all that she had wanted them to be.

Chapter 25

The sun was hot. It was high in the sky. Four of them, and a like number of horses, were under the sun in the grasslands. Rose Ellen and Alvarez were digging a wide, shallow hole in the ground. Sample and his son, Charlie, were digging a trench up from the hole, up a hill toward a cropping of green brush and thick green grass.

The boy was seven years old and strong enough to work a small spade. Like all the others he wore a wide-brimmed hat, and a bandanna around his neck, and a cotton shirt. They were soaked with sweat but the drying moisture made their skin cool, and the shirts were loose enough to let in the breeze.

"This deep?" the boy said to Sample.

"About right. But don't go too far off to the right there. Keep the line headed toward that green grass in a clump. That is where the water seeps."

The boy put his spade into the ground again. "This big?"

"No. Half that. There ain't much water comes out of the seep. You understand what we are doing? We want to catch the water that comes out of the seep. We are going to open up the seep to let the water out, what comes. Then the water will run down this line we are digging, down into the tank that your ma and Paco are working on over there."

"Then the cows can drink it," Charlie said.

"Yes. But don't start too wide. Like this, like I showed

you. If you don't want to work you don't have to. Go and set with your ma if you want."

"No," the boy said. "Let me."

They worked in the hot sun, their movements deliberate, endless, and identical. Rose Ellen broke the rhythm when she shouted for water and the boy walked to where the horses had found shade. He pulled a canteen off a saddle horn and brought it to where she stood.

She put it to her mouth. "Terrible," she said. "Hot. It would boil if we left it out in the sun."

She handed the canteen back to Charlie. "You want some?" she said. "Take some and then bring it to Paco. He must be dry. You are helping your papa, I see. Are you doing what he tells you to do?"

"Yep."

"Pull up your britches, boy. You look a sight. Give me a kiss, if you please, then take some water up to your papa."

They worked until the sun was at their backs and their shadows stretched across the grass. Sample came down the hill and stood at the edge of the hole where Alvarez and Rose Ellen were working. They stopped and looked up at him.

"How does it look?" she said.

"Wide enough. And deeper than it has to be."

"You?"

"About done. I have to hack away at the seep and dig a few more feet of ditch."

"Is it going to work?"

"God, I hope so," he said. "But if it don't, we will start over someplace else."

They walked up the hill, and found Charlie trying to dig through the roots of the brush.

"Here," Sample said. "You done good, boy. Leave that part to me. He is a real steady hand, Mama. He will make as good a worker as his pa ever was."

He shoved the spade into the ground, opening the narrow trench up to the base of the seep. There he dug a shallow basin to catch the water and channel it into the trench. But still there was no water, only damp earth that smeared his boots and the tip of the spade.

He raised the spade and when it came out of the hillside

again it brought out dark earth. Soon he had stripped away the grass and there was a trickle of water in the black soil. But the trickle lost itself before it reached the basin and the trench. He exposed a larger trickle, and stripped away more grass, and finally the trickle was large enough to survive. It fell down the face of the exposed dirt and into the basin. There it disappeared into the ground. Sample dug some more and then the trickle was even greater, and it made a growing puddle in the basin, and when the basin was full the water lapped into the trench.

Slowly the water advanced down the trench. The four of them stood at its edge and watched the slow progress of the water downhill. The ground was porous and it absorbed most of the trickle.

"It might make the tank by midnight," Sample said.

"Will it fill up?"

"I doubt it. But it might cover up the bottom and get a couple of inches deep."

"Enough to let some cows drink," Alvarez said.

"If we are lucky. If the sun don't shine too hard and burn off too much of the water. If the seep don't play out. If the cows wander over here and find it. We might be able to water five or six more cows if it all holds up."

They rode toward home over the rolling grass fields, the sun in their faces, their bodies drained by the heat and the work. The work tired them even though it was a constant in their lives. It was a simple existence now. The big herds were gone from their land. Without the Mansos for water the land would support few cattle. Each year Sample sold off enough calves, and older steers and cows, to keep the herd at about three hundred and twenty head. During dry years he had to sell more and reduce the number. They depended on what water they could squeeze out of the land by digging out springs and scratching away the topsoil in places where the water table was high, and scraping the shallow depressions they called tanks to catch rainwater and seepage.

They made enough in a good season to buy clothes and food and to pay Alvarez. He was sixty now, their only employee. Rose Ellen kept a garden, and preserved food, and was teaching her son to read and write by lamplight in the evenings, as she had been taught. Because three hundred and twenty head are not much work for good cowmen, Sample had time for other things. He had added two back rooms to their cabin and was building a system to bring running water inside the house. A windmill pulled water out of a shallow well outside the cabin, and dropped it in a wooden tank that Sample had built on upright supports. The tank was as high as the ceiling of the cabin. Gravity fed the water to the cabin from the tank. Now he was running pipes and lines inside the cabin, with water taps and faucets in the kitchen. There was money for these things, the money that they would have used once to buy another ranch in the valley. Now they had it for wood and pipe and tools as they needed such things. They no longer talked about buying another spread. Here they would stay. They were not poor but they lived without opulence, and at the end of most days they were as spent as if they had been scratching their own survival out of the land.

And in a way, they were. They were holding out against Ray Newsome, who in the last five years had cast the Circle Three's boundaries out past the northern end of the valley. He had bought the Sears's spread, and the Pratts', and the Martins', and the Hesselbarths'. He had money to spend, and credit when he needed it. At the far south end of the valley was a family named Gilmer, with one hundred and twenty-five sections. They still held out against him, and would for a few years yet. But they and Orrin and Rose Ellen were the last. Ray Newsome owned all the rest.

Irene was three years dead. Her passing had brought sadness and relief to Ray. He was sorry that she was dead but glad to stand alone on the ranch. He no longer needed her initiative, if he ever had. He still had Rose Ellen not many miles away, and she still aroused in him a confusing knot of feelings—hatred that felt like love sometimes, envy and frustration.

He met other women but they did not move him. He slept with some of them but the act was mechanical. He could not forget Rose Ellen, and had stopped trying. The truth was that he indulged in his unhappiness. He felt wounded and would not allow the wound of his only failure to heal. She was his by right, he argued to himself. Until she was restored to him he would not allow himself to forget the slight. And in the meantime he would use her to prove himself.

He built the town to show her his power.

The Central Texas railroad came to the valley in '87. It entered the north end, but Ray stopped it from going farther. The railroad had a charter from the state legislature, but Ray Newsome had title to the land. And he had his lawyers, and he had his nerve. Ray was glad to see the railroad come because that brought the cattle markets closer. But he wanted to show his muscle and to make the Circle Three more important.

So when the rail crews punched into his property Ray Newsome told his men to set charges and blow holes in the path of the tracks. His cowboys could blow holes faster than the rail crews could fill them. The crews made some slow progress until they had laid track to within a quarter of a mile from a narrow pass. The track was supposed to run between a hill and a rock cliff. Ray Newsome himself set the charges that blew tons of rock off the cliff and into the pass.

The next day two directors of the Central Texas arrived in a private car and asked to see Ray. He came with Belford Tefler.

The car was gaslit and paneled in rich, dark walnut. The directors did not seem unfriendly, so Ray shook their hands and drank their whiskey. They sat at a long, polished conference table in the middle of the car. Ray and Belford Tefler sat together at one end.

"I thought it was high time that we met," said one of the directors. "Informally, as it were."

"Good idea," Ray said.

"Mr. Newsome, you are a young man, and somewhat impetuous," the other director said. "A man of direct action, evidently. But you can't stop the railroad."

"I already have," Ray said.

"What you are doing is illegal."

"I ain't so sure it is," Ray said. "I asked my lawyer here about it and he told me what I already know. There ain't no law against a man blowing up his own property if he wants."

"We have a right of way," the first director said, his voice slightly louder, with shades of indignation. "A state grant."

Belford Tefler spoke before Ray could: "And we have deed and title to the land. The state was careless. It can't grant a right of way across private property."

"There is precedent."

"There is also common law."

Ray spoke. "You boys could get your lawyers to argue with my lawyers if you want," he said. "They prob'ly could argue up a ball of fire if they set themselves to it, but that won't lay track for you, will it? You don't have time to piss away, I don't think. So if I can just hold you off a few months or so, the way I see it, even if you win you lose in the end."

"I'm certain that we can find another way," the second director said.

"You may be right," said Ray.

The first director dropped his voice and said, "You cattlemen don't like track running across your land, we know that. But you'll find what other cattlemen already know, which is that cattle don't mind the rails at all."

"Maybe not," Ray said.

"Collisions between locomotives and livestock are infrequent, but we would compensate you generously when they did occur."

"You bet you would. I still don't want you on my land."

"Our commission specifies that we go through this valley," the second director said. "We can't do that without going through your land."

"So you can't."

"Mr. Newsome," the director said. He tried to impress Ray with an imploring tone, pleading for reason. "The railroad is progress. It is important to the social and economic well-being of this region. Why, at this moment, the town of McPherson is languishing, waiting for the arrival of the rails."

"That is what I wanted to talk to you about," Ray said.

"I don't follow you."

"McPherson is a far piece to go to trade. It is half a day's ride to get there. Too far to go for a box of cigars or a sack of flour."

"But if you don't let the rails through, there soon won't be any town at all. And then you will be even farther from a town. You don't want that.''

The chairs around the conference table were high-backed and sturdy. Ray's did not creak when he tilted back, balanced on the chair's two legs. He looked at the directors' faces across the table and he folded his arms across his chest.

"I might," he said, "if I was to build a town of my own."

This was the first that Belford Tefler or anybody else had heard of his plan. Ray wanted to build a town. He wanted stores, a doctor, a hotel, a sheriff's office. All the things that McPherson had, he wanted for his town.

"Not just that," he said. "A railroad depot. Pens for stock waiting to be shipped. Offices for cattle brokers and buyers. The thing is, gents, I want to make this a good big town that lasts for a while. But if your railroad goes through, my town won't be any different from any other stop on the line. That is why I don't want the rails going any farther than they are right now."

He left the car with Belford Tefler. A day later the directors asked for him again, and when he left the car that time he had what he wanted. His new town would be a railhead for that spur of the road. The rail rights down the rest of the valley were his. He would be obliged to complete buildings, offices, and stock pens so that ranchers could ship their cattle from the town on Central Texas trains.

He let the tracks come within five miles of the Circle Three ranch house. He found a level spot and he laid out the town with a surveying crew. First he marked off the streets with a long stick that he scraped in the ground. There was a Main Street that ran parallel to the tracks, two hundred feet west. He marked ten streets running parallel to the tracks and ten more that ran east to west and ended at the tracks. He divided each block into building lots.

On the land east of the tracks he built pens and loading ramps for cattle. Just west of the tracks went warehouses, and offices for half a dozen cattle buyers. Carpenters, masons, and carloads of wood, brick, and sacks of mortar arrived by rail. Along Main he built a few stores, a stone jailhouse, and a brick bank building with a vault. A couple of blocks farther west he built twenty neat bungalows in a row.

After the workmen arrived, their hammers pounded for five months. The Central Texas helped him to promote the town as a freight center. It printed brochures and fliers, and one day when the town was almost ready it brought in a special trainload of businessmen, speculators, and cattle brokers.

Ray had a land office on Main with a salesman and a map showing the streets and the lots. Most of these existed within surveyors' lines. Three lots on Main sold to saloon keepers the first morning. Other merchants were leery of buying lots for their businesses, so Ray leased them space in the buildings on Main. He reserved the wholesale businesses for himself. Belford Tefler moved his practice from McPherson, and brought with him a barber and a doctor.

They christened the town on the Fourth of July. It was only a formality; cattle already lowed in the pens, the jail cells had held and disgorged a dozen fractious cowboys, the saloons had twice already swept the dirty sawdust from the floor and replaced it.

Red, white, and blue bunting hung from the eaves of the depot on the occasion. County officials and executives of the road and even a delegate from the statehouse sat on a platform built across the tracks. A few feet away a steam locomotive chuffed and puffed bursts of steam.

There were six speeches; all went on too long. After the last one Ray stood holding a slab of wood. He fitted it on two hooks that hung down from the depot's eaves. There was a loud cheer. The slab of wood swung imperceptibly on the hooks; the engineers in the locomotive yanked a cord and loosed a whistle scream that shook the ground.

The name of the town, painted on the slab of wood, read: INDIAN OAK.

The town grew, and thrived. No other place for sixty miles in any direction had such large pens and so many cattle buyers. Quickly the town reached that stage of progress where growth invites more growth. Businesses sprouted to service other businesses and brought in employees, and more businesses sprouted to serve the employees. Some of the tradesmen and merchants came down the rail and settled in the town. Others closed their shops in McPherson and drifted north. By '90 Indian Oak was the county seat.

* * *

Rose Ellen's pants were dirty from digging the tank, and her shirt was stiff with dry sweat. When she got home that evening she washed her hands and splashed water on her face, put on a sleeveless cotton dress, and tried to make her hair neat. But it had become damp when she worked, and the band of the hat had pressed a wave in it all around her skull.

Then she fixed a dinner for the four of them, and taught Charlie some addition before she put him to bed. When the sun went down the house was quiet, and she was alone with Sample in their bed.

"I'll ride to the new tank tomorrow to check it," he said.

"It'll be full of water, I know it."

"I'd settle for enough that a cow can run his tongue through it without coming up full of mud."

"Maybe we can go to McPherson in the next couple of days," she said. "We are getting to the end of the beans, and I will need Arbuckle's and sugar before long."

"I need boots," he said. "But I couldn't find them there last time. There ain't a store left with goods worth buying."

"I don't want us going north," she said, "no matter what. If we can't find it in McPherson we will wait for a trip to San Antone or else we will go without. But I'm not going up there."

They had been once to Indian Oak, about a month after the christening. They had ridden in, gone from one end of Main Street to the other, ridden out again, and never returned. Going once had been Rose Ellen's idea, and staying away was her idea, too.

"You ain't sorry about the way things come out?" Sample said to her now. "I wonder sometimes."

"I'm where I want to be, Orrin."

"You could have done a sight better. You shouldn't have to work out in the sun like a convict or a field hand."

"I want to help. You try to keep me off but I don't let you."

"I can't try too hard," Sample said. "I need your help."

They were both naked between the sheets. She moved beside him until she was on her side, her breasts against the muscles of his arm. She put a hand on his chest. It rested lightly there.

He turned to face her, took her in his arms, kissed her. A touch from her hand moved him on his back. She straddled him. He thought she was beautiful, above him like that. And he found pleasure in the friendly and familiar ease of their intimacies.

"We don't do this near often enough," he said.

"No. Seems we are always too busy, too tired, something."

"I always want you. Even when I am bone-tired. My heart is like to bust when I know I have you with me."

She moved astride him with graceful, knowing motions.

"Even if we didn't have this," he said, "you would still be everything to me. Just you beside me. More'n I ever saw for myself. You give and give. You changed my life with your giving."

Her moving ended the words. He put hands on her hips, and held her against him.

A year later she bore their second child. They called her Dora. The baby was light-haired but ruddy, and to Rose Ellen she had something of Charlie Fowler's face when he brooded, thoughtful and clouded. On an infant the effect was comical, but Rose Ellen liked to see it anyway. She liked the evidence, however circumstantial, that there was something of her father in the children she brought to life.

With the baby, Rose Ellen could not be outside as much as she had been, and the work fell even more heavily on Sample. One evening he was shoeing a mule while Rose Ellen nursed the baby. The only blacksmith was in Indian Oak, so Sample did his own work.

While the baby fed, Rose Ellen watched Charlie write in a notebook. He knew the alphabet, and now he was learning words of three letters. His fingers gripped the pencil. He bit his lip and frowned and labored over the letters.

After a while he put down the pencil and asked to leave. Rose Ellen looked at the scratching on the paper and said, "You've done enough. Go find your papa. Maybe you can learn something from him, if you won't from me."

The boy returned in a few seconds. Rose Ellen saw panic in his eyes and braced herself for what was to come.

"Mama, Mama," he said. "It's Pa. He's hurt bad."

She tried to keep calm, make herself strong. She took the baby from her breast and laid it, wailing, in the crib. She pulled her shirt down and then she ran with Charlie to the shed. Sample kept a small forge there. She found him curled on his side. His breath came in short, shallow panting. He was lying a few feet from the hind legs of a mule that was tied to a post in the shed. The mule twisted its neck and looked back at them.

"The damn jenny," he said. He gasped for air before he spoke again. "It was my fault. I dropped a nail and bent down to get it. I know better than that. She cut loose. Got me right in the gut."

He still panted. He looked up at Rose Ellen and took one of her hands. His, beefy and calloused, swallowed up her own.

"How long ago?" she said.

"Couple of minutes before Charlie come in. Maybe longer. Things got fuzzy. When I come to I thought I'd best keep still until the pain passed."

"Is it bad?" she said.

"God, yes," he said, and she knew it was even worse than that.

"I'll help you," she said, "when you're ready. We can lay you in bed. I have some laudanum in the kitchen."

"We'll do that," he said.

She helped to pull him to his feet. When he slumped against her she realized again what a big man he was, how massive and solid. The springs creaked in the bed when he sat down. She took off his clothes and stretched his legs out on the bed. There was the beginning of a bruise already with a crescent welt low on his abdomen.

She lay beside him later, when he was drowsy with the drug. She could not sleep because she could not rid herself of fear and dread. In the middle of the night he passed blood into a chamberpot, and groaned when he did.

By the middle of the next morning, when Alvarez had returned with the doctor from Indian Oak, Sample was already sweating with the fever. Rose Ellen stood beside the bed while the doctor lifted Orrin's nightshirt and looked at the billowing black and purple bruise, and pressed his fingers into Orrin's side.

When he took her outside to talk to her she knew it was bad.

A kidney, he said. And infected now, to judge from the swelling and the fever. She could try to keep the fever down, and pray, and could send for him in three days if her husband was still alive. He might be able to help then.

The fever was the worst. For three days Orrin groaned and tossed and moaned. She kept a cold towel on his forehead, and wiped him dry as often as she could. He was helpless and in misery.

He died the morning of the fourth day.

She and Alvarez dug his grave not far from the cabin. When they got near the bottom they found water, and the bottom of the hole was sloppy mud. It would have been as good a tank, she told herself, as any that she and Orrin ever had dug together.

Chapter 26

"Ray?" said the voice. "Did you get that? The part about the Baldwin?"

Ray Newsome found himself looking out the window. It was the only open window in the room, and it had brought in a breeze that caught him and turned his eyes toward the sunshine.

"Yes," Ray said. "Ah . . . no. Maybe I didn't, at that."

"The Baldwin we wanted is four months to build from the day we order it, and shipping on top of that. But Wheelock says there is a short line in Nevada that is selling off some of its rolling stock. They have a 2-4-2 in good shape and some cars, too."

"Is the gauge right?" Ray said.

"I wouldn't mention it otherwise."

"Then maybe you ought to send somebody out there to look at it. No, you do it yourself, then you know it is done right. And if it looks good you can buy it. This ain't the Union Pacific we are talking about here. No need to buy a new engine if we can get around it."

Once a week Ray met with his business managers in his office. Just to make sure, he sometimes joked, that he wasn't broke yet. It was his only way of keeping his businesses run as he wanted them run.

He had split the ranch into two sections, north and south in the valley. Each had a foreman and a manager. There was a manager for his land-selling business in Indian Oak, and a manager for the packing plant he had built a year earlier on the east side of the tracks.

Now he was building a railroad, a narrow-gauge short line to run from Indian Oak to the south end of the valley. The Central Texas was helping him with financing, because Ray's line would help bring in even more cattle to be shipped north and east.

"I talked to the engineers," his railroad manager was saying. His name was Harmon. "They say we need to trestle twice over the stream, once about five miles south of here and then about fifteen miles south again of that."

Harmon stopped. Ray was looking out of the window again.

"Go on," Ray said. "I'm listening."

"They say if we don't we will have to dig a new bed for the stream, and even then you are asking for trouble because a river usually ends up going where it wants."

"Yes," Ray said. "That makes sense."

"That's all," said Harmon. "It will take a couple of weeks to bring in the crews when we are ready. Ties and rails are already coming in. But there is no point in starting until we know we have stock on the way. If the Baldwin in Nevada looks good, we can get going right off. Sixty miles of track is nothing to these boys when they get moving."

"Good. That sounds just fine," Ray said. There was a robin outside the window, teetering on the end of a tree limb. Ray watched the robin steady itself and fly away. When he brought his attention to his office again, the manager of the northern division of the Circle Three was talking about a feedlot he wanted to build.

"We have pens we can use," the man was saying. "We can add some later, but for now we have enough. We can bring water in, too. That is no problem. The big expense, of course, is grain. But I've been looking into this and I . . ."

He stopped when Ray rose out of his chair and walked to one of the other windows. He pulled back the velvet drapes, folded back the shutters, and opened the window. Then he walked around the room and opened all the windows. One of the managers slapped a hand down on a stack of papers to keep the sudden wind from scattering them.

Light filled the room. Ray turned off the gas jets.

"We have a beautiful day outside," he said. "Seems a terrible shame to waste it. This place was too dark."

He usually liked it dark. The leather upholstery of the chairs was dark. So was the long conference table that he had been given from the railroad directors' car, and so was the walnut paneling that he had copied from that same car.

"You were saying about grain," Ray said.

"Yes. I think it would be feasible to grow corn. I planted a test patch myself and it is growing right nice."

"This is a cattle ranch, not a farm," said the manager of the southern section.

They all waited for Ray to speak. He was looking up at the ceiling. The manager of the northern section cleared his throat.

"Hell, I don't know," Ray said. "Ask me about it next week."

They talked on. It was a drone to Ray. After a while he gave up trying to follow them. This wasn't normal. He usually hunched over the table and stared at them the way a hungry dog waits for a scrap of food. He would pounce on their mistakes.

But lately he had been different. Listless, one of the managers had said. But listless was not quite the word. He had energy enough, but undirected energy, no place to put it.

Today was worse than before. His managers gave up asking questions or waiting to be interrupted. Each spoke for a few minutes and got noncommittal nods, grunts, silence.

He finally spoke again when Bartell, the manager of his wholesale warehouses, began to talk about increases in shipping prices from factories in the east.

"We have any candy?" Ray said.

"What was that?" said Bartell.

"You know. Candy. Do we carry that wholesale?"

"Licorice and gum balls, peppermint sticks," Bartell said.

Ray shook his head. "The kind that comes in a box," he said. "Fancy candy. Chocolates and such."

"No, sir. Not enough demand. That's a specialty item. Mrs. Roth has some, I think. She makes it herself and sells it in her bakery."

"Hmm. How about perfume?"

"Same thing. Jenkins the druggist keeps some, but it is a low-volume item so we let him order it direct. Not worth our trouble."

"The French kind is what I was talking about. The good stuff."

"Well, um, he has it, if I'm not mistaken."

Ray looked up at the ceiling again. "Would you like me to get some for you, Mr. Newsome?" Bartell said.

"Would you?" Ray said. "I'd be much obliged. I surely would. Make sure it's the best. Not some cheap toilet water. And a good big box of chocolates while you're at it, too. Would you do that for me?"

He would be happy to do it, Bartell said.

"Good," Ray said. "Good. I'd do it myself but I'm going to be busy. Can you go out and do that now? I'd appreciate it. I'm riding down to the big house in an hour or so and I'd like to bring those items with me if I could."

He gave Bartell twenty dollars and sent them all away. No way he could keep his mind on business today.

When they were gone he paced the room, back and forth—up one side of the table, around the end, and down the other side. He stopped at a window and looked outside. The robin was there again. There were blossoms on the trees. He thought about how it was going to be tonight.

He was going to see Rose Ellen.

He had told himself that before, and each time he had lost his nerve. This time was going to be different. To keep his courage he had pictured in his mind how it would be, and it was good, always good, every time he ran it through.

The Rose Ellen of his mind was hesitant at first. Of course she would be. You couldn't expect a woman of Rose Ellen's spirit to open her arms at the first sight of him. Not Rose.

But she wouldn't throw him out, either. She would give him a chance. And in his mind he said the right things. He had all the lines right now, all the apologies and explanations and then the sweet talk that she would be ready for when she had been with him for a while.

Of course he was due some apologies, too. But he wouldn't expect much from her at first. You couldn't expect from Rose the things you would take for granted from anybody else. He wanted them to have some time alone. He was sure that they belonged together. They needed only a chance to rekindle the old love.

The scenes he imagined had different forms, but they all ended with Rose letting him take her in his arms. The impression was vivid, almost tangible. It gave him what he needed, the courage to make the journey and to make all the imagining real.

He looked at a clock on the wall. Eleven-ten.

Eight hours, he thought. Maybe nine. Until I see her again.

After Bartell brought the candy and the perfume Ray rode to the house. He spent more time in town now, in a place he had built near the tracks. This house was too big for him alone, even with the maid and the cook who lived there.

He wondered where Rose Ellen would want to live.

She would make this place a sight brighter, he thought. This is bigger than what she is used to these days. She won't know what to do in a place this size, not after that joke of a squatter's nest.

Maybe, he thought, she will want to live in her old place. The foreman of the southern section lived there now. If she wished, so it would be.

He dressed three times. First, in a business suit, the clothes he wore most often now. But when he looked at himself in a mirror he tried to picture himself in her cabin. He would look ridiculous. The suit belonged at a business meeting.

He wondered, How will she remember me?

Not riding in a buggy dressed like a chairman of the board. Like a cowboy, on a tall, strong stallion.

He still had those clothes. He hadn't stopped riding the land, not entirely. Sometimes riding gave him respite from talk and business, and it kept him strong and slim as he drew near thirty. He put on some faded pants and a plain shirt and tied a bandanna around his neck. But before he was finished, even without the mirror, he knew that he looked wrong. He was no longer a sixteen-year-old boy who lived in the saddle. She would know that.

The third time he settled on blue cotton trousers and a collarless white silk shirt, clean boots, and a Buckeye-model

Stetson, broad and tall and elegant. This time when he looked at himself he saw only a prosperous young man going to call on his lady love.

Now in the late afternoon the air held a promise of warmth through the night. He decided to carry a woolen jacket just in case. He shouted down for the maid to tell the stableboy that he wanted the big grey. He stepped close to the mirror and peered at his face, wondering what she would see there after these years.

She would be looking at this face before too long now, he thought. Looking at him the way he was today, not so much different if one didn't count the years and the knowledge that were just beginning to show itself in lines at the corners of his eyes. Not so much different, after all.

The grey was saddled and ready when he came outside. The stableboy held it for him. Ray put the candy and the perfume into a saddlebag and tied the jacket behind the saddle. He mounted and rode down the valley.

At once he had to fight back the impulse to turn away and try it another time. He had waited too long already, he told himself. When he first heard of Sample's death, he had considered a note. A simple and short note telling her that he was sorry. A hand could have delivered it. But he had decided against a note when he crumpled up half a box of stationery trying to find the right words. He wasn't sorry that Sample was gone; he had hope for the first time in years. And she would know that.

When the chance for the note passed, he thought he ought to wait a few weeks before he visited her. This time it would have to be in person, for he thought she would laugh at a message inviting her to dinner. But he had to wait awhile to visit. He wasn't going to crowd her while she mourned her husband. He would wait the proper time.

But how long, he wondered, was proper? She would not mourn forever. After a while she would want men to come visit. Widows did, didn't they? Three months, he thought. Three months would be right. But after three months he talked himself into four, then six. Sample had died in August, and when Ray faced the first week in March he knew that he should wait no longer. Twice he had dressed and made ready.

But he had never asked for the horse. Now he was riding toward her and fighting to keep his horse on the path.

He rehearsed the words that he thought she would want to hear.

The fence. It was Irene that talked me into the fence. I didn't want to do that, and I know it was wrong. But I was upset and I wanted to hurt you, Rose dear. I did—it's true. But you are doing fine without the river and I'm glad you are.

The children are beautiful, Rose. Fine children. No, I don't care that they ain't mine. I could love them like they was my own. And we'd have plenty of room for them in the big house. We'll hire us a teacher to come live with us and make sure they learn. We got a school now in town, you know, but they won't have to go there. These beautiful children will get nothing but the best.

The past? You can't let it get to you, Rose. The past is gone and there is nothing for us to do about it. What does it matter, anyways? Here we are, the way we ought to be. We been through a lot, but we're still young. Still got our best years ahead of us. And if we are together they will be the best.

Rose, you are still beautiful as ever. No, no, I take that back. More beautiful than you ever was before, and you was a real beauty. You're a woman now, Rose—that's the difference.

Do I love you? There, Rose, is a question I have no trouble answering. I do, I swear I do. More now than I did ten years ago. I have never stopped.

He thought, that one, at least, I will be able to say as if I mean it.

He reached the fence that marked his property line. When he passed through the gate and shut it behind him he was on Rose's land, and he knew there was no turning back.

The first few seconds would be the hardest, he thought. She would be surprised. And maybe that was good. She would not have time to work up an anger and think of ways to send him away.

That was how he got the idea of tying his horse and leaving it some distance from the cabin, walking the rest of the way. She would not hear him. He would knock on her door and she would be facing him before she knew what was happening.

It had been years since he had ridden the road into Sample's property. Then he had been living three days a week with Sample and courting Rose Ellen. As he rode now he remembered how anxious and nervous and excited he had been, riding to meet her. And how happy and complete he had been riding back, with the smell and the feel and the taste of her still fresh with him.

He rode on, as nervous now as he had ever been as a boy. It was evening. Night came down around him. He thought he was close to the cabin now, so he tied the horse to a tree, took the candy and the perfume from the saddlebag, and walked.

He had misjudged slightly. He walked for twenty minutes before the cabin came into view, partly hidden by trees that lined the wagon ruts of the road. He stopped. Lamps burned in the house. He heard a child's voice, a boy's happy shouts. A baby crying.

He waited in the trees. Something about this settled life stopped him. She had existed so long apart from him. She didn't need him now. The thought made him pause while he waited for his courage to restore itself.

The baby stopped crying. The lamps went out, all but one in the front room. He guessed that she had put the children to bed.

He was ready to walk to the house when the door opened. She stepped out. He recognized her outline. He felt his heart thump. She stepped out onto the porch.

And a man stepped out with her.

He was tall and broad-shouldered, this man. He had a deep voice that carried out to the trees where Ray stood. Her voice followed the man's. Hers was light and it had a laugh in it. This was not the lonely widow he had expected.

He stood in the trees. He could not move; they might see him from the porch. They were on a bench. The man's arm was around her, and she, with her legs tucked under her, rested against him. Ray saw the man turn his head. Their talking became too soft for him to hear. Rose Ellen turned to the man and moved her face up to his. They kissed, and then stood and went into the cabin, and the last light went out.

Ray could not force himself to move. He stood among the trees and watched the cabin for what seemed like hours. He waited until he was sure he knew what Rose Ellen and the man were doing in the cabin.

And when he was sure, he left.

He walked to where his horse was tied. When he got there he realized that he was still carrying the perfume and the candy. He tore the cover from the box of chocolates and flung them into the field. He pulled the cap from the perfume and threw the open bottle away.

He let the horse plod up the road. He was near the gate when he thought he heard another horse behind him.

There was an arroyo beside the road. Laurel grew around the side of it. He pointed his horse down the arroyo and climbed off. He was hidden. He stood at the edge of the arroyo and looked through an opening in the laurel as the horse drew near.

The rider was the man he had seen on the porch with Rose Ellen. He recognized the square, wide shoulders. The horse was trotting. Ray glimpsed the man's face, but in the darkness he could make out no features that he recognized. But as the horse came by, Ray did see the brand burned into the animal's left flank.

The brand was a circle enclosing three bars. A brand, Earl Newsome had once said, you could read in the moonlight.

Chapter 27

She had met him when Orrin was still alive. She was pushing a heifer out of a wallow that day. The wallow was just inside her property, and she was up to her knees in mud, heaving against the rear end of the bleating cow, when he spoke.

"You ain't going to do it that way," he said.

She caught her breath as she looked up at him. He was on a horse, on the other side of the four-strand fence.

"You can keep your opinions to yourself," she said. "They aren't worth much over here."

Once more she pushed against the rump of the heifer. She could not budge the animal. She looked up again. He was still on the horse, staring at her in the mud.

"I'm so happy for Ray Newsome," she said, "that he can afford to pay his hands to sit about in the saddle all day and admire the sights."

"I'd be happy to help," he said, "but I been told to keep my flapper shut."

She pushed some more on the heifer. Her pushing only drove it deeper into the mud. She wanted the cowboy to go away. She was sure that she could not save this heifer and she did not want anyone to see her fail, especially this cocky youngster grinning down from his horse.

Then she thought that failing would be easier if he failed, too. "If you are so damn smart," she said, "you are welcome to try."

He climbed between two strands of wire and walked to the

271

wallow. His own boots and pants and shirt were muddy. "This is all I been doing since I got here," he said. His boots made sucking sounds when he walked in the mud. "I learned a few things."

He stood beside Rose Ellen. "Like some cows will help you. Others won't help at all. This here's the worst kind. Makes it harder on you. See, you wouldn't know from that end. But she's making her front legs straight and you're just pushing her in deeper."

He grinned again at Rose Ellen.

"Don't give me a lyceum lecture," she said. "Just help me get the cow out if you can."

He told her to reach behind the cow's forelegs. Somehow that made the cow move its legs while he pushed, and in a few seconds the heifer was out of the mud, running away with eyes wide.

"Obliged," she said. "I thought I knew all there was to know about cows."

He was hardly more than a boy, if you looked past the tanned and leathery face. Twenty-two, twenty-three, maybe.

"Always glad to help a neighbor," he said. "Who is Ray Newsome?"

"You must be new to the Circle Three."

"Five days new."

"If you stay around much longer you will find out that Ray Newsome owns the ranch you work for. You will also discover that he would not look kindly on your helping out anybody on the O–Bar–S. Which is my spread, mine and my husband's."

"Bad blood?"

"Bad as it gets."

He made a motion of turning to look one way, then another. "I don't know the gentleman," he said, "but I don't believe he is anywheres about."

He stuck out his hand. "Quiller Meacham," he said.

"Rose Ellen Sample. I have some water that was halfway to being cold last time I tried it."

"I'll have some, if you're offering."

He drank. When he was finished he said, "Hills, more damn hills. I never seen the like of it. Even the valley has hills in it. My brother and me come from up Panhandle way, nothing like this.''

"This is good country," she said.

"I could get to like it," he answered.

She saw him again three weeks later. He brought in one of their cows at the end of a rope. He had cut it out of the herd and brought it to them when he could.

Dinner was on the table. Sample invited him to stay, and he accepted.

After that he came every few weeks to visit. Sometimes he brought toys for Charlie, a knife or a spinning top or a looking glass.

A few days after Sample died he came again to visit.

With his hat in his hand he said, "Mrs. Sample . . . Rose . . . I just heard, just this morning I want to tell you how bad I feel. How sorry I am. Orrin, he was a good man.

"That's all," he said. "I wanted you to know that."

He was almost at his horse when he said, "Oh. And I wonder if you need some help. Ray Newsome don't own me all day every day."

"Nothing now," she said.

"I could stop by. Once a week or so when I get a few hours to myself."

She knew she would need help. Alvarez could not do the work he had done even five years earlier.

"I'd be grateful if you would do that," she said.

He came at least once a week after that. He chopped wood, fixed a leak in the roof, helped her count cattle and brand calves. Once she asked him if he would leave the Circle Three to hire on with her. She would hire him and his brother, she said.

They were on horseback, looking over a knoll on a cold December day. He had a fleece jacket, and he turned the collar up around his neck before he answered.

"I don't believe so," he said. "But thank you."

She tried to smile. "You think I would be tough to work for?" she said.

"I know you would," he said. "But that ain't why."

"You wouldn't want to work for a woman?"

"I don't care one way or the other about that. Some might, but I don't."

"Then why not?"

"Because," he said, "I don't want to be your hired hand. I don't want it that way between us."

Then she understood, and she was not surprised a few days later when he held her hand and then kissed her on the cheek when he left. It began that way. He was slow about it, never forcing, never straining. They stayed friends throughout it.

She liked him. She was a talker, and they could talk together.

One night she told him, "I have been a lucky woman. I have known at least two good men. One in a lifetime is more than some women get. I had my papa. I had Orrin. He was different from Papa but a good man. Then there is you.

"You could be as good as either one of them," she said. "I don't know yet, but I think so. Don't let me down, Quiller."

They made love that night for the first time. In this as in everything else, she found him patient, gentle, confident. By now she was watching him closely. He was smart, and he had sense. He was good to Charlie and Dora. He was good to her. He had a feeling for the land and he seemed to care about the ranch.

More and more, he was acting as if he belonged there.

One night while they lay together she thought, Go on and take it if you want it. If you are good enough and strong enough to take it all, I won't stop you. I'm yours and so is all I have if you know how to go about getting it.

During dinner one evening they talked about water, grass, cattle.

"It is a shame," he said. "All this grass and there is so little you can use."

"The cows need water," she said. "You know it. They won't go far from it. Grass is no good if there is no water near it."

"There ought to be water," he said. "Think about it. Look at the way the Lord put things together. Look at this grass. Don't water belong with it?

"If you had water everywhere, you could run four, five

thousand head on what you've got. Fifteen acres for a cow. How many would that be? If you only had water.''

They were in love. He had most of his evenings free, so he ate with her and slept beside her until early mornings, when he had to return to his bunkhouse. The size of the Circle Three was a blessing to them in that way. He was one among dozens of cowboys. No one cared where he went or how he spent his nights, and the impoverished rectangle that lay within the Circle Three's sprawling prosperity was more embarrassment than worry.

One night he brought another hand to dinner. His name was Josiah Benton. He was an old man with a stubble of beard and sunken cheeks. He had no teeth. The skin of his hands was cracked, and there was black grease in the cracks and under his fingernails.

He ate dinner with them. Rose Ellen thought Quiller was acting strangely. Like a boy Charlie's age, she thought, about to pull an outrageous practical joke and unable to contain himself. Not like Quiller at all, she thought.

"Josiah and me been setting 'crost from each other during breakfast these days. Ain't that right, Josiah?''

"Yessir,'' Josiah said.

"Won't nobody else talk to Joe since he ain't a cowboy,'' Quiller said. "But I ain't particular.''

"No, he ain't,'' Josiah said. "Quiller is real good to me, he is.''

"And what is it,'' Rose asked, "that you do on the ranch, Mr. Benton?''

"I was hoping you would ask him that. Tell her, Joe. Tell her what you do.''

"I'm a machinist,'' he said.

"He fixes machines,'' Quiller said. "The handiest son of a gun I ever seen. If it moves, Joe here can fix it. Most of the time he is up in town, but lately they had him down at this end, so we got to be friends.''

"That's right,'' Josiah said happily. He gave a toothless smile and went back to his dinner.

"Now, the reason I brought him along—besides the fact that I want all my good friends to meet you, Rose—is what Josiah told me a couple mornings back when we was shoveling in the flapjacks. He come here from Nebraska. He worked up there for a comp'ny that made machines. Tell her what kind of machines, Joe.''

Josiah Benton swallowed. ''Hydraulic rotating machines,'' he said, and he took another bite.

A smile creased Quiller's face from one cheek to the other. ''And tell her,'' he said, ''what those machines do.''

Josiah took a long drink of water before he answered. ''Oh,'' he said, ''they can do many things. But me, I would use them to drill deep-water wells.''

To a woman who had learned to be thankful for a tepid inch of brown water in a hole, the idea seemed impossible, a fancy that could not be taken seriously. Not just the idea that there was water deep in the ground, hundreds of feet beneath them. That part Quiller could make her accept, however grudgingly and tentatively.

But she could not believe the notion that the means of getting that water should appear one night at her table. She had taught herself that nothing is that easy. If it was not the product of backbreaking labor and frustration and pain it could not have value.

The next night and the next Quiller brought Josiah Benton to dinner. Out of courtesy and with a hope that she would not admit even to herself, she asked him questions.

''Seems to me everybody would want a machine like this if it worked. Why haven't I heard of it? Why isn't it famous?''

''The fellas that own the patent give up on it,'' Josiah said.

''See, they run the company on a hope and a prayer,'' Quiller said. ''They had to hit big first time out or they was out of luck.''

''I gather,'' she said, ''that it was a miss, not a hit.''

''They didn't know how to run it,'' Josiah said.

''Who did?''

''Me. It was my machine. It was their idea, but I made it work. But when it come to their big chance they told me to ankle it out of the way. They didn't want to have to cut me in. It wouldn't work for them, not the way it ought to.''

''But it is still there,'' Quiller said. ''Still in Nebraska. Ain't that so, Josiah?''

''Last I seen, a few months back. Don't nobody want it.''

"But I am supposed to," she said. "If this machine is such a wonderment, why haven't you told anybody else about it? The Circle Three would like to have water."

"Nah," he said. "Bunch a bastards, from where I sit. They pay me wages and they get my time. I got no reason to help them. But Quiller here, he is a friend to me. I let him in on it, and if he lets you in, it's all the same to me."

She said, "I cannot get away from the feeling that this is going to cost me money if I say yes."

"They owed money," Josiah said. "The sheriff come and put a lock on the door. They can't get to it 'til they pay their debts. But if you was to come up with the money, they would send their number one model down to you, first thing."

"And how much," she said, "would that be?"

"Eighteen, nineteen hundred."

She had the money. She could cover it with what remained of the funds she and Orrin had once hoped to use for a new ranch. And there would still be thousands left. But she had not kept it all these years by sending it after vague hope.

Quiller persuaded her. And then she knew how much she trusted him.

It arrived at the depot in six long wooden packing crates. They sat there until Quiller had a free day. Then he took her wagon to town and loaded the crates and returned with them that evening.

The spending was not finished. She had to hire Josiah and pay him Circle Three wages. She had to hire two helpers for him. She had to buy pipes and lumber and fittings.

They built a derrick fifty feet high. It was in the middle of a field, about a mile from the house, where there were no springs or seeps, no water that she knew. That made it like nine-tenths of all the land on the O–Bar–S. It had to work there if it was going to work.

She could see the operation from her kitchen window. The first day she made three trips with Dora in her arms and Charlie trailing behind. She stood beside the derrick and watched the machine. It threw up dirt. Sometimes loam, sometimes dark sand, sometimes rock and gravel. But dry, all of it. Not enough water, she told Quiller that night, to wet a tick.

The second day she made only one trip, and after that she only watched from her kitchen window. They worked for a week. Josiah told her they would be needing more pipe soon.

"I bought six hundred feet," she said.

"And I put all but sixty down the hole," he said.

"No more," she said. She felt ridiculous, ashamed to have let herself be taken in like that.

The next day Quiller was off, and he came over to work. She was angry. As much at herself, she said, as at him. But he had to take his part of the blame for foisting such a scheme on her.

Quiller told her quietly that he would help them drill the last sixty feet.

She was working that afternoon in the front room, darning socks for Charlie, mending his pants. She heard the back door, then Quiller.

"Rose," he said. His voice was not loud. It sounded strained. The sound wavered and hung up in his throat.

"Rose," he said again.

"What's wrong?" she asked. She tried to be calm. "Something wrong with you, Quiller?" She put down her sewing and went to the kitchen.

He was standing in the middle of the room. He had his arms outstretched and he was holding his Stetson, brim up.

She saw that his clothes were wet. He let go of the hat. Water poured out of the crown and splashed on the kitchen floor.

"You got to come," he said.

They ran hand in hand to the derrick. They found the two helpers there tramping and splashing in a pool of water. In the middle of the pool was a swelling of water that poured from the hole, around the legs of the drilling rig. Josiah Benton sat on a lower rung of the derrick and smiled a toothless smile.

"My God, save it," she said.

"The water?" said Quiller.

"Yes, the water. We have to find a way to catch it and save it."

"That ain't your problem," Josiah said. "In fifty years this well will run just as strong. You have to figure out what you are going to do with it all."

"Is this true?" she said to Quiller.

"It is."

She kneeled in the water. It was cold. She cupped her hands and drank. Cold and pure and sweet. She put her head down in the pool and felt the water rush from the well hole and buffet her face.

Then she made them dig a tank to catch it. And she told them to keep the well a secret.

The next week there was a cattle auction at Indian Oak. She sent Paco with some of her savings, and he bought five hundred and fifty calves. She went to Austin a week later and bought five hundred more. The prices were low then, but a few days later one of Josiah's helpers got drunk in Indian Oak and told the story, and the rumor drove up prices. In a week, a valley that had been saturated with cattle found itself with more grass than all the livestock could eat, and the value of a cow went up. When it did she sold all her old herd, except a few seed bulls, to bring in capital.

She hired four hands, and a woman named Inez to help with the children. She built a bunkhouse and kept Josiah and his crew working. They could do eighty or ninety feet a day in most places. She kept them drilling until there was not a spot on the ranch that was more than a mile and a half away from fresh, flowing water. The water gushed from some of the wells. Others needed pumps, so Josiah built windmills to bring the water to the surface.

That year she changed the name of the ranch. She did something that the place had not deserved before. She gave it her father's initials, and enclosed them in a box, and the spread became the Box CF.

Quiller was with her in all this, but as a bystander. There was ground yet to be crossed between them. He had gone so far, no more.

One afternoon when he was free she put lunch in a basket and rode with him into the pastures. They stopped and spread a blanket not far from a new windmill. The wooden tanks that the hands were building could not contain all the water, and the excess made the grass grow tall and green. It was a soft cushion under them when they lay on the blanket.

He was on his back looking at the sky. She moved to be closer to him, so she could look into his face.

"I owe this to you," she said.

"I helped," he said. "But not so much."

"It feels like you have been as much a part of this as I have. Lately it seems wrong when you leave and go back to the Circle Three."

He did not answer, but picked a long blade of grass and put it between his lips.

"I shouldn't have said that, maybe," she said. "It isn't a woman's place to talk that way. But I don't know that I ever learned my place, Quiller. If I ever did, I forgot it a long time ago."

He looked at her for the first time since she had spoken. "You want more out of me than you are getting," he said. "I think about it. All the time. I been tempted, I have to say that."

"What holds you back, Quiller? This place is going all right now. It is going to go somewhere. It could take both of us along with it."

"Hell, the place is fine," he said.

"Something with me, then?"

"You? Any man who knew you would want you. I do. And I am close to trying to take you sometimes."

She bent her neck so that her face was close to his. "What stops you, Quiller?"

"I am a cowboy," he said.

She drew back. "What can that have to do with it?"

"There is a reason I'm a cowboy. I like to be loose on my feet. I like to do what I want, and when. A loose rein, you might say. If I want to wander, I do it."

"Quiller, that is nonsense. Where do you wander to so often? Two years you've been at the Circle Three and I don't see you trying to jump the fence. To go where? Do what? Be a cowboy someplace else?"

"If I want."

"You're a man, not a coyote. Animals have to wander, maybe, but not you. And even an animal knows to stay in one place where the food and the water are good."

"Say . . . say I married you, if we're talking about that.

Say we did get married. And I decided this ranch and this valley didn't suit me no more. And I wanted to try some place else. I couldn't up and leave, could I?"

"No," she said.

"There. You see? You see why I'm shy of settling down?"

"I never heard such claptrap. Who teaches men these things?"

"Rose, don't push me," he said. "I got to take things at my own speed."

"You can leave at your own speed," she said. "You can do that too, you know."

"Maybe I will," he said. "Maybe I have that feeling right now."

He left her alone to gather up the food, fold the blanket, return to the cabin.

He was back a few evenings later. She knew better now than to press him. Then they fought again. This time it was about fences; she wanted to put some up for the first time. He thought that was a bad idea.

"You can't tell me," she said, "that it doesn't help the grass. I know it does. Anytime you can keep cattle off the grass and give it a chance to grow, it helps."

"It helps some," he said. "I ain't saying it don't."

"If I had just three or four different pastures,' she said, "I could keep the cattle in a herd and move the herd from one pasture to the next. Wouldn't let them spend more than a month or so in any one, then move them to where the grass is highest."

"I know what you want to do," he said. "I understand that. But I think you could spend your money better. What this place needs now is more cows to fill up the land you got, fences or no. That is what you ought to be buying."

"I don't think so," she said.

"I can see you don't. Go buy your fence, then. But it is a damn waste of money."

"It is my money," she said. "And my ranch. Seems to me if you know so much you would have your own place by now to do what you wanted with it."

She regretted the words as soon as she heard them. "I'm sorry, Quiller," she said. "That was terrible. I'm sorry."

"You said it. Maybe you have something there. It's plain, ain't it, that the only way I will have anything in life is by marrying you?"

"Don't think that way," she said. "I want you to understand. I had to work so hard to get what I have and hold on to it. I still hold on hard. Too hard, maybe."

That was the end of the fight. But her words and all that lay behind them were still with him later when he returned to the bunkhouse and his brother told him to pack his saddlebags and roll up his blankets. The big boss himself, Mr. Ray Newsome, wanted to see them in Indian Oak.

Quiller was ready to leave, and the leaving felt good.

For a while, Ray Newsome had forgotten about her.

The night he saw another man kissing Rose Ellen and riding from her place, he was purged. He knew then that if he tried and if he did the right things with his life in the next few weeks he would be rid of her. He would not care about her any longer.

He lived in his town home and tried to keep busy with work. The railroad was pushing down the valley, and several times a week he rode to the end of the line to see how far the wood and steel had extended. For the first time he kept Rose Ellen out of his mind. Then he heard about the water well.

First he thought about his own ranch, what it would mean to have water and use all the grassland. He wondered how he could dig such a well, and whether there was water under his land.

Next he thought about Rose Ellen, how happy she must be. And triumphant, too, because she would prosper now after all that he had done against her. That was how she entered his mind again.

He told himself that he was only curious. One day when he was riding with the locomotive down the track—it was almost finished now, with a new depot and pens and docks and ramps at the south end—he made the engineer stop. The track here ran east of the Mansos, just a few hundred yards inside the fence that he had first ordered around Orrin Sample's spread. Ray got down and walked to the fence, climbed through it, and walked some more. No harm, he argued to himself, in looking for one of these water wells. He saw only a few cows and open grassland, and he thought of Rose Ellen riding the land and making something of nothing the way she had.

Have to admire her, he thought. Give the woman her due, mulish as she is.

Now the image of the stranger who had left her home that night nagged at him. Maybe she was lonely, he thought. Of course. Maybe this character was taking advantage of her.

He decided to find the stranger. Just to satisfy his own curiosity, he told himself. He knew from the brand on the horse that night that the man was one of his hands. He did not know many of them now, but a few days at the grub table and a few casual questions gave him a name. The next day Ray asked his foreman to point out the cowboy named Quiller Meacham. The next morning Ray ate breakfast with the hands. He took a chair down the table from Quiller, at an angle that allowed him to stare at the cowboy, study his face and remember him, without seeming obvious about it.

Within a week he had convinced himself that Rose Ellen did not belong with a common cowhand. And he had convinced himself further that Rose Ellen might yet come into his life if that cowhand were out of the way.

Donnie Lee

Sue E. was with me every time after that when I went to talk to Gandy Meacham about Rose Ellen. There was something between Sue E. and the old man that I could see but could not explain. The questions I asked him was never quite right. Sue E. would get impatient and so would Gandy Meacham, like they knew all the lines already and I was the one slow catching on. After a while I gave up asking questions and let Sue E. handle it.

She was the one who got the story out of him about how he had come to leave Texas. I'd figured that he just up and left on his own. Which he did, to look at it one way. But there was more to it, and he told it all that night.

It happened when Sue E. mentioned the name Ray Newsome to him. He got the same kind of look that come over him when the pain got real bad. I started to go for his pills. But he stopped me.

He said, No pills can help what I feel when I hear that man's name.

Sue E. said, Did he hurt you, Quiller?

He said, No, not exactly. I don't even know that I can blame him. But he brings back bad memories.

He stopped talking the way he done when he had to think about what he was saying.

Then he said, Some things a man does he would as soon forget. But he can't. That's the way with life. You lose the good things but you can't get rid of what makes you ashamed.

285

I was so young then, he said. So much I didn't know and I thought I knew it all. Rose Ellen, she had it over me there. She knew what was worth caring about and what wasn't. It come down to me thinking I had to be free to up and fly away like a bird any time I pleased. I couldn't have it any other way.

He said, And there was more to it. Rose Ellen hung on tough to what she had, and when it looked like I couldn't get her to let loose of it right away I didn't want any part of it. All I had to do was be patient. She would have shared it eventually. But I didn't have it in me to wait.

Oh, he said, I wish I knew then what I learned later. But you never learn until it is too late and you find out the hard way. Nobody can just tell you.

He looked at me.

I could tell you things, Donnie Lee, he said. You'd listen and say yes you understood. But you wouldn't understand. You would go out and make your mistakes just the same.

He said, What I am trying to tell you is that when Ray Newsome said he wanted to talk to me he got me at just the wrong time. I don't believe he ever knew it. But when I walked in to see him I was still full of piss and vinegar about Rose Ellen not giving me enough slack, and holding so tight to what she had.

I want you to remember that part, he said. About the way I felt the day Ray Newsome called me in his office. Maybe you won't think so bad of me if you do.

Sue E. said, We won't think bad of you, Quiller.

He said, Don't talk so soon. What happened was, Ray Newsome called me in his office and said he would give me one thousand dollars and a train ticket to get out of town and stay gone. And I took it. My brother stayed and I went.

He said, The bad part is that I knew he was doing it to buy me off Rose Ellen. And I still took the money. He didn't come out and say so, but I knew it all the time. Rose Ellen told me about the bad feelings between them. When I thought about that in his office I knew it was not just bad feelings but good that was once between them.

He said, You see? Ray Newsome wanted me out of his way. I didn't take it at first. For what that is worth. When I seen what he was up to I said no, I didn't want any part of it. He told me I was out of a job no matter what I decided. That put it right back on me. There was only one other place in the valley, and that was the Box CF with Rose Ellen. And I was to the end of my string there. It was marry her or nothing. We could not go on much longer the way we was. I had to make my move if I was going to stay.

He said, I was thinking on my feet there with Ray Newsome looking at me, waiting for an answer. I told myself that I couldn't tie me down with a woman that way. I couldn't just jump into something as serious as marrying. I was out of a job and that meant I was out of the valley too and I told myself, Hell, if you are leaving anyways you might as well take the money and the ticket. And that is what I did. That afternoon I was on the train and I never did come back until now.

The tears busted out on Sue E.'s face right about then. I tried to stop her crying but Quiller said to let her go.

He said, When you are young you think your chances come along thick as flies. You think you got all the time to pick the one that suits you when you are ready for it. But it ain't that way. When the chance comes you got to take it. I didn't get but one Rose Ellen come my way and I sold that chance. Six months later the money was spent and I was married to a gal that I didn't care about and all I got out of it was a daughter. And eventually you, Donnie Lee.

He said, I don't know. Maybe it weren't the money. When you think a thing over too much it changes and you never remember the way it was. I sure to hell wish I'd left that money on Ray Newsome's desk. And I wish I'd've gone straight to Rose Ellen even more.

Chapter 28

The fastest and the most beautiful horse on the Circle Three was a big chestnut gelding. Ray Newsome entered it in quarter-mile match races in the region. Once he won a bet of five thousand dollars with the horse. It had muscles that showed taut and full through its glistening coat. Two weeks after Quiller Meacham had left the valley, Ray pinned a note to the gelding's hackamore and told a ranch hand to take it to Rose Ellen.

The note read: "For you. Respectful, Ray."

He waited all day for the ranch hand to return. He could not work; he was too nervous. Late in the afternoon the ranch hand came up the path to the big house. The chestnut was on a lead. The note was gone.

Ray asked what had happened.

"She read the note," said the hand. "Then she told me to take the horse back, she couldn't keep it."

"How did she say it? Like she was riled?"

"No sir, I wouldn't say so. I ain't positive but I believe she had something of a smile on her when she read it."

"She did?"

"I think so. I wouldn't put my life on it."

"What else? How did it happen?"

"It looked to me like she wanted to keep it. She looked it over and touched it—like, run a hand down the horse's back. You could tell she thought it was a dandy. So I asked her was she sure she didn't want it."

"And what did she say?"

"She didn't say nothing right off. She just stepped back a pace and looked at it some more. Then she said no, take it out of there. So I did."

"But she wasn't hot?"

"I can't say she was."

The next day he sent the hand back to Rose Ellen with the chestnut and also with a black mare and the mare's colt. There was another note that read: "For you and yours. Respectfuly, Ray."

This time the hand returned without the horses.

"She took them," Ray said when he met the hand outside the stable.

"She sure did."

"Tell me how it happened."

"First off she looked a mite cross. Then it was like she couldn't stay cross and she smiled. She read the note and she looked at the horses and she said they was beautiful critters, wasn't they? Then she said she would keep 'em, and she told me to pass a message on to you."

"Tell me."

"She said to tell you she didn't have room in her stable for no more of your calling cards. She said next time you got something to say you better say it in person."

He called on her the next day with a big bunch of wild flowers that he had picked along the way. Charlie answered the knock and went to get his mother. When she came to the door, she looked at him for the first time in more than eight years.

His presence at her door startled her. She had expected him sometime but she could not have prepared herself for it. She could feel her heart beating fast, insistent. She looked at his face.

He was not so different, she thought. Paler than she had remembered. The thrust of his jaw made her throat tighten; she had seen him do that so often before, a gesture of bravado when he was shrinking inside.

Her eyes swept over him. She glanced up and down and let her eyes settle again on his face. A moment frozen, and he locked in with it until she went one way or the other.

"Those flowers will wilt in the heat," she said, hoping to sound matter-of-fact. "They are too lovely to have that happen." She opened the screen door and took the flowers from him.

"Come in and sit down," she said. She groped for easy words that would not give away the shock that she felt. "Little Charlie has made a mess, as usual, but I think you can find a chair that isn't full of toys."

She left with the flowers. Ray took off his hat and sat down. He looked at the boy, who looked, unblinking, back at him.

In the kitchen, she filled a jar with water. Just Ray, she told herself. Just Ray. You know how to act with Ray.

She walked into the front room and put the jar of flowers on a table. "I'm taken aback," she said. "I don't know why. I realize that I left the gate open, so to speak."

He watched her, and saw lines at the corners of her eyes where there had been none before. Her right hand went to her hair; a few strands had fallen from a bun that she wore at the back of her head. Her hands smoothed some wrinkles in her skirt and went back to her hair again.

"But I didn't expect you to be here," she said. "Not so fast, anyway. Oh, I don't know what I expected."

Something was wrong, he thought. The girl in her, maybe. Her voice sounded flatter to his ear now. But she was still Rose Ellen, he thought, and he would put the music back in her voice again.

"You like them horses?" he said. "Ain't that chestnut a beaut?"

"For a fact, it is. I didn't know what I ought to do. I thought I should send them back, but then I thought that Charlie Fowler didn't raise me up to be a fool either."

She sat a few feet away from him. Time to find out if this is the Ray I knew, she thought. You could always talk straight to Ray.

"It would have been easier for me to make up my mind," she said, "if I'd known why you were doing it."

"You have a weakness for horses," he said, "or did, anyways."

"Still do, for good ones. But that doesn't say why."

"Maybe I wanted to show off some," he said. The words jumped out before he could try the sound of them in his head. "And I wanted you to think good of me. That was a big reason."

"You expect those horses to do a lot."

"I wanted to see you again and talk with you again."

"You see me," she said. She was resisting him. She did not want him to think that he could appear at her door and make her forget the years and all that had happened.

"You look the same as ever," he said.

"Don't say that. I know it isn't true. And anyway I don't feel the same. There have been changes inside of me that you don't know anything about."

"Been a lot of changes everywhere," he said. He thought, Don't fight me, Rose. Please don't fight me this way.

"You're looking at one of them," she said. "My boy, Charlie. Charlie, this is Mr. Newsome. Dora is asleep. I have a woman lives with me now and helps me with the children. I couldn't mother them alone and do a decent job of running the spread now that we are going forward again."

"I heard about your good luck," he said.

"Don't call it luck. I found a way to do what I had to do to survive."

There was a bite in the words. He gripped the hat in his hands and said, "Rose, you want me here?"

Just like Ray Newsome, she thought—so proud, wouldn't be caught anywhere he wasn't wanted.

"Oh," she said, "I don't see why not."

"I want us to be friends again."

"It doesn't happen as easy as saying, Ray. Words don't make it be."

"Can we walk somewhere?" he said. "Just to get out in the air?"

"Ray Newsome," she said, "I don't know how far I want to go with you."

"Doesn't have to be far. Up the road a ways."

"I don't mean that."

"You afraid of me?"

"I probably should be," she said. She left the room to tell Inez that she would be gone a few minutes. Then she told

Charlie to mind Inez. Ray followed her out the front door.

"I can show you one of my wells," she said. "You ought to have water, too. I don't know why it wouldn't be there."

"Oh, yes," he said. "I have plenty of people telling me I got water. What I can't find is somebody who knows how you got to yours, and can do the same for me."

She was walking ahead of him. He could not see her smile. But he heard it in her words.

"You'll find a way, I'm sure," she said. "Sooner or later. Until then, I suppose you'll just have to get by the way you always have."

They tramped through the grass in the field behind her cabin.

"If you stay around," she said, "you'll find I'm different from the girl you knew."

"You always were a hard case," he said.

"I mean it," she said. The shock of his visit was gone now. She wanted him to know that she was a woman, with hard years behind her, proud that she had survived them.

"This is not a joke," she said. "The things that happen to a person change them. With me it was either find a way through the hard times or give it all up. I am not a quitter, so I found a way. But it changed me. I am not what I used to be."

"Somewhere inside you," he said, "part of you is the same."

That made her angry. "You can see that?" she said. "You are with me five minutes and you can see right inside me, know what I am, clear through to the other end?"

"I don't have to see. I know."

"You might be right," she said. "But I don't let that out too often. Don't think I am going to let it loose now that you are on the scene again. You, far as I'm concerned, I don't even know you."

"I'm not so different either. Same old Ray, when you get down to cases."

"Some parts of that fellow I liked," she said. "Some parts I didn't."

They reached the well. It had a cap and a valve on it now. She opened the valve and the water gushed out.

"It never ends," she said. "It keeps coming, always so cool no matter how hot the day is."

"Rose," he said, "about that fence a few years back—"

"No," she said. "Don't talk about what is gone. It won't work if you do. If we are going to be friends we have to start fresh. You and me the way we are today. We can't fall back on the good parts of what we had before and we can't get tripped up by the bad. You and me today is the only way we have a chance."

"You want to try it?" he asked. "Friends, I mean."

"We have to go it slow," she said. "Don't go expecting too much from me. You will be disappointed if you do."

From that moment he pursued her. He was cautious at first, almost formal in the way he spoke to her and behaved with her. She was defiant, daring him to make a mistake, to set one foot wrong in his approach. He did not. He was as kind and patient as she demanded.

She was ready for his attentions. Quiller's leaving—without explanation, without even good-bye—had rocked her. But it left her alone again, and she was not used to being alone.

Ray was doing everything right. She remembered why she had loved him before. And he was all the things now that he had been then. He was manly in a way that few men are, with a gentleness that comes from strength. He was handsome and he could laugh and he made her feel beautiful. He loved the land, as she did. She felt her defenses giving way. He was winning her.

He liked showing off his possessions. She toured his stables with him and walked the streets of Indian Oak beside him one night when they had both drunk too much wine at dinner. "This place is mine," he said, "the whole shebang." He said it, not with an arrogance that would have repelled her, but with a childish delight.

They rode on his train one night on a platform car that carried a table and two chairs and a serving cart with their dinner. The platform car was hitched to the locomotive and the tender. There were no other cars, no other passengers. He called it his moonlight special, and they laughed together when the cinders blew into their plates.

One night he gave her an emerald ring. The stone was as big as her thumbnail.

"I can't take this," she said.

"Sure you can."

"I don't know."

"You don't like it? I'll give you another one, a better one."

"No," she said. "It is beautiful. But it must have been so expensive. I've been so used to scrimping and putting away every extra bit."

"Put it on," he said.

She did. She kept the ring.

They lived so differently, she thought. He had so much. He spent without second thoughts. He had power and he did what he wanted. He mentioned casually to her once that he had one hundred and ninety-three people on his payroll. And only sixty of them, he said, rode a horse on their job.

One evening she went with him to a dinner party in Austin. Ray had bought her a gown for the occasion, yellow silk with a high, tight waist and a cascade of flounces down the front of the skirt. Not in years had she worn such a dress, nor primped as she did that evening. She powdered her face and put long curls in her hair.

Ray sent a hand to pick her up and drive her to the railroad track. The train stopped for her on its trip north. She rode it to Indian Oak and Ray met her at the depot. They walked together across the platform to a special Central Texas excursion car. Half a dozen times on the way to Austin the train stopped to pick up passengers who were bound to the same party. A porter kept their glasses full of champagne. The people around her laughed and drank.

At the party she met politicians and railroad men and businessmen. Their eyes followed her, and she caught more than one of them staring at her as she ate her dinner.

Ray spoke into her ear. "You are beautiful," he said. "See the way they look at you? You belong in this life."

The party went on into the night. For a while Rose Ellen felt removed from it. The gown felt wrong on her after pants and a shirt. She wondered whether the men would admire her if they saw her with her pants muddy up to the knees. But the music played on and she danced and drank, and soon she was a part of it, and enjoying it, and it was the ranch and hard work that seemed distant.

At daybreak the train returned to Indian Oak. At each stop more passengers got off, sleepy and subdued. They rode alone the last few miles into Indian Oak, Ray with an arm around Rose Ellen. At the depot they stood alone on the platform. Ray took her in his arms, buried his face in her hair, her neck.

"Come on with me," he said.

She went with him to his town house. She let herself climb the stairs to his bedroom. That did not seem out of place with the rest of the night. She was going to let it happen.

He undressed her and ran his hands over her body. He lay beside her on the bed. She reached out and held him.

Later her head rested in the crook of his arm. They were together in bed, looking at the new morning.

"Make this permanent," he said. "Marry me. I mean, right away."

"This is too important to rush," she said. There was something left of the caution she had learned.

"Then just say you will. This is a good life, Rose. All it needs is you to add that last part. The part that means most to me."

"You live high," she said. "Not the way I'm used to."

"Telling me you don't like it?"

"It has its advantages," she said.

Beats what I've been used to, she thought, in every way you can name. But she kept that to herself.

"Think what a life we can have together," he said. "We'll make it right this time."

She was close to saying yes. The image tempted her: the two of them like king and queen in this valley that would be all their own, with more wealth than she had ever known before, and no more work than she wanted to take on.

But she would not be shoved into it.

"You don't give up," she said.

"Tell me you will."

"Not now. This is the wrong time. I don't want to have to live by what I say now. I need some time."

She could not sleep there; her head was too full. So she took the train south. The same ranch hand brought her home. She kissed her children, said hello to Inez, and then fell asleep in her room around noon.

The baby's shriek woke her. Rose jerked herself awake and was sitting up in bed when Inez burst through the door.

"Fire!" she screamed. "Miss Rose! Bad fire in the kitchen!"

"Get the children out," Rose Ellen said. "You hear me? Out in front so I know they are there."

She yanked on jeans and a shirt and boots. The fire snapped and popped in the kitchen, and smoke streamed in tiny insistent curls from spaces between the boards in the wall of her room. She ran out of the house. Inez was there with the children.

"You stay there," she said. "Keep them there, Inez."

Then she ran back into her bedroom. She grabbed a pile of papers that Sample had kept tied with string in the bottom of the closet. The deed was among them. She grabbed clothes for herself, went into the children's room, and took more for them. When she passed the kitchen door she could feel the heat. She ran outside again and dumped the clothes at her feet. She stood, holding the papers, and watched her home burn.

It went fast. The flames came through the room above the kitchen and then the wind spread it across the roof. Black smoke rose from the flames. Rose Ellen put one arm around Charlie. Inez cradled the baby in her arms and cried. It all happened so fast, she said, no way to stop it.

Alvarez saw the smoke and came running with two of the hands. They stood with the others and watched the cabin burn. The roaring was loud, and at its height the fire was so hot it drove them back. In less than an hour it was gone. Only a few tongues of flame flickered from the ashes.

"Where are we going to live, Mama?" Charlie said.

"Right now we have the new bunkhouse," she told him. "There are beds there, and room for all of us."

"Are we going to get a new house?" he asked.

"You know it," she said. There was not even a question. She felt that her property had been marred, defaced. She knew that it would have to be restored.

"We need a house," she said. "We live here. This is where we belong. We'll build it up again, is what we'll do."

For a moment she did not realize what she had just been saying. Then she considered her words, and she knew that they were true. This was her life. The years and the work she had spent here had claimed it for her. She could never leave it. Nothing Ray Newsome could give her would ever mean as much to her as what she had already.

The next morning Ray heard of the fire. He came to visit her, found her among the ashes, her arms and her face black. She was shoveling out charred wood, cleaning the foundation for a new house.

"We need to talk," she said.

"Clean up. I'll wait."

"No. We better talk."

They sat together under a cottonwood tree.

"I can't leave this place," she said. "I can't marry you. Oh, I could, and we would probably do pretty well. But I'm not going to."

"I have heard this before," he said.

"This isn't the same. We were kids then, and there wasn't much difference between us. That isn't so anymore, and that is why I'm telling you no. You want me to come into your life. But I have things I can't leave behind. They mean too much to me. I worked too hard for them."

"You mean this spread."

"This spread is part of it. I can't run it from your ranch house, can I? And maybe I don't want to see it swallowed up by all the rest that you own."

"Done in by a piece of land," he said. "You know, I could buy a spread like this the way a grocer sells a can of coffee."

She ignored his antagonism. He had some anger coming, she knew. This wouldn't be easy for him, and she wanted to explain.

"You ever lay awake nights," she asked, "thinking about what you're going to do with the Circle Three and your town and your railroad?"

"All the time," he said.

"Same for me," she said. "I get to thinking about my

place and I can't sleep for all the ideas running around my head. Would you give yours up? For me? Even for me?''

"You can keep your ranch," he said, "if that is what bothers you."

She took his hand and held it tight. She wanted him to understand. "This ranch is the part you see," she said. "But there is more I have now that I didn't have eight years ago. Like the way I live and the way I look at what happens around me. You have those, too, and they're different now from mine."

She touched his cheek. "We aren't like most," she said. "We got a lot inside us, and it is strong. That didn't matter when we were together and changing the same ways. But eight years we've been changing in different ways, and that is too long for people like us. Eight years, and every day you find something that is important to you, and you put it away with all the rest that is important to you, and pretty soon you've got too much to give up for somebody else."

He stood up. He slapped his hat against the tree. "Tell you one thing," he said. "The second time is easier than the first. I been as low as I can get with you and I know what it's like. Second time around can't be as bad."

"It hurts me, too," she said.

"You say that, but I don't know it."

"It's true. There's a part of me that wants to go along with you, a part of me that needs you."

"Then you won't be happy," he said. "Not all the way. You know that, don't you? If there's a part of you that wants me, then it won't let you forget."

"You have it right," she said. "There'll be days when I'm miserable. When I'll be sure I made a mistake. But a long time ago I stopped trying to be happy all the time. You can't have it."

He put the hat on his head and he looked at her. "I hope you don't think it will be different with anybody else," he said. "Any other man, it'll be the same."

"I know that."

"You know what that means, don't you?"

She answered softly. "It means I will be going it alone from here on," she said.

*   *   *

Not long afterward she heard that Ray had married the daughter of one of the Central Texas's directors. Her name was Lucille Wheelock. The news brought to Rose Ellen a certain melancholy. For a few days the ranch seemed more like a prison than a refuge and a home. But the feeling passed.

Ray changed the name of his town. He took the first two letters of his wife's first name and put them with his own first name and called the town Luray. There was some resistance to the change, but the citizens came around eventually. It was his town.

The year 1895 brought two events that stood out in the procession of days. In April, Lucille Newsome gave birth to a boy. She and her husband named him Robert E. Lee Newsome. And in June, Charlie Sample died of a rattlesnake bite before his mother could get him to a doctor.

Chapter 29

Ray Newsome left his office in Luray and walked around the corner to the livery stable. He stood in the door and tapped the heel of one boot against the floor. He didn't like to wait. The cowboy who was sitting in the corner reading the Luray *Clarion* looked up and saw him, threw aside the newspaper, and jumped to his feet so fast his spurs rang.

"You ready, Mr. Newsome? Didn't nobody tell me. I'd have her ready for you if I'd knowed."

"Just get it," Ray Newsome said.

The cowboy went to the back of the stable. Ray could not see him, but he heard the wheeze and the cough, the wheeze and the cough and the wheeze and the cough and the wall-shaking bang in the same sequence as always. Even the horses were accustomed to it now. White smoke that burned the nostrils drifted to the front of the stable. Then a surge of mechanical noises: rattles and tickings and a nonstop series of muted bangs. A metallic clank; more smoke; and the automobile rolled out of the stall and up to the door of the stable. The cowboy moved across to the passenger seat. Ray Newsome sat behind the wheel. He had to take off his hat to pull a pair of goggles over his eyes. There was another clank from the gearbox and the car lurched forward, through town, south to the ranch house.

His car was the first in the valley, a new 1910 Thomas Flyer with wooden spoke wheels and brass fittings and an engine compartment like a metal chicken coop. When the weather was good he traveled in the car from his home to his office and back.

He lived in every way now the life of the rich and privileged In 1901 he had torn down the home that Earl and Irene had built. In its place he put a mansion styled in the Victorian manner, designed by an architect in Kansas City. They had house servants, not just kitchen help but maids and butlers. He and his wife and their son had visited Europe three times, bringing back paintings and furniture and rugs for their home. Lucille understood these things, and he trusted her taste.

In his room he washed the road grime off his face and put on a fresh starched shirt and tie. His clothes were custom-tailored and were cut more fully every year. He wasn't yet fat, he told himself. But he was heavier than he had ever been. He blamed his job; he got out of the office so seldom now.

His wife was seated at the table already when he went down. This was not the main dining table, which could seat twenty-four with formal arrangements, but a smaller table for ten in an anteroom of the kitchen. Lucille was at one end of the table. She turned the side of her face to him so that he could kiss her cheek. He went to the other end of the table, where his place was set.

"Where's Bobby?" he asked.

"How good of you to notice," she said.

"Ah, hell, what has he done now?"

"Sent home again," she said. "Fistfighting."

"He likes to mix it up," Ray said.

"Such surroundings he is in there," she said. "The sons and daughters of cowboys, tavern keepers, even Mexicans. It isn't right for him."

"I don't want to send him away, have him turn into a nancy who can't stand up for himself when he has to."

"He should be with his own kind," she said.

"He is with his own kind. This is where he lives. Sending him off to school won't change that. How would it look? It's my town, practically my school. I gave them the land to put it on. How would it look for me to send him away to school?"

A butler came in with plates of cold cucumber soup. He served Lucille and then Ray.

"I'll talk to him," Ray said.

"Please do. And while you are about it I wish you would correct the way he speaks to me. So smart and full of sass. He has no respect."

"I will," Ray said. "I'll do that."

They finished the meal without another word, and then Ray went to his son's room. He found the boy lying on the floor with his feet propped against a wall. He had a pocket-knife in one hand and was shaving long, thin slices off a piece of wood. The shavings were scattered on his chest and on the floor.

Ray looked down at him. "Your mother tells me you had a problem today at school."

The boy glanced at him and then went back to the knife and the wood. More slivers fell away from the edge of the knife.

"Is that so?" Ray asked. "Is it?"

"Nothing much," the boy said without taking his eyes off his hands. "I got in a beef."

"With who? You throw any punches?"

"Ezra Paine's son. I had to clean his plow for him."

"Him? Tiny as he is?"

"He had it coming," the boy said.

The anger blossomed in Ray, and he let it show in his words. "Stand up when you talk to me," he said. "And put away that knife. Don't you have anything better to do with your time? Look at the damn mess you're making."

The boy expelled a big sigh. He slowly took his feet off the wall, folded the blade into the knife, brushed the shavings from his chest, and stood in front of his father. The boy was as tall as Ray already. He was not yet so full in the shoulders and the chest, but the outlines were there in the big bones, and he was still growing.

He stood now with hands on hips and calculated boredom on his face.

"Why can't you stay out of trouble?" Ray said. "Don't you know how bad it looks for me to have my son sent home from school once a week for one reason or the next?"

He waited for a reaction.

"Anything else?" the boy said.

"Yes. Your mother says you have been smart to her again. I want an end to that. You show her some respect or you'll have me to deal with."

"What are you going to do?"

"Put you over my knee and whup you if I have to," Ray said.

The boy looked into his face and said, "Maybe. But not for long."

"I am going to Kansas City tomorrow. I'll be gone a week at most. When I get back I want to hear that you've behaved yourself. If I hear any different you'll pay with your hide."

The boy said nothing.

"And clean this damn mess up," Ray said. "You could have a rat's nest here and not know it."

Ray went downstairs to his study and closed the door behind him. He could shut out his problems in here. He wanted now to be far from them. He wanted them to belong to someone else.

The problems were all at home. At the office there was nothing that he could not fix or change or talk through. He was master of that part of his world. Home was different. Here the problems seemed nebulous. They evaded his touch. How could he make things right, he had thought more than once, if he could not even see what was wrong?

He knew that something was not right with his son. Bobby was turning out bad. But Ray knew no way of getting what he wanted from the boy. Obviously he had failed to provide the ingredients that go into a good son. But he didn't know what those were, or how he might start doing it now. Sometimes he told himself that Bobby wasn't such a bad son. Lazier than Ray would have liked, maybe. Ray had taken for granted that the boy would be as eager as he himself had been to take part in the ranch. He had assumed that his problems would be coping with Bobby's eagerness to take control of the holdings. He had looked forward to that, a rivalry to spur him and keep him fresh; the business would be all the better for it. And soon enough he would have made the boy a full partner, a reward for his impatience. But Bobby had never showed an interest in what his father did or how the money came.

Ray called that laziness. He told himself that it was not a

serious flaw. A disappointment, maybe, but no disaster.

The boy did fight too much. When he felt generous Ray convinced himself that his son had spirit and feist, and that a few scraps were inevitable. And that would account for the disrespect he flashed at his parents. At other times Ray told himself that there was no ignoring the truth, which was that Bobby was spoiled and slothful and a disgrace to his family.

But even that brought him no closer to a solution.

His failure with his son might have been easier to take if Ray had not felt that he was fighting the battle alone. Lucille was no happier with Bobby than he. But that was the end of it. Did she, Ray sometimes wondered, agonize and wrestle with the problem as he did? She gave no sign of it. She seemed as detached from this as she was from everything else.

Here the failure was even more vague, though just as apparent to Ray. He could not even say how he would make his marriage different. He would want Lucille to care more, maybe. To show more feeling. But that seemed a flimsy bill of charges. Maybe, he thought, he was asking too much of her and too much of marriage. He did not know what other marriages were like. Even after sixteen years he was not sure what he should ask from this one.

He did know two things. One was that his marriage and his son were not what he had assumed they would be. And he was sure that he could be happier, that he had reservoirs of joy and fulfillment that had not been tapped for many years.

But he also carried with him the lesson, long and hard in the learning, that nobody ever gets everything he wants.

Rose Ellen and her daughter were talking about college. Dora was finishing her last year of high school and she wanted more education.

"I'm not saying," Rose Ellen told her one night, "that I'm against it. I want you to do all you can do."

"That is what I want," the girl said. "I want to study English literature."

Rose Ellen was washing dishes in the kitchen. Inez had the evening off and Dora had not offered to help.

"I don't think English literature will help you much on the ranch," Rose Ellen said.

"Mama, they don't teach agriculture at Barnard."

"Why do you want to go so far away?" said Rose Ellen. "They have a good university right up in Austin."

"I want to go East," Dora said.

"What's back there that you can't find here?"

"Mama, let's not go around with that again. I want to see something besides cows and grass for a while."

Rose Ellen scrubbed a plate and dipped it into a pan of hot water. "I wish you cared to learn more about this place," she said. "Someday you will own it."

"Mama, you're going to live forever. Don't talk that way."

"I'm not," Rose Ellen said. "Someday this will be yours and you will have to know how to make it work."

"Then I'll hire somebody," she said. "That's what foremen are for."

Every time, the talk about English literature and Barnard and going East came down to Dora wanting what she did not have, and finding no satisfaction in what was hers already. Rose Ellen had known for several years now that Dora would leave when she got a chance. The girl loved her mother, but she felt nothing for the ranch and the valley. She could hardly ride, and rarely did. She spent her time reading books and magazines from Boston, New York, Philadelphia. She had never been east of St. Louis, but she knew Manhattan better than she knew the back sections of the Box CF.

"It means money," Dora said. "I know that."

"We have that money," Rose Ellen said. "That is not what stops me from saying yes right off."

Rose Ellen wiped her hands on a dish towel and she faced her daughter. She put her hands on Dora's shoulders and gripped her hard. "I am forty-five years old," she said. "People die that young. So tell me the truth. If I died tonight, what would you do?"

"Cry a long time."

"About the ranch. Would you stay here and run it? What would you do?"

"I don't know what I'd do, Mama."

"You know."

Dora's lower lip trembled. "I'd sell it, Mama, if I could. I wouldn't stay here. I'd be too lonely here, and anyway there are other places I want to live."

"That's what stops me," Rose Ellen said. "I am not anxious to send you off someplace where you will want to stay."

Dora held her. "I don't want to hurt you, Mama," she said.

"It is not you," said Rose Ellen. "I don't know where you got your ideas but I can't blame you for them. We just don't see the world the same, you and me. That's what is so hard to take. It is hard for anybody to swallow that someone they love doesn't care about the same things they do. What is important to me means nothing to you. And to be honest, I have to say that what you care about doesn't mean so much to me. So there we are."

"I don't know how I got that way either," Dora said.

"I will send you to school in the East if you want it so much," Rose Ellen said. "You knew I would. It is just that some things take getting used to."

She held tight to her daughter. She meant what she had told her. She didn't blame Dora for her feelings. She didn't blame her, that was true. But she still faced years alone now, alone on the ranch and alone with her love for the valley, and that was not easy to take.

Chapter 30

The smoke and the noise bothered her. She was not accustomed to such commotion in her own home. So Rose Ellen Sample stepped out on her front porch and looked over her land. The laughter and the music and the shouting followed her, seeping through the walls.

A blast of wind caught her in the face. It was cool and damp; what had been a warm, bright June afternoon was suddenly dark now. To the north the sky boiled purple. The grass on the lawn bent flat in the wind; leaves shook loose from the trees and specks of grit stung her cheeks. In the near pasture the cows huddled together, turning their heads away from the wind. Nothing blew like a norther. Nothing else so drained light from the day and color from the landscape.

It was Dora's wedding day. She was marrying a Philadelphia boy and going there to live with him. What Rose Ellen had expected and feared during four years of college was fact now. Dora was never going to live on the ranch. Since her freshman year she had spent only summers anyway.

The front door opened behind Rose Ellen, and Inez stood beside her. "She's ready," Inez said.

They came in out of the wind. Dora was standing at the bottom of the stairs that led up from the front room. She had changed from her wedding dress, and now was wearing a long black skirt with a jacket and a white blouse. The visitors from the East—college friends and the groom's family—were behind her, talking among themselves in the accents that Rose Ellen had found so flat and clipped.

All week there had been strangers in the house. Two days earlier the groom's father had stood on the porch with Rose Ellen, looking out on the grassland.

"A great deal of land here," he had said. "A great deal. Although I must say I find it a trifle . . . monotonous."

Now he was walking behind Dora and her husband, carrying a valise in each hand. They were all leaving for Philadelphia that evening, and Dora was going with them.

Dora put her arms around Rose Ellen. "Thank you, Mama," she said. "This is such a happy day. I'm sorry I have to spoil it for you by going away now."

"You have a husband to follow," Rose Ellen said.

"We'll be back soon, Mama. I promise. I'll make Gerald bring me back real soon."

Rose Ellen said nothing. She knew that the valley of the Mansos was a long way from Philadelphia.

Outside were three carriages and a wagon. The visitors loaded their bags into the wagon. Dora and her husband got into one of the carriages alone; the other two filled with visitors.

"Why, it looks like rain," Gerald's mother said. "And an hour ago there wasn't a cloud."

"We call them northers," Rose Ellen said. She was standing on the porch with Inez beside her. "They move fast and they throw a chill in the air. But they blow by just as quick, most of the time."

"I should hope so," the woman said.

The bags were loaded and the carriages were full. Dora looked up to Rose Ellen and waved; Rose Ellen tried to smile, and she nodded. The first of the carriages lurched forward, and led the procession down the road, away from the house. The wind blew into Rose Ellen's face. The rain would be coming soon, she knew. She could almost taste it on the air now.

She squinted as she watched the wagon and the carriages withdraw. She brushed away moisture that formed at her eyes.

The wind was strong, she thought. Even for a norther.

*   *   *

Rose Ellen began to mark time's passing as much by events as by dates. The numbers did not mean as much as the changes she saw around her. Dora's marriage came the summer the Circle Three Bar began to bathe its cattle in a tick dip. The Box CF did the same a few months later, and that was the end of Texas fever.

The spring after that Paco Alvarez died, and so did Lucille Newsome.

The drought summer followed that. They had water from wells now but no irrigation system, so when there was no rain there was no grass. It was a bad year, prices down on cattle because the ranchers had to dump their stock on the market for lack of feed.

All the time the two ranches were becoming more modern. The longhorns were giving way to Herefords, quicker to fatten and more placid than the native cattle with their stringy lean muscles and wild ways.

The cattle were healthier. On both ranches the hands now scattered bone meal to cure the phosphorus deficiency that the cattlemen called "creeps."

Rose Ellen bought her first automobile the year the geologist came to the valley, wanting to look for oil. That was 1916.

At first Rose Ellen refused. She had heard that the drillers defaced the land. She ran a cattle ranch, she told them. Her interest was in the grass and the water that the land provided.

Ray Newsome let them drill. First the geologists rode over the land, studying the contours and the formations. They set off a series of blasts and listened to the way the explosions reverberated through the earth. For two years they set off dynamite and drilled and explored. In '18 they hit their first gusher, on land across the valley that had once been part of Charlie Fowler's Diamond Five spread. They found more oil north of there, and they pressed Rose Ellen for permission to drill on the Box CF. Finally she relented when they promised to keep the drill sites clean. They found oil on her property, too.

There was never enough to make her rich. She remained a working cattle rancher. But for the first time she did not have to depend on cattle for her existence. She had an income to keep her going if the price of beef ever dropped drastically. As it did, a decade later.

The oil companies changed the look of the land. They built roads to their wells. That ended whatever was left of the kind of cattle ranching that the three partners had once known. With roads the ranchers could truck their cattle from one part of the spread to another. Trucks were faster than cowboys. The ranchers rotated cattle from parched, bare land to pastures where the grass was thick. That meant more fences. Now every acre was good for pasture because every pasture in the valley had artesian wells.

Not long after that, electricity came into the valley. And soon after that it got telephones, first in Luray and then throughout.

And in 1924—Rose Ellen marked it as the year she planted Rhodes grass in some of her pastures—Robert E. Lee Newsome, his father's sole heir and abiding disappointment, drove his Packard into one of the power poles that now lined the main roads of the valley. He killed himself and the young woman riding with him.

"A tragedy," Inez said. "A true tragedy, I'm telling you." She put a cup of coffee in front of Rose Ellen, poured a second for herself, and sat down in a chair on the other side of the desk at which Rose Ellen was examining a ledger.

"A tragedy," she said again. "I don't know how the Lord can allow such things to happen." She sipped and put the cup down in the saucer.

"The only thing I can say is that there's a purpose to it somewhere, something God can see even if we can't." Once more she sipped from the cup.

"I don't know what that could be, though," she said. "I don't know what plan He had in mind."

Rose Ellen looked up from the ledgers. Her hair was mostly grey now, and there were lines and pouches on her face. But there was little that was matronly about her. She still had her sharp jaw, and she had perfected an even glare that could intimidate a stranger.

She used it now on Inez, who was (she knew) immune to

its effects. "Are you still talking about that baby?" she said.

"Yes. Miguel is his name. The poor child. An orphan."

"A bastard."

Inez pursed her lips in a frown and looked away. "Rita was a good girl, Lord keep her," she said. "I don't blame her. You want to blame somebody, you blame that Newsome boy. He gives her a child and then he won't marry her. She had to run off to San Antonio to have the baby baptized, can you believe that?"

Inez brought her hand down hard on the desk. "Anyway," she said, "you can't hold the father's sins against the child. The poor thing."

"I don't hold anything against the baby," Rose Ellen said. "How could I? I don't even know the child's name."

"His name is Miguel."

"I don't hold anything against him. But I don't understand why I have to hear about him ten times a day, no matter what I'm doing to keep this place running as it should."

She looked down at the ledger. "I've never even seen the child," she said.

"His name is Miguel," Inez said once again. "And you will. I'm bringing him here for a few days. I have to care for him for a while."

That brought Rose Ellen's face up from the figures once more.

"You're not!" she said.

"I am. Miguel is of my family. I told you that. His mother was the daughter of my only sister. I must take a turn with him. His grandmother isn't well and she can't do it alone."

"Fine," Rose Ellen said. She waved a hand in the air. "Do what you want. But don't ask me to help. I'm a busy woman."

"Whatever you say."

"This is no concern of mine," Rose Ellen said. "Let Ray Newsome take the baby in; it's his responsibility if what you say is true. Let him do the right thing."

A few days later Inez brought the child into Rose Ellen's home. She carried it in a cradle into her own bedroom. Rose Ellen looked into the cradle for a few seconds. Then she excused herself. She told Inez that she had work to do.

She went into her office to read. But soon Miguel began to cry, and though the baby was upstairs the sound of his wailing made its way to her ears. Rose Ellen could not concentrate on her reading. She left the house and went to ride. She was sixty years old, but she could still ride for hours when she wanted.

The horse trotted past the barns and the bunkhouses, up a road and into a pasture. The ranch was orderly, tamed, placid. Usually these qualities made her proud. Today they irked her. Her spread was too polished for her liking, too well run, if that was possible. As she rode she thought that she had made everything of it that she could: a tidy, efficient operation built and maintained for the purpose of profitably raising cattle. It was self-perpetuating now, strong enough to survive drought and bad times. It needed her no more, she thought, than did the windmills that ceaselessly pumped water from the earth. She knew that if she left it, it would still whirr away and spin out its respectable, predictable profit.

The thought startled her: I have taken this place as far as it can go. Nothing more to do here.

That evening the baby cried again. They were eating dinner. Inez got up from the table to go upstairs.

"Bring him down," Rose Ellen said. "Probably he wants to be around people. Bring him down and we'll take care of him."

Inez carried him down, squalling in her arms.

"Bring him here," said Rose Ellen. She took the baby and cradled it, rocked it as she had rocked her own children so long ago. She thought of Charlie and she thought of Dora, who had a daughter of her own now. Rose Ellen had seen Dora just once since her marriage, on a visit to Philadelphia.

"Miguel, Miguel," Rose Ellen crooned. She kept rocking the baby in her arms. He stopped crying and closed his eyes.

"You see?" Rose Ellen said.

Miguel stayed for two weeks in the ranch house. That pleased the family. It was a good home and Miguel was looking healthy. For two weeks he filled the house with his infant's wails and sputterings.

Rose Ellen always woke early, so she began to feed him in the mornings. She would put Miguel in his crib afterward and watch him as he slept. She began to look at his face for traces of Ray Newsome.

Inez lamented the boy's future. No mother, she said, no father. Nobody to care for him.

Ray will do something, Rose Ellen thought. Ray will do the right thing. When the two weeks were up, she drove to visit him at his ranch house.

She still saw Ray a few times a year. Usually it was to mediate fights between their hands. There would be a fence-cutting, or some punches thrown in a bar, or stray shots fired into the night. There was a rivalry that nobody could explain except as a residue of the old bitterness. So she saw Ray Newsome sometimes, and it was not difficult for her to drive in her Model T pickup north on the valley road one afternoon, to pass beneath the wrought-iron gate which bore the Circle Three Bar brand, to walk up the steps of the big house and call on him.

They sat together in the parlor, and there was something yet between them, some shared leftover feeling that, like the old rivalry, still worked its unobtrusive ways.

She said, "Ray Newsome, there is talk you have a grandson in Luray. Is this true?"

"Bobby never married," he said.

"I hear anyway that he was the father of a boy. We both know the child I mean. I am sorry to bring this up, but I have to know."

"Rose Ellen," he said, "I never knew you to care so about somebody else's strays."

"There was a time," she said, "when your strays were meat on my table. You didn't answer my question."

"What is it to you?" he said.

She studied him to find traces of the boy she had known, now grown into this hard man.

"Say I am an old lady with more time on my hands than is good for me. Just tell me what you plan to do for the child."

"I don't plan to do anything," he said.

"Mine is living in Philadelphia," she said. "My grandchild, I mean. A year old next month. I have to ride three days on a train if I want to see her. I'm trying to tell you how lucky you are."

His grandmother and the county agency were happily surprised to have Rose Ellen Sample ask for custody of the
orphan and begin adoption proceedings. In spite of her age
she was healthy. She would give the child a good home.

She and Inez brought him to the ranch. But he was Rose
Ellen's child. She dressed him in the mornings and took him
with her when she drove in her pickup. When he was old
enough she gave him a pony and taught him to ride, as she
had taught Ray Newsome once.

She watched him grow, and she gave him her love. He was
an obedient and attractive child. She taught him all that she
could about the ranch. He was a good student in school, too,
but he would have been even better if he had not cared about
the ranch so much. He would skip his homework to muck out
the corrals, if she allowed him. He grew up working beside
the hands in the pastures and looking over Rose Ellen's
shoulder in the office. On his sixteenth birthday she changed
her will. Miguel Sample became the sole heir of the Box CF.

Donnie Lee

We got our A on the history project. It was Sue E.'s idea to use Gandy Meacham's own words, like he was telling about Rose Ellen Sample himself. That made the story sound more real, she said, and she was right, for we got our A and the teacher even asked if Gandy Meacham could come talk. When I said no, I had to read the paper out loud in front of the class instead.

I told Gandy Meacham about that, about the teacher's invite to talk to the class, and he laughed as loud as he could manage and said that was right funny, for he was twelve years old last time he'd been in school and that time they invited him to leave.

So we done the paper and summer finally come. But Sue E. and me still saw each other almost every day. Somewhere during that history paper she become my girl. Once school ended we went every night to the pictures, or to eat, or just to talk and look at each other.

We didn't stop visiting Gandy Meacham either. Him and me had come to be pals, if you can say that of an old man and a young fella like me. And he would not have let Sue E. stop visiting if she had wanted to, which she didn't.

He had his good days and he had his bad. At first I couldn't see a change in him, and I hoped maybe he was not so sick after all. But I seen about the beginning of July that his good days was getting fewer and fewer, and his bad spells was lasting longer.

That made me want to be with him as much as I could when he was right. He and Sue E. and me talked about all manner of things. Sometimes it was him asking me questions, about our friends and what we did with our days and what Luray was like now. Other times, when he was up to it, he went on with his stories about cowboying and ranches the way they used to be.

One thing we all passed over was any mention of Ray Newsome and Rose Ellen Sample. That is, Sue E. and me both steered around it. But one day Gandy Meacham himself said, Donnie Lee, what do you think of that boy Rose Ellen called her son?

The Mexican, I said.

He said, That's the one.

I told him the truth. I said there wasn't nobody I knew ever said a word against him for anything he done. Though there was those who was down on him for things he couldn't help.

Like being half Mex, Gandy Meacham said.

I said, That is part of it.

Sue E. said, If you listen to the talk around town there are some that are jealous that he ended up with so much because of Miss Rose and wasn't blood kin to her.

People set stock in blood kin, Gandy Meacham said. As if there ain't any other sort.

I said, That is part of it too. I said, And there is some that don't think too much of him since they say his daddy and his real mama wasn't married.

You mean he was a bastard, Sue E. said.

Gandy Meacham got a laugh out of that one.

He said, Now, there is one thing you can't blame him for. I bet if he had a choice he wouldn't have picked Ray Newsome's no-good boy for a pappy. But that is how it turned out.

I said, That is the talk.

Gandy Meacham got a sour look. He said, How much proof you need? Boy, look at what happened and tell me it wasn't 'cause the boy was Ray Newsome's grandson. Look at Rose Ellen taking him in that way and all the rest of it and tell me she didn't do it because Ray Newsome was his granddaddy.

I said, It does look that way. Or maybe she was just lonesome.

He lay back on his pillow and looked at me and looked at Sue E. His eyes was solemn and sad.

He said, She was lonely a good while before that. I know. My brother Lynn that stayed on the Circle Three, he would write me letters. First off it was just about the cows and the weather, but after a spell I made him throw in something about Rose Ellen every time.

He said, It hurt to read about her but I wanted to know. Maybe I wanted to hurt, like I had some hurt coming to me. Anyways, he put things in his letters about Rose Ellen. About her being without a man the way she was. About her daughter going away, and her running the Box CF on her own.

She was alone a long time, he said. If you don't think that means lonely you don't know people. I don't care who you are. Rose Ellen Sample or the queen of England. You go very long without anybody to love and you are bound to be lonely. But she was lonely a long time before she took in the Mex. So it had to be more than lonely that made her do it, he said.

He said, I bet there was trouble along the way, her making the boy her son like she did and everybody knowing that the ranch would be his. I can't imagine she made any secret of it.

She didn't, I said. I told him it caused her trouble on her own ranch once.

I told him a story that I knew real good since it was what got Tom Holloway's daddy his job as straw a couple of years back.

I said, The straw boss then was a man name of Judkins. The story is that one day he sent a crew out to lay some pipe for a new bunkhouse. They set in to digging and they dug their ditch and they was starting to lay pipe when Miguel come along and told them he wanted the ditch deeper. Even if it didn't freeze but once in a blue moon he didn't want the pipes choking up when it did.

Then Judkins happened along, I said. He wanted to know what the problem was. Miguel told him there wasn't no problem and Judkins said that in that case he could let his crew be and Miguel said just whose crew did you say it was.

They had it out right there is the way Tom Holloway's daddy tells it, I said. So they marched into the house to Miz Rose. And the next thing Tom Holloway's daddy knows, Miz

Rose is calling him in out of the ditch and standing him next to Miguel and Judkins and asking him if he can take orders from a Mex.

I said, Tom Holloway's daddy the way he tells it come right out and said he didn't know about every Mex but he wouldn't care if it was Miguel. Then Miz Rose says good. He was the straw boss now, and Judkins, since he had such trouble taking orders from a Mex, could take orders from Tom Holloway's daddy instead.

I said, But that ain't the end of it. A few minutes later Tom Holloway's daddy is outside her office and he hears Miz Rose telling Miguel that is the last time she sticks up for him and he has to do it for himself from now on.

Gandy Meacham said, And did he?

I said, Every time far as I know.

That sounds just like Rose Ellen, Gandy Meacham said. And it sounds like somebody that was brought up by Rose Ellen too.

It appeared that he was wore out. He looked up at the ceiling and didn't say nothing for a spell.

Then he said, You two going out tomorrow night?

We said we was.

He said, I need something from you. I need it bad and I hope that you will not let me down. I want you to come see me tomorrow when your folks has gone to bed, Donnie Lee. And you too, Susan, if you can make it.

I knew there would be no keeping her away.

Like he meant it he said, This is important to me. Don't you kids let me down.

Chapter 31

Ray Newsome sat in the hot sun. With a handkerchief he dabbed at his forehead, his upper lip, his temples. A few feet to one side, the Mansos Valley High School marching band was tooting and thumping through "Anchors Aweigh," so loud it made his ears hurt.

He was sitting on a bench beside the track that circled the high school football field. The stands behind him were full of the people of Luray and the valley. He could feel the sun bearing down on him from above, and he could feel the eyes of all those in the stands staring at his back.

He dabbed again with the handkerchief and told himself that soon the ordeal would be over. He would have to look for a second into the eyes of his grandson. Then he could look away and it would be finished.

Being seen with his grandson made him uneasy, always had. He had tried to avoid it. That usually was not so difficult. Ray never visited the Box CF. When the boy was going to school in town, Ray had sometimes glimpsed him in the schoolyard or on the streets. As a youngster he'd had the same gawky build and narrow face that Ray had seen in Bobby. The sight had made him writhe inside but it had fascinated him, too. He wondered how many of his son's ways were in this boy.

Few, it seemed. From the first grade on, the boy's name appeared often on the school honor rolls published in the *Clarion*. Ray had the habit of scanning the list each month, looking for Miguel's name. He'd been curious about what the boy was becoming.

Still, he had not wanted to be seen with him. Ray believed he shouldn't be blamed for refusing to claim a bastard half-breed, yet he felt that the matter was best left neglected. It was, most of the time, except when grandfather and grandson were seen together. As they would be in a few minutes, with the valley's population looking on.

It had happened once before, when the boy was in the eighth grade. The principal had asked Ray to award the prizes in the school's oratory contest. He had accepted. He took his seat at the front of the auditorium stage. He was stunned to see Miguel Sample walk in as one of the three finalists, and sit a few feet away from him. The auditorium was small, with room for no more than a couple of hundred students and teachers, and a few parents. But he'd been sure that their eyes were all on him, full of reproach for his having rejected his grandson.

The boy was third to speak that day. While the other students were at the podium Ray was careful to study them, never letting his eyes stray toward Miguel. When the boy's turn came to speak, Ray did not know how to behave. He didn't want to stare at him but he didn't want to ignore him, either; that would look wrong. He tried to be politely attentive, looking at Miguel for a few moments but then allowing his eyes to wander around the auditorium. This so concerned him that for the first couple of minutes Ray did not hear what the boy was saying. Then the words filtered through him. Miguel was talking about the valley.

It was a good place, Miguel was saying. Some places in the world were easier to live in, but the valley was good to people if they worked hard and respected it. It gave a living to hundreds of people. And when you looked around you, you saw what people could accomplish with the land if they worked hard enough.

It was the best speech of the day, and Ray found himself pinning the blue ribbon on the boy's shirt while the crowd watched.

He vowed never to let himself in for such embarrassment again. But now he faced it one more time.

He'd had little choice. The valley's young men had returned from the Second World War and the townspeople wanted to honor them. A ceremony of some kind. A band and speeches— a proper welcome home. Mansos Valley's first citizen could not refuse the request to shake hands with them, one by one, as they marched past the stands of the football field.

They were grouped by service. First had come the army, then the air corps. Now fourteen young men in navy uniforms were at attention in front of him, waiting out the last bars of "Anchors Aweigh." The music ended. Ray Newsome put away his handkerchief and walked to one end of the line. He moved down the row, addressing each by his first name, shaking hands with him and sometimes clapping him on the shoulder.

"Johnny," he said. "Good to see you back home."

"Luke. You look good, boy. It was a cruiser, wasn't it? North Atlantic? You was a long way from home."

They were his cowboys, some of them, and some the sons of his friends. He tried to look every one of them in the eye, but he could not keep his attention away from the far end of the stadium. Seven marines waited there. And one of them was Miguel Sample.

"Peter," Ray Newsome said to the last sailor in the line. "Your pa is glad to have you back, I know. You want a job riding for the Circle Three, you just see my foreman anytime this week. And tell him I said to take you on."

The sailors walked to chairs that were set out on the field. The bandleader stood and waved his arms. The brass section hit the first notes of "The Halls of Montezuma." The marines marched up the track to where Ray Newsome stood.

He had already picked Miguel from the row. Third from the left. They came to within a few feet of him, and then marched in place while the band played. Ray could hear their shoes stamping in unison on the cinder track.

When the song was finished they stood at attention, their shoulders thrust back and their chins thrust out.

Ray began at his left. "Andy Merrill," he said. He took the first marine's hand and pumped it. "We're proud of you, young fellow, I mean it."

"Thank you, sir."

Then the second. "Jimbo. You was busting windows with a slingshot not too far back. You remember that?"

The marine grinned. "You bet I do, Mr. Newsome. You told me I was hell on wheels."

"But next I heard you're a sharpshooter on Saipan and you're winning medals. I guess the practice come in handy."

He gripped Jimbo's hand and smiled at him. Then Ray Newsome took one step to his right and looked into his grandson's face.

Miguel's eyes did not move. Ray forced the words up his throat.

"Well," Ray said. "Look at the medals you got there. You must be a real hero."

Miguel did not answer. He did not know what to say to that. He stayed at attention, his eyes fixed on a point beyond Ray's face, the way he had learned.

Got to make him say something, Ray thought. This looks all wrong. "What you plan to do with yourself now that you're back?" he said.

Miguel had an answer for that. "Going to ag school this fall," he said. "A&M."

"Good," Ray said. He was relieved. "Good for you." And he moved down the line, to the next marine in the row.

For the next hour and a half Ray sat in the sun and listened to the speeches. He was relaxed now. The worst was over. He had survived it. He could go home now and never see the boy again, if he was careful.

After the last of the speeches they all stood for a benediction. When that was finished, all the people in the stands cheered and rushed down onto the field. Men and women sought out their sons and embraced them. They all ignored Ray Newsome, and he began to move away. His driver was waiting with a car under the stands.

He was leaving when he saw Rose Ellen coming down from the bleachers. She shouted Miguel's name, and waved at him. Miguel came out of the crowd, ran to her, took her in his arms.

Ray Newsome watched until he could bear it no more. Then he turned away and walked to his car.

Chapter 32

The big picture window in Ray Newsome's third-floor office in Luray presented a view of the downtown area (now five blocks by three, comprising a collection of retail stores, a movie theatre, a soda fountain and two pharmacies, professional quarters, and a civic office building), with the railroad depot beyond that, and the warehouses and stockyards and packing plant on the east side of town. In the ten years since the construction of the red brick office building, the changes in the view from that window had never been drastic enough for Ray Newsome to notice. Usually he studied the view no more closely than he studied the walls which framed it.

But the day that he went to visit Rose Ellen was different. He found himself nervous, distracted, and he focused his attention on what he saw in the window.

Two days earlier Rose Ellen had fallen downstairs and broken her hip. Though he disliked hospitals he felt he ought to visit her as she recuperated. It would be a small kindness, and there remained between them a bond that was wispy and unspecific, but still real. It had its basis in shared experience and remembered passion. Though they saw each other infrequently, and when they did their meetings were likely to have a formal tinge, there remained some unacknowledged feeling between them that they had for each other only.

So he felt obliged to visit her in the hospital, and he was edgy as he waited to do so. She could still do that to him. Visiting hours were from one to three in the afternoon, he'd

325

been told. He had half an hour to wait yet, so he was passing time by examining the view that he usually neglected.

His eyes rested on the stock-auction barn across the tracks. It looked wrong. He squinted to see it better, then removed the gold-rimmed bifocals he had resisted until the summer of '47, when he'd found himself unable to read a contract or see across the street. He breathed on the lenses and polished them with his tie, then replaced them and squinted again at the auction barn.

The last time he had noticed, it had been painted a gleaming enamel white, and the red letters of RAY NEWSOME STOCK SALES, INC. had been bright and distinct.

Now, he thought, it looked terrible, even from seven blocks away.

There was an office intercom on his desk. He rarely used it.

"I want Harris!" he shouted into the speaker.

Among his employees were four young men Ray called his bird dogs. At least one of them was always with him. They were his agents, his emissaries, his errand boys. They did for him all those things on which he would not spend his dwindling time and energy.

Harris was one of them. He hurried into the office.

"Look at that," Ray said. He pointed a damning finger toward the window. "Would you look at that stock barn?"

"Uh-huh," Harris said. He wasn't sure what was supposed to be wrong with the building.

"Look at that paint job," Ray said. (The paint, Harris thought. He doesn't like the paint.) "Even with an old man's eyes I can see it is in rotten shape."

"Yes, sir," Harris said. "Looks bad."

Ray jumped out of his chair. When he was angry or excited he was still capable of brief, startling agility.

"Who let that happen?" he said.

"Well, Mr. Newsome, I don't know, exactly; it's not my responsibility."

"Let's find out," Ray said. He left the office.

Before Harris followed he looked at his boss's auction barn again. The paint looked no shabbier now to him than it had for the last three years.

They rode to the ground floor in the elevator, the first in the county.

"It's a disgrace," Ray said. They left the office building and walked east on Chisholm Street. "What would a visitor think, coming to town and seeing that? He'd think that the Ray Newsome who owned that building must be seeing hard times to let his property go to hell that way. I want to know how this kind of thing is allowed to happen."

Harris walked beside him. Ray Newsome paid his bird dogs well but they earned their salaries with improbable excesses of patience. The old man had a way of suddenly fixing on some obscure detail of his businesses that he had always before ignored, then behaving as if it were the crux of his wealth. Now he seemed convinced that his reputation hung on a paint job.

"Makes me sick," Ray said as they walked to the barn. "Just sick. Why is it I'm always the first to notice these things?"

When they reached the barn Harris went to find the auction manager. Ray stayed outside and stared grimly at the peeling paint. Soon Harris returned with the manager and a maintenance man, really just a boy.

"Look at this," Ray said. From the outside wall he lifted a large flake of paint, held it out for them all to see. He tossed it aside.

"Look," he said, and he gestured with his hand to include the entire wall. "This is just awful."

To the boy he said, "You're the handyman around here?"

"Yes, sir, I am."

"Why hasn't this barn been painted?"

"Nobody told me to, sir."

Ray glowered at the auction manager. "I'm telling you," he said. "I want it painted. Now. Right away."

"Yes, sir," the boy said.

"I'll get him right on it," the auction manager said.

"Find him some help," Ray said to Harris. "It'll take him a week to do it by himself."

"Right away," said Harris.

Suddenly Ray felt tired. He sent Harris back to the office to get the driver. Then he went inside the barn. It was an arena with bleachers on three sides, enclosing a dirt-floored pen. On auction days buyers sat in the bleachers to examine the stock and make their bids.

Now it was dark and quiet. Ray sat on a wooden plank seat. He was sorry that he had fussed about the paint. It was a triviality, he knew. But details were important to him. He wanted everything to be right. The small mistakes, the blemishes and imperfections, seemed to bother nobody but himself.

In a few minutes Harris came looking for him. He had brought the car and the driver, he said. Ray sat in the back seat with Harris while the driver headed out of town, south to the hospital.

It was a short trip, and was almost over when Ray realized that he had brought nothing for Rose Ellen. He made the driver stop beside a field where bluebonnets grew in patches. Harris tried to help him but Ray made him stay in the car. He went out into the field alone and he picked a handful of flowers, and he brought them with him when he walked into the door of Rose Ellen's room.

When he entered the room he wished he had not come.

Miguel was in a chair beside Rose's bed.

"I see you got comp'ny already," he said. "Maybe I'll come back in a while."

"No," said Rose Ellen. "If I let you go now I'll never get you back here. Pull up a chair on this side, Ray."

Ray sat beside the bed, opposite Miguel. He did not want to look at the young man's face. He looked at Rose instead. "Brought you some flowers," he said. "They ain't store-bought, though."

"Picked fresh is better," she said. "Give them to me, I'll put them in a glass of water. They're beautiful, Ray."

When she had done that she said, "Ray, you know my boy Miguel."

"Right," said Ray. "A pleasure." He looked quickly at the boy and returned to Rose Ellen.

"Well, Rose," he said, "how you comin' along?"

"I will live," she said. "The doc tells me this kind of thing happens to people our age. This is just the years' way of letting me know I can't run away from them, hard as I try."

"I know what you mean," he said.

There was a silence of a few seconds that Miguel broke. He had to go to town, he said. He would return in half an hour. He kissed Rose Ellen on the cheek and said a polite good-bye to Ray.

"Seems like a good boy," Ray said to Rose.

"That he is. He makes me happy, and he has never disappointed me."

But that was all. No more. She just looked at Ray without another word and he looked back at her and thought, That's how it is, Rose; you know and I know, but today we decide not to talk about it. We are going to pretend it is nothing special—and thank you for that, thank you.

"Does it hurt you bad?" he asked.

"It hurts more to know I won't get on a horse again."

"It didn't take me a bad hip to stop," he said. "I don't suppose it is ten years since I rode."

He rubbed his hands on the knobs of his knees. "You always was one for riding," he said. "If I shut my eyes I can see you like yesterday on that long-legged mare, the one you had—"

"Don't," she said, almost sharply, almost a rebuke.

He knew what she meant. Don't hurt yourself, looking back. It always hurts to look back.

"I talked to Faulk up at the statehouse yesterday," he said. He wanted his voice to be upbeat again. "He says we are getting pavement down the east side of the valley if he has to tar it himself, next year at the latest."

"Is that a fact?" she said, and once more they were casual friends with the safe wall between them. They talked about politics and they gossiped. They mutually condemned grain prices and electrical rates.

Then they fell silent again, before Ray said, "This morning I was shaving, and thinking about Jay McClellan that passed on last week. He wasn't but fifty-five, fifty-six, and I thought, there sure are a lot of younger folks dying in the valley these days.

"Then I realized that everybody who dies in this valley is younger than we are, Rose. You and me, we're the oldest. Oh, there might be a great-aunt or some such that somebody brought in from out of town, but I'm talking folks that grew up here and lived here in the valley. Nobody goes back as far as we do. Between you and me, we remember things that nobody else walking around here has seen.

"Did you know that?" he said.

"I noticed it a while ago," she said.

"I asked myself how it happened," Ray went on. "I can remember when everybody around me was older'n I was. I couldn't wait to grow up. Now I look around and of all the people I knew then, you're the only one, Rose, that's left."

She said nothing.

"It is good to talk to you now and again," he said.

"Same for me."

"You look happy," he said, "hip and all."

"I am happy."

"Don't it bother you?" he said suddenly. "When everybody you knew before is gone, you got to know your time is near, too. There ain't no pretending. You know. 'Cause it gnaws some at me. I'd be lying if I said different. Don't it bother you?"

"Some," she said. "But I'm lucky. I have my son. I don't want to rub your nose in it, Ray, because done is done, but having him around changes things."

"He keeps you from getting lonely," Ray said.

"That's true."

"Keeps you thinking young, too."

"That is part of it," she said, "but just a small part. The most important is the peace I get knowing that the one possession I love in life is going to end up with somebody who cares about it as much as I do."

They went back to trivialities after that, and they talked for a few more minutes before Ray left. He drove to visit the southern section of the ranch, and after a couple of hours there he told the driver to take him back to Luray. From the edge of town he could see the auction barn, with half a dozen workmen on ladders, painting one wall. It was green paint, not white, that slopped from their brushes.

"Look at that," he told Harris. "Look at what they're doing."

He made the driver stop at the barn. Then he got out and

yelled at the workmen on the ladders. "You idiots," he said. "What the hell you doing? Sweet Jeezus, it looks awful."

The auction manager heard him shouting and came out.

"Look what they're doing," Ray said.

"Yes," the manager said. He didn't understand why Ray was angry.

"The color," Ray said. "That's green. This is supposed to be a white barn with red letters."

"We couldn't find enough white," the manager said. "You said you wanted it done right away, so we took what we could get."

"Aw, no," Ray said. He looked at the wall. "Don't anybody else here care about my place but me?"

He looked at Harris, and at the manager, and at the workmen on the ladders. He heard the question he had just asked.

And he already knew the answer.

Chapter 33

Even in his own airplane Ray Newsome grew weary of the trip home from Laramie. It was a long flight for a man seven weeks short of his eightieth birthday. But he still ran the Circle Three, and when there was land to be bought in Wyoming he did the buying. Now the deal was closed, and the Circle Three Bar had a place to fatten its cattle in the summer before they were shipped to market. The Circle Three was a better ranch now than it had been a day earlier. That was how it was supposed to happen. But the work tired him, and so did the long flight home, with the DC-3's engines rumbling and vibrating outside the cabin.

His limousine was waiting for him when the plane touched down. It was quieter than the airplane and he could relax. It brought him to the ranch house. The driver opened the door and Ray walked up to his room on the second floor.

An air conditioner buzzed and rattled in one window. Ray had a maid turn off the machine and open a window to let in the evening air. He ordered a poached egg on toast for dinner, and when the maid was leaving he asked for the back numbers of the *Clarion* that he had missed while he was in Wyoming. He read the paper every afternoon when he was at home.

This time there were five in a stack. He ate the poached egg while he read the first one. His eyes ran up and down every one of its eight pages. It was a small-town paper and he liked that. He liked to read about people he knew, who walked the streets of his town and lived on checks from his companies' payrolls—about their bowling scores, their marksmen's medals from boot camp, and their bake sales; the visits of their relatives and their church socials. He also liked to know what they were reading about him in his own newspaper.

He was feeling sleepy in the middle of the third paper in the stack. He was reading the back page, ready to put it aside, when he saw the headline on the bottom corner: Two single-column photographs showed a pretty blonde girl named Loretta Foster and the young man, Miguel Sample. Both, said the article under the photographs, were June graduates of Texas A&M University. Miss Foster was the daughter of Mrs. Eunice Foster and the late Mr. Charles Foster of Amarillo. Mr. Sample was the son of Mrs. Rose Sample of the Box CF Ranch. The wedding, the notice said, would be held this coming Saturday, three P.M., in the home of Mrs. Sample.

The next day was Saturday. When Ray woke the air conditioner was humming and the sun was hot and white around the edges of the drapes.

The clock on the nightstand said nine-twenty. He had slept eleven hours and he still was not rested. That didn't surprise him. Even sleeping was an effort now, and he was perpetually tired. He dressed and ate breakfast: dry toast and half a cup of coffee. He told the maid to send for his car. He wanted to go for a drive.

Two of the bird dogs were in the hall outside his room, waiting for him when he came out. He told them to go away; he did not need them today. He walked on his own strength to the car, and sat in the front seat. He told the driver to start going north.

The ranch that he owned, the miles of it, rolled up to meet him in the limousine's windshield and then peeled away and disappeared in the mirror. Railroad tracks. Asphalt roads. And fence, fence forever. Cows that grazed in the green grass, and horses that ran with flying manes for the pure frightened pleasure of it as the car sped past. He saw a flock of blackbirds perched on electric lines, and the mantis-heads of a dozen oil pumps dipping and raising. A cowboy that he did not know rode a horse that he did not recognize through an irrigation ditch that he had long ago forgotten.

At the edge of Luray the driver asked him where he should go.

"Drive," Ray Newsome told him. "Drive anywhere that is mine."

They went through the town. Ray looked hard at the railroad depot and the lumberyard and the packing plant and the livestock pens. He looked, too, at the faces of the people on the street, at the mothers and the children and the old people, none of them as old as he.

The road ran parallel to the Central Texas tracks. He told the driver to turn east when he got the chance, so at the next mile road the driver pointed the limousine toward the hills that had seemed so distant and foreboding to Ray Newsome when he was a child. Now they were brackets for the land that he owned. He tried to make himself realize that all the land that stretched up to them was his.

They drove east to the base of the hills. There Ray told the driver to turn south. Then they were going down the valley, their course meandering through oil fields and pastures.

"Keep going," he told the driver. "Keep going."

It was the time of the day when he usually napped, but he fought to keep his eyes open. He wanted to see it all, to comprehend that it was all his and that the time was short when he would be able to hold it.

They were near the south end of the valley. The car needed gas, so the driver stopped at an equipment yard with sheds that housed some of Ray Newsome's heavy machines. The driver filled the tank at a gas pump in the yard, and when he came back to the car Ray had directions for him. Up this road, down the next for a few miles. A right here, a left there.

Then a right that carried him off his property for the first time in the hours that he had been driving. It took the limousine up the gravel road that led to the Box CF and Rose Ellen Sample's ranch house.

Forty-two people were sitting in the parlor of the house. Most of them were on metal folding chairs that she had rented in Luray. The chairs were in rows. Rose Ellen sat in the front row, and while she waited for the minister to appear, she hoped for a breeze to cool the room and she listened to the low, expectant chatter that the guests made behind her.

It was the kind of noise that dies in stages. Rose Ellen heard the noise fall away, voice by voice. But that was wrong, she thought. The minister was still in the kitchen, five minutes to go yet. She looked around and she saw the people beside her turning their heads, whispering, staring.

She, too, turned in her chair. Ray Newsome was standing at the back of the room. His body was bent and his eyes searched the faces. She thought he looked frightened. It was an effort but she pushed herself out of the chair and walked to him.

He saw her coming toward him. Not stern but smiling. She was welcoming him. He was grateful that she would do that. He wanted to thank her. But he could not talk.

She put out a hand and said, "Come, Ray, here. Your place is over here."

Someone gave up a seat beside Rose Ellen.

"I come for my grandson's wedding," he said.

"Yes," she said.

"Not because I have an ounce of good in me," he said. "I come because I need something."

She raised a hand and put it on his cheek. "We all need something," she said. "It's okay. We all do."

"I need somebody to give my ranch to," he said.

The next Saturday was theirs. He married Rose Ellen in the same parlor. She held his hand as they spoke the vows. Her grip was strong and reassuring. Then he put a ring on her finger, and they kissed tenderly. And for the first time, Ray Newsome knew peace within himself.

They had already spoken to the lawyers. Ray had wanted to put her in his will, give her part of the ranch, with the rest for Miguel. He was sure that he would die before her. But she and the lawyers talked him out of that. Too complicated, they explained, when it would all be Miguel's eventually.

He added one clause a few days before he died. It concerned a hill on the west side of the valley that had been within the original holdings of Charlie Fowler, Earl Newsome, and Orrin Sample. The top of the hill stayed bare and unused until after Ray Newsome died. Because his wife's passing followed so closely his own, she did not ever see or know what he planned for the hilltop.

But in February of 1951 a crew of workmen erected there a pedestal of native stone and mortar, and fastened to it a bronze plaque with raised letters that said:

ROSE ELLEN.

They situated the pedestal exactly as the will had specified, beneath the branches of a solitary old oak tree. In a few days a stakebed truck drove to the top of the hill. Using winches and a block-and-tackle, the workmen erected a life-size statue of a young woman and lowered the statue onto the pedestal.

It was a curious work. The head of the young woman was slightly bowed. The eyes were somber as they gazed down on the valley. And the arms were spread wide in the all-embracing posture that the old Mexicans used to call *brazada*.

Donnie Lee

We went back to see Gandy Meacham that night, the way he asked. It took some doing. Sue had to wait outside by the window while my folks batted the breeze in their room. Finally I saw their light go dark. I waited for a few minutes, snuck down the stairs and into Quiller's room. I opened the window for Sue to crawl through.

The old man's face got a dozen new crinkles in it when he seen her, but they all pointed straight up. He liked that gal. I believe he was happier to see her, who was no kin to him, than he was to see his own great-grandson.

We came like you said, she told him.

I tole you I wanted something of you, he said. And this is it. I want you to take me where she is buried.

Naturally he did not have to say her name. We knew.

First thing, I thought of all the reasons why not. Like getting the old man up and dressed, and getting him to the car, and what hell I would catch if my folks found out, and what I would ever do if the old man died on me.

We'll do it, Sue E. said. Won't we, Donnie Lee?

You bet, I said.

We better get you dressed, she said.

Gandy Meacham pulled down the covers. He was dressed underneath them. He was wearing a flannel shirt that was way too big for him, and brand-new jeans that wasn't broke in, which bunched up around his waist where he tightened his

339

belt. It was some belt. It had a silver buckle in the shape of a longhorn's head, with two red stones for the eyes.

He said, I dressed myself. Took me a while but I done it. These is my burying clothes. I made your mother buy them for me, Donnie Lee. I told her I wouldn't have none of any fancy black suits.

He said, They fit me a month ago.

His boots had stood in a corner of the room from the first day he came to our house. I fetched them and slid the old man around until his legs, from the knees down, dangled off the side of the bed. It was no trouble to slip the boots on. It appeared that even his feet had shrunk.

Then he raised up a bony crooked finger and pointed at the closet. My hat, he said.

Sue went for it. When he clapped it on his head, damn if he didn't look like an old cowboy instead of a sack of bones.

We had a time getting the old guy out. First me and Sue E. carried him to the window. We stuck him through so he was on the ledge. Then I had to chance going through the house, out the front door, and around, so's I could get hold of him from the other side. I done that, and held him in my arms while Sue climbed out and run to hold the car door open. I set him down in the middle of the seat and got behind the wheel and Sue got in the other side. I let the car roll down the hill with the lights off, until we were a fair piece down the road. Then I dumped the clutch, and the motor caught quiet as you please, and we headed toward the cemetery. It was a couple miles before I realized I had forgot to turn on the headlights, for there was a big full moon out and it shined a pearly white down on the valley, with nothing but a scrap of cloud sliding past now and then to get in the way of that light.

We made quite a group, the two of us kids with the old man wedged between us. Nobody had a word to say, though I imagine we all had our own thoughts.

The old man, I could see him wanting to do this, when you figure that he loved Rose Ellen Sample once and maybe never got rid of her. At first I couldn't get the point of going out to a grave. Then I decided he wanted to do something for her, anything he could. It didn't matter that she would never know of it. He was doing it as much for himself as for her. And what was left but to go out to her grave and stand there?

I understood that part, about wanting to do something for somebody you love. Me, I was doing it on account of Sue. I could tell it was a big deal to her, doing this. Not to say that I begrudged the old man his hour. I had come to care for him, and he had been good to me, and I wasn't a bit sorry to help him out when he wanted something.

So we drove on, and presently arrived at the foot of the hill where the cemetery sat. We drove up slow, the gravel crunching under our tires. At the top of the hill the iron gate was shut tight, so I parked and took Gandy Meacham in my arms again. The fence around the place was not too high, and it was easy to get the three of us over.

We walked through the cemetery. Any other time this would have been spooky as all-get-out, the big moon shining and a wind rustling the tall grass, that being the only sound save our own footsteps. But there was something bigger that rode over all the rest and left no room for spooks. Maybe it was the three of us together that way, knowing so much about each other when you think about it. I was carrying Gandy Meacham. Sue, she was right beside us and had one arm holding me. Holding me and the old man both, I guess.

Then Gandy Meacham said, Tell me when we's close.

I stopped when he was maybe half a dozen graves away. I said, them there. The two new ones. Hers is the far one.

Let me down, he said.

I did. At first I thought he was going to fall. He held my arm, and Sue's, for maybe half a minute. Then he took a step. And I and Sue knew we ought not to follow him, that we had to let him alone.

He tottered like a baby. A couple of times I thought he would pitch right over on his face. But he didn't. He kept looking at her tombstone, and walked right over Ray Newsome's grave, and just when it looked again like he was going over, he reached out and caught himself on Rose Ellen Sample's hunk of marble.

He stood there, and straightened himself some, and I could

see he wasn't touching the stone for a hold now, but just to be touching it. His fingers rested on it. His head was bent down. Sue E. began to cry about then, without making a sound. She hugged me, and all the time we watched the old man in the moonlight.

I wondered what was on his mind, what he was thinking about then. He was thinking about her, sure, but I wondered what was going through his head when he thought about that grey-headed old lady that I used to see on the streets of Luray.

Then it hit me. He never did see her that way. I seen her as an old lady but to him she was still young and beautiful, always was and always would be.

Maybe it was the way he was standing, not hunched over at all anymore but right straight and with his shoulders square, that showed me something else. He was no old man now. Not in his head, anyways. He was young again, same as her, and healthy, and they was in love just the way they'd been before.

Maybe it was his winning that put the starch in his backbone and made him stand up straight. I mean, he did win, if you want to look at it one way. Ray Newsome had his ranch, and married Rose Ellen for a short spell. But what good did it do him tonight, all that work and all that scrapping, all the hating and the loving and the pride that was in him? Maybe Quiller Meacham was not long for this world but tonight he could think thoughts of Rose Ellen while he breathed in the night air, hold her in his heart just as sure as I held Sue E. in my arms. For the night, Rose Ellen and living was his.

I seen all that in the poor old man who stood there in that Texas moonlight. I seen that, and more. And it come over me like a big cloud over the moon. It made my chest swell up, and made me hold tight to Sue E.

I was scared, not from ghosts and graves, but from what I seen. All this time I had been thinking that me and Gandy Meacham was so different, him being old and me young, him being sick and me healthy.

But I seen now we wasn't so different. Like I had Sue, he had Rose Ellen. The hand that touched her gravestone was the same that must have touched her a hundred times. The eyes that looked on grass and marble and moonlight had looked on her young face, and seen love.

We was the same, him and me and all the rest of us, him past things that I had in front of me yet, but both of us walking the same road, with others before us and others behind. So what made us different? A few years, is what. A.few years.

Which, I seen in that moonlight, ain't so very much a-tall.

3 ABSORBING NOVELS BY PHILLIP FINCH

_____ 04590-0   **BIRTHRIGHT** $2.75
"Boisterous fun with a heart of gold!"
—*Kirkus Reviews*

_____ 05492-6   **TEXAS DAWN** $3.25
Three generations of women and men with passions as untamed as the giant land they loved!

_____ 04927-2   **TOXIN L** $2.50
The nightmare shock-thriller about the ultimate unnatural disaster!

Available at your local bookstore or return this form to

**Berkley Book Mailing Service
P.O. Box 690
Rockville Centre, NY 11570**

Please send me the above titles. I am enclosing $_____
(Please add 50¢ per copy to cover postage and handling). Send check or money order—no cash or C.O.D.'s. Allow six weeks for delivery.

NAME_____

ADDRESS_____

CITY_____STATE/ZIP_____

143

ROMANCE, WAR, HONOR AND ADVENTURE AT THE DAWN OF A NEW FRONTIER!

NORTHWEST TERRITORY

For the millions who thrilled to John Jakes' <u>Kent Family Chronicles</u> comes NORTHWEST TERRITORY, a riveting new series of novels about the men and women who forged out of the American wilderness the vast Northwest Territory, America's heartland and our first great frontier.

NORTHWEST TERRITORY is guaranteed to hold you spellbound with its sweeping tales of love and unforgettable adventure. Discover it for yourself... Order today!

_____05738-0/$3.50 WARPATH (Northwest Territory #1) by Oliver Payne

_____05532-9/$3.50 CONQUEST (Northwest Territory #2) by Oliver Payne

 Berkley Book Mailing Service
P.O. Box 690
Rockville Centre, NY 11570

Please send me the above titles. I am enclosing $_____
(Please add 50¢ per copy to cover postage and handling). Send check or money order—no cash or C.O.D.'s. Allow three weeks for delivery.

NAME_____

ADDRESS_____

CITY_____STATE/ZIP_____ 126